W9-CAJ-456

Murder Song

by the same author

YOU CAN'T SEE ROUND CORNERS
THE LONG SHADOW
JUST LET ME BE
THE SUNDOWNERS
THE CLIMATE OF COURAGE
JUSTIN BAYARD
THE GREEN HELMET
BACK OF SUNSET
NORTH FROM THURSDAY
THE COUNTRY OF MARRIAGE
FORESTS OF THE NIGHT
A FLIGHT OF CHARIOTS
THE FALL OF AN EAGLE
THE PULSE OF DANGER
THE HIGH COMMISSIONER
THE LONG PURSUIT
SEASON OF DOUBT
REMEMBER JACK HOXIE
HELGA'S WEB
MASK OF THE ANDES
MAN'S ESTATE
RANSOM
PETER'S PENCE
THE SAFE HOUSE
A SOUND OF LIGHTNING
HIGH ROAD TO CHINA
VORTEX
THE BEAUFORT SISTERS
A VERY PRIVATE WAR
GOLDEN SABRE
THE FARAWAY DRUMS
SPEARFIELD'S DAUGHTER
THE PHOENIX TREE
THE CITY OF FADING LIGHT
DRAGONS AT THE PARTY
NOW AND THEN, AMEN
BABYLON SOUTH

JON CLEARY

Murder Song

2/91

William Morrow and Company, Inc.
New York

Copyright © 1990 by Sundowner Productions Pty., Ltd.

Originally published in Great Britain in 1990 by William Collins Sons & Co., Ltd.

All rights reserved. No part of this book may be reproduced or utilized in any form or by any means, electronic or mechanical, including photocopying, recording or by any information storage and retrieval system, without permission in writing from the Publisher. Inquiries should be addressed to Permissions Department, William Morrow and Company, Inc., 105 Madison Avenue, New York, N.Y. 10016.

Recognizing the importance of preserving what has been written, it is the policy of William Morrow and Company, Inc., and its imprints and affiliates to have the books it publishes printed on acid-free paper, and we exert our best efforts to that end.

Library of Congress Cataloging-in-Publication Data

Cleary, Jon, 1917–
        Murder song / Jon Cleary.
           p.   cm.
        ISBN 0-688-09458-9
        I. Title.
        PR9619.3.C54M87   1990
        823—dc20   90-39931
                                                                          CIP

Printed in the United States of America

First U. S. Edition

1 2 3 4 5 6 7 8 9 10

For Kathleen and Bob Parrish

ONE

1

It was a perfect day for aviators, bird watchers, photographers and sniping murderers. The air had that clean bright light that occurs on some days in Sydney in the winter month of August; the wind blows out of the west, across the dry flat continent, and scours the skies to a brilliant blue shine. Thin-blooded citizens turn up their coat collars and look east to the sea or north for the coming of spring. But hardier souls, depending upon their pay or their inclinations, welcome the wind-polished days of August.

The construction worker, in hard hat and thick lumber jacket, was alone on the steel beam of the framework of the twentieth floor of the new insurance building in Chatswood, a northern suburb. He was leaning against the wind, holding tightly to the safety rope, looking north, when the bullet hit him in the chest. He did not see it coming, despite the clear light; if he cried out as he died, no one heard him. He fell backwards, away from the safety rope, was already dead as he went down in a clear fall to the ground two hundred feet below.

Several of his workmates, horrified, saw him fall. None of them at that moment knew he had been shot. None of them looked for the murderer, so none of them saw him. The shot could have come from any one of half a dozen neighbouring buildings, all of them occupied, but the time was 9.10 in the morning and bosses and workers were still settling down at their desks. It was too early in the day to be staring out of windows.

The dead man was Harry Gardner, a cheerful extrovert with a wife and four children and not an enemy in the world. Except the unknown man who had killed him.

A week later, on a cold rainy night when no one had a good word to say about August, Terry Sugar, a twenty-four-year veteran of the New South Wales Police Department, was getting out of his car in the driveway of his home in Mount Druitt, a western suburb of Sydney, when the bullet hit him in the neck, went down through his chest, came out and lodged in the car seat. He saw his killer, though he did not recognize him, but he died almost instantly and had no time to tell anyone.

First Class Sergeant Sugar was married and had two sons, one at high school and the other in his first year at university. Naturally, as a policeman, not everyone was his friend: that was the Australian way. He had, however, received no death threats; for the last year he had been in charge of the desk at the Parramatta Police Centre and had been working on no outside cases. The detectives assigned to the murder attempted no written guesses, but amongst themselves they put the killing down as the work of a crank who had a grudge against all police, a thrill-killer or someone who had mistaken his victim for someone else.

Detective-Inspector Scobie Malone and Detective-Sergeant Russ Clements, both of whom had known Terry Sugar, attended the funeral. There was a police guard of honour and four of Sergeant Sugar's fellow officers were the pall-bearers; Police Commissioner John Leeds and several other senior officers and a hundred uniformed officers marched in the cortège. Around Parramatta there were four break-ins, two bag-snatchings and an attempted bank hold-up during the forty-five-minute church service.

It was another fine clear day, but the wind, coming today from the south-west, had a touch of Antarctica to it; tears were cold on the cheeks. The light was ideal for the press photographers and the newsreel cameramen, though funerals don't photograph as well as fashion parades.

Malone and Clements, the Commissioner and other outsiders dropped out after the token march down the main street; the family had requested that the actual burial be as private as could be arranged. As he stepped aside Malone bumped into one of the television cameramen, a tall, bald, overweight man with a beard.

'Sorry.' The man took his eye away from the view-finder. 'I didn't see you, Inspector.'

Malone didn't know the man's name, but he had seen him occasionally at the scenes of crimes; he recognized the logo on the camera. 'Will it be on Channel 15's news tonight?'

'Probably.'

Malone glanced at Clements. 'Remind me not to look.'

The man smiled through his thick black beard. 'I understand. But I have a job to do, just like everyone else. I don't enjoy these jobs.'

'Maybe,' said Malone. 'I just don't like my kids to see their father following another cop's coffin.'

TWO

1

'There's been another one,' said Claire, coming into the kitchen.

'Another what?' said her mother.

'Homicide. Pass the Weet-Bix.'

'Terrific!' said Maureen. 'He's gunna have his name in the papers again.'

'I think I'll start another scrapbook,' said Tom.

'You haven't started a first one yet,' said Maureen.

'No, I was going to, but.'

'Who mentioned homicide?' said Malone. 'Who was that on the phone?'

'Uncle Russ,' said Claire. 'He's still hanging there.'

Muttering an incoherent curse, picturing the 100-kilogram Russ Clements hanging by his neck from a phone cord, Malone got up and went out into the hallway. 'Russ? How many times have I bloody told you – don't mention homicide in front of the kids!'

'Get off the boil, Inspector,' said Sergeant Clements in a patient voice that made a gentle mockery of Malone's rank. There had once been a Commissioner of the New South Wales Police Force, as it was then known, who had insisted on the use of rank when addressing another officer; he had given rank another of its meanings when he had been found, on retirement, to have been the State's patron saint of corruption. He, however, had been before Malone's and Clements' time, though his legend persisted. 'Claire's got too much imagination. Where does she get it from?'

'Her mother. Go on. Is there a homicide or not?'

'Yeah, there is. But all I asked Claire was whether you had

left for the office. You know how I feel about your kids, Scobie –'

'Yeah, I know. Sorry. Where's the job this time?'

'Down at The Warehouse in Clarence Street, it's an apartment block. It seems routine, a woman shot.'

'If it's routine, why ring me? Take Andy Graham or someone and get down there.'

'Scobie, there's three guys off with 'flu. I need a back-up.'

'An inspector backing up a sergeant? You trying to ruin my day? Righto, I'll be there. But I'm going to finish my breakfast first. It's a privilege of rank.'

He hung up and went back into the kitchen. It was a big old-fashioned room that, despite all its modern appliances, suggested another time, almost another country. The house was eighty years old, built just after Federation, part-sandstone, part-redbrick. It was of a style that had become fashionable again with its pitched slate roof, its wide front verandah, its eaves embellishments and its hint of conservative values, though not in dollar terms. The Malones had bought the house eight years ago and now it was worth three times what they had paid for it. With its backyard pool, a gift from Lisa's parents, adding to its worth, Malone sometimes wondered if the neighbours thought he might be a policeman on the take. Easy money had been a national gift for several years and suspicion of a neighbour's good fortune had become endemic.

'I'll have another cup of coffee,' he said, spreading some of Lisa's home-made marmalade on a slice of wholegrain toast.

'So where's the murder?' Maureen was almost ten, going on twenty; she lived in a world of TV cop shows and soap operas. She had a mind as lively as an aviary full of swallows, but she was no bird-brain; Malone felt that, somehow, she would grow up to be the least vulnerable of his three children. 'God, why did we have to have a cop as a father? He never wants to talk about his work with us.'

'You think Alan Bond sits down at breakfast and discusses take-overs with his grandkids?'

'What about the Pope?' said Tom, the seven-year-old.

'I've told you before – the Pope doesn't have kids. What sort

11

of Catholic school do you go to? What do you do during religious instruction?'

'Play noughts and crosses.'

'Holy Jesus,' said Malone, then added, 'That was supposed to be a prayer.'

'Just as well,' said Tom piously. 'You know what Grandma Malone thinks about swearing.'

'She should come up to Holy Spirit some day and listen to the senior girls,' said Maureen. 'Holy –'

'Watch it,' said Lisa, who swore only in bed under and on top of Malone and never within the hearing of the children, which meant she sometimes got up in the morning with a hoarse throat.

'Dad,' said Claire, going on fourteen, more than halfway to being a beautiful woman and beginning to be aware of it, 'what about my fifty dollars? I've got to pay the deposit for the skiing holiday.'

'Who's taking your class on this trip?'

'Sister Philomena, Speedy Gonzalez's sister.'

'A sixty-year-old skiing nun? Does the Pope know about this emancipation?'

'What's emancipation?' asked Tom, who had a keen interest in words if not in Catholic politics.

'Forget it,' said Malone and took a fifty-dollar note from his wallet. 'That skins me. I can remember my school holidays, we went to Coogee Beach.'

'Not in winter, you didn't,' said Claire, as practical-minded as her mother. She took the note and put it carefully away in her wallet, which, Malone noticed, was fatter than his own. She had inherited his reluctance to spend, but somehow, even at going-on-fourteen, she always seemed to be richer than he.

'Don't let the light get to the moths in there,' said Maureen, the spendthrift. 'Now tell us about the murder, Daddy.'

'When I'm retired and got nothing better to do. Now get ready for school.'

Later, when the children had left to walk to school, an exercise that Lisa insisted upon, Malone stood at the front door with Lisa. 'It's unhealthy, the way they keep harping what murder I'm on.'

'What do you expect, a father's who's been ten years in Homicide? You could always ask for a transfer, to Traffic or something unexciting. Or Administration, that'd be nice. Nine to five and you wouldn't have to wear a gun.' She patted the bulge of his holster, as she might a large tumour.

It was a sore point between them; he couldn't blame her for her point of view. Cops everywhere in the world probably had this sort of conversation with their wives or lovers. 'You'd be bored stiff if I turned into a stuffy office manager.'

'Try me.' She kissed him, gave him her usual warning, which was more than a cliché for her: 'Take care.'

He drove into town in the six-year-old Holden Commodore. Like himself, it was always slow to start on a winter morning; they were a summertime pair. The car was beginning to show its age; and on mornings like this he sometimes *felt* his. He was in his early forties, with a fast bowler's bulky shoulders and still reasonably slim round the waist; he had been rawboned and lithe in his cricketing days, and he sometimes felt the ghost of that youth in his bones and extra flesh. But that was all in the past and he knew as well as anyone that one couldn't go back. Lately he had found himself observing Lisa, forty and still in her prime but just beginning to fade round the edges, and praying for her sake (and, selfishly, for his) that age would come slowly and kindly to her.

Randwick, where he lived, was eight kilometres from the heart of the city; in the morning peak hour traffic it took him twenty-five minutes to get to the scene of the murder. Clarence Street was one of the north-bound arteries of the central business district; it was one of four such streets named after English dukes in the early nineteenth century, a tugging of the colonial forelock of those days. Originally it had been the site of the colony's troop barracks; pubs and brothels had been close at hand to provide the usual comforts. Then the barracks and brothels had been cleaned out, but not all the pubs. Merchants had moved in to build their narrow-fronted warehouses and showrooms; silks and satins had replaced sex in the market, salesmen had taken over from the soldiers. There had been a tea-and-coffee ware-house that Malone could remember passing as a boy; there had also been the scent of spices from another warehouse; he had stopped to breathe deeply and dream of Zanzibar and Ceylon and dusky girls amongst the bushes. He had matured early, a common occurrence amongst fast bowlers: matured physically, that is.

The Warehouse was not a warehouse at all, but a block of expensive apartments built where two commercial houses had once stood. Two police cars were parked by the kerb ahead of two unmarked cars on meters with the *Expired* sign showing: they, too, would be police cars, probably the government medical officer and staff members from Crime Scene. He parked the Commodore in a Loading Zone strip, grinned at the van driver who pulled up and yelled at him to get his fucking car out of there, and went into the apartment block. A uniformed policeman was in the small foyer.

'Morning, Inspector. It's up on the ninth floor. They're all up there, the doctor, the photographer, everyone.'

Malone looked around. 'Is there a porter or anyone?'

'No, sir. Everything here is automatic, the security, the lifts, everything.' He was a fresh-faced young man, still a probationary, still eager to be eager.

'This your first homicide?'

'Yes, sir.'

'It won't be your last. Keep everyone out but our people. Oh, and any of the tenants. Get their names if any of them appear.'

He went up in the lift to the ninth floor and the murder scene. It was a two-bedroom apartment with a living-dining-room, a small kitchen and an even smaller bathroom. It had a balcony that looked west towards the Darling Harbour entertainment and convention complex; in the distance was the Balmain ridge, with the tower of the local town hall jutting up like a secular minaret beneath which more abuse than prayers was exchanged. The furniture of the flat was good but undistinguished; the carpet was thick but not expensive and was stained in several spots; the prints on the walls were of birds but one had the feeling they had been chosen by a decorator who didn't know a budgerigar from a bald crow. It was a pied-à-terre, not a home: no one had left a handprint on it.

14

The body was lying just inside the closed glass doors that led out to the small balcony. There was a silver sunburst in one of the doors, like the sketch for a motif on a headstone. Russ Clements pulled back the sheet.

'Her name's Mardi Jack, her driving licence says she lived out in Paddington. She was thirty-three.'

Malone looked down at the dead woman. She had dark red hair, cut short in a shingle style, tinted, he guessed; she had a broad sensual face, pinched a little in pain; her body, too, might have been sensual when she was alive, but death had turned it into a limp ugly heap. Her clothes looked expensive but flashy, the sort bought in boutiques that catered to the disco crowd; Malone, knowing nothing about fashion, was conservative in his taste, though his wife and elder daughter said he had no taste at all. Mardi Jack's green sequinned blouse was low-cut, her cleavage made ugly by the congealed blood from her wound; her black trousers were too tight, too suggestive, Malone thought. The dead woman had not come to the flat expecting to spend the night or the weekend alone.

'There's a black fox coat, dyed, I think, in the main bedroom,' said Clements.

'How do you know so much about dyed fox coats?'

'I bought one once that fell off the back of a truck. For my mum.'

Malone looked down again at Mardi Jack, then drew the sheet back over her. 'How long's she been dead?'

Clements glanced at the government medical officer, who had come in from the kitchen, where he had just made himself a cup of coffee. 'How long, doc?'

'Thirty-six hours, maybe a bit more. Saturday night, I'd say.' The GMO was a man who looked ready to burst from years of good living; belly, cheeks, chins all protruded and his breath wheezed out of a fat throat. Malone often wondered why Doc Gilbey had chosen an area where most of the corpses he examined were at ankle-height. One day the GMO, bending down, was going to collapse and die on top of one of the bodies. 'Just the one bullet in her, right into her heart, I'd say. A lucky shot. It's still in the body.'

15

'Let me know when you've sent it on to Ballistics.'

Gilbey slurped his coffee. 'They'll have it today.'

The small apartment was becoming crowded; two men from the funeral contractors had arrived to join the Crime Scene men, the girl photographer and the two uniformed officers. Malone pulled back one of the glass doors and stepped out on to the balcony, jerking his head for Clements to follow him.

'What have you got so far?'

'Bugger-all.' Clements bit his bottom lip, an old habit. He was a big, plain-looking man, a couple of inches taller than Malone and almost twenty kilos heavier. He was a bachelor, afraid of commitment to a woman but envying Malone his comfortable family life. He was mildly bigoted and racist, but kindly; he could complain sourly about too many Asians being allowed into the country, then tenderly, if awkwardly, console a Vietnamese woman who had lost her son in a gang battle. At that he was no more complex than Malone and sixteen million other Australians, including the Asian-born.

'Who found her?'

'The cleaning lady.' Clements belonged to that class which thought that to call a woman a 'woman' was demeaning to her; it was another manifestation that contradicted the native myth that Australians did not believe in class distinction. 'I've interviewed her and let her go home. She's a Greek, a bit excitable about dead bodies.'

'So am I. I don't like them. You talk to anyone else?'

'I've got a coupla the uniformed guys going through the building. So far they haven't brought anyone up here.'

'The flat belong to her?' Malone nodded in at the corpse, now being covered in a green plastic shroud.

'No, it's a company flat. There's some notepaper and envelopes in a desk inside. Kensay Proprietary Limited. Their offices are in Cossack House in Bridge Street. She had a key, though.'

Malone, raincoat collar turned up against the wind coming across the western reaches of the harbour, looked out at the buildings surrounding them; then he looked at the bullet hole in the glass door. 'A high-powered rifle?'

'I'd bet on it. I don't think anyone would have been standing here and shot her through the glass. There's a lot of dust and dirt here on the balcony – looks like the cleaning lady doesn't come out here in winter. There's no sign of any footmarks.'

Malone looked down at the marks his own and Clements' shoes had made. Then he looked out again at the neighbouring buildings. 'Where do you reckon the shot came from?'

'Over there.' Clements pointed at a block of offices in Kent Street, the next street west. 'He'd have had an ideal spot there on that flat roof. It's about a hundred and fifty metres away, no more. If he was experienced, with a good gun and a night 'scope, she'd have been an easy target.'

'Righto, send for Andy Graham, get him to do the donkey work, tell him to search that roof and next door to it for any cartridge cases. Stay here till he turns up. I'm going out to Paddington, see if there's anyone there to tell the bad news to.'

'Better you than me.'

'Some day you're going to have to do it.' *I just hope to Christ you don't have to tell the bad news to Lisa.*

He left Clements, went down in the lift with the two men from the funeral contractors and the body of Mardi Jack. The lift wasn't big enough to take the stretcher horizontally and one of the men was holding Mardi Jack in his arms as if she were a drunken dancer.

'Wouldn't you know it?' he said over the green plastic shoulder to Malone. 'The bloody service lift isn't working. I guess it's gunna be one of them weeks.'

'At least you're still breathing,' said Malone.

The man, tall and painfully thin, a living cadaver, wasn't offended; his trade brought more abusive jokes than even a policeman's lot. 'Sometimes I wonder who's better off,' he said and looked reproachfully at the shrouded corpse as if Mardi Jack had missed a crucial step in their dance.

Malone went out into Clarence Street, pushing through the small crowd that had stopped to see why an ambulance was double-parked in the busy street. There were also two TV vans double-parked behind it; a cameraman aimed his camera at Malone, but he shook his head and put a hand up to his face.

Two reporters came at him, but he just smiled and said, 'See Sergeant Clements, he's in charge,' and dodged round them.

There were two parking tickets on the Commodore; the Grey Bombers, the parking police, must be making blanket raids this morning. He lifted them off, stuck them under a windscreen wiper of one of the TV vans, got into the car and pulled out into the traffic. He glanced in his driving mirror as he drove away and saw the body of Mardi Jack, now on the stretcher, being pushed into the ambulance.

The start of another week, another job. He wondered how senior men felt in Traffic or Administration each Monday morning. But even as he drove towards that aspect of murder he always hated, the telling of the dreadful news to the victim's family, he knew he would always prefer people to paper. The living and the dead were part of him.

2

Goodwood Street was a narrow one-way street lined on both sides by narrow-fronted terrace houses. Paddington in the last century had been a mix of solid merchants' houses and workmen's cottages and terraces; perched on a ridge, the merchants and one or two of the workmen had had a distant view of the harbour, but most of the citizens had just stared across the street at each other, not always the best of sights, especially on Friday and Saturday nights when the drunks came rolling home. Then in the twenties and thirties of this century it had become almost solely a working man's domain, the narrow houses crowded with large families, constant debt and a solid Labour vote. In the last twenty years it had been invaded by artists moving closer to the wealthy buyers of the eastern suburbs, by writers who weren't intellectual enough for Balmain and by yuppies turning the terrace houses into shrunken mansions. Houses with sixteen-foot frontages now brought prices that would have kept the families of years ago for a lifetime. It was another turn of the wheel in the history of any city that manages to survive.

Malone had to park again in a No Standing zone; the Commodore, in a year, collected more parking tickets than it did birdcrap. He knocked on a bright yellow door in a dark green house; the iron lacework on the upstairs balcony was painted white. As he was about to knock for the third time the door was opened by a girl in a terry-towelling dressing-gown; she had frizzled yellow hair and sleep in her eyes. She blinked in the morning sun.

'Yeah, what is it?' She had all the politeness of someone who hated her sleep being disturbed, even at ten o'clock in the morning.

Malone introduced himself. 'Does Miss Mardi Jack live here?'

'Yeah. But she's not in. Why?'

'Are you a relative?'

The sleep quickly cleared from the girl's eyes; she was alertly intelligent. 'Is something wrong? Is she in jail or something?'

Malone told her the bad news as gently as he could; he had had plenty of experience at this but it never became any easier. 'Does she have a family? Parents or a husband?'

The girl leaned against the door as if mortally wounded by shock. 'Oh my God! *Shot?*' She had a husky voice that cracked now; she cleared her throat, wrapped her dressing-gown tighter round her as if she had just felt something more than the morning cold. 'You wanna come in?'

She led the way down a narrow hall, through a small living-room and out into a kitchen that seemed to be about two hundred years ahead of the vintage front of the house. Beyond its glass wall was a neat courtyard, complete with trees in pots, a bird-bath and a gas barbecue on wheels. Tradition could be respected only just so far, about half the length of the house.

The girl prepared coffee. "Espresso or cappuccino?"

All mod cons, thought Malone; this girl, and probably Mardi Jack, knew how to live well. Except that Mardi Jack had gone where all mod cons counted for nothing. 'Cappuccino. Do you mind if I ask who you are?'

'I'm Gina Cazelli – Mardi and I share – *shared* this place. You asked about her family. She just had her father, he lives somewhere up on the Gold Coast. He and Mardi weren't too

19

close. Her parents separated when she was a little girl, then her mother died about, oh, I think it was five or six years ago.'

'Did she have any close friends, I mean besides you. A boy-friend, an ex-husband?'

'I don't think she'd ever been married, at least she never mentioned that she had. She had no particular guy. She was – I shouldn't say this about her, but I'm trying to help, I mean, find who shot her. She sorta played the field. Christ, that sounds disloyal, doesn't it?' She busied herself getting cups and saucers, got some croissants out of a bread-tin and put them in a micro-wave oven. Malone noticed that the kitchen was as tidy and spotless as Lisa's; Gina Cazelli at the moment looked like a wreck, but either she or Mardi Jack had kept a neat house. 'She wasn't a whore. She was just unlucky with the men she fell in love with. She'd be absolutely nuts about some guy, it'd last three or four months and then he'd be gone. She'd bounce herself off other guys out of, I dunno, spite or self-pity or something. You know what women are like.'

She looked at him carefully and he smiled and nodded. 'I try to know 'em. It ain't easy.'

She nodded in reply, took the croissants out of the microwave. 'I haven't had breakfast. Yeah, you're right. Men are easier to know.'

'What did Mardi do? For a living?'

'She was a singer. Good, but not good enough, I mean to be a top-liner. She sang around the clubs, you know, the girl who comes on and sings for the wives before the smutty comic comes on and tells sexist jokes. She hated it, but it paid the rent. Her main income came from singing jingles for commercials. That was how we met. I'm an assistant producer with a recording studio.'

'Were you close? As friends, I mean.'

She handed him his coffee and a croissant, pushed strawberry jam in a small decorated crock towards him; he began to suspect that Gina was the one who kept the house up to *House and Garden* standards. She handed him a fancy paper napkin, yellow to match the front door and the colour strips on the kitchen cupboard doors and drawers.

'No, we weren't that close. We sorta lived our own lives. There was ten years' difference between us – she was thirty-three. It made a difference. She liked older guys.'

Malone sipped his coffee, trying not to be too obvious as he studied Gina Cazelli. She was dumpy and plain, her plainness not helped by her frizzed-out hair; it was the sort of hair that would always look the same, in or out of bed, any time of day or night; it was the latest fashion, Claire, the fashion expert, had told him when he had commented on a certain TV actress's hair-style. Malone had seen Gina's type before when he had had to brush against the fringes of the entertainment industry: the too-willing, efficient plain jane whom everyone would use because they knew that what she was doing was her whole life, her only escape from whatever drudgery was her alternative.

'Any particular older bloke?' It was one of his idiosyncrasies that he never used the word *guy*; fighting a losing battle, he stuck to the slang of his rabidly patriotic father, Con Malone, who hated more foreigners than even the Aborigines did. 'A recent one?'

Gina shook her head; the hair shivered like an unravelled string cap. 'No, there's been no one for at least four, maybe five months. Nobody she's brought home.' She munched on her croissant. 'But –'

'But what?' he said patiently after waiting a few moments.

'I think there's been one guy. He used to ring her here, not often, but maybe two or three times. She never told me anything about him and I never asked. She had a call from him on Saturday morning at the studio, we were doing a recording for a TV commercial. God, when I think of it!'

'What?'

'The jingle was "I'll be alive forever"!' She gulped down a mouthful of coffee; for a moment she looked as if she was about to burst into tears. Then she shook her head again, the hair shivered. 'Well, it was him. I took the call and he asked for her.'

'Did he ever give his name when you took a call from him?'

'No. When she came back from the phone she seemed upset, but she didn't say anything. I had to work back and by the time I got home Saturday, about six, she'd gone out.'

21

Malone put down his empty cup, declined the offer of more coffee. Cappuccino and croissants on Monday morning in Paddington was okay for assistant recording producers and artists and ballet dancers, but not for working cops. 'Could I have a look at her room?'

Gina hesitated, then nodded. 'I suppose you've got to. But it's like intruding on her, isn't it?'

'It's better intruding on the dead than on the living, but we don't enjoy any of it.'

She smiled, a painful one, and for a moment looked less plain. 'Why do we call you pigs? Not all of you are.'

She led him up the narrow stairs to a back bedroom that looked out on to the courtyard. The room looked as if it had been freshly painted, but it was a mess, a sanitized rubbish tip. The bed was unmade, clothes were strewn over the two chairs, the dressing-table looked like a wrecked corner of a beauty parlour. He began to suspect that Mardi Jack's life might have been just as unkempt.

'She took two showers a day,' said Gina Cazelli, 'but she hadn't the faintest idea what a coat-hanger was for.'

'You mind if I look through here on my own? You can trust me.'

She looked around the room, sad and puzzled at what might be all that was left of her friend's life; then abruptly she left him. Malone began the sort of search that always disturbed him, the turning over of a murder or suicide victim to see what was hidden beneath the body.

The closet was packed tightly with clothes, all of them expensive and, by his taste, a bit way out. There were leather and sequins and eye-dazzling silks and taffetas; Malone wondered how the man who never left his name could have had a discreet affair with her. Then he found a black woollen coat and remembered the black fox one in the flat where she had been murdered. He wondered if the man had bought them for her, thrown them over her to hide her.

He went through the drawers of the closet and the dressing-table. In the bottom drawer of the latter he found what a policeman always hopes for: the personal give-away that we

22

always leave when we depart this life unexpectedly, the secret at last exposed to the light.

It was a journal rather than a diary; there were no dates other than the year, 1989, in gold figures on the green cover. There were no names, only initials; it seemed, however, that Mardi Jack wrote only about the men in her life, it was an all-male world except for herself. It seemed, too, that she fell in love, genuine love, as other people, fumble-footed, fall into holes that more nimble-footed elements avoid. The men, it also seemed, walked away, leaving her floundering; she would be bitter for a time, then the next temptation would appear. Christ, thought Malone, what makes women such masochists? He had forgotten that Lisa had already given him the answer: love is both a form of possession and a form of masochism and women feel the latter more deeply than men. Men once wore hair shirts, but it was women who had woven them and tried them on first.

The later entries spoke of B., *'the love of my life'*. He appeared sincere and gentle enough in the early days of their relationship – *'He makes me feel as if I'm walking on clouds. All I want to do is sing love songs, happy ones. Get lost, Billie Holliday.'* Then the words and music started to change: *'God, he is just like the rest of them. The second brushoff in a week.'* One could feel the anger in her pen; the writing was shaky. *'No excuses. I just won't be there tonight, he says. Jesus, why do I bother? Won't I ever learn? Come back Billie Holliday, Edith Piaf, all you women who cry the blues! I know, boy do I know, what you mean!'*

Malone was embarrassed by the melodrama of her feelings, the banality of the entries; but she hadn't been writing for him or anyone else, not even the man who had dumped her. He should not expect the laconic reporting style of a police running sheet.

The last entry must have been written on Saturday just before she had gone out to her death; the writing seemed to quiver on the page: *'I'm seeing B. tonight – I hope! We must have it out between us. Will this be our last meeting? Please God no! He says there is someone else . . . When I first met him all those years ago in London there was already someone else – ah, but he was a different man then and I wasn't even a woman, just a different girl.'*

23

Malone closed the journal, continued his search, found nothing else that was helpful. He took the journal downstairs with him. 'I'll be taking this with me. I'll sign for it. Did you ever see her writing in this?'

Gina Cazelli shook her head; she sat at the kitchen table sipping a second cup of cappuccino or perhaps even a third. There was still the look of pain on her round face, almost like a bruise. 'You find anything in it?'

'Just a reference to someone called B. She never mentioned him?'

'Never. But he was probably the guy she's been seeing lately.' She frowned, squeezing her memory. 'I can't remember any of the guys she brought home, none of their names started with a B. There was a Charlie and a Roger and a Raul – he was South American. They were all bums, fly-by-nights or in the morning, but she couldn't see that and I never told her.'

'Well, it's too late to tell her now. I'll send a policewoman out here to go through her things again. If you think of anything that might help, ring me.' He dropped his card on the table. Then he said, as he might to Claire in five or six years' time, 'Be careful with your men, Gina.'

She smiled wearily, wryly. 'What men?'

He left her then, went out to the Commodore; sure enough, there was another parking ticket stuck behind one of the wipers. There were also two splashes of bird-crap on the bonnet. Grey Bombers and their tickets were not universal; but birds were everywhere, always haunting him. If he took the Commodore to Antarctica, the penguins would be sure to leave their frozen mark on it.

3

Russ Clements was already back at Homicide waiting for him, cleaning out his murder box, a cardboard shoe box, of last week's homicide and making room for this week's bits and pieces that

24

might add up to incriminating evidence. So far there was very little.

'We went right through the apartment building, but came up with nothing. There's only six permanent residents – the rest of the flats are company ones, used by company staff or visiting freeloaders. Nobody heard any shot, nobody saw Mardi Jack – the other two flats on that floor are also company ones. Andy Graham had a look at the roof of that building in Kent Street. Someone had been up there – there was a half-eaten sandwich and a Coke can.'

Malone looked at the murder box. 'You got the sandwich in there?'

Clements grimaced. 'You kidding? It's gone to Scientific. They'll hold it and we'll match the bite prints against whoever we pick up.'

'Any cartridge cases?'

'None. Possibly a bolt-action rifle. He coulda been a pro or a semi-pro – he knew what he was about. One shot and he didn't have to extract the shell. The roof is about twenty feet below the balcony, so he'd have been shooting upwards. That meant he was probably aiming to put the shot between the bars of the balcony railings.'

'At night?'

'The railings and Mardi Jack were both silhouetted against the lights in the living-room, assuming he shot her Saturday night. You ever use a night 'scope? You'd be surprised how accurate you can be with 'em.' Clements was the gun expert of the two of them. Malone hated guns and spent the minimum allowable time on the practice range.

Malone sat down, taking off his jacket. After almost a year here in the new Police Centre, he was still getting accustomed to the extra space in his own office. For years the Police Department had been scattered over the inner city; Homicide at one time had been quartered in a leased commercial building. It had lent a certain informality to murder, an atmosphere not always appreciated by the murderers brought in, some of whom expected the Brueghel-like scenes of *Hill Street Blues* and felt cheated to look like no more than tax evaders. The Police Centre had an antiseptic look to it which Clements, a naturally untidy man, was doing his best to correct. Malone, for his part, kept his office neat, as if expecting Lisa to come in any day and do housework.

'Anything on the company that owns the flat?'

'Kensay. I've been on to Companies Registration. It's one of ten companies that are subsidiaries of Cossack Holdings. That's why it's in the Cossack building.'

'What does Kensay do?'

'It owns a music publishing company and a recording studio and it makes TV commercials. It was registered in 1983.'

'Cossack Holdings – who are they? You're the big-time investor.'

It was a private joke between them that Clements was the richest honest cop in the NSW Police Department. He had always been a lucky horse punter and since the October 1987 market crash he had dabbled on the stock exchange, picking up some sweet bargains through his brokers. He was not greedy, did not even have an ambition to be rich; he just gambled because he loved gambling. He was also incorruptible.

'They're a public company, unlike Kensay. They're the leading shareholder in the O'Brien Cossack. That's a merchant bank. Their shares are very dicey at the moment – there are lots of rumours. The bank and the guy who started all the companies are being investigated by the National Companies and Securities Commission. Brian Boru O'Brien.'

'Brian Boru. B . . .'

'What?'

Malone told him about the B. in Mardi Jack's journal, pushing the book across his desk at him. 'It's a long shot –'

Then he looked up as Chief Inspector Greg Random wandered into his office. Greg Random had never been a man in a hurry, but lately he had seemed to be ambling aimlessly up and down the corridors of the Centre. He had been the chief of the thirty-six detectives in the old Homicide Bureau; but regionalization had broken up the Bureau and reduced the staff to thirteen detectives, too few for a chief inspector to command. Random had been moved to a supernumerary position, where he was lost and unhappy. He had come in now because he could still smell a homicide a mile away.

'What happened down in Clarence Street?' He was a tall, thin man with a shock of white hair and weary eyes. Nothing ever surprised him, neither the depravity of man nor the occasional kindnesses.

Malone told him. 'We aren't even in the starting blocks yet. All we know is she was shot by a high-powered rifle.'

'Like those other two, the Gardner case and Terry Sugar?'

Malone raised his eyebrows. 'I hadn't thought about them.'

'That's all I've got, time to think. There's bugger-all else for me to do.'

'You think there's some connection?'

'I don't know – that's your job.' Malone was now in charge of the remaining thirteen detectives and he sometimes wondered if Greg Random resented his luck. 'Get Ballistics to get their finger out. Tell 'em you want a comparison of the bullets by tomorrow afternoon at the latest.'

Malone wanted to tell him that he no longer ran Homicide, but he couldn't kick a man who was now virtually a pensioner, even if on a chief inspector's 44,800 dollars a year. 'Righto, Greg, thanks for the suggestion.'

Random hung around for another minute or two, then wandered out and disappeared. Malone looked at Clements. 'Righto, you heard what the Chief Inspector said. Get your finger out.'

Clements sighed, picked up the phone and dialled Ballistics two floors above them. He spoke to someone there for a minute or two, trying to sound patient as he pressed his point, then he put down the phone. 'They say they're short-staffed – they've got two guys away in the bush and two off with the 'flu. They'll do their best, but do we think all they have to do is help us solve homicide cases.'

Malone stood up, put on his jacket and raincoat and the battered rainhat he wore on wet days. 'Come on, let's go down and talk to Cossack Holdings. If nothing else, you might pick up some bargains.'

They drove down in an unmarked police car. The sun had

disappeared and it was raining again, the rain riding a slanting wind down through the narrow streets of the central business district. Sydney was still a clean city compared to many, but high-rise development was doing its best to turn it into a city of shadows on sunny days and canyons of gloom on days such as today. The roadway and the pavements glistened like dirty grey ice; a red traffic light was bright as a desert sun in the dull day; a shoal of umbrellas made a shifting pattern as it drifted down Bridge Street. Clements parked the car, but ignored the threatening meter with its *Expired* red glare.

They rode up to the thirty-fifth floor, rising past the bank offices on the lower floors to the executive offices of Cossack Holdings. The reception lobby would not have been out of place in a five-star hotel. The black-haired girl behind the big desk was dressed in a beige suede suit that complemented the green suede walls. A Brett Whiteley hung on one wall; an Arthur Boyd faced it. This was not a reception lobby that welcomed would-be clients rattling a tin cup.

The girl did not look surprised that Cossack should be visited by the police. 'May I tell Mr Bousakis the nature of your visit?' Her vowels were as rounded as her figure.

'Who's Mr Bousakis?' said Clements, who had made the introduction of himself and Malone.

'The chief executive. You said you wanted to see the *boss*.' She obviously thought all policemen were vulgar.

'I think we'll tell him the nature of our business when we see him,' said Malone, smiling at her. 'It won't take long.'

She didn't smile back, but got up and went into an inner office. It was almost a minute before she came back and held open the door. 'Mr Bousakis will see you.'

The inner office was as big as the reception lobby; the shareholders in Cossack kept their executives in the style to which they aspired. George Bousakis did not rise from behind his big desk; from the bulk of him it looked as if he got to his feet only in an emergency. He was a huge man, at least six feet four and three hundred pounds: Malone still thought in the old measures when assessing a stranger. He was in his mid-forties with black slicked-back hair, a hint of handsome features behind the jowls and fat cheeks, and dark eyes that would miss nothing, even that which was hidden. He wore a pink shirt with white collar and cuffs, a blue tie with a thin red stripe in it, and a dark blue double-breasted suit. Converted to sailcloth, Malone reckoned there was enough material in the shirt and suit to have equipped a twelve-metre yacht.

'Good morning. Miss Rogers didn't say which section you were from.' He had a pleasant voice, at least in timbre; but there was a hard edge to it.

'Homicide,' said Malone and explained the reason for their visit. 'Miss Jack had a key to the flat. Who would have given her that?'

'I haven't the faintest idea.' Bousakis showed no shock at the news of murder in one of the company flats; Mardi Jack could have been something discovered missing from stock during an inventory check. 'I wouldn't know Miss – Jack? – if I fell over her.'

It would be the end of her if you did, Malone thought. 'Do you ever use the flat yourself, Mr Bousakis?'

'Never.'

'Who does use it?' Malone sat back, letting Clements take over the questioning. Their teamwork was invariably good: Malone always knew when it was time to change the bowling.

'Some of our executives. Sales directors, people like that. And out-of-towners, people from our interstate offices. We put them up there instead of in hotels. We're very cost-conscious,' he said, evidently blind to the indulgence amidst which he sat. The room, green and grey, had suede-covered walls like the outer office; the carpet almost buried one's shoes; the furniture was antique or a good reproduction of it. The paintings on the walls were from the traditional school: there was a Gruner, a Streeton, a Wakelin: they were familiar, but Malone did not know enough to name the artists.

'Any of the O'Brien Cossack personnel?'

'Occasionally. We try to keep ourselves separate from the bank.'

'Why?'

Bousakis' voice hardened just a little, his fat lips looked suddenly thin. 'It's just company policy.'

'What about Mr Brian Boru O'Brien?' Clements seemed to have a little difficulty in getting the name out.

Bousakis' gaze was steady. 'What about him?'

'Would he use the flat?' What a bowler to have at the other end, thought Malone in cricket terms: Clements thumped the ball down straight at the batsman's head, the West Indians would have offered him full citizenship right off.

'Why should he do that? Mr O'Brien has the penthouse suite at the Congress, only a couple of blocks from here.'

'He lives there?'

'Yes. Mr O'Brien's not the sort of businessman who goes in for flamboyant mansions. He likes to live quietly, without too much self-advertisement. We have enough of that in this town,' Bousakis added with a curled tongue, and Clements nodded in agreement.

Malone wondered what the penthouse suite at the Congress hotel would cost. Five thousand a week, six, seven, even allowing for corporate rates? It was an expensive way of living quietly, of being cost-conscious. He then began to wonder what the rumours were that Clements had mentioned about Cossack Holdings.

'What does Mr O'Brien *do*? I mean in regard to Cossack?'

'He's the executive chairman. He leaves the day-to-day running to me, but he's here every day, doing the strategic thinking. He wouldn't even know we own that apartment you're talking about.'

'I think we'd like to see him,' said Malone, taking over the bowling, deciding it was time to start seaming the ball.

'I don't think that can be arranged at such short notice –'

'You mean your girl outside hasn't already warned him we're here?' Clements was still thumping them down.

'You're pretty blunt, aren't you, Sergeant?'

'This is one of his milder days,' said Malone, deciding that Clements had bowled enough bean-balls. 'We don't want to be *rudely* blunt, Mr Bousakis, but we *are* investigating a murder committed in a flat owned by one of your companies.'

Bousakis said nothing for a moment, then he nodded. 'Sure.

30

It's a good point.' It's the only point, thought Malone; but didn't press it. 'I'll take you up to him.'

He pushed back his chair from the leather-topped antique desk; only then did Malone notice the semi-circle cut away in the desk-top to accommodate Bousakis' belly. The big man looked down at it and smiled without embarrassment.

'It's an idea I picked up in London, at one of the clubs there. Brooks'. There's a table where Charles James Fox, he was an eighteenth-century politician, used to play cards – they cut a piece out of the table so that he could fit his belly in. An admirable idea, I thought. I've always been built like this, even as a kid.'

'How did you get on at a desk when you were working your way up to this?' Clements was getting blunter by the minute. Malone had only *thought* of the question.

'I sat sideways,' said Bousakis and for the first time smiled. 'That way I was able to keep an eye on the competition.'

The three of them went up in a private lift to the boardroom and the office of the executive chairman. The reception lobby here was much smaller; the board directors were either modest men or the chairman did not feel that visitors had to be impressed. A lone secretary sat at her desk, a girl as elegant as Miss Rogers downstairs but a few years older, experience written all over her. She stood up as soon as Bousakis led the way out of the lift and said, as if she had been expecting them, 'I'll tell Mr O'Brien you're here.'

She went into the inner office and was back in a moment. Bousakis led the way in, filling the doorway as he passed through it and looming over the secretary like a dark blue hippo. This office was as large as Bousakis', as elegantly furnished but more modern. There were expensive paintings here, too, and several pieces of abstract statuary. And, between two of the paintings, a gold record in what looked to be a gold frame.

Brian Boru O'Brien rose from behind his brass-and-glass desk. He was in his early forties, it seemed, lean and fit. For all his ultra-Irish name, he looked pure Australian: the long jaw, the cheekbones showing under the stringy flesh, the squint wrinkles round the narrow eyes. He had thick dark hair, a wide, thin-lipped mouth full of very white, rather big teeth and a smile that, used too much, would puzzle strangers as to its sincerity. He was not handsome, never would be, but more women than not might find him attractive.

He came round the desk and put out a large hand. 'Hullo, Scobie. Remember me?'

THREE

1

Malone stared at him. He had trained himself to remember faces. In a game where names are just part of a criminal's wardrobe, to be changed at will, a face is as important as a fingerprint. There was something faintly familiar about O'Brien, but it was a face seen through the dusty glass of many years.

'Over twenty years ago,' said O'Brien. 'Twenty-three, twenty-four, whatever it was. At the police academy. I was Horrie O'Brien then, a cadet like you. A long long time ago,' he said and seemed to be speaking to himself.

Malone relaxed, suddenly laughed. 'Crumbs – you! That's you – Brian Boru? Is that your real name? No wonder you didn't use it at the academy.'

'No, Horace is my real name. Horace Clarence. Or Clarence Horace, I've done my best to forget which.' He looked at Bousakis and showed his big white teeth; it could have been either a smile or a snarl. 'You mention that outside this room, George, and you're out of a job. We all have our little secrets.'

'Sure we do, Brian. My middle name's Jason, if that'll make you any happier. My mother was always telling me to go looking for the Golden Fleece.' He sounded smug, as if he had found it. 'Do you have a middle name, Sergeant?'

Malone felt the game was getting away from him; he chipped in before Clements could answer. 'It's Persistence. Can we see you alone, Brian?'

'You want to talk about old times?' O'Brien gave him a full smile.

'Not exactly. If you'd excuse us, Mr Bousakis? We may be back to you.'

33

Bousakis flushed; he was not accustomed to being dismissed. He went out without a word, the bulk of his back seeming to tremble with indignation. O'Brien moved to the door, closed it and came back and waved Malone and Clements to green leather chairs set round a low glass coffee table.

'George doesn't like being shut out of things. He thinks this place can't run without him.'

'Can it?' said Clements.

O'Brien seemed to freeze in mid-air for a split second as he sat down; then he dropped into a chair. 'You mean the rumours? Don't believe everything you read in the newspapers, Sergeant. Were you at the academy when I was there?'

'You wouldn't remember me. I was in another group. I moved across to Scobie's group the week before we graduated.'

'I never did graduate. I often wonder what would have happened to me if I'd hung on there. But you're not here to talk about old times, you said. You're not from the Fraud Squad or anything like that, are you?'

'No,' said Malone. 'Homicide.'

For the first time O'Brien lost his composure. 'Jesus! *Homicide?*'

Malone gave him a brief summary of why they were here. 'Did you ever meet a woman named Mardi Jack?'

There was a moment's hesitation; the frown of puzzlement came a little too late. 'Mardi Jack? No. Has she murdered someone?'

'No. She was the one who was murdered. Shot by a high-powered rifle in a flat owned by one of your companies in Clarence Street.' Malone bowled a bumper of his own.

O'Brien didn't duck. 'I didn't know her. I don't even know anything about the flat.'

Malone had had no conviction that the B. in Mardi Jack's journal stood for Brian; it could have been the initial for half a dozen other names, surnames as well as given names. It could even stand for Bousakis. He stumbled mentally in his run-up to his next question: it was difficult to imagine that a mistress could be so desperately in love with a man as huge as Bousakis. Which only showed the prejudice of a lean and fit man.

34

He started again: 'This murder isn't going to be good for your corporate image. I mean, in view of the rumours . . .'

'You believe the rumours, too?' Hardly any of the big white teeth showed in O'Brien's dry smile.

I don't even know what they are: Malone, a non-investor, rarely read the financial pages. 'It's what other people believe that counts, isn't it? You want to hear what Sergeant Clements thinks? He's the Department's biggest investor, outside the police pension fund.'

O'Brien looked like a man who knew his leg was being pulled. 'What sort of investor are you, Sergeant?'

'A cautious one. I've also punted on a few of your horses.'

'Cautiously?'

Clements nodded, but didn't elaborate; the inference was that he did not take O'Brien's horses at face value. 'These rumours, Mr O'Brien. They involve a lot of people – I've heard a State cabinet minister mentioned and a Federal Opposition front-bencher. Insider trading.'

'It'll all come out in the wash,' said O'Brien, his leg safe but the rest of him now looking vulnerable. 'And the wash will be cleaner than you've all expected. It's the old tall poppy syndrome – chop down anyone who does better than the mediocre. That's the sacred koala in this country – mediocrity.'

Malone had heard it all before; there was a certain truth to it. He wondered, however, if a nation dedicated to worship of the brilliant would have been any better. The jails weren't full of just failures; there were a lot of over-achievers amongst them. Tall poppies who had lopped off their own heads.

'Is the NCSC gunna hold an enquiry?' said Clements.

'They've already started.' O'Brien appeared relaxed; but he was gently bouncing one big hand in the other. 'I thought you'd know that.'

Clements took another tack, a wide outswinger: 'Didn't you have something to do with music at one time?'

The hands paused. 'Yes. Quite some years ago. That was how I first got started.'

'You managed and promoted pop stars in Britain and America?'

That explained O'Brien's accent. Malone had been trying to place it: it had an Australian base, the vowels occasionally flattened, but there was something else laid over it, a transatlantic sound.

'Yes,' said O'Brien. 'What's this got to do with what happened today? The murder, I mean.'

Malone took up the attack again, seeing where Clements was leading. 'Miss Jack was a singer. One of your firms, Kensay, owns a recording studio where she was working on Saturday before she was killed. How long ago were you in London – what do I call you, Horrie or Brian?'

'Brian,' said O'Brien coldly. 'Horrie was someone I knew in another life. Someone I've just about forgotten.'

His voice had changed as he spoke, became almost English; it was a formal statement. There seemed a note of venom in what he said, but Malone couldn't be sure. The hands now were locked together.

Malone repeated his question: 'How long ago were you in London?'

'I went there over twenty years ago, a couple of years after I dropped out of the police academy. I came home eight years ago.'

'And you've built all this up in eight years?' Malone waved a hand, as if the O'Brien empire was spread out below them.

'I read all the stuff put out by Australia House in London. The Land of Opportunity. I figured if the Poms like Alan Bond and the Hungarians and the Balts could come out here and make fortunes, so could I.'

'And you did.' Flatly.

'Yes.' Just as flatly.

Malone eased his tone a little. 'You still in pop music? I don't keep up with the pop scene.'

'I gave it up in the mid-seventies. I got out before it sent me deaf. I went into property – that's silent and you don't have to deal with little jerks who think they own the world because they've made a hit single. What's all this leading up to?'

'Mardi Jack was in love with a man she met in London ten

years ago, maybe a bit more. A feller whose initial was B. It could've been Brian.'

'It could have been Bill or Boris or Buster, any bloody name at all. You're not making me too happy, chum.'

'Maybe you've forgotten – they didn't invent the police force to make people happy. They told us that at the academy. I'm just doing my job, Mr O'Brien, trying to find out who murdered a woman who'd be a bloody sight happier if she were still alive.'

O'Brien said nothing for a moment; then he nodded. 'Sure, I understand. You've just caught me on the wrong foot. I've got so many other things on my mind –' It was an admission that he seemed instantly to regret; he was the sort of man who would always claim to be in control of a situation. He waved one of his big awkward hands, taking in his office and everything that could be seen from its big picture windows. He stood up, walked to one of the windows; he had an aggressive walk, the way, Malone remembered, the police academy had taught them to approach a riotous assembly. But there was no riotous assembly here, just a crowd of suspicions. 'I'm sorry about what happened to Miss Jack, but I've got enough bastards out there hounding me without you two trying to lay something else on me.'

'Righto, one last question. Where did you spend the week-end?'

For a moment it seemed that O'Brien hadn't heard the question; then he turned back from the window. It had started to rain once more; the glass looked as if it was dissolving, the city behind him was about to collapse. He had a sudden stricken look on his face. 'I can't tell you that, Scobie.'

'Why not?' Malone saw that Clements was scribbling in his notebook: negative answers were sometimes as helpful as positive ones.

'I was with a lady. I'm not going to tell you her name.'

'Are you married?'

'I was. Twice. I've been divorced for, I don't know, twelve years, I think.'

'Your ex-wives – where are they?'

'In London. They were both in the pop scene – one was a singer, the other was in PR. There were no kids, thank Christ.

They're married again, both of them, and, as far as I know, never give me a thought. Is this going to keep on? If it is, I think I'll send for my lawyer.'

Malone rose and Clements followed him. 'There'll be no need for that, not yet. But we may have to come back, Mr O'Brien.'

'Mr O'Brien? I suppose I'd better get used to calling you Inspector? We were mates once, remember? Well, almost.'

Bits of memory were coming back, like the jetsam of youth drifting in on a long-delayed tide. 'I don't think we were ever mates, Horrie. You were too much of a loner, you always had your eye on the main chance.'

2

'Brian Boru –' Except in passion, when she called him names even his mother would never have called him (or perhaps least of all his mother), he was always Brian Boru to her, as if the two words were hyphenated. It had a certain Gaelic-Gallic ring to it, if one could imagine the combination. 'I can't get there for at least an hour.'

'Can't you make it before then?'

'It's impossible. What's so serious?'

But he said he didn't want to talk about it over the phone, he would expect to see her in an hour. She hung up, stood for a moment looking out at the rain-drenched gardens without seeing them. He had sounded worried; more importantly, he had sounded as if he *needed* her. Almost every night, in the last moments before falling asleep, she asked herself why she had fallen so desperately in love with him. She had met many more physically attractive men, as many who were more attractive in their personality and their approach to women. But if love could be defined in definite terms, it would have died years ago: the psychoanalysts would have turned it into a clinical science. She had been in love before, with three men before her husband, and she knew in her heart, if not in her head, that part of the joy of love was that one could never truly fathom it. She no longer loved her husband: that was something she was definite about, had been for months before she had met Brian Boru. But there could be no thought of divorce from the Prime Minister, not while he was in office.

She could hear the chatter behind her in the main rooms of the house. Kirribilli House, the Prime Minister's Sydney residence, had never been as much a favourite with her and Philip as it had been with previous Prime Ministers and their wives; she always compared it unfavourably with Admiralty House next door, the Governor-General's residence. Both were harbourside mansions built by nineteenth-century men with delusions of grandeur; Gibbes, the Collector of Customs who had built Admiralty House, had had grander delusions than Feez, the merchant of Kirribilli House. Both the Norvals had aspirations to grandeur, though Anita kept hers more secret. It was difficult to compete with her husband's conceit, but up till now she had not discouraged him in his ambition to some day be Governor-General. It would be even more difficult, as the wife of the G-G, to get a divorce.

She went out of the small study where she had taken the call and back to the main reception room. She paused in the doorway, caught the last of the gossip before this charity morning tea broke up. It was for one of her favourite charities, homes for deaf children, and she was glad the children couldn't hear the gossip.

'Have you met her husband? His idea of repartee is to pass wind.'

'Why do we need men? I'm beginning to understand lesbians.'

'That writer over there, what's-her-name, she's one, you know.'

'Really? I thought they all looked like punk rockers.'

'I tried to congratulate her on her new book, but she got in first. She writes her own reviews, so they say.'

'They sleep in separate rooms,' Anita heard from another corner. 'She tells me they make love on their anniversary each year. I'm surprised they know where the essentials still are.'

The women began to file past Anita Norval, chattering, murmuring, gushing. She found groups of women no worse than

39

groups of men; the men were a little more deferential to her, paying awkward court to her beauty and the position of her husband, if they were conservatives. Gossip was endemic to both sexes; the men varied it by trying to buy or sell influence with it. There were no men here this morning and she was glad of that; she did not want to compare any of them with Brian Boru. It was a weakness she recognized in herself that she was always comparing people. It had started when she had first gone into radio over twenty years ago.

Penelope Debbs, the last to leave, stood before her. 'I always enjoy coming to Kirribilli House, Anita. You're so fortunate.'

'It comes with the territory, as they say.' In her days in radio, when she had hosted her own chat show, she had perhaps used too many American expressions; she had cured herself of that since Philip had gone into politics, but some still clung. They put her very much on side with Philip's minders, all of whom had done a quick course in Americana. 'You should put forward a bill to have a permanent residence for the State Premier. There are several going around Point Piper for ten or twelve million.'

'I'm Labour, remember? If ever I suggested anything like that, I'd be thrown out on my rear.'

She had been born a Whymper; with such a name she had been destined for some sort of climbing, though Alps were in short supply locally. Unfitted for mountaineering, she had taken up political climbing. She had driven her pitons into at least a dozen rivals on her way up, buried others in small avalanches started by her scrabbling boots.

'Never you, Penelope.' No one ever called her Penny, except one man: that would suggest a value much below that which she put on herself.

She was the State Minister for Development; her main development, it was said, was her own advancement. Her ambition was so naked that the Premier, Hans Vanderberg, had once remarked that it should be censored and not allowed on television in front of children; it was rumoured that when in the Cabinet Room with her, he wore a chain-mail vest and never turned his back on her. She was a goodlooking redhead till she turned her face full on to one: then one saw the green ball-bearings that were her eyes and the white steel smile. She gave Anita the smile now.

'No, that's true. It's very comforting representing constituents who think I'm Mother Teresa.'

That was when God should have sent the bolt of lightning; but God, Anita often thought, was a Labour sponsor. 'How's Arnold? I rarely see him in Canberra.'

Arnold Debbs was a Federal Labour member, sitting on the front bench opposite Philip and his ministers. The Debbs were a formidable pair. 'He finds Canberra boring – one always does when one is in Opposition. He tries to escape as often as he can. I'll tell him you asked after him. Give Philip my love. How is he? Still playing God? Or is it the other way round?'

'He's busy.' Though God knew what at or with whom. He had a new secretary who was either slow at her word processor or quick in bed; either way, Philip and she had been working an awful lot of overtime lately. Anita did not care, so long as Philip didn't ask what *she* was doing. 'I'll tell him you asked after him.'

Then the house was empty but for the servants cleaning up, her secretary and the Federal policeman who was her security guard. All at once she wished she were rid of it all, it had all suddenly become tiring, tiresome and empty; she had tried to become a political animal but the metamorphosis had been too much for her, though few would have known. She longed now for escape with Brian Boru, away from the constant wearing of a face that was false, the rein on a tongue that wanted to be truthful, the *politics*.

She hurried upstairs, checked her make-up, went to the bath-room for a nervous pee, as if she were a teenager sneaking out on a date, put on a raincoat and hat, and as she came downstairs was met by her secretary, Grace Weldon.

'Going out? I'll tell Sergeant Long –'

'No, Grace. I'll drive myself. May I borrow your car?'

Each time they came up from Canberra for an extended stay, Grace Weldon drove up in her own car, a bright red Celica. Not really a car to be driving in to a secret assignation, but better that than to be driven there in a government car.

Grace looked dubious. 'I don't know – no, I don't mean I

don't want to lend you my car. By all means, take it. But Sergeant Long will hit the roof when I tell him you've gone off –'

'Then don't tell him, not unless he asks.'

'May I ask where you're going?' Grace was tentative, but she asked out of the best of intentions. 'Ted Long said you were gone Saturday night and all day yesterday. He was nearly out of his mind. He rang me at my mother's, wanted to know what I knew. Did he say anything to you?'

'Yes, this morning. Very politely. I just told him I was visiting an old schoolfriend who's in trouble and I thought the fewer people who knew about it, the better.'

'Is that what you're telling me now?'

She hesitated, then put her hand on Grace's arm; it was almost as if she were speaking to her own daughter. 'No, Grace. I'm going to meet a man I'm very much in love with.'

Grace pursed her lips as if she were about to whistle. She was a romantic, which, with being a cynic, is the best of two things to be in politics; it was the in-betweens, like Anita, who couldn't stand the disillusion. She squeezed Anita's hand. 'You look marvellously happy. That's good enough for me. Here are the keys. I'll take care of Sergeant Long.'

Anita drove north up Pacific Highway, the main artery to the tree-thick suburbs of the North Shore. The area was called the North Shore, though it did not begin till one had travelled at least five or six miles from the actual north shore of the harbour. The Japanese business community, which had moved into the area in the last few years and started its own school, was still bewildered at the natives' careless attitude to geography and put it down to the fact that the continent was so vast that a few miles here or there didn't matter. There was no South Shore or West Shore; the underprivileged who lived in those desert regions had to find their own social status symbols. To live on (never *in*) the North Shore was a sign that one had arrived at a certain altitude on the social climb: half the climbers might be bent double under the back-pack of mortgages, but social status supplies an oxygen all its own.

Anita turned off into Killara, one of the older suburbs. She had grown up here and when she and Philip had bought their own small mansion in one of the quiet tree-lined streets, when Philip had been at the height of his TV fame, there had been no feeling, at least on her part, that she was a new arrival. Her mother and father, he a retired banker, lived half a dozen streets away. They were pillars of the local community, Doric columns of respectability, and they would have been frozen stiff with disapproval if they had known what she was doing.

She turned into the driveway. *This* was home to her: The Lodge in Canberra and Kirribilli House were only *pieds-à-terre*. All political leaders' spouses felt the same, she guessed: the tenants of the White House and Camp David, of Number 10 Downing Street and Chequers could never think of those places as *home*. She loved the big old house, but just tolerated the extravagances Philip had added when the money had been rolling in: the 100-foot swimming pool, the cabana that her son and daughter had always called the Taj Mahal dolls' house, the all-weather tennis court, the jacuzzi and the sauna. She had put her foot down only when Philip had ordered a haute cuisine barbecue. Though she had been in radio when she married him, she had been with the ABC, whose poor budget didn't encourage extravagance and so had built for its stars a reputation for good taste.

She parked the red Celica in the triple garage, closed the doors to hide it and went across to the house. As she put her key in the front door Brian Boru came hurrying up the driveway, seeming to half-run on his toes, as if he did not want to arouse the neighbours with the sound of his shoes on the gravel. He was wearing a raincoat with the collar turned up and a hat with the brim turned down all round and looked like a minor character out of the Midnight Movie.

'Where did you park your car?'

'Quick, inside!' He almost pushed her into the house, slammed the door shut behind them. 'Is there anyone here?'

'Of course not.' She wanted to laugh at the melodramatic way he was acting; but reason told her he would not be acting like this without cause. 'That's why I suggested we come here. I don't want to be found out, any more than you do. Now what's this all about?'

43

He took off his hat and now she saw clearly the worry and concern in his bony face. She was a practical woman, even when wildly in love. She wanted to embrace him, hold him tight against her till she could feel the hardening of him; but, as always, she first wanted to know exactly where she was. The actual place didn't matter, the situation did.

'Has Philip found out about us? Has he been on to you?'

'Christ, no! I could handle him.' He took her by the hand and looked about him. He had met her here two or three times since they had fallen in love, but he still didn't know his way round the house. It was one thing to know one's way around a man's wife, but another one altogether to invade his house willy-nilly. 'Where can we go?'

She could feel the tension in him. 'Relax, there's no one here. Our cleaning woman comes in once a week when we're not here, just to rearrange the dust. We'll be *all right*,' she said reassuringly. This was her first affair since she had married Philip, yet sometimes she felt so much more experienced than her lover. 'Let's go in here.'

She led him into the sun-room that looked out on to the back garden and the pool. As in almost every room in the house, there was a television set here; Philip never wanted to miss any screening of himself, no matter how brief. The screen now was, mercifully, grey and blank.

They sat down beside each other on a couch, still holding hands. He looked at their hands, then at her face. For weeks she had tried to put a name to that look: it was more than love. Suddenly she realized it was gratitude and the thought hurt her.

'You're a real comfort,' he said. Then his grip tightened; she was always surprised at the strength in those big hands, they had often bruised her in their love-making. 'I'm in trouble.'

'Trouble?' She had heard the rumours; even Philip had discussed them at the breakfast table as he read the financial pages. 'You've never talked about the rumours –'

'No, not them. Well, yes, maybe –' A thought struck him, one that hadn't occurred to him before. 'A girl was murdered in our flat at the weekend.'

'*Our* flat?'

44

Then she realized which one he meant. They had met there half a dozen times, he always making sure that none of his corporate executives ever tried to use it at the same time. She had felt sleazy at first, sharing a bed with God knew how many other lovers; the sheets were always clean, but she had seen the semen stains on the mattress, like dirty handprints. The flat was obviously as much a fringe benefit for the local executives as it was an accommodation for interstate and overseas executives. Then she had come to realize that all the beds they shared, with the exception of that here in her own house, would provoke a feeling of sleaze: she had never achieved the blind innocence of the really promiscuous. Even here she never took him into her and Philip's bed; they always went into one of the spare bedrooms. As if he were no more than a visitor in her life. Which (and the thought chilled her) was all he might prove to be.

'A girl – *murdered*? Which girl?'

'One I used to know.' He had known dozens, she knew that, though he had never boasted of them. Indeed, he had seemed almost ashamed of them, as if he would rather have come to her a virgin. *You're the only woman I've ever loved*, he had told her the second time he had made love to her, and she had believed him. He was a liar and a robber in business; she had heard the Minister for Business Affairs describe him that way to Philip. Yet with her (or was it conceit on her part?) he was sometimes self-scaldingly truthful. As he was now: 'I told her it was all over, but she didn't want to believe it.'

'Who killed her?'

'How the hell – sorry. I don't know. The police are working on it.'

'Have they been to see you?' He nodded. 'What did you tell them?'

'Nothing. That's where I was stupid – they'll find out eventually. All I wanted to do, I was thinking on the spur of the moment, was to protect you.'

'You told them you didn't know the girl?'

'I even told them I knew nothing about the flat. I was bloody stupid, but I could see them asking other questions . . .' She wondered if men in desperate love were always so naïve. But

45

naïveté, of course, was a part of love: that was one of its weaknesses.

'She was murdered at the weekend? Did they ask where you'd spent Saturday and Sunday?'

'I told them I'd spent it with a lady I wasn't going to name.' He could be very old-fashioned at times; it was one of the more endearing things about him. She wondered if the original Brian Boru had been chivalrous towards women, but decided it was unlikely: Irish and medieval, he would have been too busy fighting, drinking and talking.

She squeezed his hand in thanks; then felt ashamed that so far her concern had been only for themselves. 'How was the poor girl killed? Was it an intruder or someone?'

'The police said she'd been shot, it looked as if it was from a neighbouring building.'

'Did you and – did she go to the flat regularly?'

'Fairly regularly – up till I met you.'

'Did she have a husband or a boy-friend?'

He looked at her with admiration; he was recovering his composure. 'You would make a good detective.'

She hadn't meant to sound like that. 'You don't want me playing detective – there'll be enough of the real ones. You should have told them the truth right from the start. In the long run it's always best.'

'You don't believe that.' He was gently cynical for the moment. 'Not with a husband in politics. This is the same, darling. There are always cover-ups in politics. I was trying to cover up on you.'

So far she had felt little fear; she was more concerned for the situation he had got himself into by his lying to protect her. Six months ago she would have laughed at the idea that she would be having a passionate clandestine affair with a man who was hated, even despised, more than he was admired. She was forty-five years old and a grandmother, even if only recently. True, she was still beautiful in face and figure, thanks to Jane Fonda's videos and her own genes; her parents, in their late sixties, were still a handsome enough pair to look good even in the candid camera shots on the social pages. She was intelligent, could be witty, if sometimes waspish, and always rated in the

46

top five of the list of Most Popular Women of the Year. She was married to the most popular prime minister in decades, a man who fitted perfectly into the Image, a quality that, his minders told her, was the most necessary qualification for today's leaders. She had two children, one of whom had fled the Image of his father and was now working in a merchant bank in London, the other married to a doctor and living in the Northern Territory, where the Image never penetrated; she had two grandchildren, both too young to know what an Image was even when it interrupted their cartoons on television. She was moral and decent and had taken seriously her task of trying to set an example. Then she had met Brian Boru, the last man she would have thought she would fall for, and had stepped off a cliff.

And now, somehow, she was involved in a murder. For the first time she was suddenly, terribly afraid; but for *him*: 'Was it someone trying to kill you?'

He hesitated, took his hand away and put his arm along the back of the couch behind her. 'I thought of that, only a few moments ago. I've got enemies, but I never thought anyone'd want to *kill* me. Christ, I *hate* violence!'

She was studying him, looking for the stranger she hadn't yet discovered: she knew there was one hidden there in Brian Boru O'Brien. He had none of Philip's classical good looks; the only feature that gave him distinction were the streaks of grey thick hair along his temples; there was no grey in her own equally thick dark hair, yet she was two years older than he. In public he had a certain arrogance to him, but never with her: not even at the moment they had first met, she remembered. He had been extraordinarily successful in a generation that, it seemed to her, had bred successful men like too-fecund rabbits. Yet, unlike the country's *nouveaux riches*, he did not flash his wealth. Sure, he lived in luxury at the Congress, but no one could drive or sail past and say, with sour envy, 'There's that bastard O'Brien's ten-million-dollar waterfront palace.' He owned no yacht, no Learjet, not even a car; once, he told her, he had owned a Rolls-Royce in London, but in those days in the pop world you were expected to own a Rolls. It wasn't so much a status symbol, he had said, as a jerk of the thumb at the Establishment who

47

had thought up till then they had owned the world. The financial columnists told her that his dealings with the business Establishment in this country were done with a jerk of the thumb; yet he was always a gentleman of the old school with her, though her father had belonged to the Establishment. He was not a gentleman in bed, but it was her guess that no man worth his balls was ever a gentleman in bed, even one of the old school: she couldn't imagine anything more boring than being made love to by a gentleman. Brian Boru was a sum of contradictions and she hadn't yet got them all in place. There was still a stranger hidden amongst them.

'I think you should go to the police and tell them the truth.'

He shook his head emphatically. 'I'll never tell them about you.'

'I don't want you to – I hope you don't have to. But if you have to explain where you were Saturday and Sunday . . .'

They had spent the weekend at a hotel on the Central Coast; in winter it had few guests and certainly none who would recognize O'Brien. She had worn a blonde wig and the rimless fashion glasses she wore when watching movies or television; they made her look older, but, she had told herself, she wasn't spending the weekend with some youth half her age. The wig had been a joke gift from Dolly Parton, whom Philip had invited to dinner at The Lodge during one of the singer's tours: she had got on like a fond sister with Dolly, a woman who understood men. She had trimmed the wig; she hadn't wanted some guest at the hotel asking her to sing 'We Had All the Good Things Going'. Brian Boru had laughed at her disguise, but not in an offensive way; it had been a wonderful weekend. At forty-five she had been like a young girl in love for the first time, keeping him in bed till she had exhausted him and then, laughing, mothering him.

'Go and see the police. You may need their protection.'

'Darling, the police don't protect you – it's not their job. Not unless they want you as a witness.'

'They protect *me* –' But she knew that was different. 'No, you're right. But I still think you should go to them, tell them you knew – what was her name?'

48

'Mardi Jack. She was a singer, you'd have never heard of her.'

'I wish I hadn't.' She couldn't help that: there are several sorts of love-bites.

He nodded, understanding. She wondered if he had been so understanding with his other women. 'I first met her in London years ago, just after my second marriage broke up.'

God, you and your women! All at once, for the first time, she was jealous. But all she said was, 'Don't tell me any more about her.'

'You'll read all about her in the papers, I suppose.'

'I'll try not to.' But she knew she would: you didn't know what masochism was till you were truly in love.

'The papers will get on to me as soon as they find out who owns the flat. It's going to be pretty harsh from now on.'

He looked out at the grey garden. The rain had stopped, but the trees and bushes were still dripping. Some leaves floated on the pool like scabs on the dark green water; a magpie strutted importantly across the big lawn. More rain was coming up from the south-west, thick grey drapes of it. He understood weather; it was one of the reasons he had come home from England. He had been only thirty-five then, but already he had known that he could never grow old in the English climate. Now, suddenly, he was in a climate that frightened him.

'I think we'd better not see each other for a while. Just in case . . .' He put his hand on her shoulder. 'I'd never forgive myself if you were hurt.'

'I'm going to be hurt if I can't see you.' But she knew he was right. 'How did we two fall so much in love?'

3

It was the next afternoon, Tuesday, when Clements got the call from Ballistics. He listened to what they had to tell him; then he hung up and came into Malone's office. Malone was reading the running sheets of three other cases being handled by Homicide in Southern Region. When the Department had been regionalized almost two years ago, no one had quite been able to work out how the State had been cut up; it had been described as a cross between a jigsaw and a gerrymander, with no winners. Southern Region covered most of Sydney south of the harbour, then ran in a narrow strip about a hundred and eighty kilometres down the coast, then cut in an almost straight line across the State to the border with South Australia, taking in the whole of the area down to the Victorian border. On the map on Malone's office wall it looked like a huge axe stood on its head. An axe that many, including Malone, would like to have buried in the heads of the planners who had devised the regional plan.

Malone threw down the running sheets. 'Well, what have you got?'

'Ballistics. They match, all three bullets are from the same rifle. Jason James says they're .243s, probably fired from a Winchester, but maybe a Tikka or one of the other European guns. He knows his guns, that kid.'

'Interesting,' said Malone. 'But where does that leave us? Three people bumped off in three different locations by the same hitman. Did they know each other?'

'I haven't a clue.' It was a cliché no policeman would ever repeat at a press conference.

'Who would want to shoot a construction worker, a desk cop and a second-rate singer?' Malone turned to look at the second map on his wall, one of metropolitan Sydney. 'Those locations are all ten or twelve kilometres apart – Parramatta is more than that from Clarence Street. Where did the construction bloke live?'

'I'm not sure. Somewhere down on the Illawarra line. We didn't handle that one, the guys from Chatswood did it. We know where Terry Sugar and Mardi Jack lived. Can we tie O'Brien into that? I mean, say he was meant to be the target and not the girl?'

Malone shook his head. 'That connection would be even further out than with the girl. If he was meant to be the target, how come the killer shot the girl by mistake? If he's a pro, that is.'

'I was at the flat before you, Scobie. The lights were still on.

When the cleaning lady phoned in, they told her not to touch anything. She didn't. There were two table lamps on, that was all – both against the inside wall. Mardi Jack was in pants and her hair was cut short – against the light she could have been mistaken for a man.'

'Even through a 'scope?'

'We don't know the circumstances, maybe the guy thought he was gunna be disturbed and had to hurry things. There's a security patrol checks all those buildings on that side of Kent Street every two hours.'

'The roof-tops, too?'

'No-o,' Clements admitted grudgingly. 'Look, I know I'm trying to drag O'Brien into this. I'd like to think he was the intended target. That'll be a bloody sight easier than trying to nail him as the guy who hired the hitman to hurt Mardi Jack.'

'You're looking for an easy way out.'

Clements nodded. 'It's the weather. I'm sick of getting a wet arse. I'd just like to sit here and have the case come in and drop itself in my lap.'

Then Malone's phone rang and he picked it up. It was Chief Superintendent Danforth. 'Can you pop into my office, Scobie? I'd like to see you.'

'Right now, Harry?'

'Now, Scobie. I've got Sergeant Chew here with me from Northern Region and Sergeant Ludke from Parramatta.'

Malone hung up, cursing softly. Harry Danforth was one of the old-style cops who believed that the operative word in the phrase *police force* was the last word. He had been noted for his stand-over tactics; he never went in for strategy, because he didn't know what it meant. Twice there had been departmental charges of corruption against him, but Internal Affairs had never been able to prove anything. He had remained under suspicion and had been offered the opportunity to resign on full pension, but he had refused. He was within a year now of the retiring age of sixty-five and the Department had, in its own fit of resignation, solved the problem of Harry Danforth by promoting him to chief superintendent and moving him upwards out of harm's and the public's way. He had an office in Police Centre and the title of Crime Co-ordinator, a caption no one quite understood but which was thought, in view of his past history, an apt description.

'Danforth wants to see me. He's got Jack Chew and Hans Ludke with him.'

Clements raised his eyebrows. 'Maybe we're gunna draw a prize. Maybe they've got some connection.'

'Now all we have to do is link it with Mardi Jack. While I'm gone, send someone down to one of the newspapers and have them dig out a photo of Brian Boru. Then have them go back to The Warehouse and go through all the tenants there, the permanent residents and the companies that own flats there, and show 'em O'Brien's picture. If he's used that flat at all, he'd have to have met *someone* going up and down in the lift.'

'You don't believe he didn't know Mardi Jack?'

'No. Do you?'

'No,' said Clements. 'I'd never back a horse on intuition. But I'd lay money my intuition is right about him. He's a born liar. I'm never wrong, tipping them.'

'I'll take you any day over forensic evidence,' said Malone and went out of his office.

Chief Superintendent Harry Danforth was a big man, but most of his muscle now was fat. He had a pink, mottled face and cunning rather than shrewd eyes; he had a short-back-and-sides haircut and a voice foggy with years of free whiskies and cartons of purloined cigarettes. He was the last of his kind, out of place in the bright clean clinic that was Police Centre. He still had the suggestion about him of dark walls and fly-spattered lights and grime of old police stations.

'You know Jack Chew and Hans Ludke?'

Malone had met Ludke on only one or two occasions; he was German-born but looked Latin: tall and dark with a bony handsome face and thick finger-waved hair that Malone thought had gone out with the advent of unisex salons. He had the reputation of being a good honest cop and a hard worker.

Jack Chew was an Australian-born Chinese, compactly built and with a face that, Malone was sure, had an acquired Oriental inscrutability. Russ Clements had once worked on a case with him and had come back with a story of Chew's approach. The suspect, a part-Aboriginal, had taken one look at Chew, but the Chinese had got in first: 'No Charlie Chan jokes or I'll run you in for obscene language.'

'What fucking obscene language?'

'That'll do for starters,' Chew had said and grinned at Clements. 'They fall for it every time.'

Malone said hullo to the two detectives and sat down. 'What's on, Chief?'

There were times when Danforth liked to be reminded, and have others reminded, of his rank. He was not unaware of his low standing with younger officers, but he was too lazy to attempt any strict discipline. Malone knew that so long as one touched the forelock occasionally, Danforth could be handled.

'The Assistant Commissioner, Crime, has put me in charge of these three murders. Two of the victims were hit by the same rifle.'

'So was the third,' said Malone. 'I just got the results from Ballistics.'

Chew and Ludke looked at each other, then all three officers looked at Danforth. He ran a ham of a hand over his head; it was a habit, as if he were trying to push his thoughts into some sort of working order. 'Well, it looks like we've got something, doesn't it?'

What? Malone wanted to ask.

'Now we might be able to get somewhere.' Danforth leaned forward on his desk. 'You men will work independently on your own cases, okay? But you'll send me copies of your running sheets each day and I'll have 'em co-ordinated.'

'What have you fellers got so far?' Malone asked.

'Not much,' said Ludke and handed Malone a copy of his running sheets. 'Everything's in there, Terry Sugar had had no threats. Matter of fact, he was probably the most popular cop in the district. He had no connection, as far as we can trace, with any crims, drug pushers, scum like that. His family life was happy – his wife says she'd have known if he was carrying on with any other woman. There's no motive so far, none that we can see.'

Malone glanced at the brief history of the life and death of

53

Terence Ronald Sugar. Born 16 January 1945, two years in a factory after leaving high school, enlisted as a police cadet February 1965, steady promotion but career indistinguished except for two commendations for bravery . . . 'How did he get on with the Asians out your way? You have some Vietnamese gangs out there.'

'He wouldn't have come in contact with them unless they were brought in and charged. The gangs have only started to operate in the last two or three years. He'd been on the desk all that time.'

'They were my first suspects,' said Danforth, putting in his two cents worth; it was worth no more. He had no time for anyone who wasn't white, preferably of British stock and Protestant. He would never understand how Jack Chew, a Chink, had risen to be a sergeant. Chinese should only run restaurants or market gardens.

Chew passed over his sheets to Malone. 'My guy is just as unexciting. He'd led a pretty nomadic life –'

'What's that?' said Danforth, who had never learned to hide his ignorance.

'Wandering. A drifter,' said Chew with Oriental patience. 'But once he married, he settled down, was a good husband and provider. As far as his wife knows and as far as we can find out, he never fooled around with other women. He was a good-looking guy and he was popular with the women at the leagues club near where he lived. But it never went beyond some mild flirting. No jealous husbands or boy-friends. The main point is, he had no connection with Terry Sugar, at least not for twenty years or more.'

'What was the connection then?'

Chew nodded at the sheets in Malone's hand. 'It's all in there. Compare the two of them.'

Malone saw it at once: *Enlisted as a police cadet, February 1965*. 'He was at the academy? Harry Gardner?'

'He dropped out as soon as he'd finished the course and then went walkabout for five years all over Australia.'

'Where are your sheets?' said Danforth to Malone.

'You didn't tell me to bring them –' Malone was trying to

picture the academy classes of twenty-four years ago. 'I remember him now – dimly. He was in my group . . . Jesus!'

'You remembered something?' said Ludke.

'There is a connection with my case. Mardi Jack, my girl, wasn't the target.' Russ Clements had been right after all. He told them about his visit to Brian Boru O'Brien. 'One of his companies owns the flat where the murder happened. The killer was expecting O'Brien to be there.'

'So?' said Chew.

'Terry Sugar, Gardner and O'Brien were all at the academy at the same time. They were all in my group.'

Danforth and the two junior officers sat back, saying nothing. Then Hans Ludke broke the silence: 'Does that put you on the hitman's list, too?'

FOUR

1

Malone got out of the car, waited till Lisa and the children had got out, then set the alarm and locked it. He debated whether to remove the hub-caps and lock them in the boot, but decided it would be too much trouble. Everyone in the street knew he was a cop and he had to take the chance that they either feared him or respected him. Erskineville had never been an area, even when he was growing up here, that had loved cops. Even his father had hated them.

Con Malone, the cop-hater mortally ashamed of having a cop for a son, was waiting in the doorway of the narrow terrace house for them. This was a house much like Mardi Jack's and Gina Cazelli's in Paddington; but Erskineville had never become gentrified like that other inner city district. All that had changed since Malone had lived here was that European immigrants had replaced the old British and Irish stock and that brighter colours had been painted over the old standard brown. Con, an immigrant-hater as well, had only just become accustomed to the Italians and Greeks and Lebanese newcomers, when, you wouldn't believe it, the bloody Asians had started to move in. What with one bias and another, he was in a state of constant warfare never quite declared.

'G'day, kids.' He was not a kissing grandfather; that was for the Wogs. He shook hands with Lisa, but just nodded to Malone. He was as afraid of sentiment as he was of foreign invasions. 'Gran's ready to put dinner on the table. You know what she's like, no waiting around.'

'No pre-dinner drinks?' said Malone. 'No canapés?'

'None of your fancy stuff with Mum,' said Con, but had enough sense of humour to grin. 'You been busy?'

'Same as usual,' said Malone and followed his family and his father down the narrow hall, stepping back, as he did every time he came here, into another life. Even though he was an only child and had loved his parents in the same undemonstrative way they loved him, he had wanted to escape from this house ever since he could remember. The dark small rooms, the ever-present smell of cooking, the constant shouts and screams from the ever-warring couple next door which would keep him awake at night; he had known there was a better place to live somewhere out there. His mother and father, he had known even then, would never leave; not even now when the Wogs and the Yellow Horde were pressing in on them. They felt safe in the small, narrow house. And, he hated to admit it, he too had felt safe: the whole world, it seemed, had then been a safer place. At least there had been no hit lists with his name on them.

His mother had dinner on the table; they were expected to arrive on time. She clasped the children to her, as she had never clasped Scobie to her; then pushed them into their chairs around the dining table. She gave her cheek to Lisa's kiss, but didn't return the kiss; she loved Lisa as much as she did the children and Scobie, but, like Con, she could not handle public sentiment.

'Get started! Don't let it get cold.'

It was a roast lamb dinner, the usual: none of your foreign muck here. Con had bought a bottle of red, his compliment to Lisa, the sophisticate in the family. Malone noticed it was a good label and he wondered who had advised the Old Man. Gradually Con Malone was changing for the better, but his son knew it was too late.

When dinner was over Lisa went into the kitchen to help Brigid with the washing-up, the children went into the front room to watch television and Malone and his father sat on at the dinner table to finish the bottle of wine.

'I notice someone shot a copper out at Parramatta last week. You working on that one?'

'No, that's for the Parramatta boys. I've got my own case.'

'That singer they found in Clarence Street?' Though he would

57

never admit it, Con Malone followed all the police news. He knew the dangers of his son's job and he was afraid for him, though he would never admit that, either. 'They're shooting a lotta coppers these days,' he said, giving his wine a careful look, as if he were a wine-taster.

Malone remarked his father's concern and was touched by it; but he could never let Con know. All at once he was struck with the sad, odd wonder at what he would say to the Old Man on his death-bed. Would there be a last moment when both of them would let the barrier down and they would admit the truth of the love that strangled them both?

'It's a different world, Dad.'

'You ever get any threats?' He had never asked that question before.

'Once or twice.' There had been more than that; but why worry his father with them? 'You just have to pick the serious ones from the loud-mouths.'

'You ever tell Lisa about 'em?'

'No. When you were having those union fights on the wharves, did you tell Mum?'

'No.' Con drained his glass, took his time before he said, 'If someone ever tries to get you, let me know.'

'Why? What'll you do?'

'I dunno. Bugger-all, I suppose. But I'd just like to know.'

Malone looked at his own glass; the wine had the colour of drying blood. 'No, Dad. I don't bring my worries home to Lisa –' Which wasn't strictly true; she anticipated them. 'I'm not going to do it with you. I can handle whatever comes up. But if something ever does happen to me, I hope you and Mum would help prop up Lisa and the kids.'

'You think we wouldn't?' Con Malone looked offended. 'Jesus Christ –'

'Who's swearing?' said Brigid, coming in from the kitchen. 'What if the children hear you?' They were her angels, to be protected from the world. She sprayed the house with holy water, as if dampening down the dust of sin; her rosary beads were always in her pocket, more important than a handkerchief. All her life she had been religious, but little of it had rubbed off on her husband and only a little more on her son. But at least I'm a believer, Malone thought. He doubted that his father was.

Lisa ran a hand affectionately round the back of Con's neck; his blunt wrinkled face coloured. 'I don't think you could teach them anything, Dad. They hear it all on TV these days.'

'Not in this house,' said Malone with a grin. 'Mum's got the TV aerial aimed straight at St Mary's, the Cardinal's her favourite news-reader. Sermons and hymns and no news unless it's good news.'

They all laughed, including Brigid: unlike so many narrowly religious, she could laugh at herself. She had never believed that Christ had gone through life without a smile or a joke.

When it was time to go home Malone carried Tom, who was already asleep, out to the car and settled him in the back seat between Lisa and Maureen. Brigid kissed all the children good-night, gave her cheek to Lisa and smiled at Malone. Con stood with his hands in his pockets, but it was obvious he had enjoyed having the family, his and Brigid's family, come to visit them.

An Asian man and woman passed the Malones, said good evening in soft shy voices and went into a house several doors up the street.

'That's Mr and Mrs Van Trang,' said Brigid. 'They're a real nice couple. They're Catholics,' she added, naturalizing them, forgiving them for being foreigners.

Con had just nodded at the Vietnamese. He looked at his son as the latter said good-night to him across the roof of the Commodore.

'Drive carefully,' he said: it was the closest he could come to saying, *I love you all.*

'Night, Dad. Look after yourself.' Some day he would put his arms round his father, when he was dying or dead.

Claire got in beside Malone as he settled in beside the wheel. 'Enjoy yourself?' he said.

'I shouldn't say it, Daddy, but why does Grandma's house always smell of cooking?'

He took the car out from the kerb, pausing to let another car, drawing out from the kerb some distance behind him, go past.

But it too paused, and he pulled out and drove on down the narrow street.

'There's been about a hundred years of cooking in that house, my grandmother lived there before Gran. It sorts of hangs around, the smell.'

'You think we should bring Grandma a can of Air-o-zone next time we come?'

'You'll do no such thing!' said Lisa sharply. 'Just stop breathing if you don't like it while you're there. That's Grandma's home, smell and all.'

Malone turned into a main road; the car following him did the same. 'It doesn't smell like your cooking,' Claire said. 'I wouldn't mind if it did. But it's, I dunno, cabbage, stuff like that.'

'Corned beef and cabbage,' said Malone. 'I grew up on it.'

'Yuk,' said Maureen from the back seat.

Malone was almost halfway home to Randwick before he realized that he was being tailed. At every turn he had made, another car had made the same turning. He was tired, he had not been alert; now all at once it came to him that the car following him was the same one that had pulled out from the kerb behind him in the street in Erskineville. Suddenly his hands felt clammy on the wheel.

What to do? He could continue on to the police station at Randwick, but that would only alarm Lisa and the kids; he did not want to frighten them, in case his own fear was a false alarm. Hans Ludke's question this afternoon, *Does that put you on the hitman's list?*, had been at the back of his mind all evening, like the smell of his mother's cooking.

He reached Randwick, turned into his own street as rain began falling again. He had led the hitman (if, indeed, he was the hitman) to his own home; but, he guessed, the man probably knew where he lived, anyway. Their phone number was in Lisa's name, L. E. Malone, but that wouldn't have fooled anyone really intent on finding out where he lived; if the hitman knew where Con and Brigid Malone lived, he certainly would know where their son lived.

Malone swung the Commodore in the entrance to his driveway; then braked sharply, throwing Tom forward and waking him. The driveway gates were closed. Time and again he had lectured Lisa and the kids against leaving them open. Now he wished for them and the garage door to be wide open.

He glanced back along the street. The other car had come round the corner and pulled into the kerb about fifty yards up the street, dousing its lights. Malone hesitated.

'What's the matter?' said Lisa. 'We don't have automatic gates, remember?'

'I told him we should get them,' said Claire. 'Everybody has them now.'

'We can't afford 'em on a cop's pay,' said Maureen. 'He's told us.'

'I'll open 'em,' said Tom and fumbled with the door handle.

'Stay where you are!'

There was a note of panic in Malone's voice. He hastily got out of the car before Lisa could comment on it, hunched over as much to make himself a smaller target as against the rain, and moved quickly to open the gates. Too late he realized that he had stupidly left the headlights on: as he stood in their glare, fumbling with the bolt of the gates, he felt as exposed as if he were in the middle of the Nullarbor Plain in broad daylight. He was wearing no hat or raincoat; the rain fell on him in drenching sheets, he was almost blinded by the water pouring down his face. His fingers were frozen (by fear or cold?); the gates refused to open. Then he jerked the bolt up out of its socket, he dragged the gates open, swung them back and stumbled back to the front door of the car. As the other car, its lights now on, pulled out from the kerb and came at gathering speed down the street.

He turned to face it, his back against the closed front door of the Commodore; he spread his arms wide, trying to protect his family, as if he meant to gather the hail of bullets into himself. The approaching car swung towards the Commodore and for one horrible moment he thought it was going to crash into them, killing them all in a mad suicidal attack. Its headlights blazed at him, blinding him; then it swung abruptly away. It went past, spraying up a wave of water from the flooded gutter, and sped down the street. Malone staggered on rubbery legs to the back of the Commodore, tried to identify the make of car and its registration plate, but it was gone into the dark swirling night before he could get even a hint of identification. The driver had been too smart: he had known the blaze of headlights would blind Malone.

Still weak, Malone went back up the driveway, opened the garage door and came back to the Commodore. He got in, suddenly glad of the support of the seat beneath him.

'What's the matter, Daddy?' said Claire.

Malone noticed that Lisa, in the back seat, was sitting forward but saying nothing. 'It was just a drunken driver – I thought he was going to smash into us.'

'They shouldn't drink and drive.' Maureen had all the slogans at her tongue-tip.

Malone drove the car into the garage. Lisa got out, gave the front door key to Claire. 'Get ready for bed. See Tom cleans his teeth and has a wet before he gets into bed.'

Maureen said, 'What are you and Dad going to do? Wash the car?'

'Inside!'

Claire took the key, looked thoughtfully at her mother and father but said nothing. She'll make a good cop, Malone thought, she's miles ahead of me in perception. And prayed that she would never want to follow in his footsteps.

When the children had gone inside Lisa put her hand on his arm. 'That was no drunken driver. I've never seen you like that before.'

He sat back on the wet fender of the car; all the rest of him was wet through, a damp arse wouldn't make much difference. All at once it came to him that he had been scared to death, not at the thought of his own death but that he would be murdered in front of his family. He could never leave them a legacy like that.

He knew this was one time when Lisa had to be told the truth: 'I think I'm on a hit list.'

'Oh God!'

She leaned against him and he put his arm round her, holding her tightly. It seemed to him that he could feel the heavy beat of her heart through their winter clothing and it was beating as much for him as for her.

2

'You have to take the rough with the smooth,' said O'Brien. 'I never promised there would be no risk.'

'Don't give me any of that,' said Arnold Debbs. 'You've got me with my career on the line. If this blows up, I'm finished. I promise you, so will you be, too!'

Five years ago, even six months ago, O'Brien would have shrugged off such a threat. From the time he had moved out of the world of pop music into the bigger, rougher world where money and power and influence were concomitant he had more than held his own. In England there had been very few, if any, politicans who could be bought; the system didn't work that way in Britain. But venal councillors and planning authorities could be found wherever development was growing; the skull-and-crossbones had flown from mastheads before the Union Jack was thought of and the Brits never forgot their heritage. When he had come home to Australia it was almost as if the politicians, hands held out, their convict heritage unashamedly displayed, had met him at the airport. It was, of course, nowhere near as bad as that; but cynicism narrows one's view. He had been introduced to his first crooked politician, Arnold Debbs, within two days of his return. A week later he had met his second crooked politician, Arnold's wife, Penelope.

He had always known there was the chance of making enemies of them: bribes never bought friendship, that came free, if you were lucky. He had never been afraid of them because he had never been afraid of failure: he was a gambler, ready to go off somewhere else and start all over again. But that had been before he had met and fallen in love with Anita Norval. Now all he wanted was respectability and no one, least of all the Debbs, would or could offer him that.

63

'You did us once, Brian, with that mining lease –'

'Arnold, that was business. You got the profit you were promised –'

'We didn't get the profit we could have made!' Debbs' temper was notorious; it had always been held against him in Caucus. Political parties do not like hotheads; they can't be controlled. Debbs had once had ambitions to be the leader of the party, to be Prime Minister when it returned to power in Canberra; but he had a head for figures and eventually he had realized he would never have the numbers to reach the top. Three times he had run for leader and three times he had finished bottom of the poll; it was then he had decided to be a Party of One, to look out for himself and use the front bench for all he could make from it. 'You're a robber, Brian, a fucking crook who should be locked up! Now you've got me and my wife linked to this investigation –'

'I told you, Arnold, you and Penelope will be kept out of it. Your names are on nothing –'

'The shares are in a company name, but they can be traced to us! These bloody young reporters these days – they're muck-rakers! *The Eye* has already had a piece – no names but plenty of hints. How many others have you got strung up with my wife and me?'

'You know how many there are, Arnold –'

'You bet your fucking life I do!' Debbs' language, too, was notorious. The *Sydney Morning Herald* had once published a short verbatim statement from him that had contained as many dashes as words. The Anglican and Roman Catholic archbishops, the Festival of Light and half a dozen women's organizations had written letters to the Editor in protest; even Prime Minister Norval had had an attack of mealy-mouth and deplored the lowering of standards. 'I introduced them to you – they could fucking turn on me!'

'Relax, Arnold,' O'Brien said, then tensed as he saw the unfamiliar car coming up the long driveway between the paddocks towards the house. 'Who's this?'

Arnold Debbs turned. 'I don't know. Let's hope to Christ it's not some shitty reporter.'

It wasn't. The unmarked police car pulled in besides Debbs'

blue Volvo and Malone got out. 'Jesus!' said O'Brien softly.

'Who is it?' said Debbs equally softly.

'Police.'

Malone wondered why the familiar figure stiffened as he approached. He had never met Arnold Debbs, but no one could mistake him. Tall and heavily built, he had a pompadour of egg-white hair that made him look as if he had just been crowned with a large pavlova. Beneath it his lamp-bronzed face suggested not so much health as a bad case of brown jaundice. His wide smile was no more than a display case for his expensive dental-work; there was no humour or friendliness in it. Malone shook hands with an enemy who had already declared himself and he wondered why Debbs' grip was so tense.

'I'm sorry to interrupt, Mr O'Brien –'

'It's okay, Mr Debbs is just leaving. He came up to see one of his horses – we've got it on agistment here. I'll see you to your car, Arnold.'

Malone watched the two men walk across to the Volvo, heads close together, voices low: they seemed to be arguing. But O'Brien, as if aware they were being watched, patted Debbs on the shoulder, waited till the older man had got into his car, then stood back and waved as the Volvo was driven away. Then he came back to Malone.

'Bloody owners – they're a pain!'

'You're one, aren't you? A whole string of horses, Sergeant Clements tells me. You've done well, Horrie.'

'Brian.'

'No, it's Horrie who's done well. I'm not so sure how Brian Boru is doing.'

Malone looked out over the stud farm with its lush green paddocks, the white railing fences and the double row of stables of red brick. Mares and foals grazed amidst the grass; a stallion high-stepped along the length of a fence, as arrogant as any disco stud. Further up the red gravel driveway, the main house, a low colonial building with wide verandahs, looked as it must have looked when it was first built a hundred and fifty years ago. This district of Camden, about sixty kilometres south-west of Sydney, had been the birthplace of Australia's sheep industry; now it had become almost a dormitory suburb of the city. But some pockets were still zoned for rural use and Cossack Lodge stud was one of the show places. Yet Malone could not remember ever having seen O'Brien featured in any newspaper or television story about the stud.

He remarked on that now. 'How come? Most racehorse owners risk getting kicked in the head to be photographed with their horses.'

O'Brien smiled. He was dressed in checked cap, a dark blue turtleneck sweater, pale moleskin trousers and stockman's boots: every inch the country gentleman except for the cynical eyes and a certain nervous energy that, had he been a grazier, would have knotted the wool of his sheep. He could never be totally relaxed, he would never adapt to the rhythm of rural seasons.

'An Irish philosopher – there have been one or two – once said, Man who keep low profile rarely get egg on face. Have you come up here to try and smear some egg on me?'

They began to walk up towards the house. Two girl strappers passed them, smiled at O'Brien and went on to the stables. A man came out of a small office at the end of the stables and raised his hand to O'Brien.

'Later, Bruce. He's my foreman,' O'Brien explained to Malone. 'Why are you here, Scobie? Is it about Mardi Jack?'

'Partly. You remembered her name?'

'Yes. You want to sit out here in the sun? We're out of the wind.' It was a clear sunlit day, with the wind on the other side of the house. Yesterday's rain had gone and the countryside looked as if it had been swept with a new broom. The rows of poplars that lined the driveway were just beginning to be tinged with green; they bowed before the wind like armless dancers. 'I'll get us some coffee.'

He went into the house and Malone sat down. O'Brien came back, they exchanged some chat about the stud until the foreman's wife brought them coffee and cake, then O'Brien leaned forward, his cup and saucer held in front of him almost like a weapon.

'I'd better tell you about Mardi Jack. Yes, I did know her. I used to meet her at that flat.'

'I'd half-guessed that. Why did you try that stupid lie? We'd have found out eventually.'

'I'm trying to protect someone.'

'That the woman you mentioned, the one you spent the weekend with? Did she know Mardi Jack?'

'She knew nothing about her.'

'*Knew?* You mean you've told her about Mardi since we came to see you? How did she take it?'

'How do you mean?'

'Was she jealous? Was she shocked when you told her Mardi had been murdered?'

'No, I don't think she was jealous. Or maybe she was – I guess we're all jealous of someone at one time or another. Shocked? Yes. She's not the sort of lady who's accustomed to murder.'

'She's married?'

'Yes.'

Malone finished his coffee, held out his cup for a refill. He bit into a slice of the housekeeper's carrot cake; the semi-country air was making him hungry. Or maybe he was just nervous: he had hardly slept last night.

'I don't think we're interested in her for the moment. There's something else that's worrying us. I think you and I are on a hit list, Brian.'

O'Brien's big hand tightened on his cup; for a moment Malone thought he was going to crush it. 'Hit list? You and me?'

'Are you surprised or were you expecting something like that?'

O'Brien put down his cup on the small table between them, stared at it a moment, then lifted his head. He took off his cap and kneaded it between his hands. 'I wouldn't be surprised if I were on someone's list. I can't understand why you and me together.'

Malone told him about the random murders. 'We think you were the target in the latest one, not Mardi. Whoever he is, he's going for fellers who were in our class at the police academy back in 1965.'

O'Brien frowned, was silent for a moment. Then: 'Has he tried for you yet?'

'Not yet. But –' Malone told him about the car tailing him last night.

'That must've scared the hell out of your wife and kids.'

'Out of my wife, yes. I'm keeping it from the kids. What did you mean when you said you wouldn't be surprised if you were on someone's list?'

Again there was a silence, but for the occasional moan of the wind round the corners of the house. At last O'Brien said, 'This thing I'm in with my bank and my companies. Some people think I doublecrossed them.'

'Have you?'

'What's it to you, Scobie? You're not on the Fraud Squad.'

'If someone bumps you off, I don't want to be following two trails all over Sydney. I'd rather just have one suspect, even if I don't know who he is.'

O'Brien smiled without any humour. 'You're pretty bloody brutal, aren't you?'

'Brian, I'm not going to fart-arse about on this. It looks like an innocent bystander, Mardi Jack, was killed instead of you. He's sure to come back and try for you again. He's already killed two others, he may go for me and Christ knows how many others. That's enough on my plate. I don't want to be chasing some greedy bastards who think you've cheated them out of a million or two. Or some husband who's found out you're sleeping with his lady wife.' That last was a dart tossed casually.

It landed on the board if not on the bull's-eye. 'Keep her out of this! She's the only decent thing that's happened to me in twenty fucking years!'

Malone pushed away the half-eaten slice of carrot cake; he was not as hungry as he had thought. 'I'm going back to town, to Homicide. I think it might be an idea if you came with me.'

O'Brien continued to sit. 'Not if I have to make any statement.'

Malone looked at him carefully. He hadn't yet warmed to O'Brien: he was the free-wheeling entrepreneur that was a new breed, one for which Malone had little time. Unambitious himself, uninterested in being rich, he had tried to but had never understood greed, for either money or power: in today's world he knew that made him a simpleton. O'Brien was the very epitome of the new breed, yet Malone fancied there was a slight crack in him through which decency, a long-dead seed, was trying to sprout. He remembered that, though Horrie O'Brien had been the rebel in the academy class, he had never been unpopular, neither with the cadets nor the instructors, though he had been a loner.

'You'll have to make a statement about knowing Mardi Jack and going to the flat with her – there's no way you can dodge that. But we'll keep quiet about your lady friend – I don't want to bring her into it unless we have to.'

'Not even then,' said O'Brien quietly and vehemently. 'No way.'

Malone was non-committal on that. 'I want you to look at some names and photos with me. They're being sent up from Goulburn this morning.'

'Goulburn?'

'The main academy is down there now, they only do secondary courses at Redfern. They keep the police library at Goulburn. You and I can look at the class of '65.'

O'Brien hesitated, then stood up. 'Okay. Can you give me a lift back to town? I don't own a car. I usually have a hire car pick me up.'

'I thought all you fellers had a Rolls or a Merc or both.'

O'Brien smiled, again without mirth. 'I once bought my old man a Merc. He sent it back with a note telling me to drive it up the track where the sun never shines.'

He went into the house without saying any more about his relationship with his father. He came out two or three minutes later with a briefcase and walked across to where Malone was waiting for him by the police car.

'You call your lawyer?'

'No. If you must know, I rang my lady friend.'

Malone looked around the stud, admiring it and, yes, suddenly envying O'Brien his possession of it. He thought what it would be like to live here with Lisa and the kids, to breathe this clear air every morning, to live in this easy rhythm, never to have to think about homicides and the sleaze of human nature that irritated him every day like an incurable rash. He said, 'I wouldn't come up here again, not till we've nailed this killer.'

'Why not? We have a security patrol here.'

'All day, twenty-four hours a day?'

'No, just at night.'

Malone pointed to a clump of trees bordering a side road beyond the main paddock. 'He could park his car amongst those trees and you'd never notice him. He could pick you off right where you're standing and he'd be gone before anyone knew where the shot came from.'

'That's a fair distance, three hundred yards at least.'

'This bloke is an expert, Brian. With a 'scope, you'd be like a dummy in a shooting gallery. Take my advice. Don't come up here unless you have to and then have your security guards here to meet you. Just warn them, this bloke might take them out, too.'

O'Brien stared across at the trees, as if the assassin was actually there. There was no sign of immediate fear on his face, but he was looking, for the first time, at the possibility of his own death. 'I don't want to die, Scobie. Not now.'

'Who does?'

They drove back to the city, through the flat sprawl of suburbs and along the main roads too narrow for the traffic that clogged them. Freeways were being built, but for every mile of freeway laid down it seemed that a thousand cars had been newly spawned to flood it. They passed several miles of used car lots, metal beasts waiting to be released to add to the flood.

O'Brien was silent most of the way, not sullen but worried-looking. Malone kept the conversation casual. 'My sidekick, Russ Clements, has been looking up your history. You were bigger than I thought you were on the pop scene.'

'I was in it when it started to take off, just after the Beatles first appeared.'

'Russ told me about some of the groups you managed. There was one called – was it the Salvation Four or something?'

'The Salvation Four Plus Sinner. They were big.'

'I asked my two girls about them – they'd never heard of them.'

'How old are your girls?'

'Nine and almost fourteen.'

'Another generation. Pop groups are like Olympic swimmers – they hit gold once, then they sink without trace.' There was no pity in his voice for the failed pop groups or Olympic swimmers.

'Why did you get out of the game?'

'Boredom. And greed,' he said frankly, as if avarice was a virtue. 'I was making a million a year, but that's chicken-feed in the pop game.'

'The chickens started to bite you?'

'Scobie, a million bucks is like a short-handled umbrella – you can't swagger with it. But fifty or a hundred million, that's different.'

'I thought you didn't like to swagger? The low profile and all that.'

'The richest guy in America doesn't swagger. He lives in a small city in Oklahoma and drives a pick-up truck to his office. But when he lifts the phone, the banks fall on their knees and salaam.'

'The banks salaaming you now?'

O'Brien smiled ruefully: there was some humour in it, even if it was as dry as a western creek-bed. 'Not now. Not now.'

When they reached Police Centre Russ Clements was waiting for them with the file from Goulburn. The file cover was dark blue, the spine of it faded to a sky blue where it had been exposed to light on a shelf; the papers and the single photo in it were yellowing round the edges. Evidently no one had looked at the file since 1965.

The three men sat down in Malone's office, but first Malone pointed out to O'Brien the three red pins on the map behind his chair. 'Parramatta, Chatswood, City – three random murders. That's what we thought at first. There's going to be another one, I can feel it in my bones –' He had Celtic bones, in which superstition was ingrained in the marrow.

'We have a hundred and fifty-one names to choose from,' said Clements. 'Less Terry Sugar and Harry Gardner. We also have the same number of suspects, less, of course, those two and you two.'

71

'Thanks,' said Malone. 'You always know how to keep the spirits up.'

'I was in the class,' said Clements soberly. 'But not the same group. I think we can narrow it down to your group, if you can remember them all.'

'The names aren't classified in groups?'

'No. We're all lumped together.'

'What about the photos?'

'There's only one, a class photo. There's a caption on the back with all the names. Except there are only a hundred and fifty guys in the photo. They must have taken the names from the class roll without identifying them with individuals in the photo.'

O'Brien said sarcastically, 'The police academy must've been pretty smart in those days. I can't remember – did they teach us how to identify mug shots?'

Malone could feel Clements' resentment even across the desk: no policeman likes the force being criticized, no matter how valid the criticism. He cut in before Clements could make a comment: 'Have you worked out who's missing?'

'Not yet,' said Clements. 'I thought we'd start by you two trying to remember the names of all the guys in your group.'

Malone's was the mind trained by experience in the use of memory, but it was O'Brien, the half-trained accountant turned entrepreneur, the man who lived by his wits and the dropped name, who remembered most of their group-mates. Clements wrote the names down and then Malone and O'Brien tried to match a face in the photo with a name. The whole procedure took them half an hour. Without remarking on it, both Malone and O'Brien spent as much time looking at themselves when young as they did identifying the other members of their group. Malone felt a sense of loss looking at the distant youth who was himself: he was a stranger whom he wished he knew better. What had he felt in those days, what had he thought about, what mistakes had he made? But it was all so long ago, it was like trying to draw pictures on water.

At last O'Brien said, 'The guy who's missing is Frank Blizzard.'

Malone frowned. 'I remember the name. But I can't remember what he looked like.'

'That was him. As soon as he left you, you couldn't remember what he looked like. There was something else –'

Malone waited.

'We caught him cheating on an exam paper, remember? We hazed him, gave him a helluva hosing with a fire hose, then we kicked him out into – what was it, Bourke Street? – just in his underpants.'

'I remember that,' said Clements. 'It was all around the academy the next morning.'

'It was a stupid bloody thing to do,' said Malone. 'I mean, what we did.'

'We were young,' said O'Brien. 'We thought cheating was against the rules.'

'Wasn't it? Isn't it still?'

'Not in the big wide world, chum. Frank Blizzard was just ahead of the rest of us.'

Out of the corner of his eye Malone saw Clements' lip lift just a fraction; he did his best to show no expression himself. 'Would what we did to him be enough for him to start killing for revenge?'

'After all these years?'

'You should've stayed in the force,' said Clements; his dislike of O'Brien was blatant. 'You'd have learned some people will wait for ever for revenge. Women are the worst.'

'Not necessarily,' said Malone. 'War veterans are as bad, some of them.'

'We weren't at war with Blizzard,' said O'Brien.

He was aware of Clements' feeling towards him; for a moment he had looked unexpectedly uncomfortable. His hands gripped the seat of the chair beneath him like anchors; then they slowly relaxed, like an arthritic's whose pain had been conquered. He moved stiffly, showing his shoulder to Clements, and looked at Malone.

'None of us reported his cheating, not until they called us in and put it to us about what they'd heard. I can't remember who it was who grassed, but then all the rest of us could do was nod and say yes, we'd done it. There were six of us, as I remember.'

Malone nodded, remembering the scene in the Inspector's office, hazy though the memory was, like a soft focus flashback

73

in a television mini-series. At that time he thought they might all be dismissed from the academy; but Blizzard's sin or crime or whatever you called it had been greater. Hazing, in those days, was tolerated in institutions as civilized barbarism, no worse than poofter-bashing. Blizzard had been doomed from the moment that – had it been Jim Knoble? – had opened his mouth and told about the cheating. Frank Blizzard had gone from the academy by lunchtime next day.

'I was there when he went out the gates,' said O'Brien. 'He got out into Bourke Street and all of a sudden he went berserk, right off his bloody rocker. I couldn't hear half of what he was saying, he was standing out in the middle of the road, in the traffic, but I did hear him yell he'd blow the place up. Then he caught sight of me and he put his arms up, like he was holding a rifle, and made out he was shooting me.'

'What happened?'

'They went out, brought him back and dumped him in a paddy-wagon and drove him somewhere. That was the last I saw of him. They didn't charge him, I think the idea was to get rid of him as quietly as they could. You know what it was like in those days, the less scandal about the police, the better.'

'Was he a bit of a psycho while he was at the academy?' Clements asked.

O'Brien looked at Malone; the latter shrugged. 'How would we know now? That was over twenty years ago. Incidentally, I've just remembered. It was Jim Knoble who dobbed him in.'

'Where's he now? Is he still in the force?'

'He's out at Randwick,' said Clements. 'He's a senior sergeant. I bumped into him a coupla months ago at the races.'

'That's five of us accounted for,' said Malone and looked at the short list Clements had written down. 'That leaves Culp, Sam Culp. I haven't heard about him since we left the academy.'

'Has anyone heard anything of Blizzard?' said O'Brien.

'No.'

'So what do we do?'

'First, I'll get permission to start a sweep for him, as wide as possible. I'll get the other states and the Federal boys to co-operate.' He looked at Clements. 'We'll need some of your punter's luck.'

'Don't ask for any of mine,' said O'Brien and grinned wryly.

Malone said, 'It might be an idea if you took a sudden trip overseas, get you out of harm's way. Go and tie up another million-dollar deal.'

'You're kidding. I wouldn't cross the Harbour for chicken-feed like that.' For a moment there was a show of arrogance.

'Righto, do a ten-million-dollar deal.' Malone out of the corner of his eye could see Clements biting his lip, trying to stop himself from saying something cheap and nasty.

The arrogance suddenly subsided. 'I can't. The NCSC and the Tax Department got together and got me to surrender my passport. That's between you and me. They were going to get a court order, but I gave it up without going that far. That's how we've kept it out of the papers. All but the rumours,' he added bitterly.

'Crumbs,' said Malone, 'you do have trouble, don't you?'

'You must be in shit up to your navel,' said Clements, pleasure beaming out of him.

One of the big hands gripped the seat of the chair again, but O'Brien said nothing. Then Malone said, 'Righto, Brian, then you're going to have to take care of yourself – we can't give you police protection. In the meantime I'm going to warn Jim Knoble to look out for himself.'

'Will he get police protection? And you?'

'I'll be disappointed if we don't,' said Malone and wondered why he felt no pleasure, no small sense of triumph, at O'Brien's stricken look. Then he knew it was because each was as vulnerable as the other, that neither knew who would get the next bullet.

3

Sergeant Jim Knoble was killed that night by a .243 bullet fired from a high-powered rifle at close range. The bullet went right through Knoble's chest, killing him instantly, and lodged in the back seat of his car, being deflected as it went through out of the side windows. Knoble had parked his car in the side driveway of the block of flats in Coogee where he lived with his wife and teenage daughter. Malone had rung Randwick police station twice, leaving a message for Knoble to ring him back, but Knoble had been out since midday following a drug suspect and had not reported back to the station till 10.10 at night. He had been given Malone's message, but had said he would contact Malone first thing in the morning. He had signed off, remarked that he was dead tired and gone home.

Malone and Clements arrived in the side-street above the cliffs at Coogee at fifteen minutes before midnight. The street had been closed, blocked by a motor-cycle cop. Down the street, almost at the cliff's edge, were four police cars, their blue lights revolving, and an ambulance, its red light offering a contrasting colour note. There were also four television vans, looking underprivileged with no lights to flash. Malone noticed they were from the four commercial channels. Clements, a man of natural prejudice, had a theory that the ABC only attended the murders of politicians, Aborigines and conservationists. It was also his belief that SBS, the multicultural network with the shoestring budget, rang up first to see if the victim was an ethnic, otherwise they couldn't spare the petrol getting there. He hated all the media.

Detective-Sergeant Wal Dukes, from Randwick, was the local man in charge of the investigation. He was as tall as Malone but heavier, looking massive in the long, glistening black raincoat he was wearing. He was ten years younger than Malone, but had a broad battered face that made him look older. He had once been an Olympic heavyweight, but had never got past his first bout and it had rankled ever since.

'It looks like someone from the drug ring got him,' he said in a voice that was surprisingly light for his size. 'Jim's been on their tail for a coupla months. It's one of the Triads, they've got pushers all up and down the beaches, from Bondi down to Cronulla.'

'No,' said Malone. 'I don't think so.'

He felt sick, as if he were more than halfway responsible for

76

Jim Knoble's death. He and Clements had called in at the Randwick station on their way down here and had been told that Knoble had been given Malone's message. His head told him he was not to blame, but his heart, that muscle that can bend reason into a pretzel, insisted he should have gone looking for Jim Knoble. He told Dukes about the suspected hit list.

'Jesus! Did Jim know?'

'I was trying to get in touch with him to tell him. Have they found the bullet yet?'

'The Crime Scene guys haven't arrived yet.'

'What was Jim Knoble doing chasing a drug suspect? He wasn't on the detective squad.'

'He volunteered. Sometimes he'd go out on his own, but not tonight – we had a tip, but I couldn't take it up myself. It was a stake-out at Maroubra – Jim was in plainclothes for it.' He hesitated, shutting his eyes as a gust of rain splashed across his face; then he said, 'His son was a junkie – the kid OD'd a year ago. Jim's been after the shit ever since.'

Malone, as a senior detective, had to say it: 'You should've kept him away. If he'd grabbed anyone, he was never going to put up any objective evidence.'

'I know, Inspector. But how could I stop him? He thought the world of his boy. Anyhow . . .' Dukes' voice trailed off, he looked as if he had just lost another bout, one that he would regret for the rest of his life.

Virtually every house and flat in the short street had its lights on; stiff with cold and shock, neighbours in dressing-gowns and blankets stood on their verandahs. Coogee was one of the small beach suburbs south of the harbour; it ran down as a shallow valley from the ridge of Randwick, only a few miles from where Malone lived. In the nineteenth century some of the city's professional men, trying to avoid the already rising prices of harbour properties, had moved out here and built substantial mansions. One man had actually run sheep on the slopes of the valley and as recently as the 1930s there had been a dairy farm only half a mile up from the beach, which lay between two steep headlands. Gradually the valley had filled up, then the headlands; now Coogee was a community of square boxes of flats and small houses of no distinction. Its population, like that of most beach suburbs, was mixed, but, by and large, it was considered a safe and neighbourly place in which to live.

Jim Knoble's body had been put into the ambulance and the ambulance men were having their papers counter-signed by the police. The GMO, a younger, slimmer man than Doc Gilbey, came up to Dukes, then recognized Malone. He looked from one to the other.

'Who's taking charge on this one?' He wore a ski jacket and a beanie and had a snow tan. He looked indecently healthy, a little impatient, as if he expected to be heading back to the southern slopes first thing in the morning. 'Is it a local job?'

'I'll be taking over,' said Malone. He looked at Dukes. 'When Crime Scene find the bullet, tell 'em I want Ballistics to do a rush job. But I think I know already what it is, a .243. Did he die instantly, Doc?'

'I'd say so. The killer knew what he was about.'

'Did anyone hear the shot, Wal?'

'Nobody, leastways nobody who's owned up.' Dukes nodded down towards the heavy white traffic barrier at the end of the street. 'Listen to those waves. There's a real swell on tonight – the fishing boats aren't out. Now and again you get a real boomer –' Even as he spoke there was a thunderous crash as a huge wave, invisible in the darkness, hit the bottom of the cliffs. 'Nobody's gunna take any notice of a shot in that noise. Anyway, most of 'em say they were either looking at TV or asleep in bed. There's so much shooting on TV, who'd take any notice of a shot outside?'

'How are Jim's family? Did they hear anything?'

'There's just his wife and their fifteen-year-old daughter. She was the one who found her dad's body when she came home from a friend's place up the street. The poor kid's almost out of her mind with shock.'

'How's Mrs Knoble?'

'She's just sitting inside there, not saying anything, not even crying. Just sitting. You know how it hits some of 'em. Cops' wives, I guess, are always waiting for something like this. You wanna see her?'

'I'd better. Get all these cleared out, let the neighbours go back to bed. Can you give me a ring romorrow morning, say about ten? Send me all your stuff so's Russ Clements can put it in the running sheet.'

'Sure. A hit list? Christ, why?' Dukes shook his big head.

'Maybe I'll be able to tell you tomorrow. Here come the Crime Scene boys – and a girl, too. How'd they get her out this time of night?'

'Equal opportunity,' said Dukes with a grin, another man of natural prejudice.

'Don't forget, I want that bullet on my desk by tomorrow noon at the latest. Ballistics will understand.'

He moved towards the front door of the flats, leaving Clements to make a note of all the details that would go into the running sheets. With the connection between these murders, the sheets would eventually make a book; all he could hope was that he would be alive to read the last page. He stopped for a moment and looked up and down the rain-swept street: the killer could still be there anywhere in the darkness.

As he reached the glass doors into the small entrance hall of the flats, two of the television reporters came at him, their cameramen behind them like back-up bazooka troops.

'Any chance of some shots of the family, Inspector?' He was a young reporter, dressed in a Dryazabone ankle-length slicker and an Akubra drover's hat; he looked as if he should be covering a rodeo out in the flood country. Malone had seen him several times on television, one of the new breed with American pronunciations, knee-deep in de-*bree* or on the outskirts of a me-*lee* or tasting the new season's cha-*blee*, already with his eye on world fame by satellite. 'We won't intrude.'

'Not bloody much you won't,' said Malone. 'Get lost.'

'Is that the new police community relations policy?'

Malone looked past the whipper-snapper at the black-bearded cameraman behind him. 'Why don't you crown him with your camera?'

The cameraman grinned. 'I've often felt like it, Inspector. But Channel 15 would charge me for the breakage.'

'Up yours,' said the reporter and swished out into the street.

The cameraman smiled apologetically. 'Sorry, Inspector. He does a lot for our own public relations.'

The other reporter, an older man, and the second cameraman nodded, said good-night to Malone and went out to the street with the Channel 15 man. Malone, soured by the small encounter, pushed open the glass doors and went in to see the widowed Mrs Knoble. He noted that this was not a block of flats with a security door to its entrance, though each of the flats had its own individual security grille covering its front door. But they were protection against housebreakers, not murderers.

Mrs Knoble was a small, pretty woman in a pink dressing-gown, pink mules on her feet; her hair neatly done. She had evidently been waiting up for her husband to come home and, after whatever number of years they had been married, she still thought she should look her best for him, no matter the time of day or night. She was an old-fashioned wife, still in love with the only man in her life. Like Lisa, Malone thought: and suddenly prayed to Christ that Lisa would never be sitting like this some night with some uniformed cop sitting beside her holding her hand with awkward sympathy.

The cop was Sergeant Keith Elgar, in uniform even though he had been roused from sleep to come here: he, too, was old-fashioned. He had known Malone for years, they had played cricket against each other in district competition, but he stood up, letting go of Mrs Knoble's hand. 'Hallo, Inspector. I haven't asked Mrs Knoble any questions. I don't think she's up to it.'

'Yes, I am.' Ethel Knoble had a soft voice, a little precise, as if she had taken elocution lessons at some time from a bad teacher. 'So long as it doesn't take too long –'

'It won't.' Malone could hear hushed voices out in the kitchen, those of neighbours who had come in to support her. 'How's your daughter?'

'Sylvie? She's in bed.' She nodded towards an inner room. 'The doctor gave her a sedative. Please don't question her, not tonight.'

'Not now. We'll do that some other time.'

Malone sat down in a floral upholstered armchair, taking in the rest of the room without moving his head. The room was like Ethel Knoble herself, neat and pretty, a place for everything and everything in its place. There was, perhaps, too much emphasis on the floral; even the four prints on the walls were of flowers. There was a single photo on a bureau against one wall: Jim and Ethel Knoble and their son and daughter, arms linked, standing in front of a huge bank of azaleas. Their faces were bright as flowers with happiness, not a shadow on them of what was to come.

'I'll make it as brief as possible, Mrs Knoble.' How many times had he said that in the past? If he asked only one question, it was always one too many. For a moment it was Lisa sitting in the chair opposite him; then the hallucination passed, leaving him trembling inside. He took out his handkerchief and blew his nose while he waited to get his voice under control again. Then: 'Had Jim received any threats?'

For a moment it looked as if she didn't understand the question; then she shook her head. 'No, nothing like that. If he did, he didn't tell me. He never brought work, you know, home with him. Except after Colin, that was our son, when he died, Jim used to talk about the drug pushers. He went looking for them sometimes –' She looked at Sergeant Elgar. 'That was right, wasn't it, Keith?'

Elgar nodded. 'They could have been the ones who did this, Scobie –'

'Maybe.' Malone nodded non-committally. 'Did anyone ever ring here asking for him?'

'Oh, people were always ringing here, asking him to do something for them. Drug welfare centres, you know, places like that. The cricket club, too – he used to coach the youngsters with Keith here. He was always busy, like he didn't, you know, want time to think too much about Colin.'

'No funny messages? I mean, a crank. Police sometimes get those – I've had a couple myself.'

'Me, too,' said Elgar.

Mrs Knoble was silent for a long moment and Malone thought he had lost her for the night. Then she said, 'There was a call

81

last week. A man phoned. Jim wasn't home and I answered it. He asked me to give Jim a message. Then he sang it.'

'*Sang* it?'

'Yes. It was the old nursery rhyme, about ten green bottles. Only it was six.' She hummed the old tune, then sang the words almost like a robot: '*There were six green bottles standing on the wall / And if one green bottle should accidentally fall* . . . Then he stopped, just like that. He said to sing it to my husband. Then he rang off.'

'What did Jim think of it when you told him?'

'He couldn't make head nor tail of it. I think he just forgot about it. Does it mean anything, Inspector?'

Malone kept his voice steady. 'It might. Would you recognize the man's voice if he phoned again?'

'I don't know. I can't describe it, it was just an ordinary voice, but he sang in tune. Yes, I think I might recognize it if I heard it again.'

Malone stood up. 'I'll come back in a couple of days, Mrs Knoble, or I'll send Sergeant Clements – he knew Jim. He'll come to you first, Keith. We'll do our best, Mrs Knoble. I promise you.'

She just nodded, seeming to become smaller, drawing herself into herself. Malone stood looking at her, saw her turning into Lisa; then he abruptly left the flat before the horror turned him dizzy. Once out in the street he paused and took a lungful of the cold, sea-smelling air. Fifty yards to his right and a hundred feet down a wave boomed against the cliff-face, followed by another and another: the sea was building up for an assault.

Clements approached him. 'How's the family?'

'Safe, I hope.' Then he saw Clements' curious look and he realized what he had said. He put Lisa and the children out of his mind. 'I didn't see the daughter, they've sedated her. Mrs Knoble will have some of the neighbours staying with her tonight. Keith Elgar is going to have one of his men stay, too. I want you to come back and talk to the daughter.'

'Thanks,' said Clements with no thanks.

Better you than me, Malone told him silently: I'd be looking at Sylvie Knoble and seeing Claire. 'They come up with anything yet?'

'They've already found the bullet – it was in the back seat. Ballistics will have it first thing in the morning.'

'I don't think we'll need to check. It was him, all right. He's getting cheeky now. He's sending singing telegrams.'

Clements looked at him quizzically, knowing now that these murders were getting to his mate.

'*Six green bottles standing on the wall*,' sang Malone. 'Another one fell off the wall tonight, but not accidentally. He rang Mrs Knoble last week, sang that rhyme to her and told her to tell Jim.'

'Good,' said Clements. 'Let's hope he calls Police Centre next, asks for you. Then you can let him know we know who he is.'

'What if he calls home, talks to Lisa or one of the kids?'

Clements bit his lip. 'Christ, I didn't think of that!'

'There's another thing. What do we know about Sam Culp?'

'Nothing so far. Only that's it him or you who's gunna be next,' said Clements, laying down the truth as heavily as a gravestone.

FIVE

1

Next morning just before ten o'clock Sergeant Binyan, of Ballistics, rang Malone. 'It's the same calibre bullet, Scobie. A .243 fired from the same rifle as the other three. You wanna come up and have a look?'

Malone told Clements to wait on a call from Wal Dukes out at Randwick, then went up to the fifth level of the Centre. He waited to be admitted by Clarrie Binyan himself, who came and operated the security lock. There were over seven thousand confiscated and surrendered weapons, from tiny one-shot pistols that could be hidden in a woman's hand to weighty submachine-guns, kept here in Ballistics; there were also countless flick-knives, decorated daggers, kris, bayonets, rapiers hidden in umbrella sticks, machetes and a medieval battle-axe, a treasure commonly known as The Wife. Binyan locked the door behind them and led Malone through to his office.

Clarrie Binyan was part-Aborigine, a twenty-six-year-veteran who had started as a fighting street kid in the Police Boys Clubs. Without changing his name to something Irish and romantic he had made good in a white man's racist world, but not within fifty million dollars of Brian Boru O'Brien. Malone wondered who had had the harder battle.

He waved Malone to a chair, went to a refrigerator marked with a big sign: *Warning! This refrigerator contains Contaminated Material!* He opened it; it was stacked full of cans of soft drink and light alcohol beer. He tossed Malone a can of the beer, took one himself and came back and sat down at his desk.

'I serve light beer up to the rank of inspector. Anyone above that gets a Coke. Okay, here's what we've got. I've talked it over with young Jason James. We're pretty certain it's a Tikka, but it could be a Winchester.'

'You said that before. You blokes are always so specific.'

Binyan grinned; nobody in the force, it seemed, had ever been able to get his goat. 'Never leave yourself out on a limb, my mumma taught me.'

'How many Tikkas would be imported each year?'

'I wouldn't have a clue, Scobie. A good few less than Winchesters. But this could be a gun that's ten or fifteen years old. It'd be like looking for a nugget in gibber country.'

'I thought you black trackers were champions at that?'

Binyan grinned again, a mouthful of white man's false teeth. 'The last time I went bush they had to send out my mumma to find me. Come and I'll show you the similarities between the bullets.'

He got up and led Malone out through a large, clinically clean workroom where four men were working separately at benches, dismantled weapons in front of them. He led Malone into a side room, sat down at a large contraption with a stool in front of it.

'I dunno whether I ever showed you this. It's German, a Wild Leitz forensic comparison macroscope – it's also got a video monitor. There's also Intralux 6000 optical fibre lights. It costs over a hundred and fifty grand and if I put two hairs under here I could tell you which one was a white man's and which a Koori's.'

'How would you know the difference?'

'The split hair would be Whitey's.'

Malone and Binyan had never had any racial feeling between them. 'Righto, smart-arse. Now show me the bullets.'

Binyan took three bullets from the small plastic envelopes he had brought with him from his office and set them in place under the macroscope. 'Forget the third one for the moment. These two are last night's bullet and the one that killed Mardi Jack. Have a look.' Malone sat down at the instrument, adjusted the eyepieces. 'Notice the lands and the grooves, six of 'em going to the right. Exactly the same, right? Now if you look at this particular land, near the base, there's a series of pronounced striations. That's unusual.'

Malone nodded, though it had taken him some moments to adjust to the magnification.

Binyan took out the two bullets, put in the third one, then produced a fourth from his pocket. 'Now these are the ones that killed Gardner and Terry Sugar. They match, right?' Again Malone nodded. 'Now I'm gunna take out the Sugar bullet and put in the one that killed Jim Knoble. There. It matches the first bullet, the Gardner one, right?'

Malone sat back, then stood up slowly. 'All that'll stand up in court?'

'No worries, mate.'

'Righto. Can I have all the bullets?' Binyan handed him the four labelled plastic envelopes. 'What about the ammo? How many boxes of .243s would be sold a year?'

Binyan shook his greying curly head. 'Scobie, you're getting desperate –'

'I *am* desperate. I could be the next one.' He told Binyan of the hit list. 'Keep it to yourself.'

'It's a tribal secret.' Binyan was always poking fun at what he claimed were white man's myths about Aboriginal myths; but he did not smile and Malone knew he wasn't joking this time. 'Jesus, mate, I didn't know it was that close to home. I wish we could do more. But trying to trace who's bought the ammo –' He shook his head again. 'You don't have to register to buy ammo. All you have to do is produce a shooter's licence, you know that. Gun dealers never make a note of it.'

'I know,' said Malone morosely. 'I'm not thinking too straight.'

'You better leave this one alone, mate. Take your long service leave and disappear. Go walkabout, like I would.'

'And get lost in the bush, have my mumma come looking for me?' Malone managed a smile. 'Don't worry, Clarrie. I'll cope.'

He went back down to Homicide as Clements came back. 'I've been out front. It's pissing down again. This is gunna mean a heavy track on Saturday. I think I'll lay off the horses this weekend.'

'Stick to your shares. It doesn't rain in the stock exchange.'

'Talking of the stock exchange – they've stopped all trading in Cossack shares.' The race track and the stock exchange were

Clements' main relief from the effects of homicide investigations. Going through the 'murder box' one day Malone had discovered a racing form guide and a week's share trading list absent-mindedly pinned to the running sheets of a particularly ghastly murder. 'Our mate O'Brien looks like he's really up shit creek.'

'Don't gloat, Russ.'

'Am I gloating? Sorry.' But Clements didn't look in the least apologetic. He sat down, his bulk making the chair creak. 'Changing the subject. Wal Dukes rang in, gave me what he's got so far. He said not to go out to see the young Knoble girl yet – she's still in a pretty lousy state. I think we better leave her to Wal. At least he knew the family better than we did.'

'Righto.' Malone dropped the four plastic envelopes into the murder box. 'What else have you got?'

'I've traced Sam Culp. He's changed his name. You'll never guess who he is.'

'Russ, I'm not in the mood for games.'

Clements this time was truly apologetic. 'No, I guess not. He's Sebastian Waldorf, the opera singer. He's in Melbourne right now with the Australian Opera, but he's due back in Sydney tomorrow.'

Malone was not an opera-goer, but, strapped to his chair by Lisa, he had watched several opera telecasts on a Sunday night and he had a vague memory of Sebastian Waldorf. He was not a star of the magnitude of Sutherland, but he was undoubtedly one of the top singers of the Australian Opera company. He was, Malone thought, a baritone, which, he gathered, was not only a note or two lower than a tenor but also a class or two down the scale. Baritones never seemed to get the sighs from Elisabeth Pretorius, Lisa's mother, that Pavarotti and Domingo got, and she was a paid-up member of the Friends of the Opera. If Sam Culp was on the hit list, then the hitman was no friend of his.

'Where does he live?'

'Yowie Bay. He's in our region.' Clements leaned back in his chair, making it creak again. He bit his lip and his eyes clouded with concern. 'What do we do now? I mean about you and Lisa and the kids? And Sebastian Waldorf – Christ, what a name! And Brian Boru,' he added almost reluctantly.

Malone looked at his watch. 'I've got a meeting with Harry Danforth in five minutes. I think he's going to suggest a safe house for me and Lisa and the kids.'

'Maybe that'll be best,' said Clements slowly, still concerned, part of the family.

'Balls,' said Malone just as slowly; he was working hard to keep control of himself. 'How do we know when we're going to nail this bastard? I could spend the rest of my bloody life in a safe house!'

He said almost the same thing to Chief Superintendent Danforth ten minutes later, though in more restrained language. Danforth, lazy, deliberate, sometimes dense, was the sort of superior officer who invited expletives, but in forty-three years as a cop he had heard so many of them so often that one suspected he thought they were the normal currency of dialogue. Besides, he was a chief superintendent and just occasionally he pulled rank.

'It's not my suggestion, Scobie. Fred Falkender sent word down –' Falkender was the Assistant Commissioner, Crime, one of the seven ACs in the department. 'It's gone as high as the Commissioner. We don't want to lose any more officers.' He actually sounded sincerely concerned, though he and Malone had never been close. 'We'll move you and your family outa Sydney, to one of the country towns. They're talking about Armidale. It'll be nice up there in the spring.'

Malone shook his head. 'No, Harry, I'm not having a bar of that. I'll talk to my wife about her and the kids going somewhere – I think that's a good idea, though I don't like it. But I'm not going, that's just not on.'

'Scobie, we don't need you to go on being bait for him. We still got those two civvies, O'Brien and, what's this other feller's name, Culp?'

Despite his feelings, Malone wanted to smile, but refrained. Civilians were expendable.

'From what I hear,' Danforth went on, 'I don't think O'Brien would be missed if he was next to go. He's not too popular with some big names.'

'You don't think any of them would have him wiped out and then blame it on this hitman, do you?'

It seemed to Malone that Danforth abruptly closed up; his big red face was as expressionless as it could be. 'I wouldn't know anything about that. And don't let's pussyfoot about naming the hitman. His name's Blizzard, right?'

'We think so, but we don't have any proof that he's the one. That's what I want to follow up. After I've talked to Sam Culp tomorrow, when he gets in from Melbourne.' He explained who Culp now was; Danforth, who thought Bing Crosby had been a classical singer, was unimpressed. 'Incidentally, are we going to put him and his family and O'Brien in safe houses?'

'Fred Falkender didn't mention it. Police funds don't run to that sorta thing unless they're protected witnesses.' Danforth tried a little black humour: 'You know what The Dutchman's like. He wouldn't let us waste money protecting O'Brien and what's-his-name, Sebastian.'

'His name now is Sebastian Waldorf.'

'Christ,' said Danforth. 'Well, him and O'Brien. They're probably both Liberal voters. Two less to vote against The Dutchman.'

The Dutchman was Hans Vanderberg, the State Premier and Police Minister. He was Labour to the core of his heart, though certain research hospitals were said to have already volunteered their autopsy services when he died in the hope that it could be established that he actually had a heart. He was incorruptible but he was ruthless. Malone wondered what he would say if he knew that Arnold Debbs, a Federal Labour member, was a client, perhaps even a friend of Brian Boru O'Brien. But The Dutchman probably already knew and the knowledge would be filed away for future use in the numbers game at national conferences.

'I think we've got to give them some sort of protection, Harry. If you give it to me and not to them and the papers get on to it, there'll be a real stink. Derryn Hinch would make a meal of it on his TV programme.'

89

'I tell you we can't do it if it's gunna cost money. You know what government policy is like, they only spend money on law and order after the crime's been committed,' he said with unintended humour.

Malone considered for a few moments, wondering how he was going to break the news to Lisa that the family's home life was going to be disrupted for – how long? Claire would never forgive him for having her first skiing holiday postponed; the season was coming to an end and she would have to wait till next year. Lisa would fight the suggestion at first, but, with her Dutch commonsense, would agree in the end. Maureen and Tom would not carp against anything that allowed them to miss school for a few weeks.

At last he said, 'I'll send my family away. My wife's parents will probably take them somewhere.' Jan and Elisabeth Pretorius, retired and comfortably well-off, would jump at the chance of having the family to themselves, of being able to spend money on them without Malone's disapproval. 'Then I'll move in somewhere with O'Brien and Waldorf.'

'What if they don't want anything like that?'

'Then we'll get it in writing from them and then, bugger 'em, let 'em look after themselves.' But he knew he would never let that happen; he knew, from experience, that half the elements of the civilized world, and probably the uncivilized, had to be protected despite themselves. Hospitals and graveyards were full of people who had insisted they had known how to look after themselves.

'Well, I'll put it to Fred Falkender,' said Danforth doubtfully. 'But I don't like the idea of you getting too close to this bloke O'Brien. He's a crook.'

'Harry, you and I have been close to crooks all our lives.' *You more than me and much closer.* 'I'll handle it. The tough part will be shacking up with Waldorf. Opera singers are supposed to practise four hours a day.'

'I once went to the opera with the wife and her sister. It was bloody murder.'

An hour later, when Malone was back in his office, Danforth rang him. 'Fred Falkender's okayed it. Make your own arrangements, then let me know. We'll have one of the special units standing by, just in case. They'll be on call and they'll be wherever you need 'em within ten minutes. Also, a plainclothesman will move in with you, three of 'em, each on an eight-hour shift. Where are you thinking of holing up?'

'That's all fixed. I've been in touch with O'Brien. He's not keen on the idea, but he sees the point. I'm moving into his suite at the Hotel Congress. I don't know if there'll be room for Waldorf *and* a stand-by man. You'd better put our feller in one of the rooms on the same floor.'

'How much will that cost?'

'O'Brien will probably be able to get us corporate rates. Say two-fifty a night.'

'Two *hundred* and fifty?' Malone could imagine Danforth going purple. 'Forget it! He stays with you, even if he's gotta share a bed.'

'Harry, relax. I've talked with O'Brien about the need for protection. He's moving his own security men in next door to the suite. There won't be any need for our fellers.' He paused, then said, 'Harry, this doesn't mean I'm stopping work on these murders. I'm still in charge.'

There was silence at the other end of the line. Then: 'They wanna put Greg Random in charge.'

Malone could see Greg Random jumping at the chance to be back in harness. Since the regional reorganization he would not have been remotely connected with a homicide. Once the new territories had been created, the old territorial imperative syndrome had surfaced. The local Indians did not want another chief from outside, they already had enough of their own. Malone all at once was defending his own territory.

'Harry, I'd like to front the AC on this. These are *my* cases.'

'Scobie, don't be bloody difficult. You'd be so one-eyed about nailing this bloke Blizzard –'

It was exactly what he had said last night about Jim Knoble's being allowed to pursue the drug-pushers who had contributed to his son's OD-ing. But that, of course, had been different. It always was when your point of view shifted. 'Righto, Harry. I'll

91

put Russ Clements in charge, he can prepare everything for an indictment when we get Blizzard –'

'He'll only do whatever you tell him –'

Malone was glad they weren't face to face; he could not have hidden his smile. 'Don't you trust me, Harry?'

'No.' He wondered if Danforth was smiling. Then: 'Okay, Scobie. I'll tell Fred Falkender that Russ Clements will be handling the day-to-day stuff and I'll be in direct control. That satisfy you?'

Not really; but it was the best he could hope for. 'Thanks. We'll clean this up between us. I hope before another one of us gets it.'

2

'Making love with some men is like arm-wrestling,' said Joanna Dempster. 'Floyd is like that. He always wants to be the winner.'

Joanna was Anita Norval's sister, younger by ten years. She was blonde where Anita was dark, was taller and had to watch her weight; up till now she was voluptuous, but a matronly figure was just round the curve of her. She was amoral but honest; and frank, sometimes to the point of embarrassment. She was on her third husband and she gave Anita balls-by-balls descriptions of their accomplishments and shortcomings. Her first husband, a New Zealand banker, had had a very short penis; her second, a Chilean interior decorator, had had a very long one. It had opened up a whole complex of new positions, she had told Anita, who hadn't wanted to know but couldn't resist listening; for the first twelve months of that marriage, she had confided, she had suffered from a series of sprains and strains. She was possibly the only woman who had accomplished an orgasm with a pulled Achilles tendon, a gymnastic accident she had somehow refrained from describing to her doctor, her physiotherapist and her instructor at her aerobics class.

They were having lunch in her town house in Double Bay. Ever since she had left Killara and home she had insisted on living in the eastern suburbs. It was an area where affairs could be conducted without the local citizens hanging out placards against sin; perhaps the tolerance was due to the large middle-class community of immigrants who had settled there. Of course there was promiscuity in other areas of Sydney, but it was kept under wraps as if it were some sort of infectious disease. Joanna's affair with her present husband, an American oil executive, had been started while she was married to the Chilean. She had, she said, been looking for someone less an athlete, but had, it seemed, drawn a quarterback.

Anita began to wonder why she had come here to confide in Joanna. But she had to confide in *someone*; and Joanna, for all her loose morals, had never had a loose tongue when it came to sisterly secrets. 'Brian is nothing like that. With me, he's just so gentle. Almost too gentle, as if he thinks I'm fragile.'

'I've seen him occasionally at do's. He's not brash like some of our tycoons, but he always struck me as if he could be ruthless. Floyd says he would never want to deal with him.'

'Is Floyd implying he's shonky?'

Joanna fiddled with the cottage cheese on her plate. 'You read the papers. Only the libel laws stop them from coming right out with it.'

'I know.' Anita nodded morosely. Sometimes she wondered if she loved Brian more for his faults than his good qualities, as if love were some sort of mercy mission. She tried to smile: 'Maybe he just needs a good woman.'

'Good at what? Look, darling, I'm not criticizing him for what he's like in business. You fall in love with a man for God knows what reasons, not because he's a pillar of honesty and respectability. Look at all the male saints the nuns told us about when we were at Loreto. If women fell in love with saintly qualities, do you think all those guys could have escaped as bachelors? The women would have had them at the altar before they could get up off their knees. St Francis of Assisi wouldn't have had time to get rid of a handful of birdseed.'

In spite of herself, Anita smiled. 'You're a tonic, Jo. You may not be good for me in the long run, but you make me feel better for the moment.'

'What's an errant sister for but to make a good sister feel better?' But she said it without any rancour; there was genuine love between them. 'How does all this affect you with Phil?'

'He doesn't suspect.'

'He wouldn't. With half the dumb woman of Australia in love with him, why should he worry about whether his wife is still in love with him? Serves him right if you're finding some happiness now. But there's no future in it, you know,' she said, suddenly serious.

'I know.' Anita toyed with the salad in front of her; then she said, still looking at her plate, 'There's something else. One of Brian's ex-girl-friends was murdered at the weekend in the flat where we've been meeting. You probably read about her. The singer Mardi Jack.'

Joanna put down her fork and stared at her sister. Then she took the wine bottle from its cooler and refilled her glass; she raised the bottle enquiringly, but Anita shook her head. She returned the bottle to the cooler, then drank slowly from her glass. It was the first time Anita had ever seen her sister consciously taking control of herself and it looked so out of character.

At last Joanna said, 'Are you involved?'

'No. I didn't even know about her till he talked to me yesterday. I'm sure she didn't know about me. Oh, I knew he'd had two wives and there'd been dozens of girls, but I didn't want to know about any of them and he kept them to himself.'

'You're lucky. All my men carry their score-cards with them, like bedroom golfers. I read about this girl. Does he know who shot her?'

'No.'

'Have the police been to see him?'

'Yes.'

'Do they know about you?'

'I don't think so. God, I hope not!'

'Go back to Canberra then. Forget all about Mr O'Brien for a while. Be the PM's wife, go and open some fêtes or an art gallery or something. Preferably over in Perth or up in Darwin. As far away from Sydney as you can get.'

Anita pushed her plate away; she had eaten virtually nothing. 'I can't, Jo. I can't leave him to face all this on his own. The NCSC are after him, and now *this* . . . I *love* him, Jo.'

'You just agreed with me there's no future in it with him. Phil would never agree to a divorce – it would dent his image too much. And Brian Boru – where on earth did he get that name? – he's probably going to finish up in jail for business fraud, at least that's what Floyd thinks. Now's as good a time as any to end it all. Don't even kiss him goodbye.'

Anita shook her head. 'I can't. Even if I do break it off, I'll have to see him. I can't just break it off with a note or a phone call. I'm not a coward.'

'You're a fool if you do it any other way.' But Joanna said it kindly; she had been a fool in love too many times herself. 'All right, but do it quick. Don't put it off.'

'I have to go to a reception this evening at the Town Hall – Phil is coming up from Canberra for it. We'll stay at Kirribilli tonight. I'll let Phil go back on his own in the morning and I'll see Brian then.'

'Where? Do you want to see him here? I'll go out and you can have the house for as long as you like.' Then she slapped her cheek. 'Oh God, no! Mother's coming. She's bringing some of her committee mates for morning coffee. They want to see how her wayward daughter lives. They think I've decorated the place like a brothel.'

Anita had never been in a brothel, but she was sure that none would ever be as elegant as this house of her sister's. She searched for a word that would describe it and decided the word was *creamy*; somehow, it also described Joanna herself. The colour scheme, even the shape of the furniture, was designed to engulf one in softness; just like Joanna. The pictures on the walls, all originals, were of soft lush women: lying on creamy beds, on creamy beaches: well, maybe *they* were what one might find in a brothel. She knew that she would love to have had a couple of hours here with Brian. Better to lie in cream than in sleaze.

'Never mind, I'll find some way of seeing him.'

'Be careful, darling. I'd hate to see you splashed all over the

95

front page of the *Mirror*. It would kill Mother and Dad. It might even floor Phil for a minute or two.'

Anita loved her sister and all at once envied her her amorality and contempt for public opinion.

3

Just as he had expected, Lisa rebelled when Malone told her of the protection policy. 'No! I stay with you – the kids can go with Mother and Dad, but I stay with you!'

It is natural for animals to feel that their home, their cave, burrow or house, is a safe place. Now, all at once, the Malones knew that was no longer the case. The thought sickened them both.

He took her in his arms, could feel the fight in her slim body. 'Look, darl, this is *dangerous* –'

'I know that! That's why I'm not leaving you on your own!'

He kissed her brow, loving her so much he wanted to weep. Once he had never believed that men could weep for love: it was unAustralian, something no real ocker would ever do. But that had been before he had met Lisa and come to know that love could find depths in a man that he had never dreamed of. 'You've got to go with the kids – for their sake, not just mine. I'll be safer on my own. If you're with me, I'll have my back turned making sure you're safe.'

He could feel the fight going out of her, but she persisted a moment longer: 'Darling, can't you see what it'll be like for me? I shan't be able to sleep – I'll be awake all day and night worrying about you –'

He kissed her again. 'I know. It's a bugger of a choice, but it's the only one we have. The Department's put its foot down. It'll only be for a week, maybe two. They've got a net out all over the State looking for him – as soon as he tries again, they'll nab him –' He stopped.

She leaned away from him. 'You're the bait, aren't you? I remember Dad telling me what they used to do in Sumatra.

They'd tie a goat to a stake in the middle of a clearing and wait for the tiger to come out of the jungle. Where are they going to tie you to a stake? Not *here*!' She shook her head fiercely, pushed herself out of his arms. 'He's not going to kill you here in our own home!'

He didn't reach for her; there are moments when women are more approachable when not touched. 'No. I'm moving in with O'Brien to his suite at the Congress.'

Her laugh was so harsh it was like a cough; then she shook her head and the laugh turned into a soft gurgle. He knew he had won. 'You win. The kids and I are being shunted off to – where?'

'I've already talked to your father about it. They're going to take you up to Noosa.' That was a resort and retirement town on the Queensland coast, over a thousand kilometres from Sydney and the killer. Jan and Elisabeth Pretorius had a holiday home there; indeed, they had just returned after two months' escape from the Sydney winter. Both of them, raised in Dutch colonial Sumatra, claimed they still had thin blood and even the relatively mild Sydney winters made them miserable. Jan, when Malone had explained the situation to him, had been willing to go back north immediately. It was typical of him that he had asked almost no questions: if it was police business, that was good enough for him. Con Malone, on the other hand, would have wanted to know the ins and outs of everything.

'Noosa. Not bad. But I'd rather two weeks in a suite at the Congress. Just the two of us, no kids, no Mr O'Brien.' She was regaining her composure, trying to find some humour to strengthen her. Then she sobered. 'We tell the kids nothing, understand? Nothing.'

'Righto. Let 'em think it's a surprise holiday.'

'What about Claire?'

'What about her?'

'I think she should go on her skiing holiday.'

His first reaction was to shout *No!* He wanted all the family together; he had confidence in Lisa's ability to protect them. He had thought of suggesting that the Queensland police should be asked to keep an eye on them, but he knew that Lisa would not countenance that at all. The children, even young Tom, were all bright: with police hovering around, they would know something was wrong. A policeman's lot was not a happy one: Gilbert and Sullivan should have added a verse about a policeman's family.

'He hasn't threatened any of the families yet,' Lisa said. 'Claire goes off Friday. She can stay up at the school with the boarders till the skiing party leaves for the snow. She'll be safe. If we rob her of her holiday, she'll know something is wrong and will start asking questions. She's too old to be fobbed off.'

'You'll be worried stiff.'

'I know,' she admitted. 'So will you. But we're all going to be safe – all of us but you, darling.' She put her arms round his neck. 'The kids must never know you're in danger. The only way we can be sure of that is to act naturally, do whatever we'd planned. I'll call Claire every night and you can do the same.'

'A trunk call? Two trunk calls?' He grinned. 'Think of the cost.'

But it hurt him to smile. The possibility of the other, more terrible cost was nothing to joke about.

SIX

1

Late that afternoon Lisa took herself, Maureen and Tom over
to her parents' home at Rose Bay. Malone took Claire, with all
her new skiing gear, bought, dammit, by her Dutch grand-
parents, up to Holy Spirit convent.

'You'll be the best dressed girl on the slopes. What have you
got for après-ski or whatever they call it?'

'Daddy, don't you like Grandma Elisabeth buying me things?'
She was far too perceptive for her age. In another generation or
two, child psychologists would actually be children.

'I'm happy if you like what she buys you.'

She looked sideways at him in the car; he waited for her to
tell him that was no real answer. Then she said, 'Something's
worrying you, isn't it? I don't mean the skiing gear. Why did
we all of a sudden have to get out of our house? Is someone
going to blow it up or something?'

He swung the car up the long curving drive to the top of the
ridge where the white buildings of Holy Spirit faced down the
valley to Coogee. It was a joke between him and Lisa that
the Roman Catholics had a knack for always grabbing the best
piece of real estate wherever they chose to build a school or a
church. St Paul, he was sure, had been a developer as well as a
gospeller.

'No, it's nothing like that and don't start thinking that way.
It's just that I'm on police business – *secret* police business. Like
one of those religious retreats you go on here at school. Since I
had to be away from home, Mum and I thought it would be a
good idea if she and Maureen and Tom went away on a holiday.
Grandpa Jan suggested Noosa, so that's where they're going.

We moved you up here a coupla days early because we couldn't leave you alone in the house.'

'What does Mother Brendan think? I mean, me coming in as a boarder for two days and Maureen and Tom going off on holiday in the middle of term?'

'What *are* you? A police prosecutor?' He had come up to see Mother Brendan, put her in the true picture and she had understood. *It's a terrible world, isn't it? I'll pray for you, Mr Malone.* 'It's okay. I gave her a police badge to wear on her sleeve and she's as happy as Larry. Now get out, grab your gear and go off and enjoy yourself – it's costing me a mint. Don't break a leg.'

She kissed him. 'I love you, Daddy, but you can be a trial. Take care.'

'You, too.' He wanted to hug her, to weep. 'And stay away from boys.'

'Are you kidding?' She gave him a smile that would have broken any boy's or man's heart, picked up all her gear and struggled into the school. He should have helped her, but he couldn't bear to be with her a moment longer. Love, sometimes, is the heaviest luggage of all.

He went home, picked up two suitcases and drove into town and checked into O'Brien's suite at the Hotel Congress. He did not sign in at the reception desk.

The suite was luxurious, but it had nothing of the look of a home; if O'Brien had tried to overlay some impression of himself on the designer's taste, it did not show. It was, Malone guessed, like living in an expensive bandbox. Worst of all, despite its look of costly elegance, it had no suggestion of permanence. It was for transients, even if the present transient had a long lease.

O'Brien hadn't missed Malone's scrutiny of the suite. 'You don't like it?'

'I'm suburban, I guess. I can never understand why anyone wants to live in a hotel.'

'Service, Scobie. Everything's laid on. I lift the phone and there's a housemaid, room service, a valet, a secretary – even a call girl, if that's what I wanted. In London I had the lot – a butler, a cook, a maid, a chauffeur. Then all of a sudden one day I found out I wasn't interested in possessions and I wasn't really interested in being responsible for all those servants. I came out here and I had a couple of servants in a rented house out at Vaucluse. But Aussies aren't interested in being house servants, not even the migrants – they think it's beneath them. It just became a headache. I moved in here two years ago. The company pays for it and most of it comes off tax.'

'Which company? The one that's going broke?'

O'Brien smiled. 'Scobie, if you and I are going to live together, let's call off the insults, eh? We're not man and wife.'

'My wife and I don't insult each other.'

'Sorry.' O'Brien sounded genuinely contrite. 'I guess I think all marriages are like my own were. World Wars One and Two.'

Malone tried to be more friendly. 'Would you try it a third time?'

'If she'd have me. But I don't think it'll ever be on. Not unless her husband conks out and I don't think there's any chance of that. He's one of those dumb bastards who'll last for ever.'

Malone wondered who the dumb bastard could be; but, whoever he was, he was unimportant. 'Well, our job is to see that you and I aren't conked out.'

O'Brien had been as adamant as Lisa that he would not go to a safe house. He had shown no fear of being assassinated; it was not bravado, he was too calm for that. His explanation had been quite simple:

'I've got this NCSC thing hanging over my head, Scobie. If I drop out of sight, there are going to be more and more rumours – it's bad enough as it is. I've got to keep fronting up every day. I'll co-operate with you up to a point, but I'm going to go about my regular routine. I'll just see that I have a couple of security men close to me all the time. That's as far as I'm prepared to go.'

'What about me?' It was a natural, selfish question. Then Malone had remembered he was still *working* on the murders, that he wasn't here in the Congress just to sample the room service.

Now he said, 'Righto, during the day we go through our

regular routine, each of us. But at night we stick close, okay? I want a security man sitting outside the front door all night, they can work four-hour shifts, and our SWOS and Tac Response fellers are on call to be down here within five or ten minutes if anything happens. Anyone who delivers anything up here is to be vetted by your security men, even the housemaids, and if we have any meals up here in the suite, the food's to be brought in from outside.'

'The hotel's not going to like that.'

'Tough titty. But if it comes out of the hotel kitchens, he could get to it and poison it. So far he's killed everyone with a rifle, but there's no guarantee he's sworn to that MO. Cyanide in a croissant is just as effective.'

'If it weren't for what's already happened, I wouldn't believe any of this. Are you scared?' O'Brien held out a steady hand. 'I am. It mightn't show, but I'm scared shitless.'

'Me, too. And I'm more used to this sorta thing than you are. Oh, one more thing. Stay away from the windows, keep the curtains drawn, or at least drawn enough to stop anyone from seeing who's in here.' He walked across and pulled the thick silk curtains close together, leaving just a narrow gap. 'Don't have them any wider than that. Tell the housemaids.' Then he pulled the curtains together completely. 'At night they're to be like that, nothing showing in here. The bugger could be up there in one of those neighbouring buildings.'

O'Brien said wryly, 'You can look into here from my office. It'd be a joke if he somehow got in there and picked us off from behind my own desk.'

'Yeah,' said Malone. 'You might die laughing, but I wouldn't. Where are you going?'

O'Brien had stood up after taking off his shoes. 'I'm going out. You can come with me, if you like. It's a reception up at the Town Hall. The PM's going to be there.'

'Why do you need to go?'

O'Brien was in the doorway of the main bedroom, taking off his shirt. 'Appearances. I got the invitation to this two months ago, before all my troubles blew up. Nobody's going to snub me tonight. In the old days, I gather, I'd have got a discreet message from someone telling me the invitation was a mistake. But not any more. New money runs this town, Scobie, and someone's only guilty if he admits it. It's the New Ethics. Wall Street started it and the rest of the world is picking it up. We're one of the smartest at it. You look shocked.'

'I guess I'm too old-fashioned. Whatever happened to honesty being the best policy?'

'The dividends weren't high enough.' He stripped off his trousers, headed for his bathroom; then looked back. 'You coming?'

'I might as well. What do I wear?'

'Just don't wear your police tie. That'd clear the Town Hall in a flash.'

Malone put on his best Fletcher Jones off-the-rack suit, one chosen for him by Lisa, and lined up beside O'Brien, who was wearing a little number from Savile Row and a Battistoni shirt and tie. 'You'll do,' said O'Brien. 'You're not a ball of style like the bankers and stockbrokers who'll be there tonight, but you're – what's the word?'

'Honest?'

O'Brien grinned. 'I think living with you is going to be worse than with my two ex-wives.'

The evening was clear and cold, winter hanging on like an unwanted relative. They went uptown to the Town Hall in a hired stretch limousine with a security man sitting beside the driver and another on the jump seat opposite O'Brien and Malone. Neither of them was as tall as Malone and both of them were overweight; the one on the jump seat was too big for his suit and his shoulder holster showed as a lump under his armpit. But they looked alert and Malone hoped they would stay that way. He had a cop's antipathy to the growing number of private security forces.

The Victorian pile of the Town Hall was floodlit, making everyone going up the wide front steps a splendid target for an assassin. There were plenty of voters who had no time for the Prime Minister; but there had been only two attempted political assassinations in Australia and most people had now forgotten those. There were, however, several groups of demonstrators

103

on the footpath at the bottom of the steps, waving banners and chanting slogans and abuse at the guests as they arrived. There were conservationists, Aboriginals, retrenched social workers, anti-abortionists and two women under a banner protesting that the Second Coming of Christ had been delayed by a recently passed Act, a miracle that would have gone to the head of parliament if it had believed the accusation.

Malone and O'Brien got out of the limousine, preceded by the two security men. The crowd, not recognizing them, abused them anyway: anyone who arrived in a stretch limousine couldn't be in favour of conservation, Aboriginals, social workers, the right to life or Jesus Christ. If they had known Malone was a cop, the volume of abuse would have increased.

The two security men were left in the lobby of the Town Hall and Malone and O'Brien passed into the huge main hall. Malone at once recognized at least a dozen faces: the cream, or the scum, depending on one's social prejudice, of Sydney was here. The reception was a United Nations celebration and, like motherhood, it had to be supported; one could rant against the UN in private, as one could use contraception against the chances of motherhood, but one never did so in public. A man who knew the full value of a public face stopped by Malone.

'Inspector Malone –' Hans Vanderberg, the State Premier, never forgot a name or a face. 'I saw who you came in with. Mr O'Brien. Is he under arrest or something?'

'No, Mr Premier.' *You'd have known of it at once if he were under arrest.* The Dutchman missed nothing that went on in his State. 'I can't tell you what's going on, but Assistant Commissioner Falkender will tell you.'

'I *am* the Police Minister.' The old man ran a claw of a hand over his mottled bald head; he was an eagle too old to fly but one that could not be trapped. He glared at Malone as if the upstart inspector was trying to throw him a poisoned bait.

'I know that, sir. But I think it would be better if you got it from Mr Falkender.'

Vanderberg glared at him a moment longer, then nodded and moved on, the old political smile back on his face like a mask re-donned. When they lowered him into the grave he would be smiling back up at the voters, the coffin lid left open on his orders, as if he believed in resurrection.

Malone glanced around him. He had been to very few official receptions, but the crowd always looked the same. There were the natives standing in groups telling each other about their health ('Never ask an Aussie how he is,' Malone had once heard an American say, 'because sure as hell he'll tell you. In great detail.') Italians were huddled together telling Greek jokes; the Greeks were advising each other never to have a Lebanese do any work for them; the Hungarians moved amongst everyone else as if they owned the Town Hall. In one corner stood half a dozen token Asians, wondering if they would have been more welcome if they had volunteered to stay behind afterwards and clean up and take home the laundry. Malone, a cop, felt as much an outsider as any of them.

He looked up and around him at the galleries on the second level and at the ornate, three-storey-high ceiling. The Town Hall was sometimes referred to by the more modern, less-is-more architects as a huge barn; but on the two or three occasions he had been here he had fallen for it. It had a solidity about it, a reminder of other times; chicanery might go on in the city council rooms elsewhere in the building, but this auditorium had an honesty about it. It was Victorian but somehow it suggested none of the hypocrisy of that era.

The galleries were packed, lesser guests standing at the balus-trades and looking down, perhaps their only opportunity ever, on the leading lights below. Malone looked at them and decided no assassin would chance a shot from amongst that crowd. Frank Blizzard, if he was the hitman, was not a public performer.

Malone looked for O'Brien, saw him standing against a side wall. Just along from him were Arnold Debbs and his wife, whom Malone recognized from her newspaper photos; it seemed to him that Debbs was studiously ignoring O'Brien because all at once he took his wife's arm and the two of them moved away from O'Brien. The latter looked after them, then looked across and saw Malone. He smiled thinly and shrugged. Crumbs, thought Malone, could Penelope Debbs be the woman he's in love with?

There was a stir from the lobby and Prime Minister Philip Norval and his wife entered. Lights flashed and Malone saw the famous blond head pause and turn, offering further photo opportunities. The equally famous smile almost outshone the camera flashes; Norval's hands went out, grasping other hands, some of which had not even been lifted towards him. The PM and his wife and minders moved on into the main hall and were at once surrounded. Malone noticed that one of those who did not rush to greet the PM was The Dutchman, a sworn political enemy.

Malone looked around again for O'Brien, saw him standing in the same place against the side wall. He was staring at someone in the official group, a rapt expression on his face that made him look suddenly younger, almost vulnerable. Malone pushed his way through the throng and joined him. He spoke to O'Brien, but the latter did not appear to hear him.

Malone, curious now, looked in the direction of O'Brien's gaze. Was he, the cynical entrepreneur, the probable crook, such an admirer of Prime Minister Norval, the country's figure-head leader who, reputedly, was only honest and upright because he hadn't the brains to be otherwise? Then Malone saw the beautiful dark-haired woman beside the PM turn her head and look across the crowded room at himself and O'Brien. He was no expert on love and its atmospherics; there was too much Irish in him for that. He had, however, spent all his professional life intercepting and interpreting glances and covert looks. He slowly turned his head and saw that O'Brien was in love and realized with a shock that O'Brien's lady friend was Anita Norval, wife of the Prime Minister.

She came towards them, casually, unhurriedly, pausing to smile and speak to people on the way; Malone had seen her once or twice before at close quarters and had always been impressed by her grace and dignity. It was not a queenly approach: that would never have gone down with the natives, even those who fell on their knees when British royalty hove in sight. She did, however, suggest that she knew her husband's office was one of the symbols of what the country stood for and she wanted to polish it rather than tarnish it. She was the most popular woman in the nation and now, it seemed, she was in love with or, at best, loved by one of the nation's least popular scoundrels.

'Mr O'Brien, isn't it? I think we met once before.'

Malone could feel the warning vibrations coming out of O'Brien; but the latter somehow kept his composure. 'Hullo, Mrs Norval. Oh, this is Detective-Inspector Malone, an old friend.'

She gave Malone a smile that, unlike her husband's or The Dutchman's, was not looking for a vote; yet it seemed to Malone that there was a plea in it. 'Are you his minder, Inspector?'

But before Malone could reply, the Prime Minister had appeared at his wife's elbow. 'We have to move up on to the stage, darling. It's time for my speech.'

'Another one? This is the seven-hundred-and-forty-third so far this year.' Husband and wife exchanged the public smiles of long marital experience, the hypocritical doodads that couples carry with them like breath sweeteners. 'Nice meeting you again, Mr O'Brien. You too, Inspector.'

Norval gave the two men only a nod, nothing more, and steered his wife up towards the flag-bedecked stage. Malone looked at O'Brien, said quietly, aware of the lingering glances of those who had been staring at O'Brien and Anita Norval, 'I think we'd better get out of here. You're a bit obvious.'

O'Brien's craggy face was suddenly shrewd again. 'It shows, does it? Well, now you know.'

As soon as Norval, up on stage, began to speak in that husky, honeyed voice that had once made him the country's favourite television star, the guests turned their backs on O'Brien. He and Malone at once moved out of the auditorium as quietly and surreptitiously as they could. The security men were waiting for them in the lobby. One of them hurried away to get the limousine and five minutes later was back with it and its driver. Only then did Malone take himself and O'Brien out and down the floodlit steps to the car.

The night was still brilliantly clear. All the stars in the universe seemed to have slid into the southern skies; there were more there than any planet deserved, more than enough for all the living and dead of all time to dream upon. The day's wind had dropped, but it had done its job, swept away all the smog. It was a good night, Malone thought, for a sniper.

He pushed O'Brien into the limousine, jumped in after him and waited while the two security men got in. Only then did he relax back in his seat. Out on the pavement he saw the demonstration groups glaring at him and O'Brien with a mixture of expressions from hatred to indifference; but there was no murderer amongst them, their passion burst out of them in other ways. Flying abuse, eggs, tomatoes, the occasional fist: but never bullets.

They drove down towards the harbour, against the cinema and theatre traffic. The pavements were not crowded, but there were still plenty of people about. He won't strike tonight, Malone thought, and relaxed still further, suddenly feeling tired.

'What sorta guy should we be ready for, Inspector?' said the security man on the front seat, Ralph Shad. The question was only unexpected in that neither security man had asked it before.

Malone thought a while. What sort of man was Blizzard, assuming it was the ex-police cadet who was trying to kill him and O'Brien? How did you describe a ghost you had never really known? 'All I can say is he appears to be ruthless and bloody efficient. I haven't a clue what he looks like, whether he's a psycho –'

'He must be that,' said O'Brien.

'Not necessarily. All killers aren't psychos, not in the sense of being off their rocker. He may be a perfectly reasonable man, except when it comes to wanting to kill you and me.'

'That's psycho enough for me.'

'I'm afraid I agree with Mr O'Brien,' said Shad.

'What about you, Trevor?' Malone asked the security man in the front seat. He noticed that the driver, a young Asian, was now sitting very stiffly behind the wheel, as if up to this very moment he hadn't known he was in any danger.

Trevor Logan must have sensed the driver's concern; he patted him on the shoulder. 'You don't have to worry, Lee.' Then he turned back to Malone and contradicted what he had just said. 'I think he's dead certain to be a psycho, Inspector. They're the sort that'll have a go, regardless of the odds.'

Malone said nothing, not sure that Blizzard, or whoever the assassin was, was not psychotic. If he was, then the odds were that, sooner or later, he would give himself away, come out into the open and at last be within reach. But how much sooner, how much later, after how many more murders?

The limousine turned up into the entrance to the Congress. The hotel was set back a few yards from the street and there was a slight ramp that curved up to the front doors and then back again to the street. A portico stretched out to the pavement, over the ramp and a small garden plot of hardy shrubs. Most of the guests leaving the hotel at this time were still inside the front doors, sheltering against the cold night air while they waited for their cars or taxis; but a few stood outside beside the commissionaire. The limousine pulled up and the commissionaire stepped forward and opened the front and rear nearside doors. Both security men slid out and looked about them, as if the talk about the hitman had all of a sudden made them more alert. Malone had an abrupt impression of how obvious they looked, like the Secret Service men who were always so conspicuous when an American president appeared in public.

He got out of the car and waited for O'Brien. The latter appeared to hesitate, as if he had become shy of the people standing behind the commissionaire; they were staring at the two security men and wondering whom they were minding. Then he stepped out of the car and pushed past Malone.

In that instant, over O'Brien's shoulder, Malone saw the man with the hand-gun rise up above the parapet that separated the entrance ramp from a second ramp that led down to the hotel's garage. He dropped down, pulling O'Brien down with him. He heard no shot, the gun must be fitted with a silencer; but Trevor Logan gasped and fell back against the open car door. A second bullet thudded into the car door, but again there was no sound of a shot. He heard a woman scream and saw Ralph Shad, flat on the ground, raise his gun to return the shots.

'No!' Malone yelled. 'Get 'em all inside!'

He pushed O'Brien off him, ducked round the back of the car and came up on the driver's side. He couldn't see the young Asian; he must be cowering under the steering wheel. He crept along the length of the long car, chanced a look and saw that the gunman had disappeared. He stood up, wrenching his gun from his holster, and ran towards the parapet.

'He's gone down into the garage!' he heard the commissionaire shout.

He vaulted the parapet, landing heavily on the sloping concrete below but managing to keep his feet. He ran down the ramp, keeping close to the wall. A car came up the ramp, headlights blazing, and he knew at once he was a dead man. He flattened himself against the wall, the taste of his crushed body already in his mouth: Christ, what a way to die!

Then the car's horn blared, deafening him, the car slowed, then went past with the driver, a parking valet, yelling abuse at him. He picked himself off the wall and ran down into the garage. It was full of cars, some of them on the move towards the exit ramp; the gunman could be anywhere in the huge cave. Blizzard could dart and scurry between the ranks of cars like a rat in a maze of trenches. Except that he was still intent on killing Malone.

He stood up beyond a white Ford Fairlane half a dozen cars away, his gun held in both hands in the approved combat grip. Another car, a dark BMW, pulled out of the line of cars behind him and came along the laneway towards the ramp. The driver switched its headlights on and Malone stood exposed and blinded. He jumped to one side, in behind a Rolls-Royce; it was like hiding behind a tank. He shut his eyes, then quickly opened them; the blindness from the glare was gone. He looked towards Blizzard, standing steady behind the Fairlane, gun still raised. His two shots outside the hotel had been hurried; he took his time with this one. Just a fraction too much time: Malone hit him in the chest with a lucky shot just before he squeezed the trigger. He fell back, hit the car behind him and slid down out of sight.

Malone, gun cocked again, went forward cautiously. Two more cars came from the far end of the garage, being driven up to their owners waiting at the hotel entrance; he stepped back and waited for them to go past; the parking valets seemed oblivious of what had been going on. He came round the front of the Fairlane, ready for a second shot; but there was no need of it. The gunman lay face down, the silencer-fitted Beretta 7.65 still in one hand. Malone knelt down, felt for the pulse in the neck; there was none. Then he turned the gunman over on his back. He was young, perhaps no more than twenty, dark-haired, vicious-looking even in death and, despite his youth, far too young to be Frank Blizzard.

Malone got slowly to his feet as he heard footsteps running down the ramp and from the back of the garage. His joints felt like those of an old man, locked together; he felt the taste of death again. This wasn't the gunman they wanted. Blizzard was still somewhere out there, still intent on making sure . . .

There would be no green bottles standing on the wall.

2

Lisa had been frantic over the phone, calling him on the private number he had given her to O'Brien's suite. The line was a direct one, not routed through the hotel's switchboard – 'I want no one eavesdropping on my business calls,' O'Brien had told him. Malone was glad that no operator could hear the frantic note in his wife's voice.

'Give up! Come up to Noosa with me and the children –'

'Darl –' He tried to keep his voice as cool and calming as possible; he had had time to recover, something she hadn't yet had time to do. She had called him as soon as she had heard the news-flash on a TV channel's news update. 'This bloke wasn't after me. He was after O'Brien –'

'You were with O'Brien! He tried to shoot you –'

'Only because I was after him. I've been shot at before –' He winced at the slip of his tongue; he almost felt her wincing at the other end of the line. 'This had nothing to do with the other killer –' His tongue was getting away from him; he was supposed to be reassuring her, not frightening her still further. 'Darl, I'm all *right*. If it's any consolation to you, they're going to station

111

two of our own fellers here in the hotel with O'Brien's security men.'

'It's no consolation.' Her voice was abruptly tart and he knew, with relief, that she was about to accept the situation. 'I'll ring you at seven in the morning, you'd better be awake. I love you.'

She had hung up in his ear. He had stood for a moment fighting the sudden urge to walk out of the hotel, out of the whole business, and go out to Rose Bay and her and the kids. Then he had put down the phone and gone out of the second bedroom, where he had taken the call, into the big living-room where Danforth and Russ Clements sat with O'Brien and George Bousakis.

The hotel manager was also there, a suave Serb who looked at the moment as if his hotel had just been invaded by a bunch of Croat guerrillas. 'We can't have something like this happening, Mr O'Brien! This is an international hotel – Australia is supposed to be a safe country –'

Malone waited for Danforth to say something, but the Chief Superintendent was ignoring the manager. So Malone said, 'It *is* a safe country, a bloody sight safer than most!'

The manager had been taught how to manage all types, including jingoistic natives. 'Oh, I agree, Inspector, I agree. But I'm afraid I must ask Mr O'Brien to vacate the suite – till all this has blown over –'

O'Brien said quietly, 'I'll go when I'm ready. My lease has another – what, George?'

'Another five months to run,' said Bousakis. 'Don't worry, sir, just leave it to us and the police.'

He heaved himself out of his chair and ushered the manager out of the suite; the manager himself could not have evicted a troublesome guest more smoothly. Bousakis closed the door and came back and lowered himself into his chair.

'The corridor is full of reporters and cameramen. You want to make any statement, Brian?'

O'Brien looked at Malone; it was almost as if he didn't know or couldn't accept that Danforth was in charge. 'What d'you reckon, Scobie?'

'Say nothing,' said Malone and looked at Danforth. 'You agree, Chief?'

Danforth had been studying O'Brien, his big red face expressionless, his slightly bleary eyes unwavering. He had been drinking and his breath smelled of whisky; all of those in the room had a drink beside them but Danforth had been several drinks ahead of them when he had first appeared. Malone didn't know how he had heard the report on the shooting, but he had arrived within ten minutes of it, ahead even of Russ Clements. His manner towards both O'Brien and Bousakis had been abrupt and he had said very little to either Malone or Clements.

'Give 'em nothing,' he said at last with a growl. 'The press has been giving you a bad enough trot already, Mr O'Brien.'

O'Brien looked at the older man with cautious interest; here was another cop who wasn't on his side. 'They're a necessary evil, Superintendent. Presidents and prime ministers couldn't do without them.'

'You're not running for office, Mr O'Brien. I say stuff 'em.' He looked at Bousakis, gave an order as if the latter worked for the Department: 'Tell 'em to get lost. There'll be a police statement in the morning.'

Bousakis glanced at O'Brien, who hesitated, then nodded. The fat man got up again, breathing heavily with the effort, paused to finish off the whisky in his glass and went out of the suite.

Danforth said, 'Is this one connected with the other hits, Inspector?'

'No,' said Malone adamantly.

'He had a Victorian driving licence,' said Clements, who had taken charge when he had arrived. He had still been at Police Centre when the call came in and he had been down here in the hotel within twenty minutes. 'Joseph Gotti, from Melbourne. Born 1967. Andy Graham went back to the Centre and is getting on to the Melbourne boys to see if Gotti had a record. If he's a hitman, I don't think Blizzard would have been employing him. He wasn't too bright, trying to do that job where he did.'

'Who else would have been trying to kill you, Mr O'Brien?' said Danforth.

113

'Oh, several people could have it in mind.' O'Brien's candour seemed to surprise Danforth; the bleary eyes blinked, as if behind them the sluggish mind was trying to sharpen itself. 'I have enemies, Superintendent. I've already told Inspector Malone that.'

'Would you care to give us their names?'

'The list is too long.' O'Brien had evidently decided his candour had gone far enough.

'We can't do much without your help, Mr O'Brien.'

Malone and Clements were watching the match between the two men. There was a mutal antagonism, more so on Danforth's part, that seemed to vibrate the few feet that separated them.

'I know that, Superintendent,' said O'Brien flatly, take it or leave it.

Danforth frowned; then he rose slowly from his chair. 'If that's the way you want it . . . You gunna stay here, Inspector?'

'For tonight anyway.' Malone got to his feet and followed his superior out of the suite, the latter leaving without saying good-night to either O'Brien or Clements. Out in the corridor Malone said, 'Leave him to me, Harry. I'll get what I can out of him.'

'Bugger him. He don't deserve us looking after him.'

Some reporters and a press photographer were at the end of the corridor outside the lifts; they were held back by a uniformed policeman and a new security man who had been brought in to replace Logan, who had gone to hospital to have a bullet removed from his shoulder. Bousakis came back towards the suite's front door.

'I told 'em to be at Police Centre tomorrow morning at nine, okay?'

'Who told you to tell 'em nine o'clock? I wasn't gunna be in that early. 'Night, Scobie.'

Danforth, sullen and heavy as a constipated buffalo, lumbered off along the corridor and Malone, grinning at Bousakis, pushed the fat man back into the suite. 'You'll get used to him.'

'He's antediluvian. I thought fossils like that were all dead.'

'We keep a few as museum pieces.'

With Danforth gone the four remaining men looked at each

114

other, as if realizing the evening had now run down; there was time for shock to take over, if there was going to be any. But Malone noticed that O'Brien seemed in control of himself and he himself had now recovered. It would be Lisa, several miles away, her bags packed for Queensland, who would still be in shock.

Clements was on his feet ready to depart. He suddenly looked tired and Malone realized that, in a way, the last few days had been as hard on the big man as on himself. It was as if Clements felt that the bullet meant for Malone, whenever it came, would hit him just as hard. Malone felt a sudden rush of affection for him.

'When does Sam Culp – or do we call him Sebastian Waldorf? – when does he get back from Melbourne with the opera company?'

'Tomorrow afternoon. I thought we'd better meet him at the airport.'

'I'm going down to Minnamook tomorrow morning,' said Clements. 'I went through the files again from Goulburn. Frank Blizzard grew up in Minnamook –'

'Where's that?'

'It's down the South Coast, about thirty kilometres the other side of Wollongong. It's just a village on the Minnamook River, mostly weekenders and retired people. Blizzard was an orphan, his foster parents were his uncle and aunt, the same name. I thought I'd look 'em up.'

Malone glanced at O'Brien. 'What are you doing tomorrow?'

'I've got a session with the NCSC. It'll probably last all day.'

'I'll pick you up at 9.30,' said Bousakis and added for Malone's benefit, 'We'll take a couple of security men with us.'

'Good,' said Malone. 'Incidentally, George, how did you get here so promptly after the shooting?'

Bousakis paused a moment, as if he felt the question was out of place. Then: 'I saw the commotion from the lobby. I was down there, having a snack, waiting for Brian to come back. I had those papers for him –' He nodded at a file on the coffee table in front of O'Brien. 'Do we all have to account for where we were?'

'Just routine,' said Malone routinely; it was an answer that had stood the test of time. He turned back to Clements. 'I'll come down to Minnamook with you. Andy Graham can follow up things here. I'll be up at the Centre at eight to see if there's anything needs looking at before we leave. Get on to the local police – it'll probably be Kiama or Wollongong – and tell 'em we'd like a back-up with at least two blokes when we call on Blizzard's uncle and auntie.'

Clements and Bousakis left together. Malone checked that there would be a security man on duty throughout the night in the corridor, then came back into the suite and locked the door. O'Brien was on the phone in the living-room.

'No, please don't – it's too risky for you . . . I'm all right, honestly . . . No, go back to Canberra, I'll call you tomorrow evening at six . . . I'll give my name as – Maloney –' He smiled tiredly across the phone at Malone as the latter came back into the room. 'I love you, too.'

He hung up, sat in his chair with his elbows on his thighs and his big hands hanging limply between his knees. He looked up at Malone from under his thick brows and swore softly. 'Jesus Christ, what a mess!'

Malone sat down opposite him, took off his shoes. 'How did it ever happen? I mean you and Anita Norval?'

The big hands turned upwards. 'I don't know. It just did. About four months ago, before all the stink about my companies started, I was sitting next to her at a dinner. Before we got to the dessert I knew I was in love, truly in love for the first time in my life. The unbelievable part is, *she* called *me* the next day, not the other way around.'

He was not the sort of man from whom Malone would have expected confidences. He had asked the question about Anita Norval without really expecting any answer. He had never been interested in other men's relationship with women and he would certainly have never told anyone of his own feelings for Lisa. But Anita Norval was more than just the woman in O'Brien's life, she was the wife of the Prime Minister. If the affair ever became public, he could not imagine a worse scandal. The voters, especially the women, were emphatic that their women in public

116

life must be beyond reproach. Public men could have affairs so long as they didn't flaunt them; Philip Norval was suspected of being a womanizer, but he was still popular, even with the women not lucky enough to go to bed with him. But a public woman was expected to be a combination of Mother Teresa and the Virgin Mary, a paragon of virtue. Queen Marie of Rumania and Catherine the Great would have had a hard time with the locals.

'Does the PM know about it?'

'She says no. Maybe he suspects, I dunno – not me but someone else. He can't stand me. He used to be very matey with Big Business – I was never one of his pals, but a lot of other guys were. But since The Crash a coupla years ago he's a born-again Christian or something, at least as far as business goes. The word is that when the market crashed he was mixed up in a couple of shonky ventures and his minders got him out just in time.'

'Are there any of his ministers mixed up with you right now?'

O'Brien looked at him sideways. 'What makes you ask that?'

'Who employed that hitman to try and kill you tonight?'

O'Brien laughed, but there was no humour in him. 'Scobie, they don't go that far, not down in Canberra! They have other ways of getting rid of you.'

'You told Danforth you had enemies. Who did you mean, then?'

O'Brien took off his tie, took the gold links out of his cuffs. He was debating how much he should tell Malone; he had never told even Anita the full story. All his life, though he had never been lost for words, he had always held back something of himself; had, indeed, used the flow of words as lies, as camouflage. Yet now he felt the urge to tell the truth, as if there were some salvation in it: salvation from another bullet, the final one. But he suddenly wasn't afraid of death: that was the truth, too. He had the fatalism of someone who knew he had left everything too late.

He said carefully, 'All this is off the record, okay?'

Malone hesitated, then nodded. 'Unless you're going to tell me you once killed someone or had them killed.'

'No, nothing like that. I'm not a killer, I draw the line at that.

No, it was the people I was mixed up with – still am. When I first came back here I had enough capital to start a small merchant bank, the O'Brien Cossack. I made a mistake calling it that, but I named it after one of my most successful rock groups. They all think I'm a sabre-wielder.' He managed a weary smile. 'Which I guess I am. But the name appealed to a few characters back in those early days.'

'What sort of characters?' Malone all at once was hungry, was taking nuts by the handful from a bowl in front of him.

'Villains, real villains. I had trouble getting clients at first – the old established banks did everything they could to muscle me out. They didn't want competition, even though they knew that pretty soon the banking system would have to be opened up. Then these characters started coming to me. One or two of my executives introduced them to me.'

'George Bousakis, for instance?'

O'Brien paused a moment. 'Let's leave names out of it for the time being. These guys came to me and asked me to launder money for them. Not as bluntly as that, but I knew what they wanted. And I said yes, because by then I was getting desperate. That got the bank on its feet. Laundering money from drugs, selling arms, bank hold-ups, art thefts in Europe – you name it, we took the money in and cleaned it up for them.'

'How?'

'Investment here and offshore. Some of it went back to Europe, some into Hong Kong real estate.'

Malone had slowly begun to like the man sitting across from him; now he felt anger and contempt sickening him. He said nothing, but what he thought and felt was plain on his face and O'Brien saw it.

'Don't start moralizing, Scobie. I've been doing that to myself for the past four months, trying to turn the clock back to – Christ knows when. Back to when I was a kid, I guess. Or maybe when I first went into the police academy. Some time, anyway, before I got greedy and didn't care how I made my money. I'm not proud of it, any of it. Not any more.'

Malone couldn't help his cynicism: 'You mean a good woman has made you see the light?'

'She doesn't know even the half of it. But yes, in a way. But it's too late, sport, it's much too late.' There was no self-pity in his voice; Malone was thankful for that at least. 'I know it even more than she does.'

Malone felt ill at ease on the subject of Anita Norval, as if he were peering in a window on something private. 'Who are these characters? Mafia?'

'Some of them. Some from the Triads. But most of them are just plain Aussie and Kiwi crims, bastards who'd bump you off as soon as look at you.'

'They still investing through your bank?'

'Some of them, but it's their clean stuff. I mean no dirty money, stuff to be laundered, has come in for, I dunno, three or four years. I just let 'em know the bank was under suspicion, that the Costigan investigators were looking into us.'

The Costigan commission had been an enquiry into crime and corruption that had gradually widened and deepened its net till the catch had become embarrassing.

'Were they looking into you?'

'No, but it looked like a good way of easing out those characters, or anyway of stopping laundering their money. By then the bank was becoming respectable.'

'So they still have deposits with you, I mean the money they originally gave you?'

'Yes. They're in bonds, in companies the bank recommended. That's the trouble – the bonds are mostly junk now. They also don't like the way they were bought out of a mining company I started.'

'So they've been pressuring you?' O'Brien nodded; and Malone went on, 'Anyone else? Any politicians mixed up in this?' Again O'Brien nodded. 'Who?'

'No names, Scobie. Not yet.'

Malone wanted to ask if Arnold Debbs was one of the names, but he refrained. 'You're making it bloody difficult to keep you safe. And me, too. That bloke tonight meant to kill me when I chased him down into the garage.'

O'Brien said quietly, 'How did you feel about killing him?'

'It was him or me – I didn't think about it. I'll start to think

119

about it when I have to write my report. The Department's pretty tough on any cop who's trigger-happy. I don't like using my gun.' He was calm enough now, but he knew the real sweat would begin later in the darkness just before he would fall asleep. He repeated, 'But it was him or me.'

'I'm sorry about that.' There was a note of genuine regret in O'Brien's voice; it struck Malone all at once that he was looking for a friend, even a straight cop. 'I'd have spilled the beans on everyone if he'd killed you.'

He's gone too far: Malone had believed him up till that point. 'Yeah,' he said dryly. 'I'd have appreciated that.'

O'Brien had enough shame to grin. 'Okay, no extravagant promises. But don't get killed on my account, Scobie.'

'I'll try not to.' He took another handful of nuts and stood up. He was suddenly tired, though the hour was still early. 'I'm going to bed. My wife will be calling me at seven – she and the two younger kids are leaving first thing for Queensland.'

'I bought an island up there a coupla years ago, off the Barrier Reef. I was going to retire there. If I lived that long,' he added after a moment.

Malone turned back at his bedroom door. 'Brian, when you were a greedy-guts, when you were flat out gathering all this loot, did you ever give a thought for the poor buggers without any, the battlers?'

'Only my old man. But like I told you, he didn't want to know me.'

'What about the other battlers?'

'Never.'

'Well, it looks as if they're going to have the last laugh.' Malone tossed the last nut into his mouth. 'Maybe it's true that the meek will inherit the earth.'

O'Brien, now at his own bedroom door, shook his head. 'Only if there are no prior claims. If I don't take it away from the battlers, some other bastard will. There are no saints in private enterprise, Scobie. Good-night.'

3

Lisa called Malone at seven o'clock next morning, right on time; when she named a time, one could set the GPO clock by her. She told him to be careful, told him she loved him, then put Maureen and Tom on.

'Will you ring us each night at Noosa, Daddy?' said Maureen.

'Can I make it collect? Righto, I'll call you. Take care.'

'You too, Daddy.' She sounded suddenly very grown-up. 'It's a bugger of a job being a policeman, isn't it?'

'Watch your language, kid. Is that what they teach you at Holy Spirit?'

'It's French. *Je boo-ger, tu boo-ger . . .*'

Smart-arse kids: the American TV family sitcoms were breeding them in homes all over the globe. 'You've been listening to those cute little creeps on TV again.'

'When can I start swearing?' said Tom on the extension phone.

'When I retire as a cop. Take care of Mum, Tom. When you come back I'll take you to the rugby league grand final.'

'I'd rather go to the soccer.'

'You'll go to the rugby league.' What were sons for if they weren't for going to football matches that their fathers followed?

Malone hung up, sat for a moment hugging the thought of the children to himself. He looked at his watch: it was too early to call Claire at school. He would call her this evening, hope that she would not have heard the news of his narrow escape last night. But he knew it was a faint hope: her antenna was as sensitive as her mother's.

He went out to have breakfast with O'Brien. He had forgotten to order it last night, but O'Brien had anticipated that he was a man of healthy appetite in the mornings. There was cereal, juice, bacon and eggs and pork sausages, toast and honey and marmalade and tea or coffee. Malone, still hungry, sat down to enjoy the lot.

'Just as well you have no kids from your marriages.'

'Yeah. I've always thought W. C. Fields was right. Any man who hates kids can't be all bad.'

121

'My three would clobber you unconscious if they heard you. I think I might do it myself.'

'Sorry.' Again there was the abrupt change in tone, the almost desperate plea for friendship. 'Maybe when this is all over, I could meet them. They might change my mind.'

'What about Anita? Is she a child-lover?'

'I think so. We've never talked about it. She's a grandmother, you know.' He shook his head in wonder. 'It's hard to believe, when you look at her. Ten years ago, if someone had told me I'd be in love with a grandmother, I'd have thought it was – was obscene.'

'All those under twenty-five still think it's obscene.'

George Bousakis came to pick up O'Brien; the two of them left for Cossack House with two fresh security men. Malone went down with them in the lift, said goodbye to them as they got into a hire car with darkly tinted windows, and stepped out into the wind-swept street. He looked up at the buildings opposite, but could see no open window: Blizzard was not waiting for him there.

He walked up to Police Centre, glad of the exercise in the cold gusty morning; August was blowing itself out in ambushing blasts that lurked at every corner. The walk and the wind revived him, as if last night had been blown out of him. He was an objective cop again. Well, almost . . .

Clements was waiting for him with the report from Melbourne. 'Gotti had a record, he's been in trouble since he was fourteen. Breaking and entering, assault, armed hold-up – he got only two years for that one, the judge thought he'd been led astray by older elements. The Victorian boys have put *ha-ha* after that one. They've suspected him of two hits down in Melbourne, but they couldn't pin 'em on him.'

'They know any of his connections?'

'Mostly older crims down in Melbourne, none of 'em Mafia. He was Italian, but he stayed away from them. He had a connection in Canberra, he went up there twice in the past month, and he'd been to Sydney three times in the past coupla months. The Melbourne guys missed his trip this time, they don't know when he came up to Sydney.'

'Why didn't they contact us the other times?'

'What for? He hadn't done anything. Would we have been happy if they'd contacted us to keep an eye on all their crims who they thought might be up to something? We'd be out at Mascot watching every plane coming in from Melbourne.'

Police co-operation was improving nationally, but there was still a hangover from not-so-long-ago when each of the State forces and the Federal force were suspicious of the others' honesty and efficiency. Those, however, had been the days before crime had become organized, before the crims had given a new meaning to commonwealth.

'Righto, put someone on to seeing when he arrived and where he stayed. Something may turn up.' But he wasn't hopeful. 'Give me twenty minutes or so while I write my report on last night, then we'll go down and see what we can find out about Frank Blizzard.'

'You heard from Sam Culp?'

'No. These bloody theatrical types . . . I rang again this morning, but they told me he didn't stay at his hotel last night. I dunno, maybe he's shacked up somewhere with some soprano. We'll meet him at the airport.'

They drove down to Minnamook in an unmarked car, the windows up against the wind sweeping across the scrubby trees on top of the South Coast escarpment. Malone looked out at the grey-green featureless landscape, forbidding and secretive as the whole wide continent behind it; two hundred years, he thought, and all we've done is chipped away at the edges of it. Flat and sunbaked, it yet held more mystery than even the darkest jungle. Fantasy took hold of him as he half-dozed in the car's warmth: Frank Blizzard was held there somewhere in the mystery.

Going down the F5 freeway Clements carelessly let the car wind itself up above the 110 kilometres-an-hour speed limit; he was doing 125 when he saw the flashing lights of the highway patrol car in his driving mirror. He wound down his window and put his blue light out on the roof; at the same time he eased his foot off the accelerator. The highway patrol car flashed its lights again, then slowed down and dropped away.

'It's nice to see they're doing their job,' Clements said with a grin.

They dropped down off the escarpment, easing their way past the heavy coal trucks, their air brakes gasping, on their way down to the steelworks at Port Kembla. They skirted Wollongong, possibly the cleanest industrial city in the world, certainly in winter; the smoke from the steel mills blew almost horizontally out to sea, lying on top of the tall smoke-stacks like the splintered, broken half of a thick mast. An empty coal truck passed them going the other way, speeding like a runaway locomotive, building up momentum for the long climb up to the top of the escarpment.

'The highway boys will get him,' said Clements smugly, his foot now innocent, their speed down to just below the limit.

Twenty minutes later they turned off into Minnamook. It was half a dozen stores, all owner-run, and perhaps a couple of hundred houses, most of them modest but with two or three would-be mansions up on the southern bluff where the Minnamook River ran into the sea behind the spit of sand dunes and ocean beach. It was the sort of village one found all up and down the South and North coasts from Sydney, some of them a century or more old, but all of them now under threat from developers. So far Minnamook seemed to be safe from the development blight.

Clements went into a newsagency and general store, came out and got back into the car. 'That guy remembers Blizzard. He's been here fifty years, he wanted to tell me his life story.'

'Don't we all?' But the garrulous were often the best source of what a cop wanted to know.

'Blizzard delivered papers for him as a kid. He was an orphan, like I told you. His uncle is dead, but his auntie still lives here.'

'I'd rather be dealing with his uncle.'

'So would I. But Auntie it's gotta be.'

Elsie Blizzard lived in a small weatherboard house fronting on to the riverbank. When Clements and Malone pulled up, two uniformed men, both young, appeared out of a side-street.

Malone introduced himself and Clements. 'Does the old lady know we're coming?'

'I don't think so, sir.'

They were eager and intelligent, one eye on transfer to the Big Smoke, where pollution and corruption might get up their nose but where life was at least interesting. They had the naïveté of the ambitious innocent who had not yet begun to climb, who did not know that the rungs were greasy with other men's disillusion. It did Malone's heart good to listen to them.

'Our inspector warned us about Blizzard and what you think he's been up to. We've been here since nine o'clock and we haven't seen anyone hanging around.'

'Unless, of course, he's in the house with his aunt,' said the officer who had first spoken.

Malone had considered that possibility, but hadn't mentioned it to Clements. He looked at the big man and saw that, if he had not done so before, he was certainly considering it now. He had taken his gun out of his holster and put it in the pocket of his raincoat, keeping his hand in the pocket.

'One of you go around to the river side of the house,' said Malone. 'If he comes out, challenge him. If he doesn't stop, shoot.'

'To kill?' The two young officers had looked at each other; then the first one had asked the question.

'To kill,' said Malone and hated the thought that he might be ordering these young men to kill their first man. 'Who's going?'

Again the young officers looked at each other, then the second one, stocky and ginger-haired, his bright blue eyes now clouded with the unexpected, said, 'I'll go, Reg.'

He went off at once, as if to be gone before his will suddenly folded, vaulting the low fence of the house next door and disappearing up the far side of it. Malone looked at the other young man, a good-looking dark lad with thick straight brows and a mouth that looked more used to smiling than being pinched nervously as it was now.

'What's your name, Reg?'

'Capresi, sir.'

'Why did they send two junior constables?'

'I guess they weren't expecting any trouble, sir. There's a demonstration on in the 'Gong today, there's a strike at the steelworks, and I guess they figured that was more important. Sorry, Inspector, maybe I shouldn't have said that. But down here local issues come first, you know what I mean?'

'Sure, I understand.' Malone didn't look at Clements. He was angry at himself for not having stressed the seriousness of this visit to Minnamook. 'All right, just stand behind your car. If anything happens when that front door opens, if there's any gunfire, get on to your headquarters right away. I'll want back-up here immediately, local issues or not. Understand?'

'Yes, sir.'

Malone and Clements, the latter still with his hand in his raincoat pocket, walked up the concrete path between the small, neatly trimmed lawns and the winter-brown shrubs. They reached the blue front door and there Mrs Blizzard met them head-on. She flung open the door and Malone and Clements instinctively stepped aside, one going one way, the other the other. Mrs Blizzard looked at them in angry puzzlement.

'What's the matter with you two? What do you want?'

'Police, Mrs Blizzard. Inspector Malone and Sergeant Clements.' He produced his badge.

'Police? What's this all about? You expected me, an old woman, to be timid, didn't you?' They followed her into the cottage. 'Shut the door, keep the wind out. I believe in saying what I think, that's my right, right? Tea or coffee? It's only instant, that's all I can afford on my pension. The cost of living's going up all the time, but do they care in Canberra, right?'

'Whichever you have the most of,' said Malone. 'Tea, coffee, it doesn't matter.'

'Don't be polite. Make up your mind!'

'Coffee,' said Clements hastily and looked at Malone. If Blizzard was in this house, he would be properly cowed.

The house appeared to have three bedrooms, a bathroom and an open-plan kitchen and living-room that looked out to the slow-flowing river, where a pelican was just gliding in, like an old-time flying-boat. The rooms were stuffed with furniture: solid old-style chairs, tables and sideboards of polished cedar; the antique dealers of Paddington and Woollahra would pick the house clean if they were invited in. The walls were covered in old paintings, all of them cheap and amateurish, and old faded photographs; the house was a museum. Mrs Blizzard hopped around in it like a long-legged bower-bird.

The two detectives sank down into deep leather chairs; some of the horsehair stuffing showed through one or two cracks. Mrs Blizzard, chattering all the time, brought them coffee and a biscuit tin, at least a hundred years old, full of biscuits.

'Made them myself. Now what's this all about?'

'It's about your nephew Frank. We think he could help us in some enquiries we're making.'

'What's he been up to now?' Mrs Blizzard bit into one of her biscuits, working her mouth with her lips closed as her dentures slipped. She was a tall woman, all bony angles; she might once have been good-looking, but now her face was wrinkled and gaunt. She had a head of thick white hair, bright blue eyes and, so far, no smile. She sat on a high-backed chair, taller than the two men sunk in their deep chairs. If she could only have remained still for a moment she would have suggested a dignified arrogance.

'What did he get up to when he was young? Or lately?'

'I haven't heard from him in, oh I dunno, ten years, maybe more. No, he was a good boy when he was young. A bit moody, but only children often are, so they tell me. Sometimes he was a bit, too, well, *quiet*, we thought. But him and Jeff, my husband, got on well together.'

'How did he get on with you?' Malone put the question gently.

She glanced away for a moment, then back at the two detectives. 'Not the best. I was a bit strict with him, he didn't like being told when he was wrong. Jeff would take his side, so in the end I used to keep my mouth shut. I don't think he ever got over the death of his parents, losing them when he was so young.'

'Did he ever talk about wanting to join the police?'

'He used to talk about it with Jeff. He wanted to be a detective – like you two, I suppose. He was always reading detective stories when he was young, Jeff would get them for him from the library in Kiama. American stories, Raymond Chandler, a writer named Macdonald or O'Donnell, something like that. I

127

used to read them myself before he'd take the books back to get a new one.'

'They were about private eyes,' said Malone. 'Sergeant Clements and I never have those sort of adventures.'

'Did you know him when he went to train at the police college or whatever it was?'

'Slightly. He never told us how much he wanted to be a detective.'

'He got into some sort of trouble there. He told Jeff about it, but I never got the gist of it, even. Jeff wouldn't tell me. He was dead, anyway, two days later.'

'Who?' said Clements, as if he and Malone had missed something.

'Jeff. My husband. He had a heart attack and he went – just like that. It was a terrible shock.' She stopped, bit her lip: twenty-odd years ago was only yesterday, grief was there in the blood like an ineradicable cancer. Then she recovered, she was a woman who would never weep in public: 'It hit Frank very hard. I thought at one time he was going to go out of his mind. He went – what's the word?'

'Berserk?' said Malone.

She nodded. 'Yes, I suppose that's it. He blamed Jeff's death on what had happened to him up at the police college. He just said it once, but it was frightening, the way he said it.'

'Did the doctor think it was that that killed your husband?'

She shook her head. 'Not really. We didn't know it, Jeff and me, I mean, but his heart attack was just waiting to happen. Any shock could have killed him, any sort of sudden stress, they said. But maybe Frank was right. I'll never know.'

'What happened after your husband's death?'

'The day after the funeral Frank left home. I never saw him again. I never forgave him for going off and leaving me like that. We'd looked after him ever since he was two years old. You expect a bit more gratitude than that, right? What's he done?'

Malone ignored that for the moment. 'You never heard from him again?'

'Oh, I'd get the occasional Christmas card, sometimes a short letter. From up in Queensland most of the time, but I remember

I got a couple from Darwin. The last Christmas cards were from places in Europe, I can't remember where. I never kept them. I hadn't forgiven him for going off the way he did. I said, what's he done?'

'What sort of jobs did he have? I mean before he went into the police force and then up to Queensland?'

'He was a timber-worker. Jeff, my husband, worked as a timber-cutter all his life. So did Frank's father. The Blizzards have been in the district for over a hundred years. They worked in the cedar forests up there in the hills. They're all gone now, the cedar and the Blizzards.' She put her cup and saucer down on a cedar table, said demandingly, 'Now stop beating about the bush. What's he done?'

Malone wanted to cushion the blow, but he could think of no way of doing it. It had happened before: no matter how much you hated it, you hit the woman harder than you intended. 'We suspect him of murder. Four murders, in fact.'

'*Four?* Who?'

'Three men and a girl. None of them related.' He didn't elaborate. 'You might've read about 'em in the papers.'

'I never read about violence.'

The wrinkles in her face seemed to increase; the bright blue eyes dimmed with sudden pain. She's tried to cut him out of her life, Malone thought, but it hasn't worked. She turned her head and looked at a wooden-framed photo on the wall; one amongst many, but there was no doubt which one she was looking at. Malone had missed it amongst the gallery hung on the walls. A tall teenage boy, hair cut short, dressed in baggy overalls, stood in an awkward pose, a rifle held with both hands in front of him, four rabbits lying at his feet in a heap like a rumpled mat.

'That's him?' said Clements. 'Was he a good shot?'

'My husband said he was the best shot he'd ever seen. They used to go hunting together, up the river. Sometimes Jeff would come home empty-handed, but Frank would always have something, a rabbit or a duck.' She looked back at the two policemen. 'Murder? Four murders? No, not Frank!'

'Yes,' said Malone. 'Don't you believe he's capable of committing them?'

129

'No,' she said, but it seemed that her voice held no conviction.

'We don't have any proof yet, but he's the chief suspect. We still have to trace him. We don't even know what he looks like now.' He glanced at the photo on the wall, then looked back at Mrs Blizzard. 'We'd like to borrow that photo to make a copy. Would you recognize him now if you saw him?'

She was still getting over the shock of what she had been told. She had never had any children of her own, but she had known what it was like to be a mother. 'I dunno. We all change, don't we? I've changed.' She nodded at another photo on a wall: a proud girl, dark-haired, very tanned, stared at the three of them. She reminded Malone of pictures he had seen of early Egyptian princesses, but he didn't know whether Mrs Blizzard would consider that a compliment. 'When you look in the mirror, do you remember what you looked like when you were young?'

No: you remembered other faces better than your own. Except that he could not remember Frank Blizzard's. 'What would Frank be now?'

'Forty-five, I think. Maybe forty-four. Is that still middle-aged? It was in my day. But everyone wants to be younger now, don't they?'

Then the phone rang. For some reason Clements started in his chair, as if he had expected there would be no phone amongst all the old heavy furniture. Mrs Blizzard got up, went to the sideboard and lifted a needlepoint cover that Malone had thought was a tea-cosy. Under it was the telephone.

'Hallo? . . . Yes. Who's this?' Then her hand shook and she almost dropped the phone. 'No, Frank, no. Where are you?' She looked at Malone, mouthed, *It's him*. 'No, Frank, I didn't send for them –'

Malone jumped up, grabbed the phone, jerking it from her hand more roughly than he had intended. 'Blizzard? This is Inspector Malone –'

'I know who you are, Malone. You've been in my sights for a couple of weeks. You're dead, Malone, whether you know it or not.'

There was silence for a moment; then the dial tone burrowed against his ear. He put down the phone, replaced the needlepoint

130

cover. Then he put his hand on Mrs Blizzard's bony arm, felt the trembling flooding through her. She was on the point of tears and he thought for a moment he had hurt her when he had snatched the phone from her. Then he saw that the pain was much deeper, was all through her. He gently eased her back on to her chair.

'Did he threaten you?'

She shook her head, was dumb for a long moment. Then: 'No. He asked me if I'd sent for you . . . As if I would –' She had forgotten that she had tried to cut him out of her life.

'Was it a local call? Or were there pips from an STD call?'

She shook her head again, not even looking at him. 'No pips. No one ever calls me on a trunk call.'

Malone said to Clements, 'That means he tailed us down here. Did you see anyone on our tail all the way down?'

'I wasn't even looking for anyone,' Clements confessed. 'If that highway guy hadn't flashed his lights at me, I wouldn't have noticed him.'

Malone turned back to Mrs Blizzard. She had poured herself another cup of coffee and seemed to be gathering some strength from it. He remembered an old aspirin powder slogan: a cuppa tea, a Bex and a nice lie-down; but he didn't think Mrs Blizzard would ever lie down, not even for a murdering foster-son. There was something of the durability of cedar in her.

'I think we'd better have a policewoman move in here with you –'

'No,' she said firmly and put down her cup and saucer, her hand stiff and firm as a wrench. 'Nobody's moving in here with me, not a stranger. I can look after myself, I've done it ever since my husband died. I'm just glad now that he's dead,' she added and there was just a slight tremor in her voice. 'Don't worry about me, Inspector. Frank won't hurt me.'

Malone wasn't so sure, but he knew he would never win an argument with her, not if he stayed here all day. 'Well, we'd better tell the local police to drop by every now and then.'

'I don't want them here –' But her objection now was only half-hearted.

'If Frank calls again, you'll let us know.' He put his card on the table beside her cup and saucer.

She took her time about replying; then: 'Depends what he talks to me about. If I think he's going to commit another – another murder, all right, I'll ring you. But not if he just wants to talk to me. I'm still his foster-mother, right?'

Malone had seen it before, the apron strings pulling the mother down into the drowning pool; but he knew Lisa would be the same if any of the children ever got into trouble. 'Fair enough. Is there anyone else here in Minnamook that he's likely to contact? Old mates? An old girl-friend?'

'He had only one mate, but he was killed in Vietnam. He never had a regular girl-friend. He could be a little queer at times.'

'Was he homosexual?'

She was shocked, it was something beyond her ken. *'Frank? Here in Minnamook?* We'd never stand for anything like that, not when Frank lived here. Not even now. We're churchgoers around here,' she said, as if hell and its sins were miles away across the river and up in Sydney.

Minnamook had still managed to breed a multiple murderer: but Malone didn't mention that. He didn't know why he had asked the question about the possibility of homosexuality; it smacked of Clements' prejudices. 'Did he play the field with the girls?'

'Play the field?' She wrinkled her nose. 'I don't like that expression. He didn't have loose morals, if that's what you mean. He was a decent, religious boy all the time he lived with us.'

Well, he's a sinner now. 'Righto, Mrs Blizzard. We'll probably be in touch again. Can Sergeant Clements take that photo? We'll send it back.'

She took the photo from the wall, handed it to Clements. 'You'll ring me if you catch him? I don't want to read it in the papers or hear it on the wireless. I have the right to be the first to know, right?'

'We'll let you know at once, as soon as we catch him. Goodbye, Mrs Blizzard. And don't be too rough on the local police. They only have your interest at heart.'

132

'Just so long's they don't want to come into my home. I did you a favour letting you in.'

'And we appreciate it,' said Malone as she shut the front door in his face.

He knew with certainty, as if he were staring at her through clear glass, that behind the door she had already begun to weep. She would, however, never let anyone see the tears. She reminded him, in a way, of his own mother and he wished, somehow, that he could help her. But that was beyond him. Whatever he might do from now on would only hurt her even more.

4

They thanked the two young policemen for their support and sent them back to Wollongong and local issues. Then they drove back north, Clements now alert to anyone who might be following them. But there was too much traffic on the freeway and it was impossible to tell if any particular car was tailing them. Once they pulled into the side of the road and stopped, but the following cars and trucks just hurtled by without slowing.

Clements shook his head. 'He's too smart. We're never gunna catch him this way.'

Malone looked at his watch. 'We're not going to make it to the airport in time. Let's see if Mr Waldorf has already arrived home.'

They drove on and at the southern outskirts of Sydney, at Sutherland, they turned east and drove down to Yowie Bay. In the twenties and thirties it had been an area of very modest weekenders, interspersed with the occasional fibro or weather-board cottage of a retired blue-collar worker. Fishermen frequented it to catch trevalli and leatherjackets; the odd shark or two had been sighted in the narrow bay, but they had been scared off in the years after World War Two by the real estate developers, as had the fishermen. The waterfront now was occupied by expensive houses, some of them with pretensions to mansions; behind them were more modest houses, solid in their own pretensions. This was an area of postwar money and the locals were proud to show it.

Sebastian Waldorf's home had a waterfrontage, but it was not a mansion. It had pretensions to being an Italian villa, a suitable abode for an opera singer; the builder, an immigrant from Lombardy, had tried to imagine Yowie Bay as Lake Garda. There was a pool at the water's edge and a five-metre boat moored at a small jetty. A red Lancia stood in the driveway.

Malone said, 'I always thought opera singers made less than plumbers in this country?'

'No, it's cops who make less than plumbers,' said Clements, parking the car at the kerb. 'Sebastian – I guess we'd better get used to calling him that – made his money overseas. He does all right back here, but he doesn't make the loot that Joan Sutherland and some of the others do.'

'Are you an opera lover?'

'I always thought *Il Trovatore* was some sort of pasta. I once ordered it in a restaurant.'

Sebastian Waldorf, né Samuel Culp, himself opened the rather ornate front door. 'Yes? Are you reporters?'

'No,' said Malone. 'Were you expecting someone from the press?'

Waldorf's face had been wide open in a welcoming smile; now all at once it closed up and he frowned. 'Who are you?'

Malone introduced himself and Clements. 'You might remember me? We were in the same group at the police academy back in 1965.'

'When you were plain Sam Culp,' said Clements with a policeman's ever-present suspicion of aliases.

Waldorf's face remained closed up. He was tall and well-built, a man who obviously took care of himself; he had Italian good looks that went well with the villa and the car. He was wearing a red cashmere sweater, tight designer jeans, expensive loafers and a gold watch on one wrist and a heavy gold bracelet on the other. He would never be lonely while he had a mirror to look into. Here was someone who would remember how he had looked every day of his life.

134

'What's this all about?' He had lost his Australian accent, he had an international voice that, Malone guessed, would take on the accent of wherever he happened to be.

'I think it would be better if we came inside, Mr Waldorf,' said Malone.

The singer nodded and led them through a wide entrance lobby into a large living-room that looked out on to the bay through a screen of white-limbed gums. It was well furnished, but it did not look lived in, as if it saw its owner infrequently. There were paintings on the walls, all of them modern and none of them suggesting any Australian landscape. One wall was given up to shelves of books, records and cassettes and at least a dozen photographs of Waldorf in opera costume, sometimes with another singer, always a woman.

A good-looking young woman with long blonde hair and the beginnings of the build of an old-style Brünnhilde stood up nervously as the three men came into the room. Her bosom was slightly lop-sided under her yellow sweater, as if she had not succeeded in getting both her breasts back into her brassière in time.

'This is Miss Vigil, one of my pupils. She is in the chorus of the company. We've just come back from Melbourne.'

Miss Vigil said hullo, gave Malone and Clements a charming smile, thanked *Mr* Waldorf for his lesson and left the room. Malone waited for the closing of the front door, but heard nothing; Miss Vigil had just gone to another part of the house to await another lesson in whatever it was Mr Waldorf was teaching her. Waldorf waved the two detectives to chairs and offered them a beer, which they accepted.

Then Malone told him why they were here. 'You're on the hit list, we think. Do you remember Frank Blizzard?'

Waldorf had sat down, exposing red cashmere socks to match his sweater. Malone tried not to look at Clements, who was viewing all this sartorial splendour with the sick expression of a diabetic showered in jelly-beans. The singer shook his head. 'I can't remember him, not what he looked like.'

'We keep running up against that all the time. None of us remember what he looked like. I saw a photo of him this morning

135

as a teenager, it's out in the car, but even that didn't ring a bell.'

'I remember the incident when we threw him out into the street in his underpants.' He half-laughed, then changed his mind. 'No, one shouldn't laugh. It's bloody serious.'

'Is your season over?'

'No, I have another three weeks to go, then I go overseas. I have to do *The Magic Flute* and *La Traviata*. Are you opera fans?'

'No,' said the police chorus.

Waldorf smiled, relaxing for the first time since he had let them into the house. 'I wasn't, at one time. I was in the police choir – you probably don't remember me being in that – and I used to think even Victor Herbert was highbrow stuff. Then someone told me I had a voice, not a great one but a good one. I got a scholarship to the Conservatorium, then another one to London. That was when I left the force. I went overseas, England, Germany, a couple of times in Italy. I did all right. Nothing like Sutherland – but then who does as well as her? I'm a baritone and we're never in as much demand as tenors. Tenors and sopranos, they're the spoiled ones. But I look good –' He spread his hands to display himself; Malone wondered if, with the tight jeans, he was working towards being a tenor. 'And I'm versatile. The women with tin ears come to look at me prancing around in tight pants and the music lovers come to hear Pavarotti and the really great voices. Between us we guarantee bums on seats and that's the name of the game now in opera, the same as it is in everything else. On top of that, it beats the bejesus out of singing in the police choir.'

He was a mixture of conceit and tongue-in-cheek. A woman, had she been there, would have understood his attraction for her sex; Malone and Clements were still suspicious. Malone said, 'Do you have a family?'

'My wife is German. She's taken the two kids home to Cologne.'

'You mean she's left you?'

'Is that any of your business?' There was a quick glance towards the door where Miss Vigil had exited, then he was looking at Malone again.

'Yes. If Blizzard comes here trying to get you, we don't want anyone else to get in his way. That's the only reason for asking,' he added, backing down. If the singer had lost his wife and children, he felt sorry for him, even if it was Waldorf's own fault. The break-up of any family wounded him because it reminded him of the preciousness of his own.

Waldorf, too, backed down. 'Yes. She won't be back. One of the reasons I'm going back to Europe is to be near the kids.'

'In the meantime, does anyone live here with you?' *Like Miss Vigil?*

'No. Sometimes a – a friend stays overnight, but I'm here on my own mostly.'

Clements had got up and walked to the sliding glass doors that led out on to the terrazzo patio. The doors were closed against the wind coming across the bay, turning the water into a blue-white ruffled shawl. Two kookaburras sat on the long arm of a gumtree, their backs to the wind, looking as if they had given up laughing for life. Down below, the small yacht bumped against the jetty, its tall mast swinging from side to side like a metronome.

'Is that your boat down there? Do you ever go out in it?'

'Every chance I get,' said Waldorf. 'That's my main relaxation.'

Clements turned back to face him. 'Leave it alone for a while. This guy could pick you off easily while you're out there on the water.'

Waldorf looked at the glass of beer in his hand, which he had hardly touched. Then he set it down on the marble-topped coffee table in front of him, put his hands lightly on the table and looked at them. 'I'm shivering all of a sudden. Did the others do that when you warned them? Did you, Scobie?'

'Yes.'

'I'm not used to playing hero – most baritones have to play villains.'

'That's the last thing we want, you playing hero. Leave that to Russ.'

'Thanks,' said Russ.

'We can't afford to give you around-the-clock protection – What do we call you? Sebastian, Seb, Sam?'

137

'What do you call Horrie O'Brien?'

'Brian. Sometimes when I'm feeling Irish, I call him Brian Boru.' He could see that Waldorf, or Sam Culp, was just talking while he tried to glue the pieces of himself together again. Talk often held a person together more than the person himself realized. 'Will Seb do?'

'My wife always called me Sebastian.' He spoke in the past tense, as if reconciliation was out of the question and he had said goodbye to her. 'She never liked the Aussie habit of cutting names down.'

'Righto, Sebastian it is, but I dunno how long it'll last. It's a mouthful.'

'So's Brian Boru.'

'I think you'd better pack a bag and we'll take you back to town with us. He doesn't know it, but you're going to move in with Brian Boru and me for a night or two till we can get something arranged for you. He has a suite at the Congress. You'll have to sleep with a cop, me, but there are twin beds.'

'I once slept with a tenor, a lyric tenor – a cop'll be no worse. I have to sing tomorrow night, you know. I'm Papageno, the bird-catcher in *The Magic Flute*.'

'Can't you get out of it?'

Waldorf shook his head. 'We're short on singers. This bloody 'flu that's going around has flattened two of the other baritones. I'm not being heroic – I'd be more than happy to bow out. I'd leave for Germany tomorrow, if I could. But I can't.'

'The show must go on?' Clements' tone was faintly sarcastic, he still hadn't warmed to the opera singer. I'll have to have a word with you, Russ, Malone told him silently.

'You think that's all bullshit? Show business is no different from any other business, Russ. You keep it going if you possibly can. You don't cancel performances and throw the money back at those who've bought tickets, not if you can help it. I'll go on tomorrow night, but not because I think I'm starring in some old Hollywood movie with Mario Lanza.'

Then the phone rang, just as it did in old Hollywood movies. It was picked up elsewhere in the house; Miss Vigil evidently had answering privileges. Waldorf half-turned towards a phone

138

on a buffet against one wall, then changed his mind and turned back to Malone and Clements.

'That's probably the company's assistant manager – there's a quick run-through tomorrow morning.'

'I'll get O'Brien to have one of his security men go to the Opera House with you.'

'You think that'll be necessary? Blizzard won't try his luck there, he's not going to be the phantom of the opera.' Waldorf seemed to be regaining some of his flair; or he was as good an actor as he was a singer, something Malone had read was not usual with opera singers.

'How will it affect your singing?' There was no sarcasm in Clements' voice this time, more just a tinge of reluctant admiration.

'There's a duet in the last act where I sing my name with the soprano. We have to stammer. I sing the first syllable of Papageno forty-eight times before I get my name out. I'll be perfect tomorrow night!'

Then Miss Vigil came to the door, her attractive looks pinched with puzzlement. 'I'm sorry to interrupt, Mr Waldorf, but that was some chap who said to give you a message right away before Inspector Malone left.'

'What message?' said Malone.

'It was a man, he didn't give his name. He just said to sing this –' She looked at the three men, smiled in embarrassment, then began to sing in a soft voice a song Sebastian Waldorf would never have taught her: '*Three green bottles standing on the wall / And if one green bottle should accidentally fall / There'd be two green bottles . . .*'

SEVEN

1

Hans Vanderberg was a male chauvinist right down to his toe-nails, which his wife cut for him. He was proud to be up there with the likes of St Paul, Matthew, Mark, Luke and John and at least a hundred popes, archbishops and ayatollahs; but don't tell the religious voters. He admired the good sense of Henry VIII, of Napoleon, Stalin, Mussolini and Churchill and at least nine out of every ten American presidents. Given his way he would have had no women ministers in his State Cabinet; but things did not work that way in the Labour Party. Caucus nominated its choices and he had to shuffle the roosters and hens as best he could. Like all leaders of all political persuasions he would have preferred to run the whole show himself, convinced he could do it better. Democracy had more drawbacks than were admitted by the faithful, most of whom, of course, aspired to some day be the leader.

One of the hens, who could hold her own in any cockpit with any of the roosters, who aspired to sit here in his own chair some day, now sat across from him. Penelope Debbs was ready for battle this morning.

'It's a beat-up by the press, you know that, Hans.'

'No, it ain't, love. You forget I'm also the Police Minister – I get to hear things you people never do.'

'You should tell us all you know in Cabinet. That's what Cabinet meetings are for.'

'And scare the daylights outa half of you?' His grin had all the malevolence of an old vulture trying to be human. 'Come off it, Penny –' He was the only man who ever got away with calling her that. She had remonstrated with him several times, but he

140

had been stone deaf, a political handicap he could call up at will. 'You and hubby down there in Canberra, you held out your hands and Mr O'Brien dumped some shares in them. How many?'

'I've told you, Hans, we have no shares.'

'I didn't say you have them now. I said you *had* them. Past tense.'

She arranged the skirt of her green Zampatti suit, patted the bow of her white silk shirt. The Dutchman, a sartorial wreck, the despair of the party's image makers, watched with dry amusement this playing for time. His own playing for time, when needed, was accomplished with no more than a vulture's or an eagle's stare. He looked like an old bald bird and the avian description never worried him. He had soared above all his rivals and critics and unloaded on them from a great height.

'It was over three years ago, when you first made me Minister for Development. I thought I was doing something worthwhile for the States.' She sounded pious, fingering her pearls as if they were rosary beads.

'Giving mineral rights to a shelf company, one that had never even dug a hole in a garden? Bull, Penny.' He was a vulgar old man, but he never swore in front of a woman. His wife Gertrude, if she had heard that he had committed such a social sin, would have chopped him down as no party faction ever could. 'That company was a front for laundered money – that's what the NCSC is enquiring into now. They can't prosecute on that score, but they'll pass it on to me and then I've got to do something about it.'

'I knew nothing about the laundering of money!' Her hand jerked at her pearls.

'Did Arnold?'

'No!'

'All right, Penny, don't jump outa your girdle.' But his tone wasn't soothing; he wasn't letting up: 'How many shares did you get?'

She let go the pearls, fiddled with the bow of her shirt again. 'Fifty thousand. Twenty-five thousand each.'

'How much did they cost you?'

'Ten cents a share. I don't know what the fuss is all about, Hans. It was all so long ago.'

'It's a long lane that's always turning.' His aphorisms were famous; no one wasted time trying to work them out. They made Zen riddles simple and explicit by comparison. But, though he never read philosophy, he knew, better than any philosopher, that the sound of one hand clapping was the death-knell of any politician. The voters were going the other way, the wind behind them. 'There's always a journo who meets someone who knew someone who knew something. That's why I've never taken anything, Penny, not a penny, and that's why I've lasted so long. What happened to the shares?'

'O'Brien bought them back from us six months ago.'

'How much?'

'Fifty cents a share.'

'So you made four hundred per cent profit? That's not bad.' Then he grinned again, swung his chair round and looked out the window. They were in his office on the eighth floor of the government office block; the window afforded him one of the best views in Sydney. The harbour stretched away to the east; immediately below him was the green sweep of the Botanical Gardens. Few politicians in the world had a view like this. But he was not a man for views, unless they were political. The vista before him did not appeal: he was looking out towards electorates where the voters always returned Opposition members. The Opposition leader, he knew, was just waiting for the scandal to break open. He swung back to Penelope Debbs. 'But that's nowhere near as much as you'd have made if you'd hung on to the shares, eh? They've gone as high as seventeen dollars. O'Brien did the dirty on you.'

'Arnold and I were satisfied,' she said, trying to look truthful.

'No, you weren't, Penny. None of you ever expected anything to turn up on those mining leases. When they hit that gold reef, you must've all got a hernia.'

'You can be quite crude at time, Hans.'

'You wouldn't be the first who's told me that. Don't tell me you didn't feel quite crude when you heard the news of the strike. O'Brien diddled the lotta you, buying back all those

142

shares a month before the company announced the strike. You two weren't the only ones, I'm told. He knew the same day as the strike was made and he rushed out there and paid off all the crew to keep their mouths shut.'

'How do you know all this?' She and Arnold knew and so, she guessed, did all the other dupes.

'I *know*. Now he's sitting on a fortune and it's not gunna do him a bloody bit of good. If the NCSC don't get him, someone else is gunna do it. They're gunna shoot him, they tried to do it last night. It wasn't you and Arnold, was it?'

She had been accused of many things, but never of murder. She was shocked he should think her capable of it; and frightened, too. It made her wonder how far his own ruthlessness would go. 'Good God, no!'

It was impossible to tell whether his stare was disbelieving or not. 'I think it would be a good idea, love, if you resigned. Get sick or something.'

'Why should I?'

'It's an ill wind that gives everyone pneumonia.'

She lost her temper. 'Oh, for Christ's sake, Hans, stop all that wise man's crap! If I resign now it'll look suspicious, as if you want to get rid of me before this thing gets too hot –'

'You put your dainty digit right on it, love.'

'But nothing may come of it! There's nothing to link us with what the NCSC is enquiring into – the laundering of money, the insider trading –'

'I wouldn't lay money on it if I were you. No, get sick, Penny. Resign for health reasons. Get that thing RSI, everyone else does.'

'Repetitive strain injury?'

'From shaking too many voters' hands. Or think up something else, anything to do with your health. You don't look too healthy right now.' Again the malevolent grin; for a moment she did feel like actual murder. 'Have the letter on my desk here in half an hour. We'll announce it for the afternoon press and radio. Don't give any TV interviews. The TV cameras can always tell when you're lying.'

She stood up. 'I'm surprised they've never found you out.'

'I always tell the truth, love. A little bent sometimes, but the mugs out there looking at the news think it's just been a technical hitch. Half an hour, Penny. Make it short. You're supposed to be too sick to write a long letter.'

'What about Arnold? Are you gunning for him, too?'

'He's not my problem.' The Dutchman never concerned himself with the Federal Labour Party. Sydney and Canberra, he always said, were as far apart in their interests as Washington and London. He was neither a patriot nor an egotist: he had no ambition to be Prime Minister. He ran New South Wales as old American political bosses had run their domains; his idols were not Keir Hardie and John Curtin, but Huey Long and Ed Crump. He was more honest than Crump had been and he despised the out-and-out crooks such as Frank Hague and Jim Curley, but he ran his parish with all the flint-hearted efficiency of those bosses. Power was his sustenance and at State level was where one found it. 'I'll be talking to Canberra in a coupla minutes, they can make up their own mind what they're gunna do with Arnold.'

'He might kill you,' she said recklessly, knowing Arnold's own reckless temper.

'He'll have to find someone to do it,' said Hans Vanderberg, off whom threats bounced like soft rubber balls. 'Someone more efficient than last night's hitman.'

2

O'Brien and Waldorf at first did not hit it off together. There were differences in the basic make-up of the two men that prompted a mutual suspicion, more on O'Brien's part than on Waldorf's. The former was serious, especially more so now: to have one's life under threat, to have one's career and empire falling apart, to be in love with a woman and know their affair had no future: such despair did nothing to lighten the mood of a man who had always been serious about anything he attempted. Waldorf, on the other hand, was apparently all frivolity: though afraid, he played to the threat against his life as if it were another operatic exaggeration; he would have his hand between the soprano's legs while she stroked him with a dagger. Malone knew within five minutes of bringing Waldorf to the Congress that he had made a mistake. But it would have been a bigger mistake to have left him alone to take care of himself.

'Why the hell did you bring him here?' O'Brien demanded in a fierce whisper. Waldorf had gone into the second bedroom to unpack his two bags, but the bedroom door was open. He was humming to himself and Malone hoped he and O'Brien were not in for a musical fortnight or however long. 'Why didn't you *ask* me?'

'There wasn't time.' Malone explained about the phone call to the house at Yowie Bay. 'Russ Clements and I went down to see Blizzard's aunt, down the South Coast. He called her while we were there, then he called Waldorf's house. He's getting closer, Brian.'

'Okay, but why bring that guy here? What am I supposed to be running, a communal safe house?'

Malone sighed, giving in. 'Righto, I'll move him as soon's I can find a place for him. The Department's going to have to come to the party and provide a safe house for all of us.'

'I'm not moving out of here.'

'You're getting to be a pain in the arse, Horrie.'

'Don't call me Horrie!'

'Well, then stop telling me how to do my job!' The humming had stopped in the second bedroom; there was the sound of a drawer being slammed shut, like a pistol shot. 'If they take me off this one, you could be stuck with a cop who'll handle you like some rent-a-crowd demonstrator. I'm in this thing up to my eyeballs, as deep as you or the opera singer inside there – the only thing is I have to catch Blizzard as well as dodge his bullet. All you have to do is keep your bloody head down!'

Malone's outburst made O'Brien step back a pace. He was interrupted from making a reply by Waldorf's coming to the bedroom door. 'I heard most of that. If I'm in the way, Horrie –'

'For Christ's sake, stop calling me Horrie!'

All at once, worn out by the whole day, Malone fell down into a chair and started laughing. It wasn't hysterical laughter, but it sounded like it against his usual dry amusement. The other two men stopped glaring at each other and looked at him as if he had done something totally bizarre, like fainting. Then, Waldorf, the frivolous one, the one with the easiest laugh, began with a smile that quickly volumed into a deep laugh. O'Brien, the odd one out, looked for a moment as if he would turn his back on them and retreat to his bedroom. Then slowly the big wide smile spread across his face. He started to laugh, a distinctive sound that Malone suddenly remembered from the past, as uninhibited as a child's. He could be ruthless, but there was no malice in him nor petty temper. If there had been, Anita Norval would not have fallen in love with him. The big living-room rippled with laughter, though none of them really had anything to laugh about.

'Okay, you win, Scobie. I'm sorry, Sam –'

'Don't call me Sam,' said Waldorf, still laughing.

He had got over the shock of the threat on his life quicker than Malone had expected. Once Malone had told him he would have to move out of his house he had acted efficiently and quickly. Miss Vigil, who had evidently brought her bags straight from the airport, expecting overnight lessons, had been sent packing. Waldorf had taken her to another part of the house and two minutes later was back with Malone and Clements.

'She's taken my car and gone home to her mother. She's a bit upset.'

'He might follow her,' said Clements. 'You didn't tell her you'd visit her, did you?'

'Well, I –'

'That's out,' said Malone firmly. 'You'll just have to give her lessons at the Opera House, if you want to see her. Is it serious between you two?'

Waldorf smiled, as if the thought couldn't be taken seriously. 'Nothing's serious, Scobie, not unless you're married. She's a nice girl, but I'm twice her age. My elder boy is only four years younger than she is. She –' Then he stopped, the smile fading. He was one of those who could never help themselves, who always told too much about themselves. It was plain that he was

146

serious about only one thing, his family. And, it seemed, he had lost them. He went on after a moment, 'Rosalie will be all right. I shan't go near her, not till after you've caught Blizzard.'

Then he had disappeared again into another part of the house, and come back ten minutes later with two large suitcases, a topcoat, a raincoat, and a suede hat.

'How long are you expecting us to take to nab Blizzard?' said Malone.

Waldorf laughed, looked at the suitcase. 'Caruso never went anywhere without a truckload of trunks.'

'But he was a tenor, wasn't he?'

'That's true. And as far as I know, no one ever tried to shoot his balls off. I'll leave one of the bags behind.'

'Bring 'em both. Russ will help you carry 'em out to the car. I have a bad back and I have the rank.'

'Get stuffed, Inspector,' said Russ and headed for the front door without offering to pick up a bag.

Malone grinned. 'You see? Discipline hasn't changed since you were in the force.'

Driving into the city from Yowie Bay, Malone sat half-turned round in the front seat, looking back. It was a while before Waldorf recognized that he was looking right past him. 'Someone following us?'

'Not as far as I can tell. But he followed us down to Minnamook and he must've followed us back here to your place. He's good at it.'

'I'll lay money he's already gone home,' said Clements. 'He's made his point for the day. He's started you sweating. Me, too,' he added, as if what he had said might have sounded insulting. 'Do you want me to hang around tonight?'

'No, put your feet up, study your stock market hints. First thing tomorrow, though, get on to the TV stations, borrow all their tapes on the crime scenes and the funerals, if any. Call in Jack Chew and Hans Ludke. The three of you go through those tapes, pick out any faces you see more than once and trace them.'

'I'll get the tapes delivered this evening. We can't take our time on this one.'

'No.' He read the concern for himself in Clements' voice. 'Thanks.'

Closer to the city Waldorf said, 'What's Brian Boru O'Brien like? I can barely remember him as Horrie O'Brien.'

'He's likeable,' said Malone. 'Ten per cent of the time.'

'Five per cent,' said Clements.

But now, half an hour after Waldorf's arrival, the two men at last looked as if they might be getting closer to compatibility. 'Do you have to sing tonight?' O'Brien said.

'No, tomorrow night. We give the throat a rest two or three nights a week. Union rules.'

O'Brien looked at his watch. 'It's early, but let's go down for dinner. We'll go to the Gold Room.' He saw Malone's dubious look. 'He's not going to poison the whole restaurant to get at us. We'll be safe.'

'I wasn't thinking about that. The police per diem doesn't run to eating in the Gold Room – I've seen their prices. Does the Congress have a McDonald's?'

'I'll pick up the tab.'

'I'll split it with you,' said Waldorf.

'No.' O'Brien's emphasis was a little hard-edged. He had that self-conscious aggression that self-made men have who always pick up the tab, as if to allow anyone else to do it would topple them from the peak they had achieved. 'It's on me.'

Malone, the comparatively poor man in the room, watched this small encounter; he guessed that Waldorf was also a man always first to reach for the bill. He felt embarrassed, even though, as Lisa said, she always had to take the fishhooks out of his pockets before she sent his suits to the cleaner's. But, the practical cop, he raised a point that had nothing to do with picking up the tab: 'Do we take one of the security fellers down with us?'

'Do we need to?' said O'Brien. 'I'm tired of being haunted by those guys.'

'Better them than Blizzard.'

'We'll take the risk,' said O'Brien, as if the decision was his alone. The phone rang and he picked it up. 'Hullo? . . . Just a moment.'

He looked hard at Malone and the latter waited for him to say that the nursery rhyme was about to be sung again. 'Blizzard?'

O'Brien frowned; then shook his head. 'No. I'll take it on the other phone. Hang up for me, will you? It's my friend.'

He went into the bedroom and closed the door. Malone hung up the phone and looked at Waldorf. 'He has a friend he wants kept out of this.'

'Who wouldn't? In a way I'm glad my family are in Germany. I'll call 'em tonight when we come back from dinner. The kids will be home from school for lunch. They're going to special summer classes to learn German. That's what they're going to grow up to be – Germans.'

'Do you speak German?'

Waldorf nodded. 'But I always thought I'd die an Australian. Maybe I will.'

'Forget that sort of talk!' Malone was surprised at the sharpness in his own voice.

Waldorf nodded again, all the light frivolity gone from his manner. 'Sure, it's stupid to talk like that. Sorry. But I read the papers while I was in the bedroom, about what happened here last night. You were lucky.'

'Last night's thing had nothing to do with Blizzard.'

'You want to tell me about it?'

'No, I'll leave that to Brian. They were after him, not me.'

He had called Lisa and the children in Noosa as soon as he had returned to the hotel late this afternoon. Then he had called Claire at Holy Spirit. She had been told by the day girls at school what had happened last night at the hotel, that his name had been mentioned, and she had sounded worried and all at once very young again. He had done his best to reassure her, but when he had got off the phone he had felt as if he had somehow betrayed her and Maureen and Tom. It was illogical to think so, he had only been doing his job, taking risks that were part of it. But logic has nothing to do with love: if it did, mathematicians would all be Don Juans or doting fathers. He wondered what Waldorf would tell his family in Germany, how much he would explain to them.

O'Brien was on the phone to Anita Norval for twenty minutes.

149

During that time Waldorf went into the second bedroom again to change. When he came out he looked all set for a fashion commercial, in a double-breasted navy blazer that had more gold buttons than could be found on a fleet of admirals, a pale blue cashmere turtleneck sweater and cavalry twill trousers with creases so sharp they could have sliced bread. O'Brien's door then opened and he, too, had changed: into a double-breasted navy blazer with more gold buttons etc. Malone, the standard-bearer for the unfashionable, grinned.

'How about that? I'm going to dinner with Tweedledum and Tweedledee.' His mother had never read him nursery stories, but he had heard Lisa reading them to the children. It struck him all of a sudden that he had never heard her reading anything about green bottles standing on a wall, though he had known that rhyme as a child.

O'Brien went back into his room, came out in a grey sports jacket. 'That better?'

The mood between the three of them had lightened; O'Brien's mood, in particular, had improved considerably. The conversation with Anita had been the next best thing to holding her in his arms. It had been the one bright spot in his whole day.

'How did things go with the NCSC?' said Malone on the way down in the lift.

O'Brien shook his head. 'They're holding my head under water. I'm struggling.'

'I've been reading about your troubles,' said Waldorf diffidently. 'Does it help to wish you luck?'

'Thanks, but not much. I need more than luck.'

The Congress hotel was owned by some Japanese *yakuza*, who had managed to buy reputable front men here in Australia; the major hotels were being taken over by foreigners, as if they had come to the country, sampled the service and decided it should be better. The developer, a true-blue Aussie, who had built the Congress, had piously swallowed his xenophobia, grabbed the proffered millions and retired to the Queensland Gold Coast. There he had bought a penthouse in a high-rise development owned by more Japanese. All the horses on the merry-go-round carried money, but the bets were in *yen*.

150

The Gold Room had not been designed for serious eaters. The food was just reasonable though elegantly served, but the restaurant was meant to be a showcase where the performers paid to be seen. It was all gold-flecked mirrors, gold frames and gold carpet, the monotony relieved only by the white linen and the green marble pillars along each wall; green and gold were the national colours and Malone wondered if the room had been designed by an Olympic coach who had gone mad on steroids. The waiters, mostly Asian, wore gold epaulettes that made them look like Ruritanian generals; the plate and glassware were rimmed with gold. It was enough to turn over any sensitive stomach, especially that of any commodities dealer in today's falling gold market. Malone noted that most of the diners were the hotel's foreign guests, Japanese, Americans and the odd bod from the Middle East. The natives, who had flocked here before the Crash of '87, were conspicuous by their absence. Once sheeplike in their rush to be seen at the 'in' places, they were no longer willing to be fleeced. Malone looked at the gold-trimmed menu and figured that his per diem would have bought a bowl of soup.

The three men ordered; then Waldorf said, 'I wonder what Blizzard's eating tonight?' Malone and O'Brien looked at him coldly and he smiled and went on, 'We haven't talked about him since the three of us got together. Here's a man trying to kill me and I don't know a damn thing about him.'

'We know bugger-all ourselves,' said Malone, 'except that when he was young he was a crack shot. He still is, apparently.'

'I've been racking my brains to remember anything, anything at all about him, and all I've come up with is that he was a nut about movies. He told me once that he'd only discovered them when he came to Sydney. Didn't they have cinemas down where he came from, Minnamook or whatever it is?'

'He'd have had to go into Wollongong, I guess. What sort of movies was he interested in? Horror films?'

'Not as far as I remember. Detective movies, cop shows. He asked me to go with him once, we went to see a private eye movie with Paul Newman, *Harpoon* something like that –'

'*Harper*,' said O'Brien, a film buff, 'I saw it, not with him, though.'

'Remember there used to be a TV set in the recreation room? He'd get up and sneak down there and watch the Midnight Movie. I saw him there one night, all the lights out and him sitting practically *in* the set, with the sound turned down. He told me once he'd seen Dick Powell five times in *Murder, My Sweet*.'

'That was from a Raymond Chandler book, *Farewell, My Lovely*. They made it again in the seventies with Mitchum.'

'Was that what he wanted to be? A private eye?'

'Maybe,' said Malone. 'His aunt told me he was always reading Raymond Chandler and other mystery writers. But there was no work for private eyes in Australia in those days, we didn't know anything about industrial espionage then. It was always just divorce work. He'd have wanted more than just peeping through a bedroom window.'

'The thing that always puzzled me,' said Waldorf, who appeared to remember more of Blizzard than the other two could, 'was that, in his own quiet way, he was anything but dumb. Why the hell did he need to cheat in that exam?'

'Unless he wanted to come top of the class,' said O'Brien, who understood ambition. 'If you came top of the class, you never got posted to the bush.'

Their first course was brought by an Oriental Ruritanian whose epaulettes looked like sliding off his narrow shoulders. There was *pâté de fois gras* for Waldorf, with Murrumbidgee truffles, whatever they were; native bush food had lately become a fad, as if all the white citizens were expected to become honorary Aborigines. Malone and O'Brien had oysters; Malone had been abroad only twice in his life and had never tasted anything to compare with the local breed. The main course was served with a flourish that embarrassed Malone, who did not like attention from strangers. Three waiters arrived and gold covers were lifted high from the dishes and Malone waited for them to be clashed together like cymbals. There was duckling *à l'orange* for Waldorf and steak for O'Brien and Malone. There was a bottle of Leeuwin Estate Chardonnay '84 and one of Grange Hermitage '68. All three had coffee but no dessert, cheese or liqueurs. Malone caught a glimpse of the size of the bill as O'Brien signed it and he heard the fishhooks in his pockets rattle in dismay.

Going back up in the lift Waldorf said, 'If you're doing nothing, would you care to come to the opera tomorrow night? *The Magic Flute* isn't hard to take.'

Malone hesitated, then said, 'I'll come. My wife's had me watch the opera on TV a couple of times.'

'Did you stay awake?' Waldorf recognized a non-aficionado.

'With all that yelling?'

Waldorf laughed. 'What about you, Brian?'

'I have a date tomorrow night. Anyhow, I think the soprano might be a bit loud for me. My favourite singer is Peggy Lee, slow and easy.' He saw Malone looking at him. 'I was going to tell you about the date. I'll be okay.'

'You going to take one of the security men with you?'

'No.' There was an obstinacy in his voice that was a challenge.

'It was a deal, I thought, that you didn't go gallivanting off on your own. Are you going to tell me where you're going, who with?'

It was a moment before O'Brien said, 'Okay, I'll give you an address, but that's all.'

Then Malone understood: he was going to see Anita. He knew how he would feel if someone tried to stop him from seeing Lisa.

'Righto, I guess that'll have to be it.' He looked at Waldorf. 'I hope you're not thinking of pissing off somewhere after the show tomorrow night?'

'I'll come straight home with you. We'll hold hands, if you like.'

'I'd rather hold hands with the soprano, unless she's fat and fifty.'

'She's not. She's slim and sexy and thirty. We used to hold hands at one time, but I couldn't keep up with her. There's nothing worse for your constitution than a sexy soprano with too much stamina. I thought one night I was turning into a castrato.'

'Do you opera singers talk about your partners all the time like this?' O'Brien sounded positively prim. That's what true love does to you, Malone thought.

'All the time,' said Waldorf. 'The biggest gossips in the world are in opera companies. Whispering is a nice change from all that yelling.'

I like him, Malone thought as they stepped out of the lift: he doesn't take anything, least of all himself, seriously. Except, of course, the distant family in Germany.

'Do you sing in the bathroom?'

'I will if you want me to.'

'Do you know "Carry Me Back to the Lone Prairie"?'

Waldorf and O'Brien looked at each other, for once joined in distaste if not in taste, then they looked at the Philistine. Then they saw that he was grinning and, all smiles, the three of them got out of the lift.

They nodded good-night to the security man sitting in his chair outside the front door, went into the suite and O'Brien, married to the telephone, went at once to the phone in the living-room and switched on his recording machine. The first two messages were business calls, both asking him to call back at once, no matter what the time. He jotted down the numbers given.

The third call asked for no reply, gave no number: 'So the three of you are together? That makes it easier and more convenient for me.' The voice was soft, not threatening, almost comforting. It began to sing in a whisper, as one would putting a child to sleep: *Three green bottles standing on a wall / And if one green bottle should accidentally fall . . .*

3

Malone spent a restless night; as did Waldorf in the other bed. At four o'clock Malone got up and went out into the living-room in his pyjamas. O'Brien, in a green silk dressing-gown with an emblem on the pocket (was it the seal of the High King Brian Boru? Malone wondered), was sitting on a couch with his feet up, reading a business folder. He closed it as Malone sat down in a chair across from him. The drapes were closed and two table lamps were lit.

'I'm not game to look out the windows,' O'Brien said.

'Stay away from them. Christ knows where he is. He could even be here in the hotel as a guest. I'll check with Reception in the morning, find out who's checked in here in the last twenty-four hours.'

'I don't think he'd be that obvious.'

'Neither do I, but you never know. The bastard's got to make a mistake sooner or later. Let's hope it's sooner.'

O'Brien was silent for a moment, then he seemed to put Blizzard out of his mind. He nodded to a tray on the coffee table. 'There's coffee and orange juice there. I made it myself. Did the blender wake you?'

Malone shook his head, took a glass of the juice. 'Brian, I don't think this is going to work out. I don't know where the hell he is, but he's got us in his sights.'

'Can't you send a search squad through all the buildings that overlook us?'

'Like you said, I don't think he's going to be that obvious. He won't be squatting on some roof-top waiting for us to walk by a window or for us to walk out of the hotel. We don't even know if he cares whether he's caught or not. If he's got us all together, maybe he'll just come out in the open, shoot the three of us and then just give himself up or let himself be shot down.'

There was a long pause, then O'Brien said, 'Okay, then we go our separate ways. That's what I've wanted to do all along.'

Malone finished his juice before he said, 'You sound as if you don't care much now what happens.'

O'Brien looked at the closed folder, then tossed it on the coffee table. 'My life's turned into a blind alley, Scobie. Does that sound melodramatic? Yeah, sure it does. But what we're talking about right now *is* melodramatic. They make movies or operas out of our situation. Maybe that's what Blizzard wants, he is, or was, a movie buff. Maybe he'd like to sit in jail and watch the movie of all this. Mel Gibson and Bryan Brown playing you and me. Or the other way around.'

'Your tongue's just dribbling.' Malone's voice was low but sharp, like a slap to the face. 'Get yourself together!'

O'Brien frowned, as if he hadn't expected to be rebuked. His

155

face closed up and he looked away; Malone could see a muscle working in the lean jaw. He expected O'Brien to swing round and reply with an outburst. Instead O'Brien turned back slowly and nodded, the tension going out of his face.

'You're right. I'm starting to feel sorry for myself. I've never done that before.'

'It happens to all of us.' But Malone couldn't remember its ever having happened to him: Lisa would have jerked him out of such a mood before he had even put a toe into it.

'This Blizzard business is only the half of it – for me, anyway. The NCSC are going to put me down the gurgler, they'll recommend I be prosecuted. That folder there is George Bousakis' summing up of our chances – they're about zero. If I don't go to jail, then those guys who sent that hitman after me last night are going to finish me off. On top of that, the worst of all, is that Anita and I are never going to have a happy ending. My chances there are worse than with the NCSC.'

'Is that her choice? Is she breaking it off?'

'No-o. But she's an intelligent woman. We could run off together, but neither of us wants to live the rest of our lives in Brazil or Paraguay or somewhere where they can't extradite me.'

Malone said nothing, then got up and went to the bathroom. 'Can I use yours? I don't want to wake Sebastian.'

O'Brien nodded, his thoughts suddenly as remote as Brazil or Paraguay. He had begun to daydream of himself and Anita as if both of them were young, unfettered and innocent, at least of his crimes. He had compared her with all the girls and women he had known and he had had to smile at his own judgement: he had created in his imagination a goddess at whom Anita herself would smile. Love isn't always blind, but at times it can be cross-eyed. If only all women were like her . . . But then women, all women, would fall in love with each other and the men would be left out.

The fortunate thing was that all women were not like each other, no more than all men were like each other. Thank God there were few women like Penelope Debbs. She had called him yesterday at his office to tell him she had resigned from the State Cabinet. He had just come back from the NCSC hearing and

156

when his secretary had told him there was a lady on the phone
– 'She wouldn't give her name, just said you'd want to hear from
her' – his heart had leapt. Anita never called him at the office,
but today he was glad she had taken the risk: he wanted to hear
a sympathetic voice. What he heard was a voice that sliced him
like a salami-cutter.

'You sonofabitch,' said Penelope Debbs, bitchy as it was
possible to be, no lady on the phone, at least not today. 'You've
ruined me! That old shit Vanderberg has made me resign as
Minister. It's in the afternoon paper – it's already gone out on
the radio –'

'I'm sorry to hear that, Penelope –'

'Don't bullshit me, Brian!' When he had been in the pop music
business he had been sprayed by more four-letter words than
melodic chords; but, coming from a woman of Penelope's ma-
turity, the words made him wince. Anita swore at him when
making love, but that was different: bed was the incubator
for the fundamental slang words. 'You'll fucking pay for
this –'

'Ease off, Penelope. All my phones are supposed to be
tapped –' It was a lie, but he was good at lying.

She believed him: there was an intake of breath at the other
end of the line. She was silent for a moment, as if she were trying
to remember what she had said. Then: 'Well, what's said is said.
Maybe it will interest those who are tapping the line to know
just how many people you have ruined.'

'You're exaggerating. You'll come back. In another year or
two no one will remember me and you'll be back on the front
bench.'

'You're that close to being finished?' she asked maliciously.
'Oh, I'm delighted to hear it! That makes me feel better.'

'I thought it would. All you have to do is be patient, old girl.
You'll finish up as Premier yet – Vanderberg can't last for
ever.'

'I'm aiming higher than that.' That was her one weakness,
that she couldn't hide her ambition, it was like a wen. Politicians
are never expected to be modest, it is a contradiction in terms,
but trumpet-blowing is only tolerated when one has reached the

157

peak. O'Brien knew she had as many enemies in her own party as on the Opposition benches.

'I knew you were,' said O'Brien, 'but I didn't think you'd want them to tap into that.'

She hung up in his ear and he sat back and smiled for the first time that day.

But now at 4.30 in the morning of the next day, in the shank of the night when dreams sometimes turn sour, he had nothing to smile about. He stood up, picked up the folder as Malone came back from the bathroom. 'I'm going back to bed. Wake me at 8.30, would you, if I'm not awake?'

'Do you want me and Sebastian to move out?'

O'Brien sighed wearily, resignedly. 'What's the point? Let's get it over with, one way or the other. If we all go out together, that'll be operatic. That'll please Sebastian.'

He went into his bedroom and closed the door. Malone stood alone in the middle of the big living-room, fighting against the resignation that O'Brien, another Celt, had smeared on him like a weed-juice that couldn't be rubbed off.

4

At eight o'clock Malone called Holy Spirit convent and asked for Claire. She came to the phone bubbling with excitement. 'We're just about to leave, Daddy. Are you all right?'

'I'm fine. I just called to wish you happy holiday. Don't break a leg.'

'You take care, too, Dad.' The bubbling subsided for a moment. 'Don't get shot or anything.'

Against all the grain of his temperament he wanted to shout at her, *Don't talk like that!* But all he said, quietly, was, 'I'll be all right, love. Just enjoy yourself.'

He hung up and turned to find Waldorf watching him from the bedroom door. 'Your wife?'

'My daughter, the older one. She's going on her first skiing holiday. She'll be fourteen soon, time for me to buy a shotgun.'

'Kids are a worry. But we should be so lucky.' He went back into the bedroom, already halfway home (even though it wasn't home) to Germany.

By the time Malone got to Police Centre, having checked the guest list at the hotel and found no one suspicious had checked in in the last twenty-four hours, having seen off O'Brien and Waldorf to the NCSC and the Opera House respectively, like a single parent making sure his charges would not be late, Clements, Jack Chew and Hans Ludke had been through the television newsreel clips several times.

'All the scenes of the crime clips and Terry Sugar's funeral,' said Clements. 'The head with the most appearances, apart from a coupla TV reporters, is guess whose? Scobie Malone's. You notch up seven appearances all told on all the channels.'

'You mean I'm the chief suspect? I'm sorry I suggested all this.'

'There's nobody looks in the least suspicious,' said Chew. 'I mean aside from that dumb-faced curiosity you see at funerals and crime scenes when the crowds gather. As if they're ashamed to be there, but can't help sticky-beaking.'

'Who were the TV reporters?' Malone asked.

'That smart-arse kid from Channel 15 and one from Channel 7. They're both too young to be Frank Blizzard.' Clements drank his coffee and munched on the doughnut that was his breakfast. It was his idea of a slimming diet. 'No, Scobie, he's too smart. He's not gunna put in an appearance. He's read all those detective mysteries. He knows the danger of coming back to the scene of the crime.'

'What about Mardi Jack and Jim Knoble? When are they being buried?'

'Up till yesterday afternoon the coroner hadn't released the bodies. But he's been told to get his finger out. The Department is giving Jim an official funeral, it's down for Monday. So's Mardi's, tentatively. The bodies should be released today.'

'We'll go to both of them if the times don't clash. You fellers right for Jim's funeral?' Malone looked at Chew and Ludke.

'Yes,' said Ludke. 'Are we supposed to be on the look-out for Blizzard?'

Malone nodded. 'I still think he's getting too much of a kick out of these murders to stay too far away from them. And he's still got his eye on me.' He told them of the phone call to the hotel last night.

Clements wiped doughnut sugar from his mouth. 'Think of the headlines if he shot you at Jim Knoble's funeral.'

'No, you think of them. I'd rather not.'

'Sorry, mate. I said that without thinking. I'm tired, the bloody brain's in neutral.' Then he sat up straight, opened his running sheet file. 'I've got more on our little friend Joe Gotti. The Melbourne boys passed it on – they'd got it from the Federals. Gotti went up to Canberra twice in the past month. The first time he was met at the airport by Billy Lango, Tony Lango's son.'

'I thought his record was that he'd had nothing to do with the Mafia?'

'Neither he had. This was the first time he'd ever been seen with them.'

'Did they follow him?'

'The Feds weren't asked to put a tail on him. They had enough on their plate – there were three demos that day, the students, the Abos and the gays. Someone had got his dates mixed and given 'em all a permit to demonstrate on the same day.'

'I'd have liked to be there,' said Ludke, who played first grade rugby union. 'It would've been better than a punch-up against Warringah.'

'I wonder why we never have a Chinese demo?' said Chew. 'If ever I turn up at a demo, all they want to do is throw their arms around me and tell me they're against all race discrimination.'

'You should try the National Front some time,' said Clements. 'They'd throw their arms around your neck and break it.'

Malone sighed patiently. 'Righto, you police thugs, do you mind if we get back to Mr Gotti?'

All three thugs grinned and Clements went on, 'All the Feds were asked to do was report when he arrived and left Canberra. He came and went on the same day. The same when he came back a week later.'

'Did the Langos pick him up that time?'

'No.' Clements paused, ran his tongue along his teeth; it could have been a pause for effect or he could have been cleaning his teeth of the last of the doughnut's sugar.' He caught a cab, went straight to Parliament House. He had an appointment with the member for East Gregory, Old Pavlova-Head himself, Arnold Debbs.'

Chew and Ludke now sat up straight; Malone, weary from lack of sleep but also weary from too many surprises over too many years, remained relaxed. 'Did anyone ask Debbs why Gotti visited him?'

'Not as far as I know. They had nothing on Gotti at that time.'

'Where's Debbs now?'

'I've checked that. He's up here in Sydney. I've made an appointment for you and me to see him at his electoral office in an hour.'

Ah, what would I do without you, Russ? Don't ever let anyone smarten you up, don't ever let Lisa run a steam iron over you. You're just right as you are, the perfect intelligent slob. But Clements had made one mistake: in making sure Debbs would be where they could find him, Debbs had been warned and, being a politician, he would have all his answers ready in advance.

Then Chief Superintendent Danforth appeared in the doorway of Malone's office. 'You didn't tell me you'd be having a conference this morning.'

'It's just routine, Harry. I'd have brought the results to you later.' *Why am I sucking up to him like this? Why don't I just tell him to get stuffed?* 'I thought you were too busy to be bothered with detail.'

'I am, yes. Yes, I am.' Danforth tried to look busy, something he'd never achieved in forty-three years in the Department. He usually slumped into the first chair at hand, but decided he would look busier if he stayed on his feet. He magnanimously waved to Ludke, who had half-risen from his chair, to remain seated. 'No, stay there, Hans, I've got things to do. I've been up and down ever since I got in, like – like –'

'Like a toilet seat in a dysentery plague?' said Clements straight-faced.

'Yeah.' Danforth grinned, not sure that he wasn't being

161

laughed at. 'Yeah, that's a good one. The media bastards have been on to me. They want to know, Scobie, why you were so handy to O'Brien the other night when Gotti took the shots at you.'

'What did you tell 'em?'

'I said no comment.' He was good at that; it never required much intellectual effort. 'But sooner or later they're gunna find out about the hit list and make a connection between all the murders.'

'Maybe we should tell 'em?' said Ludke.

Malone shook his head. 'Not yet. Let's wait a day or two, see if Blizzard gets in touch with the papers or one of the radio gurus. If he's after publicity, maybe he'll say something that'll give him away.'

Danforth considered this a moment, then nodded. 'Okay. You got anything new on Gotti?'

Clements told him about the advice from the Victorian police. 'He went up to Canberra to see Tony Lango and Arnold Debbs.'

'Debbs? The MP? You sure?'

'The Feds gave us their word on it,' said Clements. 'After I got the advice from Melbourne, I rang the Feds in Canberra half an hour ago.'

Danforth ran the ham of his hand over his short-back-and-sides, scratching for a coherent thought. 'That's gunna complicate things. What've you got in mind?'

'Russ and I are going to see Debbs this morning,' said Malone.

'Well, don't lean on him too hard. You know what these bloody politicians are like.' He looked at Chew and Ludke. 'How are you two going?'

'I think it's moved out of our areas,' said Jack Chew; it was difficult to tell whether he was relieved or disappointed. 'I don't think we're going to find out much more than we know now, I mean about Harry Gardner and Terry Sugar. That right, Hans?'

'I think the next act is going to be here on Scobie's turf,' said Ludke.

'Act?' said Danforth. 'What d'you think this is, some sorta bloody musical comedy?'

'An opera,' said Malone. 'It won't be over till the fat lady sings.'

'What fat lady?'

We'd better stop baiting him, Malone thought, or he's going to turn nasty. 'It's just a saying, Harry. I've been listening to Sebastian Waldorf.'

When Danforth had gone, Clements said, 'I thought the fat lady sang after American baseball games?'

'Maybe she does, I dunno. Let's go and see Arnold Debbs and see if he has anything to sing. Thanks for coming in, Jack, Hans. Russ'll let you know how we get on. We'll see you at Jim Knoble's funeral.'

Malone and Clements went down to the garage. As they got into their usual unmarked car Malone said, 'Did you tell Debbs why we wanted to see him?'

'I didn't speak to him, I spoke to his secretary. I said we were voters who wanted to make a donation to the Party, one that we didn't want to trust to the post.'

Ah, Russ, how could I have doubted you?

They drove out to Debbs' electoral office, less than two miles from the heart of the city. It was an area of light industry, rows of old one-storeyed terrace cottages, half a dozen towering Housing Commission blocks of flats, rundown stores, a seedy-looking pub and a scrubby park where four winos lay under a tree discussing the state of the nation as viewed from the bottom of the heap. Debbs' electoral office was in a single-fronted shop, one of six facing the park. On one side of it was a butcher's shop and on the other a fruiterer's, each of them advertising in rough lettering the bargains of the week. On the window of Debbs' store was: Arnold Debbs, Your Federal Member.

'Is he the bargain of the week?' said Clements as he and Malone got out of the car.

'Not in my book.'

There were half a dozen people sitting or standing in the front section of the shop when the two detectives entered. They were all battlers, some of them looking as if they had already lost the battle and surrendered. Malone looked at a young mother, thin and poorly dressed, a baby in her arms and a two-year-old

163

clutching her knee; he turned away, unable to stand the misery and hopelessness in her pinched, already ageing face.

Those waiting looked up curiously at the newcomers and Malone saw the instant stiffening of four of them; this was an area where the natives recognized a policeman by his smell. The thin young man behind the reception table, his bony face sallow from overwork and too much time spent in party rooms, looked with the same suspicion as the constituents at the two policemen.

Clements introduced himself and Malone, mentioning nothing about the earlier phone call. 'We'd like ten minutes of Mr Debbs' time.'

'I'm afraid Mr Debbs is busy. These people have been waiting, some of them more than an hour.'

That's right, Malone thought, make the cops out to be gate-crashing bastards who don't care for the rights of others. He turned to the voters. 'We're sorry to butt in, we're Labour like you —' He hadn't voted formally in ten years and he was pretty sure that Clements had the same outlook towards political parties. 'Blame our visit on the Federal government. You know what the Liberals are like.'

One or two of the voters nodded, too-bloody-right-they-knew-what-the-bloody-Libs-were-like; but a couple of young men leaning against the wall just sneered. They knew what bloody cops were like.

The secretary stood up, tall and gangling. If he was aiming some day for pre-selection as a candidate, he had everything, in these days of charisma above talent, against him. 'I'll see if Mr Debbs is free.'

He was back in ten seconds, ushering a Greek woman out ahead of him. She glared at Malone and Clements and didn't move out of their way as the two detectives stepped round her and followed the secretary into the back room of the shop. He introduced them and went out, closing the door behind him.

The office was a small room papered with posters of Debbs and party promises. There was also a poster of Penelope, as if to remind the voters that the Debbs represented them also at State level. Malone wondered if the Debbs had had any children, whether they would have installed a son or daughter in the local town hall to look after local government. But ambition had made the Debbs too busy to have children.

Debbs didn't look surprised to have the police visiting him; in this electorate, with his mix of constituents, it wasn't unusual. He sat behind a table on which were half a dozen files, some letters waiting to be signed and a small metal stand of foreign flags grouped around the Australian flag, a salute to multiculturism. Malone further wondered if a new flag was added every time a constituent of a new nationality moved into the electorate. The secretary outside looked as if he would have the nose of an immigration officer.

'Inspector Malone –' Debbs rose and put out his hand; then he offered it to Clements. It was a politician's hand, moving of its own accord. 'It must be important, to bring you way out here.'

Way out here: two miles at the most. But, Malone guessed, Debbs probably felt no more at home here in this area than those voters who had recently arrived from Greece or Italy or the Lebanon.

'We shan't take up too much of your time, Mr Debbs –' Malone went for the throat. 'Do you know a man named Joseph Gotti?'

'One of my constituents? The name doesn't ring a bell. I'm not the sort of politician who remembers everyone's name.' Debbs smiled, being frank.

'No, he's not one of your voters. He came from Melbourne, came up to see you in Canberra a week or two ago. An Italian, smallish build, young. A professional hitman.' Malone delivered the last like a professional hitman, right between the eyes.

Debbs didn't blink, but the pale blue eyes abruptly hardened, became thin blue screens behind which his real eyes had retreated. 'Oh, *him*. I didn't take to him at all. But a hitman? You exaggerate, Inspector, surely? No, you don't, I can see that. Where is he now?'

'In the City Morgue. I shot him the other night.' Another professional hit right between the eyes; but again Debbs didn't blink. 'It was in the papers.'

'Of course! I heard it on the radio – but I didn't take any

notice of the man's name. Who was he shooting at? You?'

'We think it was your friend Brian Boru O'Brien.'

For a moment the real eyes were pressed against the blue screen, showing venom. 'Did Mr O'Brien send you to see me?'

'No. Why did Gotti come to see you, Mr Debbs?'

Debbs sat back in his chair. He wore an expensive shirt and tie under the cheap dark blue woollen cardigan, part of his disguise when he came to honour the locals with his presence. This was a safe Labour seat; he would never be voted out, no matter how he treated the natives. But this area was not really his scene, though he had been born not five miles from here. Like his wife he was not really Labour, if the truth was ever to come out; both of them could just as easily have been Liberal or even National, the conservative rural party, though the latter possibility would have made even the farmers' sheep laugh. They had chosen Labour because the party talent at that time had been at an all-time low and they had known they could easily beat the competition for pre-selection as a candidate. They lived in Strathfield, a solid middle-class suburb halfway between their respective electorates, and looked upon these duty visits to their parishes as penance for sacrificing their real self-interest. The cardigan, worn to impress the locals of his humble origin, felt like a hair shirt every time he put it on.

'Inspector, for a month there I was acting-Shadow Minister for Immigration. Gotti came to see me about an uncle of his who wants to emigrate from Italy. I told him I could do nothing for him myself, but to see his local member, Nick Odskirt. When you're in Opposition there's not much one can do,' he said sadly, but sad for himself not the voters.

'Did Gotti give any references, say who'd recommended he come and see you?'

'No, he just turned up. He seemed a young man with a lot of initiative. I mean, to come all the way up from Melbourne.'

'Did he say why he didn't come up to see the Minister?'

'Yes, he told me he'd been given the brush-off. He said he was a Labour voter. A hitman!' He shook the big white head, as if hitmen were unknown in the Labour Party.

Clements was bursting to smile; instead, he said, 'I have a

166

note from our informants, Mr Debbs, that a week before, Gotti came up to Canberra and went to see Tony Lango. Did he mention Lango as a reference?'

Debbs frowned, as if trying to remember another voter's name. Then he raised his eyebrows; they went up the teak-coloured face like white grubs. 'You mean Tony Lango, the one mentioned in the Crime Authority report in the newspapers? The Mafia man? Good God, no! If he'd mentioned him, I'd have had him thrown out at once. Was he an associate of Lango's? Good Christ, and he was asking me to sponsor one of his uncles! The uncle could have been a don or a godfather or whatever they call them!'

Malone recognized a blank wall, even one hung with a cardigan. He stood up. 'Righto, we won't take up any more of your time, Mr Debbs. The voters outside have probably got more problems than we have. Can we get you here if we think of anything else?'

'No, I'm going back to Canberra right after lunch. I'll be there for the next fortnight, Parliament is in session.' He stood up, held out his hand; the screen slid away from his eyes, they looked almost friendly. 'Why was Gotti trying to kill my friend Mr O'Brien?'

'We don't know,' said Malone. 'Do you, Russ?'

'Haven't a clue,' said Clements, giving Debbs back his hand. 'But something'll turn up. It always does.'

The two detectives went out through the outer office, Malone now apologizing to the now considerably larger waiting crowd. 'Great feller, Mr Debbs. He'll do everything he can for you. Vote for him every time.' He looked at the secretary. 'Right?'

'Every time,' said the secretary, waiting for his MP to retire or die so that he could put his own name up for pre-selection.

Out on the footpath there were more people waiting. Malone was surprised at the patience on their faces, as if waiting was a lifelong habit. These were the unlucky ones in the Lucky Country; he felt helpless and angry just looking at them. He knew there would be precious little help inside for them, Debbs had his own problems.

The two policemen got into their car. Across in the park the winos were weaving and stumbling around on the brown, patchy

167

grass, playing touch football with a sweet sherry bottle. The fruiterer came out of his shop and approached the car.

'You police?' He was a Greek, but he had the local nose. 'Why you don't arrest them bums? They a bloody nuisance.'

'They're just playing football,' said Malone. 'I thought they were South Sydney practising for the grand final.'

'I bet you barrack for them silvertails, Manly,' said the fruiterer, sour as one of his own lemons.

As they drove away Clements said, 'What d'you reckon about Debbs?'

'He's a liar, every slice of him. Now we've got to find out why.'

5

'They've traced young Gotti to me,' said Arnold Debbs, cardigan discarded, now at ease again in his English-tailored suit; or as at ease as he could be in view of what he now knew. 'They've traced him to you, too, Tony.'

Tony Lango edged a little closer to the log fire in the big stone fireplace; he always felt the cold, was never comfortable except at the height of summer. He was as wide as he was tall, not all the bulk of him fat. When he had first come to Australia thirty years ago from Calabria he had earned money as a part-time wrestler around the clubs and on late night television; now he was a full-time farmer and drug dealer. He had a broad swarthy face, a huge nose overhanging a thick moustache and deceptively merry eyes; children loved him, as they had Hitler. He had three sons and four daughters and seventeen grandchildren whom he doted on; and he had been responsible for the deaths of hundreds of other children, to none of whom he ever gave a thought. Late in life he had set his eye on respectability, but he had left his run too late. He would have been amused to learn that he and O'Brien had had similar ideas.

'How d'you know all this?'

'I have a contact.' The contact had given Debbs the information only a few minutes before Malone and Clements had arrived at his office that morning. 'It's reliable, Tony. That's why I got on to all of you in a hurry.'

He had called the conference as soon as the two detectives had left his office. By chance, all of those he had phoned had been available and now they were all gathered here at the Debbs' country retreat on the outskirts of Bowral, halfway between Sydney and Goulburn. He and Penelope had bought the thirty acres and the old colonial cottage three years ago, but they had never publicized the purchase and so far, fortunately, no media muckrakers had discovered it. Bowral was a retirement retreat for silvertails and none of the Debbs' constituents would have looked with favour on their MP's living the country squire life.

It was not a big house and the room in which the five men sat was small enough for them to fill it. Penelope, an unlikely pioneer type, had furnished it with colonial antiques; there was even a spinning-wheel standing in one corner, though it was useless for spinning lies and promises. There were woollen rugs on the polished floorboards and, appropriately, a print of a local, long-dead bushranger on a wall.

'Where'd you get this Gotti anyway, Tony?' said Leslie Chung. He was in his mid-forties, a refugee from Shanghai via Hong Kong; he was rumoured to be a Triad boss, but Debbs wasn't sure if that was true. Chung was a jewellery and gem importer and that was all Debbs really knew about him; he doubted if the others in the room knew much more. Chung was balding, slim and always impeccably dressed: his clothes told more about him than his thin, impassive face. He was always polite, but in the manner of a royal executioner: he would bow before cutting off your head. 'He wasn't very efficient, trying to shoot down Mr O'Brien in front of a crowd of witnesses, including a police inspector.'

'I was the one who recommended him.' Dennis Pelong was the brute in the room, a burly man with a face as blunt and hard as his huge fists. He had come straight from a golf course and Debbs wondered what sort of club would have him as a member. He wore a woollen beanie that made him look pointy-headed and did nothing for his unintelligent looks, a turtleneck sweater

169

and a bulky golf jacket. He looked like an over-the-hill heavy-weight just back from a training run. Nobody knew exactly where he came from. Debbs thought there was a streak of the tarbrush in him, but one couldn't tell whether it was Aborigine, Maori, Tongan or anywhere south of the Equator. He ran one of the biggest drug rings in the country, had an animal ruthlessness about him and Debbs was afraid of him more than of anyone else in the room. 'He done some good jobs for me, three or four. Don't start fucking complaining, Les.'

'I was just remarking, Dennis, not making an issue of it.'

'Yeah, well . . .' Pelong couldn't stand the Chink, he was so fucking uppity. Pelong was a racist, even towards his own mother, the dark-skinned woman whom he had last seen when he had run away from home on his fourteenth birthday.

'Let's talk about what we're gunna do, not what's been done,' said Jack Aldwych. 'We gotta wash out any connection with Gotti. You do anything about that, Arnie?'

Debbs kept his temper, which he never displayed in front of these men, knowing it would only endanger him. He hated being called Arnie; but he would never have chided Jack Aldwych for doing so. Big Jack, as he was called, was the biggest man in this gathering, biggest in physique and in his power. He was in his late sixties, handsome in a coarse, beefy way, with thinning silver hair, shrewd blue eyes that looked kinder than they actually were, and a voice like a gravel chute in full working order. He had a legitimate business empire of a chain of clothing boutiques, half a dozen hotels, real estate holdings and a medium-sized engineering plant that, a joke to those in the know, made safes for trusting businessmen. He had no investment in casinos or night-clubs – 'You own one of them,' he had once told Debbs, 'you always got the police sniffing around.' He was one of Australia's ten richest men, but he never figured in any of the lists of the country's richest. His real wealth, like an iceberg of green slime, was hidden beneath the surface.

'It's being attended to, Jack. Gotti's body is being sent back to Melbourne and the file on him will just sort of be put to one side.'

'Just like in Canberra?' said Chung, and all the men, with the exception of Debbs, laughed. They all had minor bureaucracies of their own, but Christ help any mug who put any business to one side, like they did down in Canberra.

Debbs admired and envied the power these men had: it was almost imperial. He aspired to such power, though theirs was based on the uses of evil and he was not, basically, an evil man. All that bound him to them was that they had all been duped by that bastard Brian Boru O'Brien. It was not the amount of money they had been duped of that made them so implacably resolved to kill O'Brien: it was almost petty cash to some of them. It was the knowledge that he could turn out to be the informer who could send them all to prison for years; or, in the case of Jack Aldwych, for the rest of his life. Debbs sometimes wondered why he had introduced O'Brien to them. But hindsight is everyone's stroke of genius.

'We still have to attend to O'Brien,' Chung went on.

'Get one of your guys,' said Pelong. 'You Chinamen are supposed to be the expert killers, you been doing it for five thousand years, I read.'

'You've been reading comics, Dennis. We're a peaceful race.'

'Bullshit.'

'Okay, cut out the cackle,' said Aldwych, the last emperor, if not of China, then certainly of this room. 'Why has O'Brien got this guy Malone with him? I know Malone. A nice guy, but he's so bloody honest he turns your stomach. I had one of my blokes approach him years ago, when he was on the Vice Squad, and he beat the bejesus outa him and then give him a ticket for double-parking. He's got a nice sense of humour,' he added appreciatively and smiled, an old man's gentle grin. 'What's he doing with O'Brien?'

'That's where we may be lucky,' said Debbs. '*Nil desperandum.*'

One of his political heroes had been a certain prime minister who had had a classical tag for every occasion. Debbs had had no classical education, but had bought a good dictionary and found the foreign phrases in the back of it.

'What the fuck's that?' Pelong had never looked into a dictionary.

171

'It's an old Confucian saying,' said Chung, ivory-faced. 'He used to say it all the time. Never fucking despair.'

Aldwych gave them a look that was like a gavel blow on the head. 'Shut up! What were you gunna say, Arnie?'

Debbs felt he was stepping on thin ice as he ventured into the sudden silence in the room; he had created the tense scene with his stupid Latin tag. 'There's some chap, an ex-police cadet named Blizzard, who has O'Brien, Malone and an opera singer named Waldorf on a hit list. It has something to do with something that happened years ago at the police academy. He's already killed two other cops and an ex-police cadet like himself and he's also killed a girl-friend of O'Brien's. That was an accident, I gather.'

'Where'd you get all this, Arnie?' said Lango and the others nodded in appreciation of Debbs' information.

He basked in their admiration, relaxing a little. Inside information was his only riches, all he had to put him on a par with these men; but he knew that he was standing on a temporary scaffolding, that any day they could tip him off it and he would drop way down below their level, unwanted any more. He was not in their pay, which was the only honest thing that could be said about their relationship.

'Let's just say it sometimes pays to be a politician.'

'I thought it paid all the time,' said Aldwych and once again all the men, with the exception of Debbs, laughed. 'So this guy – what's his name? Blizzard? Like a snowstorm? – he's trying to bump 'em off?'

'Can we get him to work for us?' said Pelong.

'Why?' said Aldwych. He had no time for Pelong, who he thought was so dumb as to be dangerous. 'He's working for himself. All we gotta do is sit and wait. When he hits O'Brien, mebbe we can send him some flowers or something.' Again he smiled the old man's gentle grin.

'What if he takes too long?' said Lango. 'The goddam NCSC is gunna get around to us pretty soon, asking questions. O'Brien's probably spilling his guts every day he's with 'em.'

'We'll wait another week,' said Aldwych, who in fifty years of crime had never waited for anyone to elect him leader; he spoke, and the others agreed with him, if they knew what was good for them. 'If he hasn't killed O'Brien by then, we get another hitman, a good one this time. Leave it with me.'

'What about Malone and this opera singer?' said Debbs. 'I understand they're with O'Brien all the time. They're all holed up in the Congress Hotel.'

'Jesus,' said Chung, a taxpayer when it was unavoidable, 'are the police paying for that?'

'If we gotta do it, we blow 'em away, too,' said Pelong. 'Nobody's gunna miss a cop and a fucking opera singer.'

Debbs brought out his fifteen-year-old malt whisky and they all drank to the death of O'Brien and anyone else who got in the way; Debbs, mouth dry at what he was toasting, didn't waste the whisky as it went down. He knew the dangers of his being implicated in the murder of O'Brien: the police would trace some connection through the already dead Gotti. But he could not withdraw: he was more afraid of these men than of the police. He knew he was expendable, just like O'Brien.

Then the visitors left one by one, Jack Aldwych going first, as befitted an emperor. Debbs walked out of the front door with him. The house was a long way from the road and hidden by a grove of English oaks; here in the cool, often very cold southern highlands, European trees flourished. The trees gave Arnold Debbs the privacy he wanted, especially today.

'I'm worried, Jack. I keep hearing things about what's going on at the NCSC. O'Brien's being heard in camera, but I've had a few leaks. He hasn't mentioned us by name yet, but he's given them a few hints. I think he's trying to get some sort of deal with them.'

'Are they likely to give him one?' Aldwych shivered in the cold air.

'I don't think so. They're not like the Crime Authority, they're not after chaps like you.' Aldwych looked at him and Debbs shivered, but inside. 'You know what I mean, Jack.'

'Sure. Sure I do, Arnie.' He pressed Debbs' plump shoulder; he was an old man but his grip felt like that of a young thug. 'All you gotta do is not lost your nerve. We'll come outa this

173

okay. I ain't lived this long to be chopped down by some little piss-ant like O'Brien.'

He walked across to his car, a modest dark blue Toyota, and got in beside his son, who was his father's driver and minder. He waved a big hand to Debbs and the Toyota went away down the long drive and disappeared past the grove of trees.

The other three men left at intervals of two minutes, like starters in a motor rally. Lango went first in his gold Mercedes, driven by *his* son Billy; Pelong went off in a white Rolls-Royce, driving himself; and Leslie Chung got into his small BMW. He looked out at Debbs.

'You didn't choose well, Arnold, when you recommended us to Mr O'Brien.'

'I thought he was on the up-and-up – I had no idea –'

'No, I don't mean *him*. I meant our associates – particularly that dumb son-of-a-bitch Pelong.' For a moment the soft voice hardened, had a razor's edge to it. 'He *advertises* everything – that Rolls, for instance. I don't know how he has lasted as long as he has. I'm afraid that if we don't dispose of Mr O'Brien very soon, Pelong will go after him himself. Then God knows what will come out into the open.'

'Perhaps you should have *him* disposed of,' Debbs heard himself say.

'It may be necessary,' said Chung, starting up the engine. 'But I never expected you, of all people, Arnold, to suggest it.'

EIGHT

1

When O'Brien and Bousakis walked out of the National Companies and Securities Commission hearing, there were reporters and cameramen waiting on the pavement outside. O'Brien instantly about-turned and stepped back into the building. Bousakis, considerably bulkier, took a little longer to turn round and follow him, like an oil tanker trying to catch up with its tug.

'What the bloody hell are they doing here?' O'Brien demanded.

'I don't know, Brian. I guess they know things are coming to a climax. Maybe they were expecting it today. All you have to do is shake your head and say no comment.'

O'Brien looked out at the restless group being held back from charging into the building by two Commission security guards. All the channels were represented there: the four commercial channels, the ABC and even the SBS. Frustrated by the guards, the cameramen backed off and photographed each other, a regular habit, as if there were a union rule amongst cameramen that they should have as much exposure as the reporters.

'Is the car out there yet?'

'Not yet – yes, there it is now! You want to make a run for it?'

O'Brien had a sediment of humour still left in him; he looked at Bousakis and grinned. '*You* run, George. That'll look better on TV than any shot of me.'

He didn't see the tightening on Bousakis' face as the latter turned away. They pushed through the doors and went out across the pavement as O'Brien's own security guard got out of the hired car and opened the rear door for them. The cameramen and the reporters swooped like scavenging gulls, squawking questions, but O'Brien dived into the car and Bousakis' bulk blocked the microphones and cameras from getting too close to their quarry. Bousakis collapsed into the seat, the car seemed to subside on the rear axle; the security guard slammed the door and jumped into the front seat beside the driver. The car slid away from the kerb and the media gulls shrugged and moved off in quest of their next target.

O'Brien and Bousakis didn't speak till they had reached O'Brien's office in Cossack House. Then Bousakis, without preliminary, said, 'I think you'd better start preparing for the worst, Brian. That session this afternoon couldn't have been worse.'

O'Brien nodded morosely, working his big hands together. 'Yeah. But I haven't played all my cards yet. We can still make a deal.'

'Brian, they're not interested in those crims, Jack Aldwych and the others. That's not their brief.'

'They'll have to be, if I get on to the Crime Authority at the same time. I'll play one against the other.'

'That'll be risky.'

'I got into this mess taking risks. Maybe it's the only way out of it.'

Bousakis shifted his huge bulk in his chair, like a hippo that had found a rock in its wallow. 'I haven't mentioned this before, Brian. But what happens to me if you go under?'

'I haven't thought about it, George.' O'Brien's frankness somehow was not offensive; Bousakis had come to expect it. 'You'll make out. We'll fix it so's when you leave here you go with a decent handshake. Then when the roof falls in it'll be too late for them to do anything about it. You'll have no trouble getting another job. You're clean.'

'I shan't get another job like this one. There's a recession coming up, Brian, or hadn't you noticed? Or anyway, banks are closing, all the foreign ones are packing up and going home. That's all I know, investment, dealing in money.'

'George, you're an administrator, too, as good as any in town.

176

I'll write you a reference that'll have corporations chasing you down the street as soon as you walk out of here.'

'You think they'll take any notice of a reference from you?' That was offensive and Bousakis meant it to be; he hadn't forgotten the crack about how he would look on TV screens if he broke into a run.

O'Brien had been about to reach for a tissue in a desk drawer; now he paused and looked up, all at once very stiff. 'It's got cool all of a sudden, hasn't it? I mean in here.'

Bousakis was as stiff and still as O'Brien; he had turned from a hippo into a rhino, ready to charge. 'I didn't get this firm into the mess it's in – you did that all on your own. I thought Cossack was going to be my future, but now all of us, not just me, we're going to finish up out on the street. All because you got so fucking greedy you couldn't stop yourself!'

O'Brien had never seen Bousakis so worked up; he was not an excitable Greek, he was the philosopher kind. Or so O'Brien had thought; but then he had never read any of the Greek philosophers, the closest he had come to Heraclitus and Socrates was listening to Nana Mouskouri. He closed the desk drawer, straightened up and blew his nose on the tissue, then dropped it into his waste basket. He knew the value of a silent pause, though in the pop world there had been none; he knew nothing of Greek drama, where the pauses could be long and trembling before the knife was plunged in. But his hand was empty, he had no knife for Bousakis.

At last he said, 'It's done, George. What do you want me to do – turn the clock back?'

'No,' said Bousakis after his own long pause. 'I want you to give me first option, in writing, on buying out the controlling interest in Cossack Holdings. The bank will go under, but the holding company is a separate entity, it'll survive. I want control of it.'

O'Brien frowned, his way of showing surprise. Starting young in business, he had taught himself never to show that he had been caught unawares. In the laid-back world of pop entrepreneurs he had been almost horizontal. When he had moved up in the financial world, where experience and not pretence prevailed,

177

where you were often in the shark's belly before you knew you had been bitten, his coolness had been admired. One hand tightened into a fist, but it was out of sight under the desk.

'That'll take a lot of cash. I thought you were complaining a moment ago about being thrown out on the street?'

Bousakis moved again in his chair; the wallow felt a little softer, the rock was crumbling. 'It wouldn't be my money, but I can raise it. We'd want a discount on today's prices, but you'd come out with something stashed away for when you come out of jail.'

'The NCSC would never approve the buy-out, not while the investigation's still going on.'

'They would if the minority shareholders got their money back. I'd see that they did – we'd promise that.'

'Who's we?'

'I can't tell you that, not yet. Just let's say it's your opposition.'

'I've got plenty of that. Practically everyone in town.' There was no self-pity in his voice.

'Yes.' The big round face was a moon of smugness.

O'Brien studied him; then said, 'Why did you take so long to bring this up?'

The big face turned blank; it was difficult to tell if Bousakis was being hypocritical: 'I was being loyal. It's a Greek trait.'

'Is it? That's something the Irish claim. I didn't know we had anything in common.' He got up and walked to the big window. On the other side of the street were the headquarters of the country's biggest insurance company, a tower twenty storeys higher than his own building. There was nothing shaky or shonky on the other side of the street; it was impregnable, an Establishment mountain, a shareholder in half the nation. No one there had stripped assets, borrowed riskily without telling the shareholders, indulged in insider trading. There were two flagpoles on the roof of the tall building, just visible to O'Brien: the corporation flag fluttered from one, the national flag from the other. He noticed that the corporation flag was slightly the higher of the two.

'I'll think about it, George,' he said without turning round. 'The offer . . .'

178

He kept his back to Bousakis till he heard the loud creak of the chair as the other man rose from it, then the heavy tread across the carpet and then the closing of the door. He continued to stare out of the window, watching a man staring at him from a window across the street.

Then abruptly he realized where he was standing, how exposed he was. He shivered with fright, moved quickly to one side and pressed the button that swept the drapes across the glass. He stood in the sudden darkness, feeling the trembling in his hands.

It seemed that everyone was gunning for him and Blizzard was not the only hitman.

Then the phone rang. It was a moment before he could move, then he stepped back to his desk, switched on a desk-lamp and picked up the phone. It was Malone.

'Just checking. How'd you go today?'

'Bloody dreadful. You making progress?'

'A bit. Are you coming back to the hotel?'

'No. I've got some work to do here. Then I'll go straight out on my date. I'm due there at seven.'

'Call me when you get there. Then I'm going to the opera. Seb has already gone. He has to gargle or whatever it is singers do before they sing. Brian?'

'Yes?'

'Take care. Don't let Blizzard take a pot shot at you while you're with the lady.'

O'Brien hung up, all at once feeling better. There had been a note of concern for him in Malone's voice. He had never had a friend, only acquaintances, and now he was looking for one. But, like love, friendship had arrived too late.

2

Jack Aldwych lived in a huge, old two-storeyed house overlooking Harbord, one of the small northern beaches, where he surfed every morning, summer and winter, with his son Jack Junior. The house had been built before World War One by a circus-

179

owning family and Aldwych, who had been born and grown up in the district, had delivered bread here as a bread carter's boy in the 1930s. The large grounds had always seemed full of midgets, grossly fat ladies, flagpole-tall men and acrobats who would come tumbling down the gravel driveway to take the dozen loaves of bread from him before the two big mastiffs, who roamed the grounds like loud-mouthed tigers, came tearing round from the back of the house to rend him limb from limb. He had coveted the house even then and twenty years ago he had bought it from the last of the circus family. Now it housed only him, his wife, his son, a housekeeper and two minders who roamed the grounds just like the mastiffs had done. Occasionally, in his more sentimental moments, which weren't many, he longed for another sight of those acrobats, slim girls and muscular men, to come cartwheeling down the driveway to the big gates as Jack Junior drove him in and up to the house.

Sitting now in his favourite chair on the big wide verandah he looked at his visitor, who couldn't have cartwheeled if he'd been given a flying start by being hit by a car. 'Why didn't you get in touch with me first, Harry?'

Chief Superintendent Danforth wished he had worn a topcoat; he hadn't expected to sit out here in the cold. 'I rang you first thing, Jack, soon's I got the word they'd traced that kid Gotti to Debbs and Lango. But they said you'd gone shopping with your missus.'

'My wife,' Aldwych corrected him. Shirl was the only woman in the world he respected. He also had some regard for the Prime Minister's wife, whom he had never met but who Shirl said was a model for all women, and he had great admiration for Margaret Thatcher, who had a proper regard for what a boss should be. But he wouldn't have lived with either of them, not even if they had asked him. 'We go and do the weekly shopping every Thursday morning. She likes that, we've done it together ever since we first got married. We do the shopping, then we have morning coffee down in a coffee lounge on the Corso at Manly. Shirl likes that, she calls it married compatibility, whatever that is. She's a great one for doing crosswords.'

Danforth had a little trouble picking up that one; finally it

180

filtered through that Mrs Aldwych had an interest in words. He also had a little difficulty in picturing the crime boss enjoying morning coffee in a coffee lounge with his wife. He gratefully sipped the whisky Aldwych had offered against the cold evening air. 'The missus – the wife is like that. Always does the crossword first thing in the morning . . . So I rang Arnold Debbs soon's I couldn't get you. I hadda get the word to someone.'

'I've just got back from seeing Arnie. Who's this other guy who's trying to bump off O'Brien? An ex-cop or something.'

'An ex-cadet,' said Danforth, as if he didn't want a real cop suspected of being a hitman. 'His name's Frank Blizzard.'

'Do you know where he is?'

'We don't even know *who* he is.'

Aldwych looked at him quizzically. He had never had much respect for the police's ability, they had never been able to nail him on any charge. Sure, they had arrested him half a dozen times, but nothing had ever stuck once they had got him into court. 'Can I help?' He sounded like Castro offering help to some banana republic. 'Get some of my boys looking for him?'

'Where would they start to look, Jack? No –' Danforth shook his head. 'The best man in the Department is looking for him and getting nowhere. And he's on Blizzard's hit list as well as O'Brien. Scobie Malone – you know him.'

Aldwych sipped his own whisky, pulled the woollen muffler closer round his thick neck. He liked sitting out here in the evenings, but lately his bones had begun to feel the chill. He was getting old and it hurt like arthritis even to think about it.

'I know him, a nice feller. But if he gets in the road we might have to get rid of him, Harry.'

'What d'you mean?' Danforth was startled, coughing as the whisky went down the wrong way.

Aldwych waited till the coughing had subsided. 'Something's gotta be done soon. I hear O'Brien is ready to talk his head off, ask the NCSC for a deal if he tells 'em about us.'

'Us?' Danforth looked on the verge of another coughing spasm.

Aldwych smiled. 'Not you, Harry. Me and my associates.'

'How d'you know all this, Jack?'

Aldwych smiled again, an old crime boss's smile. 'Harry, nothing is secret in this country. We're the greatest blabber-mouths in the world. You hold a closed meeting that's got any politicians or bureaucrats at it and you're gunna get more leaks than you get in an army camp on a winter's morning. There's always someone dying to piss what they know.'

'I never heard any leaks coming out of any meetings you've had.'

'We're different, Harry. You don't find any politicians or bureaucrats in our game, not at my level. They just work for us. Like you do.'

Danforth put down his glass: it was time to go. He did not like being held in contempt, though he knew it happened at certain levels in the Department; but he had never protested there and he would certainly never protest to Jack Aldwych. He stood up, his joints stiffened by the cold. 'You got a nice house here, Jack. Why don't you sit inside some time?'

Aldwych laughed, a rough rumble like an echo of the mastiffs' growling of long ago. 'I bought this place for the view. I'll sit inside when I finally go blind.'

Danforth looked at him sharply. 'Are you going blind?'

'No.' The laugh subsided, the mastiffs lying down. 'I'll die out here, but not for a long time yet. Not unless O'Brien says too much and they wanna send me to jail. What would you do if they sent you out here, Harry, to bring me in?'

'Commit suicide,' said Danforth, hoping Aldwych would re-cognize it as a joke.

'We'll do it together, Harry. You can go first.'

When Danforth had gone, escorted down to the big gates by one of the minders, Aldwych went into the house. He sat down in front of the fire in the big living-room; the house was centrally heated, but he preferred a fire. He felt the warmth, like a memory of the blood of his youth, creep back into his limbs. He could hear Shirl's television set upstairs in her bedroom, the volume turned up as if she were sitting down here listening to it; she was going deaf, but she refused to admit it, insisting that

182

the world had just got quieter. She was an intelligent woman who had long ago put her intelligence into cold storage, had deliberately become simple-minded about the world in which she and Jack lived. She knew how he made his money and she knew his reputation, but she thought of him only as her husband, a good one, which he was. All she demanded was that Jack Junior, though he was his father's secretary and driver, was never to be involved in anything that might send him to prison. Jack Junior would inherit the vast fortune his father had accumulated, but he must never be anything but respectable and, when his time came, a good honest citizen. So far Jack Junior was on course.

Aldwych sat pondering the immediate future. He was at risk, considerable risk, because he had tried to make his money respectable; he appreciated the irony of it. He was evil, a true criminal; he never tried to evade that knowledge. Yet he was a confirmed conservative, as most true criminals are. He had tried to educate himself late in life by reading books on political and social history; he had developed heroes, Churchill, de Gaulle, Menzies here in Australia. He found local politics dull, but that was because whatever local politicians said didn't amount to a pinch of shit in world affairs. He had taken Shirl on several trips to Europe and he had noticed how many of the public buildings had balconies fronting large squares. European leaders had always had the advantage of being able to yell at vast crowds, of being seen in the flesh, of using the balcony as a stage; Australian leaders, on the other hand, always seemed to be at ground level, literally and figuratively. Of course there was TV; but that wasn't the same. You felt no thrill sitting in your living-room listening to a local pol telling you not to worry, just to trust him and his government. If Philip Norval asked for blood, sweat and tears, the voters would suggest he go to the Red Cross; and then go out to the kitchen fridge for another beer.

Arnold Debbs was one of those at ground level; several times this afternoon he had sounded as if he were on his knees. He was, potentially, as big a risk as O'Brien; if the heat were applied, he would run for a deal. Jack Aldwych had begun to think he had made a mistake by moving out of his own circle.

Jack Junior came to the door, switched on the lights. 'Dad?'
Aldwych blinked in the sudden illumination. 'What is it?'
'George Bousakis is here.'

3

O'Brien had had difficulty in persuading the security guard that
he wanted to go out alone. 'It's okay, Ralph. I've got a clearance
from Inspector Malone – he knows where I'll be. It's personal.'

Ralph Shad looked dubious. 'If something happens to you,
Mr O'Brien, it's not gunna look good for our firm –'

'It's not going to look good for me, either.' O'Brien smiled.
'Relax, Ralph. Go back to the hotel and order a good dinner.
Ask your wife or girl-friend in, if you like, put it on the tab. I'll
be home by midnight, I promise.'

'Do you have a car picking you up?'

'He's waiting downstairs now and I'll have him pick me up at
11.30. Don't wait up. Go to bed as soon as Inspector Malone
and Mr Waldorf come back from the opera.'

But when he got into the back of the hired car and gave the
Double Bay address to the driver, the Asian who had driven him
two nights ago to the Town Hall, he suddenly felt nervous.
Perhaps the nervousness of the driver had transmitted itself to
him.

'Would you rather not be driving me, Lee?'

The driver took the car out into the traffic. 'No, it's okay, Mr
O'Brien.'

'Where do you come from?'

'Cambodia, sir, but my parents were Chinese.'

'Were you ever in danger there?'

'Oh, a lot, sir. That's why I came to Australia, it was a safe
country.' *Or so I thought*: it was as if he had spoken the words
aloud. 'Another driver will be picking you up, sir. You're my
last job for the day.'

'Do I know the other driver?'

'I don't think so, sir. He only started yesterday. His name is

Fergus Calder, I think. He's from Scotland. I can't understand a word he says.' He sensed O'Brien's sudden concern. 'The company would have checked him out, sir. They're very careful who they employ, much more than taxi companies.'

'Give me one of your company cards.'

His nervousness had increased. He would call the hire company, have them send a driver he knew. He did not want to be picked up close to midnight by a stranger, no matter how thoroughly the company had checked him out.

When he was dropped at the address in the side-street in Double Bay he almost ran across the pavement into the front gate of the townhouse. He stood for a moment, breathing deeply; he was coming apart at the seams, something he had never thought would happen to him. He stood just inside the gate for a couple of minutes before he felt steady enough to ring the doorbell and face Anita. She must see none of the frayed edges of himself.

The door was opened by Joanna, elegant in silver and black, looking at him as frankly as a buyer at the Newmarket stallion sales.

'We've never met, but Anita has told me all about you. Well, almost all,' she added with the smile of a woman who never expected to hear the full truth about any man. 'Come in out of the cold.'

He followed her into the house, showing no eye at all for its furnishings; other people's possessions never interested him. Anita was waiting for him in the living-room and came forward at once to embrace him and kiss him as if they were alone. Joanna watched them without embarrassment, almost with dry amusement, though she never laughed at other people's love for each other.

When they drew apart she said, 'I believe it. You do love each other.'

Anita smiled, explained to O'Brien, 'She's the family expert on love.'

'Or what sometimes passes for it,' said Joanna, never one to claim unmerited credit. She loved Floyd, in her fashion, but he was not her ideal: she had given up hope of ever meeting *that*

185

man. 'The house is yours till midnight. I'll have to come home then – I'm not going to spend the night with the man I'm going out with, though he'll ask me. We're going to the opera, then he's taking me to supper.'

'That's a coincidence.' O'Brien had warmed to Joanna at once. She had a directness about her, though it wasn't a hard approach. 'I was invited to the opera tonight. Sebastian Waldorf – do you know him? – he's staying with me.'

'Sebastian Tightpants? We had a thing going for a while, before I married again. I belong to the Friends of the Opera.'

'With Sebastian she was just friendlier than any of the other Friends.' Anita smiled affectionately at her sister.

'What's Sebastian doing, staying with you? Are you old mates? Anita said you used to be in pop music, not opera.'

O'Brien had not told Anita about Blizzard's hit list; she still believed that his only danger came from whoever had ordered Wednesday night's attempt on his life. Up till now he had managed to conceal from her that Malone and Waldorf were staying with him at the Congress; he saw her now looking at him curiously. 'We knew each other years ago. He's just staying with me for a couple of nights, we're catching up on old times.' He suddenly tasted alum, wished he could spit it out. 'He's singing tonight, *The Magic Flute*.'

'I know. He won't look his best tonight, not covered in feathers – he plays a bird-catcher. That's a laugh – he's been chasing birds all his life. He should have called himself Randy Waldorf, but that would have sounded too much like a pop singer. Well, enjoy each other. I'll ring the doorbell when I come home, just as a warning I've arrived.' She said it without a wink or a leer; she was still a lady in many ways. She kissed Anita, then looked at O'Brien. 'Do I kiss you, too?'

O'Brien smiled, leaned forward and kissed her on the cheek. 'Good-night, Joanna. And thanks.'

'I've never stood in the way of true love. I'm a conservationist when it comes to that.' There was a ring at the front door. 'There's my man. 'Bye.'

She went out, leaving O'Brien and Anita facing each other across a narrow space that vibrated with Anita's hurt and

186

curiosity. And fear. 'You didn't tell me about this chap Waldorf. Why?'

He reached for her hand, but she held her arms at her side. He was still diffident towards her at times, almost a little in awe, like a young man lacking confidence with his first girl. Only in bed, where the blood took over, was he confident.

'I didn't want to tell you. I didn't want you worrying any more than you are now.'

'Worrying about what?' The hurt drained from her, but she was still puzzled and afraid.

Hesitantly, watching her carefully, seeing each word he spoke chipping away at her, he told her of the hit list and Frank Blizzard. She stood stiffly for a moment, then it seemed that she flung herself at him. He held her to him, all at once certain of her and of himself.

'Oh God, Brian!' She kissed him fiercely, bruising his mouth. 'What else can happen to you? How much more bad luck can you have? What did you do, run over a nun or something?' she said, trying to be wry and not hysterical.

He grinned, the lapsed Catholic who hadn't spoken to a nun in more years than he could remember. 'My mother used to say that. My luck's just turned, that's all. I've had a good long run. I found you,' he said and, unwittingly, made it sound like a sad climax.

'Let's go up to bed.' She took his hand, led him upstairs.

'Where's your sister's husband? Is he likely to come home and find us?'

'He's on an oil rig somewhere in the Bass Strait – they have some industrial trouble down there. He called Joanna an hour ago. He won't be home till Saturday night.' She had led him into a guest bedroom; she was delicate about using Joanna's bed, though she knew her sister wouldn't mind. The room had a double bed, not a king-sized one like Joanna's, but it was wide enough for what they had in mind. Love-making is a game that can be played on the narrowest of battlefields. 'Undress me.'

'I was never any good at this, I'm all fingers and thumbs –'

'Don't tell me about your experience. Or lack of it.'

He smiled, totally confident now as he peeled off her clothes, doing it with more tenderness than she had hoped for. 'This is like peeling a lotus –'

She kissed him gently. 'You're a continual surprise, darling – you come out with unexpected things –'

It had been a line from an old pop song sung by – he couldn't believe the coincidence! By Bob *Norval*, from the Salvation Four Plus Sinner. His world was turning full circle. He had forgotten that other Norval, as had the rest of the world.

'What's the matter?' Anita said.

He sat down on the bed in front of her, kissed her bare full breasts. Accustomed to younger women, he was still amazed that a woman of her age could be so slim and firm and beautiful. Though he was no longer young himself, he had lived too long, or lusted too long, amongst the young.

'Don't let's talk.' His voice was a husky whisper. 'Not now.'

Their love-making was both tender and furious, as it should be. She was completely uninhibited, a deflowered girl from *The Perfumed Garden*; he was content to let her make all the suggestions, though no word needed to be spoken. He had remarkable stamina, a horizontal marathoner; they wore each other out, both winners, no losers. Afterwards they lay enjoying their wounds on the rumpled battlefield.

At last she said, not looking at him but at the ceiling, 'What do we do, darling?'

He knew what she meant; there was no point in playing dumb. 'There's nothing we can do. Sooner or later we've got to say goodbye.'

'No!' She reached for his hand; he felt her nails dig into it. 'Don't talk about *that*! I mean, what are we going to do about this – this hit list?' She stumbled on the phrase, as if it were foreign, a term she didn't understand.

He continued to lie on his back, but turned his face towards her. Her dark hair was tousled, her face glowed, she had that young look that love and sex can bring back, no matter how fleetingly, to a woman. Then he looked into her eyes and saw the pain and hopelessness: she looked her age *there*.

'All we can do is leave it with the police. They're doing the best they can.'

'Is that why Inspector Malone was with you the other night at the Town Hall?' He nodded. 'And he's on the list, too? Oh God. Does he have a family?'

'A wife and three children. They're safe somewhere up in Queensland.'

'But you're not. Neither is he. Would the man who's trying to kill you have followed you here?'

He tried to reassure her, not confessing the fear he had felt when standing outside the front door less than two hours ago. 'I wouldn't have come if I'd thought that would happen.'

'Let's go away somewhere.' But even as she said it she knew the hopelessness of it.

'Where?'

'I don't know. Anywhere. One reads about it every day – people disappearing.'

'Sweetheart, it would never work.' He had money in a bank account in Switzerland, more than enough for them to live comfortably anywhere in the world; the courts might sequestrate all his holdings here in Australia, but it wouldn't matter. Money was not their problem and, it struck him only now, it was a subject she had never discussed. She had been accustomed to wealth all her life; he was troubled by the thought that she might have wondered at the greed that had driven him to accumulate his. But that was another subject she had never discussed. Their love was deeper than their knowledge of each other, but that, he guessed, might be the way of the world. He had certainly never known all that he might have of his two wives. 'Someone would find us eventually. Anyway, you can't leave your children and your grandchildren, not for ever.'

She knew the truth of what he was saying; she felt it like a stab in the chest whenever she thought of it. She wondered if she would have felt differently if she were like Joanna; her own sense of morality encased her like an old-fashioned corset. She felt no guilt that she had broken her marriage vows (how old-fashioned that sounded, even in the silence of her mind); Philip had broken them long ago and many times. But marriage did not end with Philip: her son and daughter and her grandchildren were part of it. She owed something to them, if no more than an example; or at the very least, to protect them from the scandal if she left Philip and disappeared with a man already branded as a scoundrel, even if the iron had not yet seared him. She had reached that rarefied level in the nation's society, narrow though it was, where the standards were still almost Victorian; the young might wish her the best of Aussie luck, but the majority of the citizens would never forgive her. Certainly her mother and father never would.

She rolled over on to her true love, raised herself to look at his face as if it might be her last look. 'All I want is for you to stay alive.'

4

Malone was not enjoying the opera; the first act had convinced him that he would never become a regular opera-goer. Waldorf had told him that the opera was almost an English pantomime set to some better music; but he had never seen a pantomime and now was glad he had not. He had liked Waldorf's opening song, but thereafter his ear had wandered; he had found that his main interest was in looking at the soprano playing the Queen of the Night. Waldorf had told him that in the company she was known as Queen of the Nymphos. If asked by Lisa what he had thought of the opera, he would not comment on the Queen.

At the first interval he sat for a few moments while the huge auditorium emptied. Then he was sitting in a long empty row and suddenly he felt exposed, a shag sitting on a rock and waiting to be knocked off. He looked up and around him, twisting his head almost in a panic; but there was no one aiming a rifle at him, there was going to be no drama in the interval. He got up and went out into the foyer.

He stayed on the fringe of the crowd. It was a mixed lot, young and old, jeans-dressed and dressed-up; there was a large sprinkling of the foreign-born, the older ones enjoying this distant echo of nights in Vienna and Bayreuth and Milan. A very goodlooking blonde woman, who looked faintly familiar, passed

190

by with a sleek seal of a businessman who looked as if he thought he was already halfway to bed with her. Malone heard the woman say, 'He was better as Don Giovanni than as the bird-catcher. But then they're both after birds, aren't they?'

Malone debated whether he would try for a drink at the crowded bar, decided against it and turned away to see a face he recognized, though he did not know the man's name and he looked different in a suit and without his usual open-necked shirt and anorak. The Channel 15 cameraman smiled at him, hesitated, then came towards him.

'Inspector, not on duty, are you?'

'You'd have brought your camera, if I was?' Malone didn't mean to sound so sour.

The cameraman shook his head. 'Not tonight. I'm here just to hear the music – I'm a great Mozart fan. You like him, too?'

Malone shrugged. 'Sometimes. You know, I don't know your name?'

'Colin Malloy. Oh, this is my wife Julie.'

She had evidently been to the ladies' room. She was small and pretty, younger than Malloy by at least ten or fifteen years; she looked like a woman who needed protection and she had chosen an older, more reliable man. He put his arm round her. 'This is Inspector Malone, hon. We've met several times on the job. He doesn't like having the camera turned on him.'

'I don't blame you, Mr Malone.' She turned a wan face up to her husband. 'I've got a dreadful headache. I think I'll go home.'

I'd like to do the same, thought Malone as the bell rang to end the interval.

Malloy looked disappointed, but he frowned with concern above his dark beard. 'I'll get us a cab and we'll go and pick up the car. 'Night, Inspector. Enjoy the rest of the opera.'

'Before you go –' Malone hesitated, not wanting to delay Mrs Malloy, who seemed to be getting paler by the moment. 'Tell me something. When you shoot your film or tape or whatever you use –'

'Tape.'

'How much is used in the actual newscast?'

Malloy still had his arm round his wife, as if he was afraid that she might faint against him here in the rapidly clearing foyer. 'Depends on the news items. If we get two minutes on the screen, we think we're lucky. We might get that for a major disaster.'

'What happens to the rest of the tape?'

'It's just thrown out. They might keep some of it, say a shot of a particular person, for the files, but most of it would be thrown out. There's an awful lot of waste in our game.'

'There is in any game, except ours. We never have any money to throw away. Good-night, Mrs Malloy. I hope your headache soon clears up. It's a pity to miss Mozart,' he lied convincingly.

The Malloys went across the foyer and down the wide steps and he went back in for the final act. He would send Russ Clements out again tomorrow to chase up those clips the TV newsrooms had filed. Frank Blizzard wasn't a ghost. Somewhere he had left a print of himself, something more than a voice reciting an old, threatening nursery rhyme.

When the final curtain fell Malone pushed his way out through the crowd and went down to the stage door. Waldorf had left word that he was to be admitted; none the less, the doorkeeper looked at him curiously, wondering what a detective-inspector wanted with one of the company's leading singers. Was Sebastian Waldorf to be arrested for rape, for seduction of a minor? He knew the reputation of everyone in the company. Some day he would retire and write his own opera, once he'd learned to compose music.

Malone, given directions to Waldorf's dressing-room, side-stepped his way through the musicians and chorus members already rushing to catch the last bus or to grab a lift from a fellow member who had a car. Despite his boredom out front, Malone felt a curiosity, almost an excitement, at being backstage. This was theatre, make-believe, glamour: all the clichés that were contradicted by his own work-world. Here everything was heightened, even if only by the imagination and conceit of those who worked in it; there were other rewards besides those of pay and promotion, there were fame and applause and the realization of creativity. None of these thoughts was coherent or even put into words in his own mind as he went down the bustling corridor. He was just aware of a more heightened feeling than he had felt out in the auditorium.

Waldorf was taking off his make-up; Rosalie Vigil, still wearing hers, sat admiring him. She looked up, startled, when Malone knocked and stepped in the open door. Waldorf, discarding feathers like a moulting eagle, smiled at her. 'I forgot to tell you, darling –' It was not a term of endearment, it was the currency of the theatre; even Malone recognized that. 'Inspector Malone is taking me back to the hotel. I'm not allowed out on my own.'

'I thought we could have supper somewhere.' Her look implied she had hoped for something more than supper.

Waldorf looked at Malone. 'Must we disappoint each other, Scobie?'

Malone grinned. 'Don't make me sound like a Mother Superior. You're free to take your own risks.' But his voice wasn't smiling; he was growing tired of trying to protect elements who wanted to go their own way, regardless. 'But if Frank Blizzard wants to join you . . .'

Miss Vigil peeled off her eyelashes, giving up seduction for common sense. 'When you put it like that . . .'

Waldorf, featherless now, wrapped in a silk dressing-gown, leaned down and kissed her. 'It'll all be over soon, *cara*.'

Then the Queen of the Night, bizarre in her stage make-up and a mink coat, stood in the doorway, one hand above her head in a negligent pose as she leaned against the door-jamb. Does she sing 'Lili Marlene'? Malone wondered. She looked first at Miss Vigil, then at Waldorf, decided he was taken for the evening, and finally looked at Malone. He glanced at himself in Waldorf's mirror and decided that, without make-up, he looked as dowdy as a street cleaner amongst these exotics.

'Whose admirer are you?'

'Just my own,' said Malone, wondering what, if anything, was under the fur coat.

'I'm the Queen of the Night.' She held out a hand to be kissed; he took it and shook it. She gave him a smile that was intended to floor him, where she would instantly jump on him. She was telling him, as if he hadn't already guessed, that she was a piece of no resistance. 'You're not a romantic, are you, a gallant?'

'My wife and six kids think I'm both of those.'

'Would your wife and six kids let you come to a party I'm

giving? You, too, Sebastian darling. Oh, and you, Rosalie,' she added, not looking at Miss Vigil.

'I'd love to, darling,' said Waldorf, 'but I can't. This is Inspector Malone. He's just arrested me for buggering the three boys who play the Genii.'

'Is that an offence? Dear me, I am behind the times.'

It was all as artificial as the stage setting out front and Malone, ankle-deep in the mire of the everyday world, knew he would never be able to stomach this atmosphere, glamorous or not. He reached again for the Queen of the Night's hand, lifted it and kissed it, just to show he was not an entire clod, that the NSWPD could occasionally breed a gallant. She smiled and turned her hand over to stroke his cheek.

'You're a good sort, Mr Malone,' said the Queen of the Night from Coonabarabran, a down-to-earth country girl still under all her artificiality. 'Come back when you're not on duty, any night. My room's just down the hall.'

She swept out and Miss Vigil made a retching noise. 'I think I'm going to throw up.'

Waldorf lifted her to her feet and kissed her on the cheek; he looks like her father, Malone thought, or anyway her uncle. 'Good-night, darling. I promise – when this is all over, we'll go away for a weekend somewhere.'

She kissed him in return, said good-night to Malone and went quickly out of the room. She looked on the point of tears, or perhaps peeling off her lashes had made her eyes water. Waldorf turned back to the big light-rimmed mirror, looked at Malone in it.

'I'll be glad to get home to Germany.'

'That's home?'

'It's where my wife and family are. I'm missing them, Scobie. Is that what being scared, really scared for the first time in your life, does to you?'

'Yes,' said Malone, knowing exactly how he felt.

Waldorf changed into street clothes, wrapped himself in a camelhair coat, put on a tweed cap – 'It protects me against the wind, I'm susceptible to head-colds' – and they went out into the chill night air. The wind had dropped since early evening, there were no clouds and the three-quarter moon was a broken silver button against the navy blue of the sky. Over to their right Circular Quay and the buildings fronting it were a dazzling pattern of lights, the lights reflected in the waters of the harbour, *pointillisme* gone crazy; behind them, the great off-white shells of the Opera House reared against the harbour proper like sharks playing at porpoises. It struck Malone that it all looked like a stage set, grander than the one he had seen in the Opera House itself.

He led the way across the wide forecourt to the space reserved for the staff; Waldorf had left a pass for him at the gatekeeper's shack for him to bring the Commodore in. He had gone out to Randwick this afternoon and collected the car and brought it back to the Congress. He no longer wanted to trust to taxis or to walking up the city streets. The Commodore was no tank, but he felt safe in it, it was his own turtle shell.

He went to the driver's side and put his key in the car door. Waldorf, standing on the other side, looked across the roof at him. 'Tomorrow night let's –'

The bullet hit him in the back of the head; he died instantly, the tweed cap no protection at all against the .243. Malone, some sixth sense telling him where the bullet had come from, looked up, saw the gunman at the top of the steps that led up across the face of a steep bluff that was the northern end of the Botanical Gardens. He couldn't make out the rifle; all he saw was the man's hunched shoulders against the moon. He dropped flat, rolled as far under the car as he could get, heard the two shots, in rapid succession, hit the roof of the car. He lay there, waiting for another shot, but there was none. He rolled out from under the car, looked up: Blizzard had disappeared. He dragged out his Smith & Wesson and, keeping close to the foot of the bluff, ran across and up the stairs, going up them two at a time, still keeping against the bluff.

He reached the top of the steps, dropped flat; but there was no sign of Blizzard. He had gone into the shadows, it would be suicidal to try to find him.

Malone went backwards down the steps, just in case Blizzard reappeared. He crossed to the car, aware of cars still pulling away from the entrance to the Opera House. He dropped down, making himself as small a target as possible, and looked at Sebastian Waldorf, once Sam Culp. The singer lay in a curled heap, as if the bullet had thumped him into the ground. His mouth was open as if on a high note, but only blood and silence was coming out. *Tomorrow night let's* . . .

Malone, his mind off-balance, past sanity for the moment, wondered what they would have done together tomorrow night.

NINE

1

Assistant Commissioner, Crime, Fred Falkender was a jovial man; he should have been in community relations instead of chasing criminals. He was only five feet nine, the minimum height for a cop when he had joined, rotund, bald and merry-faced; he looked like an old-time Labour politician, one of the Party's Irish stalwarts before the modern image-makers got to them and taught them about silhouette and colour co-ordination and jargon phrases like 'an election mode' and 'conceptualization of ideas'. He laughed and joked and slapped everyone on the back, even crims, when they were leaving him. He was full of bonhomie, a quality not endemic in the Police Department.

'We've got to get you out of sight, Scobie, no two ways about it. Oh, and Mr O'Brien too, mustn't forget him, eh?' He laughed, showing all his teeth; the round cheeks showed pink lights. 'But you're the important one. Won't do much for the Department's image if we lose another man.' He laughed again, looked at the two glum faces in front of him. 'I'm only trying to cheer you up.'

He's not as dumb as this, thought Malone; why does he try so bloody hard? 'I know that, sir. It's just that – well, I don't fancy being cooped up in a safe house somewhere.'

'I'd feel the same way m'self, Scobie. But the Commissioner insists on it. It seems you're one of his favourite sons.' For a moment the merry blue eyes had a different sort of gleam. Senior officers in any administration, public or private, no matter how good-humoured they are, do not take kindly to favouritism being sprayed on someone half a dozen rungs below them. Thunder was once said to be the rumbling of angels against favouritism in Heaven. 'He wants you looked after.'

Malone wished that Commissioner John Leeds had stayed out of this. He had done Leeds a favour a year ago in the way he had handled a particular case, a messy one; the Commissioner, through past association with one of the principals, might have had his name brought into the courts. Malone, however, had managed to avoid that and the Commissioner had expressed his thanks and his debt. Malone now wished the Commissioner owed him nothing.

'That's considerate of you, but I'd still like some alternative.'

'Well, wherever we put you, we've got to keep you out of the limelight for a while. You agree, Harry?'

'Oh, my oath, yes.' Danforth had been sitting quietly, content to let the A/C do all the talking. Falkender had invited them up here for, as he had put it with a laugh, an exchange of ideas. Danforth hadn't brought any ideas with him; Fred Falkender might laugh a lot, but he also talked a lot and anyone else's ideas rarely got a hearing. 'The bloody media are running some pretty wild stories. All bloody guesswork, like they usually do.'

The media had made an opera of Waldorf's murder. Every headline had been an aria, every TV newsreel had done its best to be a Wagnerian spectacle, radio reporters had hit notes that had threatened to shatter glass. Malone had stayed by the body till the ambulance had arrived to take it away. Waldorf's last exit at the Opera House: the thought had crossed Malone's mind, till he had realized the banality of it and angrily brushed it away. By the time the ambulance had gone the crowd in the forecourt had grown till it looked like a fanfare of devotees waiting to say good-night to Sutherland or Pavarotti, both of whom, when they learned of Waldorf's murder, would probably be glad they had not been here tonight.

Clements, who had arrived five minutes before the ambulance, took Malone's arm and led him across to the line of police cars. The revolving blue lights added their own dramatic note to the scene; Malone wondered if, in their light, his own face had the same pale look as Clements'. 'You want me to have someone drive you back to the hotel?'

'No, I'll be okay. I chased the bastard, Russ, but he got away. Up there.' He nodded up the wide flight of steps to the Gardens.

'You get close enough to recognize him, give us a description?'

Malone shook his head. 'He was just a shape, that was all.'

'Inspector –?' Malone turned his head. The young reporter from Channel 15, backed by an equally young cameraman and an untidy-looking sound-girl, was leaning forward expectantly. 'You were here, weren't you, when Sebastian was shot?'

Malone, still suffering from shock, looked at the reporter in puzzlement. First name basis, he thought irrelevantly; he probably never met Waldorf, but he's a public figure so he calls him Sebastian. They're all the same, these kids: they'd call God by his first name, if He had one. 'What?'

'No, he wasn't here,' interrupted Clements. 'Now piss off. Mr Waldorf was a personal friend of the Inspector's. He doesn't want to talk about it.'

'I was told Inspector Malone was the one who made the first call –'

'You want me to run you in?' Clements was belligerent, unsettled. It had shocked him to his soft centre to know that Malone had come so close to being murdered.

'What for?'

'Using obscene language in a public place.'

'What fucking obscene language?' The sound-girl joined the dialogue.

Clements grinned at Malone, some of the tension seeping out of him. 'Jack Chew was right – it never fails.' He turned back to the Channel 15 crew. 'Get lost!'

The crew went off, muttering obscenely, and Clements said, 'They're just the first. The media are going to beat this up like the beginning of World War Three. They're gunna find out about the hit list pretty soon. What do we do then?'

Malone shrugged; the media were no longer of any concern to him. He had reached a point of despair. He knew it would pass, he was still an optimist, even if battered and bruised; but for the moment he was locked in his own small world. His main concern was that Lisa would be listening to any late-night news-flash, though he doubted that the news of Waldorf's murder would be on Queensland radio stations tonight.

'There are two bullets that should be in the roof of my car –'

199

'There's only one – they're getting it out now. The other one must've ricocheted off into the harbour. I've told 'em we want that bullet and the one out of Waldorf's head – Sorry.' He had seen Malone flinch. 'I didn't mean to be as blunt as that. I'll have both bullets up at Ballistics first thing in the morning. But there's no doubt where they came from. How're you feeling?'

'Shaky. I'll give you a statement and you can go back and write the report for me, put it in the running sheet.'

'Not here.' Clements had seen other reporters and cameramen converging on them. 'Let's go back to the hotel.'

'What about Waldorf's family? Who's going to tell them?'

'I've already fixed that. The assistant manager of the company has been across – he's known the Waldorfs for some years, he's a friend of the family. He said he'd phone Mrs Waldorf with the news.'

Clements had come up trumps again, always one step ahead of where one suspected he was. 'Thanks. Better him than us. What about Miss Vigil? Can you break it to her?'

Clements nodded reluctantly. 'Okay, I'll do it.'

'How did you get down here?'

'By cab. I was at home – the office rang me. I'll drive your car. You sure you're okay? You don't wanna see a doctor?'

'You've never asked me that before. Am I looking sick or something?'

'I've seen you look better.'

And I've felt better, Malone was now thinking as he sat here in Falkender's office on the nineteenth floor. All the Assistant Commissioners at Police Headquarters in College Street were on this floor, as if rewarded with elevation above the humdrum of running the Department; they were known to Malone and Clements and a few of the Department's iconoclasts as the Archangels, though Gabriel was unlikely to blow a hymn to any of them. None of the rooms was big and Falkender's was made smaller by a huge bookcase, filled with law books, along one wall. No one had ever seen him open the glass front of the bookcase, let alone a book, but he was accepted as the legal expert of the seven A/Cs. On the opposite wall was his framed degree as a Bachelor of Law.

'That's another thing,' said Falkender. 'The media. They have put two and two together, Scobie. Both the *Herald* and the *Telegraph* were on to me this morning, asking about a hit list. They want to know why you were with O'Brien the other night and why you were with Waldorf last night.'

'I've told them nothing. They tried that tack last night, but Sergeant Clements told them to get lost.'

'I believe they also asked it at the press conference this morning. That right, Harry?'

Danforth nodded. 'I told 'em we were examining the possibility of a hit list, I didn't tell 'em we knew there was one.'

'What did you tell 'em about me?' Malone could see Danforth at the press conference, doing nothing for the Department's image with his ponderous cliché replies that had once been standard procedure, as if plain everyday language would be some sort of minefield.

'I just said you were running the investigation under me. Then they started asking smart-arse questions and I told 'em to get stuffed.'

That was plain everyday language. 'You actually told 'em that?'

'Well, no, not exactly. I just got up and walked out.'

Falkender looked as if he might laugh; but then he always looked like that. He said, 'Well, we still have to take care of you, Scobie. Have you spoken to your wife about last night?'

'Yes.' Lisa had rung him first thing this morning, before he could call her; he had slept only fitfully and it had been almost dawn before he had finally dropped off into a deep sleep. The phone had woken him and, though they had talked for twenty minutes, his mind had been off-balance all the time, teetering on a rolling ball of shock and exhaustion. But when he had got off the phone her plea had still been ringing in his ears: 'She wants me to resign.'

'Resign from the case? You can't do that –'

'Resign from the Department.'

That took the laugh out of Falkender's face; it made even Danforth sit up sharply. At last the A/C said, 'What are you going to do? Are you going to resign?'

'I don't know –'

'Don't rush it, Scobie. We need you in the Department. That right, Harry?'

'Eh? Oh sure. My word, yes.' What would happen to Jack Aldwych if Malone did resign? Would he be replaced by someone more realistic, someone not so bloody piously honest? 'But it's your decision, Scobie.'

'No,' said Malone, 'it's my wife's.'

'Well, yes, of course,' said Falkender, who had a formidable wife, a woman who had an iron laugh that had no merriment in it; their marriage was reasonably happy, but sometimes he suspected it was only because she insisted that it was. If she told him to resign, he would have to consider it. 'Your wife and family come into it, of course. But do you think Blizzard is going to lay off of you because you've left the force? He's after Scobie Malone, not *Inspector* Malone.'

Malone looked at the pink-faced man across the desk; the merry eyes were showing the shrewdness that had got him there behind that particular desk. Fred Falkender hadn't made Assistant Commissioner on seniority alone; John Leeds, the shrewdest man of all in the Department, didn't subscribe to that system of promotion. 'I tried to put that argument to my wife, sir –'

'Would it help if I or the Commissioner spoke to her? We can look after you better if you stay in the force, Scobie – you know that. Maybe we can explain it to her.'

If Lisa wouldn't listen to him, she certainly wouldn't listen to other men, no matter what their rank. Her marriage was a closed circle, a stockade. She was the old-fashioned sort of woman who believed that if a husband and wife couldn't work out their problems between them, then something was missing from the basis of their marriage and always had been. And he knew that she, as well as himself, fiercely believed that the basis of their marriage was rock solid. It was built on love, trust and understanding. If those were not enough, then no amount of advice from outsiders would make a blind bit of difference.

'No, I'll talk to her again. We'll work it out. But if O'Brien and I have to leave the Congress –'

'You have to do that, as soon as possible. It places too many other people at risk. We don't want a shoot-out with Blizzard *there*. Christ, think of it!' He shook his big head.

'Fair enough. We'll check out of the hotel today. But I want you to put us somewhere where Blizzard can find us.'

Falkender opened his mouth as if he were about to laugh at the suggestion; then he closed it and looked at Danforth. 'What do you say, Harry?'

Danforth, as usual, was slow to see the point. 'I thought that was what we were trying to avoid?'

Malone let the A/C do the explaining: 'Don't you see what Scobie's getting at? If we hide him and O'Brien too successfully, how are we ever going to flush out Blizzard? If Scobie is prepared to take the risk – we don't know about O'Brien – then we can tempt Blizzard to come out into the open to get at them.' He looked back at Malone. 'What'll your wife think of that?'

'I don't think she needs to know,' said Malone and had never felt so treacherous.

'It's a good idea,' said Danforth, at last catching up.

'Do you have any place in mind where we can send you and still look after you? Remember I'm limited in the number of men I can spare full time to look after you. This feller isn't a jail-breaker, someone we have a description of. If we knew what he looked like, we could organize a State-wide manhunt and go after him with everything we've got. But he's just a blank.'

Malone had discussed with O'Brien at breakfast the possibility of their having to evacuate the Congress. It was O'Brien who, after some thought, had made the suggestion and now Malone pushed it forward: 'O'Brien has a stud farm outside the other side of Camden. When this business first started I warned him against staying there, I thought it would be too hard to make secure. But now . . . O'Brien will put in four security guards and if you can give me four of our blokes, I think we can patrol the farm pretty effectively.'

Falkender looked dubious. 'We don't like working with private security forces.'

It was an old rivalry, the old territorial imperative on the part of the police: *stay off my turf*. Yet there was a growing awareness that, with the increase in crime over the past few years, the contempt for what had become a fragile façade of law and order, co-operation would eventually be inevitable. But Falkender, as an Assistant Commissioner, had at least to salute the Department's policy.

'With all respect, sir, if I'm shoving my neck out – and O'Brien's – I don't care where the protection comes from.'

The A/C stared at him; then he laughed, though it had no mirth in it. 'Okay, but I'll have to put it to the Commissioner. Will O'Brien agree to being the next best thing to a sitting duck?'

'He's pretty fatalistic at the moment, I think. He's in such a hole with the National Securities people over his shonky business deals, I don't think he cares much what happens. Except that, like me, he doesn't want Blizzard hanging over his head for God knows how many months or years.'

'From what I've read about him, I don't think he'd be the sort of bloke I'd want to be cooped up with for too long. What about you, Harry?'

'I can't stand a bar of these bloody white-collar crims,' said Danforth piously.

'I could have to live with worse,' said Malone, not looking at Danforth. 'When you get to know him, he's not all bastard.'

'Does he have any family?' said Falkender.

'Two ex-wives in England who he never contacts. His father's alive, he lives somewhere out in the western suburbs, but I gather they haven't spoken for years.' *Then there's Anital Norval and we won't speak of her.*

Falkender stood up, came round his desk, laughed and slapped Malone on the back. 'Let's try it, subject to the Commissioner's okay. We'll get this bastard Blizzard yet, right, Harry?'

'Oh, my oath yes,' said Danforth and went ahead of Malone out the door, avoiding the parting slap on the back. Malone got a second whack: the A/C hated to waste his good fellowship.

Malone and Danforth left Headquarters and walked up College Street towards Police Centre, four blocks away. Danforth was quiet, but Malone did not mind; conversation with the

Chief Superintendent was never easy and never illuminating. The city had slowed down for Saturday morning; people crossed the roadway at their leisure and the traffic seemed to be taking its time towards wherever it was going. August was coming to an end and spring was coming out of the north; in Hyde Park across the street the deciduous trees were bright green with new leaf; the air, no longer cramped with cold, was opening up. Old men, in thick sweaters but no longer in overcoats, sat under the trees and played chess and checkers, another winter survived, another season to live. *Hail Mary* . . . Malone found himself praying for another season for himself, or three or forty. His mother would have been pleased if she had heard the silent words and would have given him a holy water shower.

'I can't give you any Tac Response fellers,' Danforth said at last. 'We can have 'em on call, and the SWOS coves, too, but they can't do a full-time job for you and O'Brien. I'll get you three youngsters and a senior constable.'

'Just so long as they're all wide awake and can shoot straight. And don't panic.'

'You think there's gunna be a shoot-out with Blizzard?'

'How do I know, Harry? But I don't think he's the sort who's going to come out with his hands up. I'm guessing, but I think he'll take us on.'

'He didn't stop and shoot at you last night when you went after him.'

'No, that puzzled me.'

They waited at traffic lights in Oxford Street. Two punk kids, a boy and a girl, stood beside them, sunbursts of purple hair shooting out of their heads, the girl staring defiantly at the world through a domino of green mascara. Danforth curled his lip, grunted, but said nothing further; Malone would not have been surprised if he had arrested them for being no more than what they were, rebels. The light turned green and the two detectives crossed the road.

'But I'm beginning to cotton on to the way he thinks. He's stretching this out, he's dangling us, if you like. He tried to knock me off when I was down there with Waldorf, but that may have been no more than a reflex action – I was in his sights and he just let go. When I got up to the top of those steps, he could've knocked me off from the shadows without any effort. But he didn't. He's dangling us, letting us swing in the wind.'

They passed a narrow-fronted porno movie house; a girl with breasts that must have given her curvature of the spine smiled at them from a torn poster. Danforth grunted again. He was silent then till he and Malone parted inside the front doors of Police Centre. As he turned towards his own office he stopped. 'Does O'Brien have to go before the NCSC again on Monday?'

'Not till Tuesday – that'll be his last appearance. He's got an adjournment for Monday. I gather he wants to get everything together before he spills some names the Commission is dying to hear.'

'He mention any of the names to you?'

'No, and I didn't ask him. I don't want to know, I've got enough on my plate.'

'Are we expected to escort him there?'

'I don't think so. He'll have his own security men.'

'Good,' said Danforth and went lumbering off to tell Jack Aldwych where O'Brien could be found before he got to the NCSC on Tuesday and spilled his guts and, in a different sort of way, everyone else's.

Malone went into Homicide and found Clements waiting for him in his office, looking tired and even more rumpled than usual. 'Didn't you go to bed last night?'

'I got in here at seven. I've been running those off-cuts I got from the TV stations. I can't see anything in them to get excited about. Nobody suspicious-looking, nobody turning up more than once, except you and the cameramen.'

'How'd you pick them?'

'The same old thing. They photograph each other. Haven't you ever noticed when you're watching the news?'

'Are they all the same blokes every time?'

'No. The Channel 10 and the Channel 15 guys crop up the most.'

'I didn't notice who was there last night. Except that the Channel 15 bloke, his name's Malloy, wasn't there. I met him at the opera and he was taking his wife home, she was ill.

Remember there was a young bloke on the Channel 15 camera last night?'

'Well, I'll check 'em all out. I'm going to read these, too, over the weekend.' He touched a small pile of books he had put down on Malone's desk. 'I got Andy Graham to get 'em from the Woollahra library. Raymond Chandler. I've never read him. If Blizzard was so keen on him when he was young, I'll have a go at these and see if there's anything in them that makes him tick the way he does. Yes, Clarrie? Where're you going – to a corroboree?'

Clarrie Binyan, curls slicked down, dressed in a dark blue suit, a white carnation in his buttonhole, stood in the doorway. He grinned and tossed a plastic envelope on to Malone's desk; it contained two bullets. 'I'm going to a niece's wedding. She's marrying an Eyetalian. She wants to put a hyphen in their names – Mr and Mrs Bindiwarra-Caccioli. That'll go down well with the Mafia. With the tribe, too.'

Malone was never sure when Binyan was joking about his Aboriginal background; maybe he had decided that joking was the only way to survive as one of the smallest minorities in his native land. An enquiry was going on at the moment into police treatment of Aborigines in certain country towns and around Police Centre Clarrie Binyan was treated with cautious respect, as if the whites were not certain of his attitude towards them. Malone knew that Binyan was amused by the irony that he, a blackfellow, was the Department's expert on the white man's weapons.

Malone always felt relaxed with him, but he was always non-committal about Binyan's jokes. He picked up the plastic envelope. '.243s out of the same rifle as the others?'

'An exact match to all the others. They recovered the shells, too. They're from a Tikka, all right. I gather you were pretty lucky?' Binyan was certainly not joking now.

Malone nodded. 'If he hadn't hurried the shots, he'd have picked me off as easily as he did Waldorf.' He felt the shiver inside him as he said it and he hoped it didn't show.

'Well, keep your head down,' said Binyan and went off to the Italian-Aboriginal corroboree, to listen to 'O Sole Mio' played on a didgeridoo, to sit and look as warily at the Italians as they would look at him. Binyan's niece was a half-blood, a talented dancer with an all-white company, but Malone knew that the Italians, like most of the postwar immigrants, had their own colour bar.

Clements had looked at the bullets, then dropped the envelope into his pocket; it would go into the murder box. 'What now?'

'I add another line or two to the running sheet, then I'm going back to the hotel and telling Brian Boru we're moving out. Fred Falkender's and the Commissoner's orders.'

'Where are you going?'

'Up to O'Brien's stud farm.'

'You might ask him if he's got any tips for this afternoon. The programme at Rosehill looks as wide open as a picnic sack race.'

'I thought you'd given up betting on the horses, you're a big-time share punter now?'

'I just like to keep my hand in. What are you gunna do up at the stud farm, other than look at the horses?'

'We're going to play goats to Blizzard's tiger.' He smiled at Clements' puzzlement. 'It's an old Sumatran game. Lisa told me about it.'

'Don't tell me she suggested it?'

'Hardly.' And again he felt the sense of treachery. 'But how else do we get Blizzard out into the open?'

2

O'Brien sat and looked at the man who would dance on his grave; rather heavily, too. 'So you've got your financing, George?'

'I have my backer. You give me first option and we can buy you out. All you and I have to do now is work out the details.'

'How much do you think you can salvage from the NCSC? They can send the cleaners in. I don't think you realize, George, how much they intend to skin me. They're setting me up to put me before a judge – Christ knows what he'll do to me. I'm going to be an example to all the others who are trying to get away with what I tried.'

'Oh, I know all right, Brian.' They had never been as formally polite as this, not even in their first awkward days, eight years ago, when they had been trying to get to know each other. The atmosphere between them had all the chilly decorum of a funeral parlour, thought O'Brien; then wondered why he was thinking in terms of graves and funeral parlours. And knew. 'But the NCSC will be looking to save something for the small share-holders – they won't let everything go all the way down the drain. Not if there's someone who can salvage it.'

'Someone like you and your mysterious mate?'

Bousakis nodded, wondering if Malone would remain alive long enough to learn who the mystery backer was. He sat comfortably in his chair, a mountain of smug triumph.

'Is it someone I know? One of those who've been trying to have me bumped off?'

Bousakis' big moon face showed nothing. He had had an hour with Jack Aldwych yesterday evening and by the time he had left he had known, as if it had been spelled out in a legal contract, that Jack Aldwych was going to have O'Brien killed. The buying out of Cossack Holdings was a business deal; the killing of O'Brien was a personal matter. The knowledge had frightened Bousakis and he had wondered whether he had plunged into a black pool where his own life would always be in danger. He was cold-blooded in business, that was why he had been such an asset to O'Brien; but he was not cold-blooded about life and death. Even as the chilling doubt had swept through him he had known, however, that it was too late to draw back: he had already dived off the springboard. It was he who had come to Aldwych with the idea for the takeover, not the other way round. In the end greed had overcome fear and doubt. The deadly sins have a strength all their own, especially if one has nurtured most of them most of one's life. George Bousakis had missed out only on sloth: it had taken too much effort to cultivate it.

'I don't think you need to know that, Brian. Just take the money and run – if you can.'

O'Brien felt his temper rise; but held on to it. 'What about the stud farm?'

'That's part of Cossack Holdings, so we'll take that, too. All you'll keep will be the gold mine.'

'Only because I was shrewd enough to register it off-shore in another name. Nobody gets that, not even the NCSC.'

'That's all you've got, Brian, that's really worth anything. Compared to what you used to have.'

'So why are you buying?'

'Assets and potential. I can turn Cossack around, make it what it should have been.' For just a moment there was a flicker of angry hatred in the big bland face; he forgot his own greed and almost snarled, 'If you hadn't started trying to get rich so fucking quickly –'

'I *am* rich, George,' said O'Brien, his own temper subsiding as he saw the other's rise. 'The gold mine.'

'There's little point in being rich in jail.' Or dead: but Bousakis didn't add that alternative.

O'Brien sank a little into his chair; it was almost imperceptible, but Bousakis noticed it. There had been no mention of Waldorf's murder. Not because of sensitivity on Bousakis' part, but just deliberate callous indifference; it had required an effort, but he had managed it. O'Brien was still too much in shock to want to discuss what had happened; he had slept only fitfully last night, waking twice in a sweat to dodge the bullets coming at him out of the darkness. There was also a sense of loss, almost of grief; though he was honest enough to wonder if it was for himself. He had hardly come to know Waldorf, yet he had come to like him. The singer had had his own loss, that of his family, yet somehow he had held on to his laughter, to his joy in living.

When Malone had come back to the hotel at midnight and told him the news, O'Brien had been in bed reading a book Anita had given him weeks before and which so far had lain on his bedside table unopened. It was Tom Wolfe's *Bonfire of the Vanities*, and after two or three chapters he had begun to wonder if Tom Wolfe was some sort of messenger for Anita. Then Malone had come home with the dreadful news about Waldorf and the book had been dropped on the floor beside the bed.

210

Malone had sat down on the bottom of the bed. 'He almost got me, too, Brian. Another couple of inches closer and there would only have been you left.'

O'Brien looked at the tall policeman who, he now recognized, was a friend. 'How do you feel?'

Malone held up his hands; they were steady. 'I guess it must be my feet that are shaking. *Something*'s giving way. I feel like I want to get out in the middle of a bloody great paddock and yell for Blizzard to come out in the open. Anything to get it over and done with one way or the other.'

'I feel the same way.' It was despair, not bravado, speaking.

Malone stood up. 'We'll talk about it at breakfast. You going anywhere tomorrow?'

'I wouldn't mind going to the races at Rosehill, anything to get a breath of fresh air.'

'Better not. I think we have to stay away from crowds, just in case Blizzard has a go at you or me and some poor innocent bugger gets in the way.' He picked up the book from the floor and handed it to O'Brien. 'Stay home and read. I've seen the reviews of that. What's it about?'

'A guy who's got himself into a bit of a bind.'

'I'll borrow it when you've finished. Maybe we'll learn something.'

Now, late on the Saturday morning, Malone came back from Police Centre, letting himself into the suite. He pulled up sharply when he saw Bousakis, but the latter rose from his chair, picking up his briefcase as he greeted Malone. O'Brien, growing more sensitive to atmosphere day by day, almost hour by hour, was aware that the huge man, his *employee* still, was the only one of the three of them with an air of authority; or anyway confidence. But then, of course, his life was not under threat.

'I'm going, Inspector. Brian and I have finished our business, haven't we, Brian?'

'Not quite. I'll think about it over the weekend.' He might be dead before he would have to suffer Bousakis' triumph. The morbid thought somehow pleased him: he was like the swimmer who knows he will drown before the shark can reach him. 'I'll try and stay alive till then. Tell your friends.'

211

Bousakis caught the implication: the option deal would mean nothing if O'Brien was killed before signing it. It was anyone's guess what the NCSC would do with Cossack Holdings if they found against O'Brien and he was already dead, beyond their judgement.

Bousakis said nothing, but managed to depart with heavy grace. 'A rhino dancing,' said O'Brien.

'What?' said Malone.

'Nothing. I'm getting light-headed, I think. I'm having flights of fancy, all of them fucking morbid.'

'What was that about telling his friends you'd try to stay alive?'

'You don't really want to know, do you? Isn't Blizzard enough complication for you?'

Malone thought a moment, nodded and sat down heavily. 'Normally I'd say no. But if you're not worried –'

'Oh, I'm worried. But you've got enough on your plate . . . Let's stick to Blizzard. What happens now?'

'We go up to your stud today,' Malone said after a few moments' silence. He had tried to protect Sebastian Waldorf and failed; he prayed there would not be another failure with O'Brien. 'You supply four security men and the Department will give us four cops. We'll work out a roster so there are two men on all the time.'

'What do we do? Just sit and wait till Blizzard turns up?'

'We give it a week. If he doesn't come out into the open in that time, we'll have to think of something else.'

'He'll wait. He's waited twenty-odd years.'

'I don't think so. He's on a run now, four of us in two and a half weeks. Five if you count Mardi Jack as you.'

'Don't,' said O'Brien, stiffening.

'Sorry. Anyhow, I don't think he's going to suddenly get patient.'

'Serial killers do.'

'What do you know about serial killers?'

'Not much,' O'Brien admitted.

'Blizzard's not a serial killer, not in the usual sense. They usually pick random victims. Blizzard's had us marked for years, though Christ knows when he decided to kill us. But now he's

212

started, I'm betting he can't stop. He's not going to sit around and wait. We're for it, one or both of us, some time within the next week. And I think I'd rather it that way. I just hope his aim is a bit off, as it was with me last night.'

'Me, too. But I'd just like to get a look at him before he gets me.'

They went into their respective bedrooms to pack. But first Malone put a call through to Lisa in Queensland. She had phoned him just after seven o'clock this morning, before he could call her; she had heard the news of Waldorf's murder on the radio. 'Why didn't you call me last night to tell me you were all right?'

She sounded shrewish, but he knew it was with the best of intentions. 'If I'd called you at midnight last night, which was when I got back here to the hotel, woken you up, you wouldn't have slept the rest of the night.'

'I'm not going to sleep tonight, for God's sake. Come up here – get on a plane right away!'

'No!' he said quietly and firmly. 'I'm not going to put you and the kids – and your parents – in danger.'

'*You're* in danger!' It was then she had said, 'Resign, darling Get out of the police force, get your superannuation and we'll go somewhere and start a new life.'

He had to bite his tongue to refrain from telling her that that was a ridiculous suggestion; instead he said, 'There's that old Dutch thrift, don't forget the superannuation –'

'Don't joke! Bloody men!' She sounded Australian then. 'I mean it, Scobie – *resign!*'

And now, late in the morning, she was still on the same theme, but more restrained now: 'Have you thought any more about resigning? I went into Noosa this morning to a travel agent – we could all go back to Holland, Mother and Dad still have a flat in Amsterdam –'

'To *live?*'

'Of course to live.' Her voice was calm, but her thinking was hysterical; he had never known her like this. 'You could get a job in the Dutch police – No! Forget I said that.'

'That's easily done. You think the Dutch cops don't run risks? There are terrorists in Europe. At least we don't have *those* here, not yet anyway. Darl, when you've had time to think about what you're suggesting, you won't want to uproot the kids. They belong *here*. So do you and I,' he added and waited for her to disagree.

There was over a thousand kilometres of silence between them; if he hadn't known her as well as he did he would have thought she had left the phone and walked away. But he knew her silences: they could be icy calm or as tender as her lips against his cheek. He almost sighed with relief when he heard her say, 'I know you're right, darling. But . . .'

'I'm going to be all right,' he lied hopefully. 'The Department's putting a guard on me and Brian O'Brien, and he's got his own security men. If they haven't caught Blizzard within the next week, I promise we'll go somewhere right out of Sydney. I'll take my long service leave and we'll go to New Zealand or somewhere while they try to track him down.'

'What about Mr O'Brien?'

'He has enough money to go anywhere in the world.' *If he doesn't go to jail.* Where O'Brien would probably be no safer than where he was now.

'On his own? Poor man.' It was typical of her that she should feel deep sympathy for a man she had never met, a man whose financial shenanigans she abhorred. She was puritanically honest, but admitted her naïveté in expecting absolute honesty in business. 'What happens if they don't catch Blizzard?'

He sighed, making a concession. 'Then maybe we'll go to Holland.'

She made no comment on that, but said, 'You want to speak to Maureen and Tom?'

I'd better, he almost said; but that would have sounded too much like a premonition. 'Put them on.'

Maureen came on the line, plunging in without any preliminary. 'I'm in the doghouse, Daddy.'

Her usual location. 'Don't tell me!'

'I got bubblegum on the seat of Nanna's car. Then when I tried to scrape it off, I tore the upholstery. Mummy told me to try and sew it up, but I lost the needle in the seat and Mummy sat on it.'

214

He had to hold on to his laughter. 'I don't see what everyone is complaining about.'

'Neither do I. Could you put in a good word for me, Daddy?'

'Leave it to me. Is Tom there?'

Tom was. 'G'day, Daddy. You know what? I'm in the dog-house, too. I was just kicking my soccer ball around in Nanna's kitchen, I was Maradona shooting for a goal, and I knocked over a bottle of wine, Grandpa said it was one of his best, he'd been saving it, and it all spilled out over Mummy –'

When he hung up five minutes later he sat down on the bed and half-laughed, half-wept. O'Brien came to the bedroom door. 'Something wrong?'

Malone shook his head, wiped his eyes without embarrassment. 'I've just been talking to the kids. You know what? Outside there, the world is still normal.'

3

'You've been acting abnormal.'

'Oh, come on. What do you mean – abnormal?'

'All this working back. Where did you go last night?'

'I told you when I went out, I was going to see Nick Katzka.'

'You've been telling me that for weeks. Working overtime, taking night shifts you aren't rostered for –'

Colin Malloy sighed. 'Honey, I've explained what I'm trying to do. I'm trying to persuade Nick to let me do a documentary on crime in the streets. I don't want to be just a news cameraman all my life, chasing ambulances and fire engines and politicians on the steps of Parliament House.'

Julie looked at him slyly across the narrow table in the breakfast nook. 'No, Colin. I rang Nick Katzka last week. He said you hadn't mentioned anything to him about a documentary.'

Malloy felt a flash of anger that she had doubted his word and gone behind his back; she was not normally like that. He sipped the decaffeinated coffee, then spread the multigrain toast with yellowbox honey. Julie was a health food fanatic and he did his best to please her while he was at home; out on the job he ate all the junk food that came his way and enjoyed every mouthful. It was a constant irritation to her that he was overweight, but she never complained. She had never complained about anything, till now.

'Are you having an affair?'

He looked at her in surprise. 'An affair? Who with?'

'That scruffy sound-girl, Luanne. She'd be sexy and very pretty if she cleaned herself up.'

'Honey, she never has a shower – I don't think she even washes, she thinks that's bourgeois. If I was going to have an affair with anyone, I'd at least pick someone who was *clean*.'

She didn't disagree with that. Their sex life was more than satisfactory, experimental without being too kinky; she had wondered why he would want to have an affair with another woman, though she admitted to herself that she was not an expert on men. 'Where do you go then? What do you *do*?'

I go out killing men I hate. But he loved her too much to tell her that. He had tried to rationalize his hatred of those men who had destroyed his life, but had failed. Reason told him that his life had not been totally destroyed. He had a wife whom he loved and who loved him, a job that paid him more than he would ever have earned as a policeman unless he had attained a top rank: it also gave him travel opportunities that no cop was ever offered. He and Julie had good friends, though he felt close to none of them; both he and Julie, in their own ways, were loners. The hatred was there, undeniable, unconquerable. He had read enough to believe that in everyone there was hate, as implicit in man as love, fear and the other lively emotions. Even Julie, the gentlest of women, hated: adults who abused children, people who ruined the environment, racial bigots. But her hatred of them would never lead her to murder; she had an equal hatred of killing of any kind. He was plagued, mortally, by the consuming urge for revenge, something that would never infect her and that she would never understand.

He chewed on his toast, taking his time. He had never imagined that she would actually *check* on him with Nick Katzka, the current affairs executive producer at Channel 15; she had always been the most unsuspicious of wives. He had met her in London five years ago, where he had been working for one of the independent television news organizations; she had come from Adelaide to London on a working holiday and had joined the news organization as a temporary secretary. She knew little about him, even after five years; he had told her he was an orphan, came originally from Perth and had no relatives. He had invented other details as the need had arisen and she had accepted what he had told her without question. She had told him on their wedding night that she was interested only in their present and their future, almost as if afraid that there might be something buried in his past that could ruin their happiness.

Malone, O'Brien and the others had always been there in the back 'shadows of his mind; the hatred of them had been a rottenness that he had managed to hide from her. Sometimes, in moments alone, he would weep for his dead Uncle Jeff, the only person, up till he had met Julie, he had ever loved. The two of them, the young man and the older one, had talked often of his ambition to be a policeman; of more than just that, to rise in the force to a position of authority. Jeff had been a simple-minded man of old-fashioned honesty; he had never respected anyone as he had the tough, wiry timber-cutter. Jeff was the only one who had understood the instability that occasionally showed in him:

'Frank,' he had said more than once, 'look out for that temper of yours, it's gunna get you in terrible trouble one of these days.'

'Not with you, Uncle.'

'No, mebbe not with me. But you've got a streak of something in you, I dunno what it is, that you gotta watch. Especially when you become a cop. You're gunna get into situations as a cop when you're likely to do your block and you're gunna have to watch yourself.'

'You think I'm a little crazy?' He had said it jokingly, but he had known even then there were times when he didn't understand his own actions. Only a week before he had killed a neighbour's dog that had attacked him, had taken it out into the bush and buried it, then, later, helped the neighbour search for his missing pet.

When he met Julie he had just started to experience loneliness, something he had never felt before; perhaps it had had something to do with being cooped up in London, a city that engulfed him. She, though attractive and quietly pleasant, never seemed to go beyond one date with any particular man. She had told him later that the main reason, at first, that she had gone out with him on a second and third date was that, unlike all the other men, he had not tried to get her into bed on the first night. There was an old-fashioned streak in her that, to his surprise, appealed to him; the old church-going days with Uncle Jeff and Aunt Elsie still had a superficial influence on him. They didn't fall in love at once, but gradually they came to depend on each other; it was, perhaps, love with pity, though neither of them thought in those terms. Each recognized the loneliness of the other and, with the conceit of love, thought they could do something about it. There had been rocks along the way, some that had almost wrecked the marriage. Once he had hit her, almost knocking her unconscious; he had been ashamed that he had not been instantly contrite. Instead he had looked at her coldly and walked away; only hours later had it hit him how shamefully he had acted. She had forgiven him, but from then on she had retreated from their occasional quarrels before they became too serious.

There had been other examples of cold-bloodedness, of which she had known nothing. Once, covering the civil war in Beirut, he had picked up a rifle dropped by a dead militiaman and shot a civilian running across the street a hundred yards away. He had not known whether the civilian was one of those shooting at those at this end of the street; it had been enough that the man, whoever or whatever he was, had been on the other side of the dividing line. When the reporter covering the scene with him had remonstrated with him, he had dropped the rifle, picked up his camera and just walked away into the ruin of a neighbouring building. The reporter had left the next day for Tel Aviv and Malloy had never worked with him again.

He reached for a second piece of toast, though he had not yet finished the first slice. 'I didn't want to tell you this. I want to *write*.'

'Write what?' She sipped her celery juice. She had tossed and turned most of last night; this morning, pale and drawn, she didn't look a health fanatic.

'Detective novels. I've always dreamed of some day being able to turn out something like Raymond Chandler. Or Elmore Leonard, though I don't think I'd have his ear for dialogue.'

'You want to be a *writer*?'

He managed to grin, though it was almost hidden in his beard. 'Don't say it as if I want to be a rapist or a bank robber.'

'Have you written anything?' She still sounded doubtful. 'I've never seen you making notes or whatever it is writers do.'

'I've got bits and pieces at the office.' He was creating fiction while they sat here at the table and he knew he was not doing a good job. How did husbands who were experienced liars fool their wives? Yet he did not want to fool her, only to protect her.

'Why didn't you tell me? All that stuff about making a documentary . . . You know I like detective mysteries as much as you do.'

The shelves in the second bedroom, which they had converted into a study, were full of crime books, fiction and non-fiction, hardback and paperback. The list of writers ran from Poe and Wilkie Collins and Conan Doyle through to Hammett and Chandler and Ross Macdonald and on to Higgins and Ross Thomas and Leonard and Freeling; detectives' names stood out on the books' spines: Holmes, Maigret, Trent. Those and crime movies were something the Malloys shared as enjoyment, though he had had to introduce her to them.

'What's your book going to be about?'

'About a private eye tracking down a vengeance killer.'

'What's the private eye's name?'

He was tempted to say Frank Blizzard. 'I haven't decided yet. I want a name that's different, like Sam Spade or Nero Wolfe. I'm just calling him Joe Smith for the moment.'

'That'd be different, a private eye named Smith.' She got up, began to clear the table. She looked suddenly healthy again, a flush of enthusiasm in her face; she was relieved that she could wash her suspicions down the kitchen sink. She believes me, he thought; but knew it would be mostly because it had hurt her to doubt him. She loved him more than he deserved, though he would never be able to tell her that. And he hoped she would never find out. 'Can I read some of what you've written?'

'When I've finished the first draft.'

'When will that be?'

'Another week or two.' By which time the last two green bottles would be dead marines and only God knew what would have happened to him.

Last night's close encounter with Malone had scared him. He had made a mistake in trying to pick off two targets at the same time. All the other murders had been safe ventures, even the daytime killing of Harry Gardner, the construction worker and ex-cop.

He had brought Julie home, worried that she should have such a sick headache; she had never been prone to headaches. But worry about her had not stopped him from going back to the Opera House; it was like the sickness of the compulsive gambler. Seeing Malone at the theatre, watching Waldorf up on the stage, had been too much of a magnet: the cold madness had taken hold of him again. He had put Julie to bed, gone down to the lock-up garage on the ground floor; each flat in the block had its own individual garage. He had taken the flat wooden case out of the locked steel box that was bolted to the concrete floor; he had told Julie it was for his camera equipment and there were indeed some lenses in there. Then he had gone out into the street and got into their car, a beige Mazda 626; their four-wheel-drive Nissan was always kept in the garage and taken out only at the weekend. It had taken him only ten minutes to drive from Wollstonecraft back over the Harbour Bridge and up to Macquarie Street, where he had parked in a No Parking zone after putting a Press sign inside the windscreen. Carrying the gun-case he had gone down to the Opera House, circled the forecourt by staying close to the fall of the steep bluff and climbed the wide steps to the entrance to the Botanical Gardens. This was an entrance that he knew was rarely used, even during the day; but he had come here several times with a Channel 15 reporter to record an interview with some overseas visitors. The iron railing gate was locked, but he was prepared for it. He had brought with him a locksmith's small tool-kit; an abiding interest in crime detection breeds some useful, if criminal, knowledge. He had used his skill on several news assignments, much to the admiration of the reporters he had worked with.

He unlocked the gate, but left it closed, just in case a guard came round on patrol. A couple of hundred yards away up to his left was Government House, the residence of the State Governor; a similar distance away to his right and below him was a construction site for the new harbour tunnel. A security patrol might come down this far, but he had to take that risk.

He went back and sat down on top of the steps, close to the base of the railing fence that ran along the top of the bluff, He took out the Tikka and assembled it, handling it almost affectionately; he had loved guns all his life. Then he affixed the 'scope, an 8 x 56 Schmidt-Bender; it was not an infra-red night 'scope, but it was good enough at night so long as the target was illuminated or standing against a light. Though he had made a mistake in shooting Mardi Jack when she had been outlined against the light. He had been as annoyed at himself at his incompetence as he had been upset at her unnecessary death.

At one point a young couple started to come up the steps, but he had coughed, they had looked up and seen him and at once turned round and gone back down the few steps they had climbed. When Malone and Waldorf had at last come across the forecourt he had followed them through the telescopic sight, tempted to pick them both off while they were out in the open. But there were cars still coming out from the main entrance to the Opera House, their headlights sweeping across the open space like giant yellow scythes. He waited till his two victims had reached the car parked with a dozen or more others along the low harbour wall. Then he lifted the rifle and peered through the 'scope; both men were clearly visible less than a hundred yards from him. He aimed at the back of Waldorf's head as the singer came round to the near side of the car and looked across the roof of the car at Malone. He felt the tremor run through him that had shaken him on the other occasions; then the usual cold calm had abruptly replaced it. He squeezed the trigger, saw Waldorf stumble, slammed back the bolt again and again, getting off two more shots, knew he had missed Malone and decided it

221

was time to run. For the first time he forgot to pick up the empty cartridge cases.

He picked up the gun-case and raced up the path and into the Gardens. Over on his left he could see lights in the staff quarters of Government House; he hoped no security guard came out of there and tried to stop him; he did not want to kill another innocent victim. He kept running, not looking back to see if Malone was following him. He came to a gate that led out and down to Macquarie Street. He fumbled for his locksmith's kit, took out a pick and unlocked the gate. He was breathing heavily, sweating despite the cold night, trembling again. He looked back now, could see no sign of Malone in the deep shadows of the trees. He paused, took three deep breaths and tried to steady himself. Then he removed the 'scope, hastily took the Tikka apart, put both into the gun-case and stepped out into Macquarie Street, drawing the gate to behind him.

Driving home he felt none of the elation he had felt after the other murders; instead, he felt almost as drained as he had when he had learned he had killed an innocent woman instead of Horrie O'Brien. That had been a dreadful shock; he was a killer, but he could suffer for the innocent who died. He had almost decided then that enough was enough. Then the next day O'Brien's photo had appeared in the newspapers on his way into a NCSC hearing and Malloy had known that he could never rest until he had completed the task he had set himself.

It was O'Brien who, unwittingly, had been responsible for the hit list. Those shadowy betrayers of years ago, the cadets who had thrown Malloy out of the police academy, had taken shape again; he had even heard the echo of their laughter as they had turned the fire hose on him and forced him out into the street where he had almost been run down by a car. He had remembered, so clearly that the memory was like being scratched with jagged glass, being called before the Superintendent at lunchtime the next day, of being interrogated and then, an hour later, being told he was dismissed as a cadet. All that had been almost buried till six months ago when he had suddenly recognized who Brian Boru O'Brien was.

He had read about the high-flying entrepreneur, but he had

never had to film him; O'Brien, it seemed, never gave interviews. Then one day at the races at Randwick, when he and a reporter had been sent out to film an interview with a leading jockey coming back after his umpteenth suspension, the reporter had pointed out O'Brien in the saddling paddock. It had taken him a moment or two to recognize him; then the bony, laughing face of years ago had burst out of the shadows of almost-dead memory. He saw O'Brien throw back his head and laugh and, as if in a nightmare, heard the sound down the years as O'Brien turned the fire hose on him. The effect on Malloy had been such that the reporter had looked at him with concern.

'What's the matter, mate? You going to faint or something?'

'No. No, I'm okay. I should wear a hat. The sun's getting to my bald spot.'

'You ought to put some of your beard on your head, you've got enough to spare. Okay, there's our hoop, let's go and talk to him. He's been outed so many times they have to introduce him to the horses again each time he comes back.' And they had gone across to the jockey, but not before Malloy had taken another hard look at O'Brien again. It was the same man, all right, who had led the laughter against him all those years ago.

And then, on the way home, the other five men, whose names at least he had never forgotten, came slipping back into his mind, like guerrillas who expected no ambush. He had brooded about them all weekend, managing to hide his preoccupation from Julie; and on the Monday he had begun tracking down his enemies, as they had once again become. It had been easy to find Harry Gardner; he had simply phoned all the H. Gardners in the Sydney phone directory; the eleventh he had called had been *his* Harry Gardner. As soon as Gardner had said yes, he had once been in the police force, starting as a cadet at the academy in 1965, Malloy had hung up. If Harry Gardner had moved to another State and stayed there, or had not come back to his home town, he might still be alive. Malloy doubted that his urge for revenge would have made him travel to the ends of the earth, or even of Australia, to kill a man he hated.

He had killed the men in no special order. O'Brien's success had added something more scalding than salt to that wound of long ago; in a different field, O'Brien had achieved what he, Malloy, had dreamed of being, one of those at the top. True, O'Brien now looked like being toppled by the NCSC, but that did not matter: he had achieved what he had set out to do and it would be no satisfaction for Malloy if some government quango destroyed O'Brien. Malone was a different case; he was still on his way up. But Malloy had learned that the Detective-Inspector was certain of steady promotion, that he was so highly regarded in the Department that some day he might even be Police Commissioner. The job that Malloy, all those years ago, in the visions of youth, had dreamed of.

When he had reached home last night Julie was asleep. Or pretending to be: this morning he was not so sure. He had undressed in the dark and got into bed beside her. He had kissed her tenderly on her dark hair, and she had just stirred, then turned over away from him. He had lain on his back for a while, running the murder through his mind as he might run a tape through an editing machine. He still felt drained and he wondered why. Was he running out of anger and hatred? He had drifted off into sleep before he could find an answer, but when he had woken this morning he had known the task had to be completed.

Now, he got up and stood beside Julie, drying up the dishes while she washed. They had a dish-washer, but Julie used it only during the week, when they were both working; at weekends, she washed up after every meal.

'When you've finished the book, would you like me to type it up for you?' She worked as a secretary for a furniture designer and manufacturer; their flat was full of comfortable, traditional furniture, but her employer was an avant-garde designer and she spent her working day amongst chrome and glass and abstract sculpture. 'I can put it through the word-processor.'

'We'll see.' All he had to do was find three hundred pages of manuscript.

He looked out the kitchen window at the grass tennis court next door; the neighbour, a prominent lawyer, was playing tennis with two daughters and a son. He and his wife had six children, all living at home in the big two-storeyed house, and Malloy knew that Julie sometimes longed for that sort of home life. She had been brought up in a large house in Adelaide, had had six brothers and sisters, and she had never really become accustomed to living in a two-bedroom flat with only him to care for. He did not dislike Wollstonecraft, a tree-clothed inner suburb, but he often yearned for life in a country town again, to go out with a gun hunting rabbits or duck. But then, he told himself, what Police Commissioner would live in a small country village like Minnamook?

'Are you on stand-by today?' Julie asked.

'I don't know till I call in. If I'm not, how'd you like a day in the country? We'll take a picnic lunch.'

'Sure, it's just the day for it. Where'll we go?'

'Not too far. How about somewhere out the back of Camden? I can do some bird-watching.'

TEN

1

'A lot of owners look on their horses as toys,' said O'Brien. 'Though they'd never admit it. But they're like kids with their dolls – they get them out and play with them.'

Malone, seated on the verandah beside O'Brien, looked out on the visitors, thirty or forty of them, who had come up to Cossack Lodge for Sunday brunch and the weekly opportunity to look at their profligacy on the hoof. A non-racing man, he had never understood the gambling urge or the desire to splurge money on anything so unreliable as a thoroughbred horse. Once, during the boring hours of a stake-out, Clements had tried to explain to him that the odds were not as bad as he supposed, but he had remained unconvinced. There were a hundred horses here on the stud, plus those on short-term agistment, and O'Brien had admitted that only one in ten might prove a worthwhile investment. Malone, a cautious man with a penny, liked better odds than that.

But he was not really concerned with the fortunes of the horses' owners. 'I wish you could have put off this brunch.'

'It's a regular thing, Scobie. They expect it. They like to come up here and talk to the stud-master and show how knowledgeable they are and how shrewd they've been in their buying. Besides, after what was in this morning's papers about the hit list, they'd have come anyway. Look at them – they're giving you and me as much attention as their horses and mares.'

'Well, I guess that's something, an Aussie cop getting as much attention as a racehorse. You think they'll ask for my autograph?' He looked down again at the well-dressed crowd moving between the stables and the white railings of the paddocks. 'Have you considered the possibility that one of them could be Frank Blizzard?'

O'Brien turned his head. 'Yes, I considered that. They've all been checked at the gate, they're all regulars plus a few of their own friends who they had to name. But yes, one of 'em *could* be Blizzard. But I don't think he's going to try his luck in front of so many witnesses. I've known all these people ever since I got into the racing game three or four years ago. Before I started the stud. If one of them was Blizzard, he'd have killed me before this.' He was surprised at his own coolness as he said it.

Malone said nothing for a while, then: 'If you go down the drain, will you lose the stud?'

For a moment or two it looked as if O'Brien would not answer that. He stared out at the landscape, where patches of spring green were beginning to appear on the brown hills in the distance. A black horse stood alone on the far side of a distant paddock, as still as if carved from rock; it drew the eye away from the chatter and movement down by the paddock railings. He would regret losing this property; not because it was another possession but because here he had begun to find a certain peace. Something he had come to realize only this weekend.

At last he nodded. 'It's going to be bought, everything at rock-bottom prices, just enough for the ordinary shareholders to get their money back. I'll come out with bugger-all.'

'Bugger-all?'

O'Brien smiled wryly. 'Well, maybe not *all*. I've got a little stashed away that they can't touch.'

'In the Cook Islands or the Caymans?'

O'Brien raised an amused eyebrow. 'You know the hideaways. No, not there, but somewhere.'

Malone felt an itch of sympathy for the man beside him and wondered why. O'Brien was representative of everything he despised in today's society, the entrepreneur who used every promotion and tax dodge that presented themselves, for whom conscience was like an appendix, excisable. Malone did not envy him his wealth, whatever was left of it, nor his life style; nor did he himself suffer from the national harvester's disease, the cutting down of tall poppies. His contempt went deeper than that,

227

he was afflicted with an old-fashioned morality that allowed no qualifications. Yet, and he was troubled by the feeling, he did not want to see O'Brien completely destroyed. Somewhere within the man a spark of unselfishness had begun to glow.

'Do you have enough to take care of you and Anita for the rest of your lives?'

O'Brien smiled again at that, but it was a sad not a wry smile. He spread his big hands in a who-knows? gesture.

Anita had called him yesterday afternoon from Canberra and they had talked for an hour. Malone had been out in the living room watching a rugby league telecast. The sound had been turned up, as if Malone had wanted the roar of the crowd and the galloping clichés of the commentators ('a shock try adjacent to the uprights!') to drown out any remarks by O'Brien on the bedroom phone. He had been glad that Malone could not hear him: he and Anita had come closer to outright argument than they ever had before.

She had said, 'I'm going to leave Philip. He can divorce me if he wishes, but I don't think he will, not till after the next election, anyway.' As if the voters were some sort of marriage counselling service. 'We'll just announce an amicable separation, I think that's what they call it.'

'No.'

'Yes!'

'No, you're not going to throw your life away on me –'

'What life? I haven't had a life of my own since Philip came into politics. I've been married to a man I haven't loved for, I don't know, for four or five years. I've been the patroness of committees that think of me as no more than a figurehead, always on show –'

'You're more than that and you know it. Countries need a First Lady –'

'I'm not the First Lady, the Governor-General's wife is that. I'm just the first reserve.'

'Australia's women think you're the First Lady.' He was sounding like a patriot, a guise that fitted him like a clown's baggy trousers; even in his own ears he sounded comically pompous. 'Sweetheart, stop putting yourself down –'

228

'Darling –' She had made up her mind, though a woman's resolution is never set in concrete: she is too intelligent for that and concrete, anyway, is a man's medium. 'I'm not going on with Philip the way things are at the moment –'

'Have you told him about us?'

'No. But he's guessed there's someone else – I've moved out of our bedroom –'

'What do The Lodge staff think of that?'

'It's none of their business. In any case, I think they're all Labour voters –'

'So it must be all around Parliament House by now.' All at once he was too weary to continue trying to protect her. He relaxed, smiling to himself, lay back on the bed with the phone still propped against his ear.

'Are you still there? What are you thinking?'

'I'm just smiling at the thought of the cook and the maids and the butler being Labour voters. I once had a butler – he was the biggest right-wing conservative you could ever meet, he thought Churchill was a pinko –'

'Then why did he work for you?'

'He lasted a week.'

'You fired him?'

'He fired me. I was 'way below his class.'

She was too shrewd for him. 'You're trying to change the subject. I'm leaving Philip, whatever you say. I want to come up to the stud to talk it over with you –'

'No!' He sat up, no longer smiling, desperate again to protect her.

'I'll wear my wig and my tinted glasses –'

'Anita, the place is crawling with cops and security men – Inspector Malone is here for the weekend –'

'You didn't tell me!' Now she was fearful for him. 'What's happening, for God's sake? When you called me this morning about Sebastian Waldorf's murder –' She was silent for a moment, as if all at once she realized the horror of what she was saying. Then she went on, her voice unsteady, 'You didn't say anything about *all* of you – and the police, too? – all of you going up to the stud. You just said you were going up there for the weekend. Darling, what's *happening*?'

229

'We're just playing safe,' he lied. She wouldn't understand what they did to lure tigers out of the jungle in Sumatra or wherever the hell it was.

'Playing safe? God, why do men always have to talk in game terms? This – this *murderer* Blizzard isn't *playing*! He's trying to *kill* you!'

The argument had gone on; like all lovers' arguments, when they are truly in love, it had gone round in circles. Finally, angrily, she had seen his point: she could not come to the stud where she would be surely recognized. She said, laughing sourly, 'Think of the jokes. The Prime Minister's mare visiting a stud –'

'Don't,' he said, stricken for her.

She relented, began to weep, something he had never seen her do and, indeed, did not see now. 'Are you crying?' he said.

'No,' she said after a moment; but women have never learned to stop weeping without sniffling, just as men have never learned to turn a deaf ear to it. He heard her blow her nose, then she said, 'I'll be up in Sydney on Wednesday. We'll meet at Joanna's again. You and I have to sit down and talk. Seriously.'

'Yes,' he promised, lying again. Whatever plans she would propose, he had no counter-plans. Under a death sentence or two, it was difficult to plan a future. Especially if one also had to go to jail first.

He came back to today, Sunday, saw Malone leaning forward and peering down towards the stables. 'What's the matter?'

'Those Chinese, are they clients of yours?'

O'Brien sat forward. 'Yes. The little round man is Sir Keye Chai – he's a big wheel in Hong Kong. He comes down once a month on business, then he comes up here – he has half a dozen horses here –' Then he stopped as he saw the familiar figure amongst the other three Chinese. He looked at Malone. 'You know the guy in the suede jacket and the checked cap?'

'So do you,' said Malone matter-of-factly. 'Leslie Chung. Does he have any horses here?'

O'Brien hesitated; but he no longer wanted to lie to Malone. 'No.'

'So what's he doing here? Give me the truth, Brian, no bullshit.'

230

What's the point of hiding it any longer? I'll be telling it all in front of the NCSC on Tuesday. 'He's one of the guys I was telling you about. Laundered money.'

'Anything else?'

'We-ell, yes. He feels I did him out of a profit on some shares.'

'You pick some beauts to fool around with. Is he one of those who tried to have you bumped off?'

O'Brien shrugged, looking down again at the four Chinese as they came out from the stables and moved towards the linen-clad tables and the chairs set out on the wide lawn in front of the house. 'Probably. But you could never prove anything against him. Has he got a record?'

'None that I know of. Half a dozen squads – Fraud, Homicide, the Drug Squad, you name it – we've been trying to nail him for years. But no go. He's lily-white. How much did he put through your bank?'

'I wouldn't know – George Bousakis could tell you that. Several million at least. He never came to see us personally, it was always handled through a go-between.'

'Who else is in cahoots with him?' O'Brien hesitated and Malone said impatiently, 'Come on, Brian – quit stalling! You owe me. You said you were going to open up everything on Tuesday – you owe it to me to tell me first!'

'What'll you do if I give you their names?'

'I don't know,' Malone confessed. 'If we manage to get Blizzard first, maybe I'll go after them then.'

'What for?'

'Conspiracy to murder.'

'You'd have Buckley's chance of proving it.'

'Maybe. But we've already traced Gotti to one crim, a cove named Tony Lango. Was Lango one of your depositors?'

O'Brien hesitated again; then he nodded. 'Yes. There were two others, Dennis Pelong and Jack Aldwych.'

Malone pursed his lips, but did not whistle. 'Christ, why didn't you dig up Al Capone and invite him in, too? Do you have a death wish?'

'I really didn't know that much about them when I first started with them. Remember, I'd been away for years.'

231

'Did you diddle them on the shares, too?' O'Brien nodded; and Malone shook his head at another of the fools who made his job harder. 'Anyone else?'

'Like who? Aren't those four enough?'

'Like Arnold Debbs.'

'No. Scobie, Arnold is shifty and has his hand out for anything you'll put into it, he's the most up-market panhandler I've ever met. But he wouldn't be in any conspiracy to murder. He's gutless.'

'Gotti went to see him in Canberra. It's the gutless ones who go in for conspiracy. They hire someone else to do the job.'

'Are you saying Chung and the other three crims are gutless?' But he knew it was a frivolous question. 'No, I know you're not. They gave up doing their own dirty work years ago. They're like generals in a war.'

'Righto, we'll strike Debbs off the list for the time being. But the other four . . . If you name them on Tuesday, there's going to be more flying off the fan than the Sewerage Board has ever had to clean up.'

'I'll be naming Debbs and his missus, too, about insider trading.'

'You're really going to spread it, aren't you? Are you doing it for the good of your soul, as my mum would say?'

'You don't sound impressed.'

'Would you be if you heard me saying what you've just said? You're pointing the finger in every direction, trying to cop a plea.'

'You fellers put it to villains every day in the week, if you want to catch the big fry.'

'That doesn't mean we have to like the principle.' Then Malone looked at him carefully. 'Brian, are you after my approval?'

'Yes,' said O'Brien quietly. 'It would help.'

Malone sat back in his chair, stared down at the four Chinese now seated at one of the tables where a waiter from the hired catering staff was bringing them their brunch. All the other tables had a woman, sometimes two or three, at them, and the four Chinese looked like a small funeral group amidst the chatter and gaiety. Champagne glasses were being raised around them, but the men from Hong Kong were drinking only tea. They knew better, Malone guessed, than to be stirred by the sight of one of their horses galloping around a paddock where there was nothing to beat. The Chinese were one of the great gambling races of the world, but they still listened to a bookie called Confucius.

'Brian, you've been a bastard most of your life. You've tried to take the mickey out of everything I've believed in. Decency, a fair go for the other bloke – well, never mind . . .' He didn't want to lecture O'Brien. One can wear a clerical collar and sound pious; turn the collar round and one sounds sanctimonious. 'Now it's like watching a leopard peeling off his coat.'

'Maybe that's why I feel so bloody cold,' said O'Brien, trying for a smile. 'We're getting literary.'

'What else would you expect of two Irishmen? My old man's never read a book in his life, but pour half a dozen beers down him and he thinks he's James Joyce. What about your old man?' As soon as he said it, it sounded like a brutal question.

O'Brien's face went flat. 'I called him the other day. I don't know why – I just thought . . . It was no use. He just said I was where I deserved to be. Then he hung up.'

'Your mum?'

'She's dead.'

Malone turned his face away, stared off into the distance, seeing nothing. He was infected with charity; the panhandlers of the world would always make him think twice. O'Brien had his hand out and he couldn't refuse him; he looked: 'All right, I approve. But you let me down, Brian, and so help me Christ . . .' He tried to sound threatening, but how could you threaten a man who might be dead before the week was out? He stood up. 'Let's go down and say hullo to your guests.'

O'Brien rose. 'Which ones?'

'Les Chung and company.'

They walked down across the lawn, between the two kurra-jongs trimmed like English ornamental trees, and out to the tables. Owners and their wives and girl-friends, the women distinguishable from each other by their self-assured possessive-ness, as if they were owners of their menfolk, greeted O'Brien with wide smiles and offers of a glass of his own champagne. He

233

was *persona grata* here on his own property, he was as pure-bred as one of his own stallions, no one would admit to knowing what graft was. O'Brien returned the greetings, but did not stop. He led Malone to the table where Sir Keye Chai presided with all the confidence that comes with great wealth and a certain Oriental sense of superiority. These visits to the barbarians Down Under made the British in Hong Kong more bearable.

'Mr Malone –' he said, putting out a hand as smooth as silk; O'Brien had not introduced the detective with his rank. 'You are interested in horses?'

'Not really, Sir Keye. I'm just a friend of Mr O'Brien's. An old schoolmate.'

'Mr Malone is a detective-inspector,' said Leslie Chung, who had risen, like all the others, and shaken Malone's hand with a formal politeness. 'He is one of our State's finest.'

Malone gave him a sharp look, but Chung's mile was bland. 'Do you race horses, Mr Chung?'

'Never. I have tried to tell Sir Keye there are too many imponderables in the racing game – corrupt jockeys, corrupt trainers, horses that break down without warning –'

'Mr Chung has no faith,' said Sir Keye, whose only faith was in himself. 'I was educated in Hong Kong, he went to school in Shanghai. He was taught all the wrong things. They gave him Hsun Tzu to read. Too bad. Hsun Tzu once wrote, "If a man is clever, he will surely be a robber; if he is brave, he will be a bandit . . ." You read the wrong books, Leslie.'

He looked at Chung and the two men smiled at each other with all the innocence of born-again infants. He knows how Chung makes his money, Malone thought; and wondered how Sir Keye made his. But the British in Hong Kong had not only given him the right books to read, whatever they were, they had given him a knighthood and a place in their own society. Malone, who had inherited a little of his father's rabid anti-British feeling, suspected that the British knew there were more ways to trap a tiger than by shooting it. But maybe Sir Keye Chai was a totally honest man; why was he so suspicious of him? That was Con in him again, the racism he tried so hard to smother.

'May I see you a moment, Mr O'Brien?' said Chung and took O'Brien's arm and led him away.

Malone looked after them, then, because he could think of no polite way of saying no, accepted Sir Keye's invitation to join him for a cup of tea.

'Indian tea, I'm afraid. A little strong for our taste, but then we find everything in Australia is like that.' Again there was the polite bland smile. Malone envied the Chinese their finesse at insults. 'Or perhaps your own tastes are subtle, Mr Malone?'

'I'm afraid not, Sir Keye. I'm part-Irish.'

'Remarkable people, the Irish,' said Sir Keye, letting one of his companions pour the tea. They were both burly men and Malone, more security-conscious than normal, wondered if they were bodyguards. 'Two thousand years in the bogs and still treading water.'

Oh, Dad would love you! Bodyguards or no bodyguards, you'd be on your back in less than a minute.

Out beyond the rows of stables, where Chung had led him, O'Brien was not being insulted, just threatened.

'A word of warning, Mr O'Brien. A Chinese philosopher once said, If you keep your trap shut, you'll never catch anything, least of all yourself.'

'Who said that? Hsun Tzu?'

'No, actually it was myself.'

O'Brien's smile was so thin it was almost indiscernible. 'Do you guys play at being clones of Confucius?'

'I could be blunter, Mr O'Brien, but I don't want any violent reaction from you. Not in front of your guests. Take what's coming to you on Tuesday, Mr O'Brien, and don't try to drag others down with you. You have already done the dirty on us. Don't try it again.'

'It was you people who put me in with the NCSC.'

'What did you expect? You're not dealing with little old ladies and their pension cheques.'

'Who are you speaking for? Just yourself or Debbs and the others?'

'Certainly not Debbs – he can look after himself, I hope. Nor for Pelong and Lango.'

235

'So it's just you and Jack Aldwych?' O'Brien suddenly felt cold, though the sun was warm on his back. 'You're an odd couple.'

Chung shrugged his slim shoulders. 'Only temporarily. We'll go our own ways again after Tuesday. Be sensible, O'Brien. Keep your trap shut. Otherwise . . . Let's go back and join your friend Inspector Malone. Why is he here?'

'Someone else is trying to kill me.'

'You do have troubles, haven't you? Well, good luck. I think you may need it, one way or another.'

Later, when all the horse owners had gone, Malone sat out on the verandah and waited for O'Brien, after saying goodbye to the last of the guests, to come up and join him. The catering staff were carting away the tables and chairs, and out in the paddocks the horses were settling down after all the attention they had received. The day was abruptly peaceful again, the landscape soothing; but Malone could feel rage and impatience beginning to swell in him. It was not the visitors who had caused it. It was the *expected* visitor who had not appeared.

'Why the bloody hell doesn't he come?'

'Who?' O'Brien was still preoccupied with Chung and his threat. Then he looked out over the stud, following the direction of Malone's gaze towards the distant road, as if that was the route they expected their killer to take. 'Oh, *Blizzard*.'

'Who else did you think?' Malone waited till O'Brien sat down beside him; only then did he notice the latter's abstraction. 'What did Les Chung have to say?'

There was no need now to keep secrets from Malone; instead, there was a need to tell him. Not to tell the police, but to tell a friend. 'He's promised to do me in if I open my mouth on Tuesday.'

'Kill you?' O'Brien nodded. 'He was blatant as that?'

'Well, not exactly. But he didn't have to spell it out. He's not that dumb and neither am I.'

'I could have him picked up.'

'What'd be the use, Scobie? He'd deny it. It'd be my word against his and who d'you think they'be believe right now? Forget it.'

'What are you going to do Tuesday? Tell everything?'

'I don't know,' said O'Brien; then added after a pause, 'I guess it depends on whether Blizzard catches up with us between now and then.'

Then a car came up the long driveway and both men, as if the mention of Blizzard's name had made them nervously alert, stood up. Malone had seen it travelling fast down the distant road, but the gates were hidden from the house by a grove of trees and he had not seen it turn into the stud. Now it swung in before the house and Clements got out.

When he was still some distance from them he almost shouted, 'I think we've got a trace on Blizzard at last!'

2

Clements turned out into the narrow country road and saluted the two security men on the gates. It was a brand new unmarked car and so Malone had not recognized it. 'Harry Danforth saw me taking delivery of it yesterday morning and got a bit shirty. He's still got his old one.'

'Why would they give him a new one? They're still hoping he'll resign. Does he know you've got the lead on Blizzard?'

'No, I didn't have it when I saw him. What he doesn't know won't hurt us or him.'

Clements drove on up the road, through the long shadows thrown by the long line of trees bordering the stud. They turned left on to another road that led to the main highway three miles away; they drove between what looked to be a plantation of trees. The road was badly pot-holed from the long wet summer and autumn, the worst in living memory; twice Clements had to swerve at the last moment to avoid holes that looked like baby craters. This electorate was represented in the State parliament by a National Party member and no Labour government, least of all Hans Vanderberg's, was going to waste money on smooth riding for voters who elected a conservative.

The road dipped down into a cutting between steep rock-ribbed banks, went into the dusk under a narrow wooden bridge and came up to run for another half-mile before it came out between open paddocks where cattle grazed and a boy and his father flew a model aeroplane that went into a dive as the police car went past and crashed with a sickening jolt into the ground and disintegrated. Malone, looking back, could imagine the boy's cry of anguish. The boy, running desperately through the long grass, could have been Tom.

They drove on, leaving the boy and his father behind. In the far distance could be seen the outskirts of the town of Camden. The light was a sort of golden silver and Malone could see nothing moving in it now, not even a bird. The world had stopped and, beyond the hum of the car, was dead silence.

Malone slowly began to relax. He had said nothing since they had left the stud gates and Clements, sensing the tension in him, had kept quiet. Now he glanced sideways at Malone.

'I think he knows you're up here at the stud. It's a guess, but I'd bet on it.'

'I'm not just going to sit and wait for him. I'm too jumpy, Russ. Now I know who he is.'

He had felt no surprise when Clements had told him and O'Brien about the lead to Colin Malloy; and had been surprised that he had taken it so calmly. He had not suspected Malloy and yet now he knew the TV cameraman should have been on the list of suspects. But when you were chasing a ghost, it was difficult to add flesh to the picture. He realized now that he had had no real list of suspects, that he had been no more than seeking a faceless man in a huge faceless crowd.

Clements had told him and O'Brien, 'I went up to Channel 15 and talked to the news editor there, a guy named Katzka. I asked how the news crews were rostered and he said a cameraman usually worked with the same reporter and sound-man – in Malloy's case, it was a sound-*girl*. But on two of those clips we saw, Malloy was with a *different* reporter, Katzka said. Malloy wasn't originally rostered for those jobs, but he volunteered. I asked Katzka if that was unusual and he said he didn't mind if crews swapped shifts, just so long as someone was there to do the job. That got me thinking.'

238

Clements had been carrying a book when he got out of the car; he had held it out to Malone. *'Farewell, My Lovely.'*

'So?' Malone had taken the book.

'A leading character in that is named Malloy – Moose Malloy. But Blizzard – I *know* it's him – wasn't stupid enough to call himself Moose. He just picked a name from his favourite author.'

O'Brien had taken the book from Malone and was leafing through it. 'Why not Marlowe? He was Chandler's private eye.'

Malone took his time, dredging up the results of experience. 'Too obvious. When people choose an alias, one they're going to use permanently, nine times out of ten it's not a random choice. It's usually a name with some association, something that's easier to respond to. You pick a name you've never heard before and the chances are you won't react when someone calls you by that name. Blizzard would've been smart enough to work that out.'

'What are you going to do?'

'You stay here, don't go outside the house. Get all your security men and our four blokes on duty till I get back. Russ and I are going to see Mr Malloy. You know where he lives, Russ?'

'He lives in Wollstonecraft. He and his wife, there are no kids, have a flat in Temple Road.'

'We'll radio in for some men from the local region – we don't want them thinking we're busting in unannounced on their turf. We'd better have some strong back-up too, just in case. Ask for a squad from SWOS. But tell them and the local fellers to hold off, stay out of Malloy's street, till we arrive. I don't want all hell breaking loose before we get there.'

Clements had gone out to make the radio call from his car while Malone went in to get his gun and raincoat. O'Brien followed him into the house.

'I'd like to go with you.'

Malone paused as he strapped on his shoulder holster. 'No, this isn't any of your business.'

'I'm one of the intended victims. For Christ's sake, don't tell me it's none of my business!' O'Brien was suddenly agitated, tension breaking out of him in a mixture of rage and fear.

239

'No, it isn't, Brian,' Malone said firmly. 'If I let you come with me and you were killed or even wounded, it'd be the end of me in the Department. The police have copped enough crap this past year – some of it deserved, I know, but not all of it. I don't want more flung at us. You saw what the papers did today to the hit list story. I don't know where they got it from, we've done our best to keep it as quiet as possible, but they made a circus of it.'

'Maybe Blizzard fed them the story?'

Malone put on his jacket over the holster. 'Could be. I hadn't thought about him. But if he is this bloke Malloy at Channel 15, he'd know who to call at the newspapers, he'd know how to feed them enough without giving himself away.'

'Well, I still want to come now.' O'Brien was dogged. His life was coming to an end and he was going to be removed from its climaxes.

'No. I mean it, Brian – *no*.' He was sympathetic to O'Brien's frame of mind; but you could kill people with sympathy, even if only indirectly. 'You stay here and worry about Les Chung and his mates. If we get Blizzard, you'll be the first to know. I promise.'

O'Brien stood silent and motionless for a moment like a sullen child; then he put out his hand. 'Good luck. Try and take him alive. I'd just like to kick him in the balls while he's still alive. Not for myself, but for Mardi Jack.'

Malone grinned. 'I'll give him one for you.'

Then as the detective went out the front door O'Brien said, 'Look after yourself, Scobie.'

Malone nodded to a friend, recognizing the real concern in the long bony face. *What a pity you were a bastard for so long, Horrie.*

Now, as Clements, foot hard down on the accelerator, blue light flashing on the roof, put them on the road to Sydney, Malone took the radio microphone, switched to the Police Centre channel. 'Put me on to Constable Graham in Homicide.' Then he looked at Clements. 'He's on duty?'

'I called him in as soon as I knew I was coming out here. He was on his way to see Norths play Penrith.'

'Then he's out of luck.' But once again he admired the efficiency of the big untidy man beside him.

Andy Graham came on the line. 'What's happening, Inspector?'

Malone explained the situation. 'Nothing may come of it, Andy, so keep it quiet. Get in touch with Superintendent Danforth, but wait at least half an hour. Give Russ and me time to get to Wollstonecraft.'

Graham sometimes had to have things spelled out for him; but, like all police officers after twelve months in the force, he knew the urge to protect one's own turf. Chief superintendents are like generals, better behind a desk than on horseback. 'I'll have trouble finding him,' he chuckled. 'Being Sunday . . .'

'Sorry you've had to miss your footy. What's the score?' He could hear a radio in the background.

'Penrith scored in the first five minutes. Six-nil. That's all so far, there's only five minutes to go . . . No, it's all over.'

Despite the Sunday afternoon traffic, Clements made good time to Wollstonecraft. It was still light when he pulled the car in, blue light no longer flashing, under the trees that lined the street where Malloy and his wife lived. He and Malone got out of the car and looked around. Except for a dozen or so cars parked along both sides of the long street, the neighbourhood could have been deserted.

'Good,' said Malone. 'Now where are the North Sydney fellers and SWOS?'

They walked round the corner into a cross-street and there were four police cars, a SWOS van, three TV vans and two press cars, plus a small crowd of residents held back by another police car parked across the middle of the roadway with a uniformed policeman standing on either side of it.

'Christ Almighty! What do they think this is – the Charge of the Light Brigade?' Malone looked around for a senior officer and at once a detective in plainclothes and a SWOS sergeant came down to him and Clements. 'What the bloody hell's going on? I thought you got the message to keep this quiet!'

'Sorry, Inspector.' The detective, from North Sydney, was named Leo Safire; he was tall and thin and naturally lugubrious-looking. Right now he could not have looked unhappier; though he had known Malone for several years, he knew enough not to call him Scobie at the moment. 'I don't know who gave the media the word, but they arrived right on our tail. I've had to threaten to shoot 'em to keep 'em outa sight.'

'Shoot 'em anyway,' said Clements.

'After we've got Blizzard,' said Malone. He looked at the SWOS man. Sergeant Killop was a chunky man in his late twenties, dressed in the SWOS uniform of dark trousers, sweater and peaked cap; Malone could imagine him hurling himself at doors, not waiting for an axe or a battering-ram. 'What have you got, Bill?'

'I've got five men, Inspector. That enough?'

Christ, I hope so. 'We'll take it carefully at first, okay? Maybe around in Malloy's street, the neighbours don't know yet what's happening. Are the TV vans sending out anything live?'

'No,' said Safire. 'I've got a guy standing by each van. If he sees anything going out, he'd been told to arrest them on the spot. We'll drum up some charge.'

'Try obscene language,' said Clements with a sour grin. 'That always works.'

'What about the other people in Malloy's flats?' said Killop. 'You think we oughta warn them?'

'How do we do that without Malloy hearing the hubbub?' said Malone. He went back to the corner and looked through the trees at the tall block, one of three, about fifty yards down on the other side of the street. 'What would there be – sixteen flats? What floor is Malloy on?'

'I checked that,' said Safire. 'Their flat's on the sixth floor. There are two flats to a floor, each of them with a balcony looking south.'

Malone looked up at the sixth floor; both flats showed lighted windows against the gathering dusk. 'Which one is his?'

'Number 11, on the right.'

'Righto, Russ and I'll go up first. You and two of your men, Bill, come up behind us to cover us. Send your other two men around the back, in case there's some back stairs. Leo, go down there by our car and stand by the radio, in case we need more support. For the moment, let's keep everyone else back here. Especially the bloody media. What's inside the building?'

'A lift in the front lobby, just the one – it holds six people at a squeeze. There's a flight of stairs that goes all the way to the top, circling the lift as it goes up.'

'Righto, give me one of your men, have him stay down in the lobby by the stairs. If anything goes wrong up on the sixth floor, he'll hear the commotion down the stair-well. He can give you the word and then you'd better come running.'

The men were deployed and Malone and Clements, accompanied by Killop and two of his SWOS men, went into the block of flats and took the lift up to the sixth floor. Malone and Clements both drew their Smith & Wessons; the three SWOS men had 12-gauge shotguns. They were all bulky men and the SWOS officers were made even bulkier by their flak jackets; it was a tight squeeze in the lift and all the guns were held high like iron bouquets. Malone could feel nervousness taking hold of him, as if he were a novice at this. He had been in this situation on more occasions than he cared to number; but this was the first occasion where he would be coming face to face with a man who had sworn to kill him, where he, and not someone outside the police force, was the stated target. He took a deep breath and saw Clements look at him.

'The waiting's over,' said Clements and made it sound reassuring.

3

On the Saturday Malloy and Julie had picnicked behind a screen of trees on a hill a mile from Cossack Lodge stud. He had brought his camera equipment with him, carrying it as he always did. It was typical of him that, like the policeman he had wanted to be, he never saw himself as fully off-duty; news, like crime or an emergency, did not fit into a roster. He had brought a telescope, a Tasco terrestrial 93T with 30 x 90 magnification; at a mile, it was claimed, a viewer could tell the difference between natural and false teeth in a smile. He had bought it when he had first decided to kill his betrayers of long ago. He had told Julie, who supervised their budget and queried any major expenditure, that he was taking up bird-watching. He had no interest in birds and she had expressed surprise. He had lied elaborately, throwing native birds' names around like a mad ornithologist; he had known all the birds in the Minnamook district when he was a boy and he had remembered their names, though he couldn't remember exactly what many of them looked like. Still, Julie had been convinced and several times he had taken her out on supposed bird-watching expeditions. He was fortunate in that she saw birds only as carriers of lice, psittacosis and other diseases and left him to go hunting them on his own. Which he pretended to do: he would retire behind some distant trees and sit there reading a paperback detective novel till a reasonable time had passed. It troubled him that he had to lie to Julie, but better to tell her he was bird-watching than man-watching.

Malone, O'Brien and the others had been observed on expeditions on his own; scrutinized from a distance as under a microscope. Like bugs that were to be squashed.

On the Saturday afternoon he had picked up the telescope in its leather case; they had eaten their picnic lunch and he had repacked the cooler. Up in the timber above them a magpie carolled and a sparrowhawk hung in the sky like a floating cross. 'I'm going to see if there are any birds around here.'

'Just so long as they're feathered ones,' she said automatically; it was a joke that was wearing thin, as jokes do, even between people in love. She lay back on the rug they had spread out on the thick grass. 'That sun's so lovely. I'll doze off for a while. I wish we could make love.'

'What?'

'I want to take my clothes off and make love here on a hilltop with the sun on your bum.'

He smiled down at her lying flat on her back, lovely and inviting. 'What if there are other bird-watchers out here somewhere? With their glasses or telescopes on us hard at it?'

'It'd fog up their telescopes.' She smiled like a cat. 'Go on, go and watch your birds. I'll lie here and dream of what you're doing to me.'

He was tempted; sometimes she showed an abandon that was contrary to her public behaviour. Instead, he bent down and kissed her, dodged her lassoing arms, said, 'I'll see you tonight,' and went off up through the trees to the top of the hill. Above him the magpie carolled a musical warning, but he knew how to take care of himself. After all this time and all this success, he was not going to give himself away.

He lay down on the brittle leaves that carpeted the stand of trees, adjusted the telescope and at once saw the familiar figure come out on to the verandah of the main house of the stud. It was Malone; he was joined a minute or two later by the other familiar figure, O'Brien. It was the first time Malloy had come up here to observe the stud; he had not expected his last two targets to be here. He had wanted to study the landscape because he had an unformulated idea that this was where he would like to dispose of O'Brien, who would be the last to die. Here amongst the tangible evidence of his wealth and success.

Malloy put down the telescope because his hands were shaking. Christ, why didn't he have the rifle with him! He would never have another opportunity like this. The distance was extreme, but he would have been able to get closer. He trembled with frustration; then sanity steadied him. If he had been alone, had had the rifle with him, he would have gone down there and taken a suicidal risk that, up till now, he had avoided. Julie, being with him, preventing him from bringing the Tikka, had unwittingly saved him from himself.

He took up the telescope again, watched the two men for a while. Then he slowly scanned the rest of the stud. He soon picked up the security man, Shad, whom he recognized; then he saw the other men, two of them carrying automatic weapons tucked under their arms, all of them wearing pistols at their belt. He realized with a jolt of excitement that they were expecting him!

He stood up, leaned against a tree till the excitement drained out of him. He had a feeling of power, an executioner who could name his own time. Then the cold reason that had protected him so far, that had kept him so many jumps ahead of those trying to trap him, settled firmly on him. He lay down again, trained the telescope on the main house and saw Malone and O'Brien now sitting at a small table eating a late lunch. They were too obvious: they were staking themselves out as lures. They were out in the open and they expected him to come out in the open, too; like some dumb wild animal, he was to fall for the bait of them. He would kill them in his own time and in a place of his own choosing, though he might have to change the murder roster. If Malone and O'Brien wanted to stay together as a single target, they would have to die together.

He went back down through the timber to Julie. He heard the magpie carol again and looked up. Nesting early, it resented his intrusion into its territory. It came down out of a tall tree, dive-bombing him; its dagger beak scraped the top of his head. When it flew up in a steep curve, weaving amongst the trees like a black-and-white shuttle, and came back at him in a second dive he stood and waited for it; he had stood like this as a boy in the fields near Minnamook, testing the quickness of his eye against that of the bird. The magpie came down swiftly, straight at his head; he raised the telescope in its case, ducked at the last moment and hit the bird full across its throat. It wings fluttered wildly, but the magpie was already dead. It thudded to the ground, beating its wings feebly, then was still. He looked down at it without pity or any feeling at all. He was a country boy but, unlike most country boys, he had never had any love for birds or animals; they were part of the scenery, no more.

The telescope was undamaged except for a dent in the leather cylinder. He slung the case over his shoulder and went on down to Julie. She was still lying on her back, eyes closed, seemingly asleep. He knelt down, put a hand up under her sweater and stroked her bra-less breasts.

Her eyes remained closed. 'Fred? Do it some more.'

He squeezed a breast, hard. 'Who's Fred?'

She didn't open her eyes, just let the cat's smile play round her full lips. 'He's someone I've made a date with tonight . . .'

That night he made love to her so fiercely she cried out half a dozen times in painful ecstasy. Afterwards, when she had fallen asleep, he lay and stared at the darkness, wondering if it was the last time he would ever make love to her. Normally he did not suffer from post-coital blues. Those, he had always thought cynically, were the symptoms, not of nascent melancholia but of lack of stamina.

Sunday morning he opened the newspapers to different treatments of the same story. The *Sun-Herald* and the *Sunday Telegraph* each ran a lead story on the hit list. When he had finished reading both of them he knew they were like most Sunday stories, no more than beat-ups, a few facts and a lot of guesswork. The police had fed the press just so much and no more; there was no mention that the murder suspect was an ex-policeman. The Police Department had had some bad publicity from a couple of incidents this year and it was obvious to him that the Department was trying to cover up that an ex-cop was going around killing off other cops. Pride and public relations occasionally conjoin, though the first is a stirring of the spirit and the latter is a stirring of the public's gullibility.

Julie, still in her dressing-gown, mouth bruised from last night's love-making, looking as dissolute as a harlot and liking it, smiled at him above the *Telegraph*, which he had already read. 'Wanna go back to bed, Fred?'

'This afternoon,' he promised. 'When I've got my strength back.'

She smiled lazily, satisfied to wait, and went back to her paper. Then she looked at him again over the top of it. 'You see this? Those killings you covered, they say they're a hit list.'

'It's a beat-up.' He wondered what she would say if he told her the truth, gave her the other two names to complete the list. But he couldn't do that to her. 'You know what the print boys are like, they've got to fill their pages, especially on Sundays. We've heard nothing at the channel.'

She wriggled her shoulders in a mock shiver. 'I hate it whenever I read about *real* murder. It's all right in detective novels, it's, I dunno, somehow removed from you –'

'Turn to the social pages. See if the usual free-loaders have got their photos in the news again.'

After lunch he rang Nick Katzka at Channel 15; the news

247

editor worked every second weekend. 'Am I on stand-by today?'

'No, you're free, Col. There are the usual weekend press releases by the pollies, nothing of any interest to anybody – I dunno why they bother. There's some good overseas items – a train wreck in Holland, a tornado in the States – some nice disaster stuff. See you tomorrow morning.'

'What's on the list for tomorrow?'

'There's the funeral of that singer, what's-her-name, Mardi Jack – there should be some show business faces there. Then there is the funeral of that last cop who was shot, Knoble. They're both being buried out at Botany cemetery. You can cover them both and we'll run 'em in the same item.'

He felt that touch of excitement again, the matador's thrill as the bull's horns graze past his belly. 'Okay, I'll do those. Anything else?'

'Not at the moment. Oh, wait a minute. There was a cop up here this morning asking about you, a Sergeant Clements from Homicide. What've you been up to? He wanted to know your history, whether you volunteered for certain shifts –'

He looked at his hand holding the phone; the knuckles were white. 'Did he ask you not to tell me he was making enquiries?'

'Well, yeah, he did. But you work for us, not them. He wasn't prepared to be specific about anything, so I brushed him off – he got me just as I was getting down to work –'

'Thanks, Nick. It's personal. I lost my temper on a job a week or two ago and said something I shouldn't have.' The lie came smoothly, as if he had rehearsed it. Perhaps he had, subconsciously. He had known that some day, inevitably, there would be questions: from the police or Julie or from that God who, Aunt Elsie had told him, would always be waiting with the final query. 'He's probably decided to do something official about it. You know cops, they can be pretty touchy about us in the media.'

He hung up, stood motionless while his mind settled. He had sounded cool enough on the phone; but now he felt shaken and unsteady. For some time he had known there was the possibility of his being discovered; he also knew the thin line that divided possibility from probability. Fate was supposed to laugh at probability, but Fate always had the last laugh anyway. He had just not expected the net to be thrown so soon. Clements might already be on his way here. Nick Katzka might have to feature his chief cameraman as the lead item on tonight's six o'clock news.

He looked about the living-room where he stood. Julie had made a good home for him here. It was more than just a comfortable stop-over to somewhere better, though they dreamed of a house and a garden and a pool that they would not have to share with others. He earned $45,000 a year with shift work and overtime and Julie earned $23,000; their mortgage was manageable, they had no other major debt, they owned two cars and every year they could afford a holiday on the Barrier Reef or to Fiji or New Zealand. It was a lot to give up and, for the first time, he wondered if his urge for vengeance had been worth it. But then, of course, when he had first drawn up the hit list there had been no thought that he would ever be caught. That had only come later when the momentum of his excitement had taken hold of him.

He went into the bedroom where Julie was taking a shower. He looked at her vague shape through the frosted glass; he hoped she would never become as shadowy as that in his memory. Suddenly he was angry with himself: he had sacrificed too much for stupid revenge! But it was too late.

He slid back the door of the shower as she turned off the water. 'I have to go on a job, up the bush. I'll be away for a couple of days.'

'Oh damn!' She stood glistening and dripping, her body still faintly tanned from last summer; her dark hair, cut short, lay flat and wet on her well-shaped head like a boy's. She had never looked more desirable, he thought with great sadness. 'I thought we could've gone to a movie and then come home and . . .'

He put his arms round her and lifted her out of the shower and kissed her fiercely. Then he let her go. 'No, don't let's get started again . . . I've got to be at the channel in half an hour.'

'Where are you going?'

It was harder to lie to her now, but he managed to grab a town out of the air: 'Boggabilla. There's been another Aboriginal riot.' Blame the Abos for anything: they were always good for a story, even to one's wife. 'I'll be back tomorrow night, Tuesday at the latest.'

She wrapped a terry-towelling gown round her. 'I'll pack for you. What do you want?'

A flak jacket, a getaway jet, 50,000 dollars . . . 'A couple of shirts, underwear, my blue sweater and my corduroys. I'll wear my jeans and my anorak. Do you have any money?'

'About seventy or eighty dollars, I think.'

'Lend it to me. I'll draw some more on my bank card.'

'Why do you need so much? You'll be on expenses, won't you?'

He had slipped up; he was finding it harder and harder to lie to her. He wanted to spill out the truth to her; but there was still the faint hope deep within him that she might never need to know. She was the one thing in the world he wanted to protect. 'Sure, you're right. Hurry up and pack, will you?'

When she had gone out of the bathroom he looked at himself in the mirror. The beard would have to go. He had worn it now for ten years; he would be another man without it. It had not been grown as a disguise; now, he realized, he would be disguised without it. He took out his razor, shaving brush, trimming scissors and put them in his toilet kit. Then he looked in the mirror again and said goodbye to Colin Malloy.

Ten minutes later he said goodbye to Julie at the front door. He tried to make it as casual as possible, as just a repeat of dozens of other farewells he had made when he had left for trips out of town. She was still wearing only the terry-towelling robe, but he did not attempt to feel beneath it. He was saying goodbye to more than her sex.

'Be careful,' she said and it seemed to him that she had never before said that to him. Or was his ear too imaginative?

He kissed her, tasting her, storing up another memory. 'Don't let any strange men in while I'm away.'

Carrying his camera equipment and the telescope, he went down to the garage. He put the camera gear and the telescope in the back of the Nissan Patrol, then he unlocked the steel box bolted to the garage floor. He took out the gun-case and three packets of ammunition; he looked at the three remaining boxes and decided to leave them where they were. He was not planning any siege, with himself either inside or outside the circle.

He backed the Nissan out of the garage, paused at the end of the short driveway and looked up at the flat on the sixth floor. Julie was on the verandah; she waved to him and blew him a kiss. He drove away up the quiet suburban street, feeling sick and sad, something he had never been prepared for. Except, of course, for that day twenty-three years ago when he had walked out of the police academy. But then he had been as angry as he had been sick and sad.

4

Malone and Clements stood on either side of the flat's front door. In answer to the ringing of the bell, the door was opened. Julie Malloy, in sweater and slacks, stood behind the security grille door.

Malone turned side on, held his Smith & Wesson .38 out of sight. 'I'm Inspector Malone, this is Sergeant Clements.' He held up his badge. 'Is your husband home, Mrs Malloy?'

Julie shook her head. 'No, he's not home. What do you want?'

'Just to talk to your husband. Where is he?'

'He left this afternoon for Boggabilla. He's gone up there on a job.'

'May we come in and use your phone, Mrs Malloy?'

She hesitated, then she opened the security door. 'I don't like being on my own, but it happens a lot, my husband working the hours he does –'

'My wife feels the same way,' said Malone sympathetically.

In the living room Julie had crossed to switch off the television set in one corner. 'I always look at the SBS world news. Channel 15 would fire Colin if they knew it's one of his favourite programmes, too.' She looked more closely at Malone. 'We met the other night, but I recognize you now. My husband has filmed you a couple of times. I always remember his clips in the news.

251

Family pride, I suppose,' she said with a pleasant smile. 'There's the phone.'

Malone glanced at Clements. 'Go out and tell the fellers to go back to their vehicles, Russ. Tell 'em to wait.'

Clements paused at the door. 'Mrs Malloy, what sort of car would your husband be driving?'

'He'd have driven our Nissan Patrol up to the channel. But from there they'd have gone in one of the news trucks.' She frowned, all at once looked worried and irritated. 'What's going on? What other men outside? What are they doing there?'

Clements ignored the question. 'Where does he keep the Nissan?'

'Down in our garage, Number 11. What *is* this, for God's sake?'

Malone said, 'We'll explain in a minute, Mrs Malloy. Would you give Sergeant Clements the key to your garage, please?'

For a moment it looked as if she would refuse; then she went to a side-table, opened a drawer and took out a key. She tossed it almost angrily at Clements. 'There'd better be a good explanation for all this!'

Clements nodded at Malone. 'The Inspector will explain.'

When Clements had left the flat, Malone picked up the phone. 'What's Channel 15's number, Mrs Malloy?'

She raised her eyebrows; rather prettily, he thought. Very soon he was going to surprise her even more and he was not looking forward to it. 'You're going to call the channel?'

'Yes. Who's your husband's boss?'

'Inspector, I'm not going to tell you any more until you –'

'Mrs Malloy,' he said patiently, 'I'm trying to save you any hurt. If your husband's boss contradicts what I've heard, I'll apologize and walk out of here –'

'Bloody police! You –' He stared at her impassively; he had heard it all before and she knew that he had. Sourly she said, 'His name's Nick Katzka. I don't know if he'll still be there –'

Katzka was; but he sounded impatient, as if he had been caught on his way out the door. 'What? Send Col Malloy up to – *where*? Boggabilla, for Chrissake. Why the hell would I send him there? He's not due in till tomorrow morning –'

'Mr Katzka, Sergeant Clements came to ask you a few questions this morning. Did you tell Mr Malloy we were enquiring after him?'

'Yeah, well . . . Yeah, I did –'

'Thanks, Mr Katzka. Some day we may be able to do you a favour, too.'

He hung up and Julie Malloy came at him as if she were going to throw herself at him. 'Why are you making enquiries about my husband?'

'Let's sit down, Mrs Malloy. You're not going to like what I'm going to tell you and I'm not going to like telling you.'

'Tell me what?' Her voice suddenly faltered.

He told her, as gently as he could. There are aspects of innocence that leave some people totally vulnerable; they have a profound belief in the goodness of human nature that denies any disillusion that may coat their perceptions. They are fools, many of them know it, but they would not want to be any other way and they are to be admired for it. Malone never scorned them; if there were no fools, who would recognize a wise man? But one's admiration, or anyway patience with them, cannot stop one from, however unwillingly, punishing them for their innocence.

'I'm sorry, but I'm certain that what I'm telling you is the truth. Your husband is Frank Blizzard and he's killed five people and is now planning to kill me and another man.'

'You've already said that,' she said automatically; she was chiding him for repeating himself, as if one insult was enough. 'I don't believe any of it . . .' But she did, every word of it. The belief was plain on her no longer pretty face. 'How could I have not known he was like – like *that*?'

'I can't explain it,' he said, not wishing to; that way there might lie more hurt. 'I've arrested God knows how many men – and women, too – whose families never suspected what they were really like. We all hide something. Some of us just do it better than others.'

'But why would he hate you so much, just because you had him expelled from the police academy?'

'Perhaps you should ask him that when we bring him in.'

253

She sat silent for a while and he made no attempt to disturb her further; he had already done that to a degree he had hoped to avoid. She was completely in love with Malloy (or Blizzard); it would have been easier had she had her own doubts about him. At last she said, 'He *has* been acting strangely. But I put it down to his moods – he could have moods that I never understood.'

'Were you happy together? Most of the time?'

She nodded vigorously, almost as if trying to convince herself. 'Oh yes. Yes.' Then she said in a despairing plea, 'You're sure about what he's done?'

'I'm sure.' He looked up as Clements came back into the flat. 'Everything okay?'

Clements put three packets of ammunition on the arm of Malone's chair. 'We found those in a steel box in the garage, bolted to the floor. Bill Killop had to bust it open. They're .243s. The gun's gone.'

'A gun?' said Julie. 'He had a gun down there?'

'You didn't know about the steel box?'

'Of course. But Colin said he kept his spare tapes and lenses in it. I – I never saw him open it.'

Clements was as uncomfortable as Malone with Julie's anguish. He looked at Malone. 'Bill Killop wants to know how long it's likely to be.'

'Did your husband take any gear with him?' Malone said.

'Some extra shirts and a sweater. He asked for extra money, but then he said he'd use his bank card.' She stared at them with no hope at all in her pinched, pale face. 'I thought he was only going for a couple of days.'

Malone tried to tone down the pity in his voice: 'I don't think he'll be back at all, Mrs Malloy.'

ELEVEN

1

'He's got to be disposed of, Arnie, no two ways about it. We'll kill him.'

'Jack, isn't there some other way? Jesus, can't we just buy him off? He'll listen to the sound of money. Everybody does.' Arnold Debbs judged everyone by his own standards: he liked a yardstick he could trust.

'Arnie, he's not some local councilman –' Jack Aldwych almost said, *He's not some local politician*; but you couldn't insult a politician to his face, not in his own home. Shirl had tried to teach him some manners and, to a certain extend, she had succeeded. 'No, O'Brien's got more money than we could offer him to keep him quiet. I've been talking to someone in his organization –'

'Who?'

Aldwych smiled. 'Arnie, do you tell me who gives you leaks out of Cabinet? This feller knows everything that's going on. O'Brien has money salted away overseas –'

'Then why the fuck doesn't he pay what should be coming to us?' Debbs could feel his temper rising, as much with Jack Aldwych as with O'Brien. Sometimes he wondered if Aldwych thought he was just the office boy, the messenger from Canberra. But he was a small man in a plump, large frame and such small men have their own invisible mirror. He knew his limitations and they gave him a headache.

'Arnie, he's like the rest of us, greedy. I've never criticized anyone for being greedy, it's a natural condition, like dandruff or piles.' Lately, in the evenings, Aldwych had taken to becoming philosophical. Which was why he rarely did business after dark nowadays.

He had come out here this Sunday evening to visit Arnold Debbs; Jack Junior had driven him and was still outside sitting in the dark blue Jaguar, which was Shirl's car. The Debbs lived in Strathfield, in Sydney's inner west, a middle-class area that had once had higher aspirations. It had originally attracted the professional classes who, for various reasons, had wished to avoid the more socially conscious eastern suburbs; it was not that they were against keeping up with the Joneses, they were careful about spending their money to do so. At one time, it was said, 50 per cent of the local population had consisted of solicitors and accountants, each keeping an eye on the other. The area was conservative in politics, even if voting Labour, and once had been conservative in religion; now, religion found the going a little harder, as if, like the Joneses, it was no longer a necessary beacon. There were several grand mansions in the district, but these were now mostly taken over by institutions, private schools and nursing homes. Postwar immigrants who had made good had built large houses on small blocks, many of them distinguished by more balustrade work than one would find in a day's drive in the Florentine hills. The Debbs lived in a blue-brick one-storey house, built in the 1920s; it was bourgeoisly solid, but not grand enough to earn a curled lip from any Labour voter who might stray into their quiet, tree-lined bourgeois street. Democracy is elastic: it doesn't insist that its representatives have to be humble. Except at election time.

Aldwych sipped the twelve-year-old Chivas Regal he had brought as a gift: Debbs, a good host, had opened it at once, realizing that that was what Aldwych wanted him to do. 'Arnie, Les Chung saw O'Brien today. He went up to O'Brien's stud – he's holed up there with Scobie Malone. Les got the idea that they're playing at stake-out goats to this other feller who's trying to bump off the two of them.'

'The two of 'em? I'm surprised the Police Department would go along with that.'

'I hear from my contact in the Department that they're getting pretty desperate. Anyhow, we're gunna have to do something. Les gave O'Brien a warning, but it wasn't worth a pinch of shit, according to Les. So, I've got a feller going up there tonight. A couple of 'em, in fact. One's gunna create a diversion, to get the police and the security guards over his way, while the other guy goes in and does O'Brien.'

'Won't that be risky, with all the police hanging around?'

'Arnie, the risk will be for the guy who's gunna do the hit. And he doesn't know who's paying him.'

'And Malone?' Debbs could feel the whisky splashing in his glass.

'Yeah, he'll do Malone too, if he has to. Don't worry, Arnie,' said Aldwych, as if he could see Debbs' trembling hand in the gloom of the living-room. 'It'll be done and nobody'll ever connect us with it.'

Then Penelope Debbs came to the door of the room, peered in at them. 'What are you doing sitting in the dark?'

She switched on the ceiling light; the room sprang up around the two men. It was a big comfortable room, panelled halfway up the walls; there were old-fashioned picture-rails round the walls a couple of feet below the moulded metal ceiling. The furniture was much better than one would find in the homes of the majority of the Debbs' voters; both politicians were careful never to have any party branch committee meetings here. All the paintings were Australian landscapes, including a subdued Pro Hart and a Hans Heysen without a gum tree; there was a photo of Penelope with the Queen, she looking more regal than the Royal; and there was a glass-fronted cabinet in one corner in which was Penelope's collection of Lalique crystal, her main indulgence outside of her own self-promotion.

'Do you usually sit in the dark at home, Mr Aldwych?'

'A lot of the time, Mrs Debbs. My wife is on at me all the time, asking me if I'm trying to save electricity.'

Penelope had never met Jack Aldwych before this evening; had never wanted to. She was not afraid of him; indeed, of any man, gangster or saint; she would have put both Jenghis Khan and Jesus Christ in their places if they had tried to boss her around. She was careful with whom she brushed her well-clad shoulders; she had made one or two bad choices, including O'Brien, but she had always avoided criminals. She had known that Arnold knew Aldwych, but she had been shocked when she had gone to the front door an hour ago and a young man had stood there, introducing himself as Jack Aldwych Junior and saying that his father was outside in their car and would like to come in to see Mr Debbs. Arnold had come into the hall behind her and, though he had tried to disguise the surprise in his voice, had said, yes, ask your father to come in, by all means. When the old man had come up on to their front verandah she had been surprised at how amiable and polite he had seemed. She didn't know why, but she had expected a gorilla in a trenchcoat. She had greeted him just as politely, then excused herself and gone out to the kitchen. Whatever he had come to discuss with Arnold, she did not want to hear it first hand. Later would do, when she and Arnold were in bed. They slept in twin beds and they never had sex on Sunday nights, so their talk could be cool and political.

Aldwych stood up, rising slowly. 'Well, I better be getting back. I'm keeping my son away from his girl.'

Penelope wondered what sort of girl would go with a gangster's son. 'He seemed a nice boy. He's got a charming smile.'

'His mother's smile. He's all right – it's just a pity he's got me for a dad.' He looked at her, giving her his old man's smile, as if waiting for her to contradict him. But she had learned just how far you could take politeness; he would recognize hypocrisy far quicker than any voter. She let her opinion of him hang in the air like a looped rope. He recognized a woman as formidable as himself and thanked Christ that Shirl was nothing like her. 'Well, good-night. I've just been telling Arnold that all our troubles will soon be over.'

'That'll be a relief. Good-night, Mr Aldwych.'

'Good-night, Mrs Debbs.'

Arnold Debbs showed him out of the house, then came back into the living-room, where Penelope hadn't moved, stood still and waiting. 'So what did he mean by saying all our troubles will soon be over?'

'He's going to attend to Mr O'Brien.'

'How?' But she knew at once; and quickly she said, 'Don't tell me! I don't want to know.'

He poured himself half a glass of the Chivas Regal, took a

258

long gulp of it. 'How did we ever get into this fucking mess?'

But that's a question that has been echoing down history ever since Adam, without the adjective, first asked it.

2

Malone and Clements got back to Cossack Lodge at midnight. Julie Malloy had called a girl-friend, who had arrived to stay the night with her; her sister would be coming over from Adelaide first thing tomorrow morning. The media had been sent away with a few sparse facts but no pictures; the SWOS men had gone back to Police Centre and most of the local police had been retired. A roster of two men at a time was to stake out the Malloy flat in case Malloy came back to see his wife.

'But I think there's one chance in a thousand of that,' Malone had told Sergeant Safire. 'She's seen the last of him, unless we manage to take him alive.'

'If he turns up,' said Safire, 'I'll be on to you right away. You'd like to be in at the kill, I reckon.'

'Yes,' said Malone, but wished Safire had used another word.

The two detectives had said very little to each other on the drive back from the city. As Clements turned the car in at the stud gates, a security guard approached them from the side, flashing a torch in their faces. 'Oh, it's you, Inspector. Everything's okay, nothing's happening. Looks like a quiet night.'

Clements drove on up to the house. The lights were still on in the front room and O'Brien opened the front door as they stepped up on to the verandah. 'You didn't get him?'

'Let's talk inside,' said Malone. 'We don't want to be standing against the light –'

Then there was a shot somewhere across the paddocks. Malone pushed O'Brien ahead of him back into the hallway; Clements followed them, slamming the door shut behind him. 'Turn out the lights – all of them!'

O'Brien reacted as quickly as the two policemen; in a few seconds all the lights in the house were out. Outside, Malone heard a car start up, heard shouting; then the car went roaring down the drive. A horse whinnied, almost a scream of terror, then there was the sound of running feet and more shouts as the stud staff rushed out of their quarters to try to quieten the restless horses in the stables. O'Brien said with real concern, 'I hope the horses out in the paddocks aren't going crazy.'

'Would it be any of the locals shooting? Do they come out here at night to knock off wallabies or anything?'

'I dunno. This is the first time I've heard any shooting.'

'I'll go out and have a look,' said Malone.

'No, you won't,' said Clements. 'You stay here.'

He didn't give Malone time to argue; he went out through the back of the house, stumbling in the dark in the unfamiliar surroundings, cursing as he bumped into furniture. He opened the back door and stepped out into a yard which, even in the moonless night, looked more uncluttered than the usual farmhouse yard. There was no rusting machinery, no discarded bales and oil-drums; the yard was part of the showcase stud. He turned left and went towards the corner of the house just as the dark figure came running up from one of the rear paddocks. He halted and waited, taking his gun from its holster.

The man vaulted the white-railed fence that separated the yard from the paddock, landed on rubber-soled shoes and came swiftly across the yard towards the back door. Clements stepped silently behind the large water-tank at the corner of the house, a still-useful relic from the days before town water had been connected to the stud. He raised the Smith & Wesson and said, 'Don't move! Police!'

The man was alert for any danger; he fell flat at once, facing Clements, and the latter saw the gun come up. There was no flash; he just heard the bullet strike the water-tank like a quick flick on a drum; it hit above the water-line inside. He fired at the prostrate figure, but the man rolled to one side an instant before. Another bullet hit the tank, ricocheting off with a thin whine; a third bullet speared the corrugated iron, lower down this time, and a jet of water spouted out past Clements' face. The gunman had rolled close to the wall of the house; he was pressed up against the back step. Clements dropped flat to the ground, grunting as he did so; he had too much belly to lie perfectly flat. He took aim through the wooden legs of the tank stand; then saw the back door open right above the gunman. The man rolled over on his back, his gun coming up to point straight at Malone's shadowy figure in the doorway. Clements' first shot was a lucky one; it knocked the gun out of the man's hand. The second shot hit him in the head.

Clements got to his feet, leaned against the tank while he steadied his shaking legs. He held out his hand and scooped some of the leaking water into his face; it was icy cold and better than a dose of smelling salts. Malone stepped over the dead man, first checking that he *was* dead, then came quickly across to Clements.

'You all right, Russ?'

'I'm okay. Christ, I thought he'd got you then –'

'He would've, if you hadn't got in first. Thanks. Where'd he come from?'

'Up from the paddocks. But what the hell's going on over the other side?'

O'Brien came out of the back door, stepped down and fell over the dead gunman. He let out a curse of shock, picked himself up and looked around. 'Scobie?'

Malone and Clements came across the yard to him. 'We're okay, Brian. Better get back inside.'

O'Brien looked down at the body. 'Is it Blizzard?'

'No. I think it's your mates having another go at you. Let's go inside. You too, Russ.'

'No, I'll go and see what's going on –'

'Inside! Get him a drink, Brian. Get us all one.'

Clements looked down at the gunman. 'What about him?'

'Leave him there till we find out what's been going on . . . Sounds like they're coming back now.' Cars were coming up the driveway. He looked down at the body again. 'Where are your dogs, Brian? I don't want them sniffing at him.'

'They're all over at the stables, all four of 'em.'

'Righto, take Russ in and give him that drink. I'll be in for mine in a minute.'

He went round to the front of the house as three cars swung

261

in and pulled up. He recognized two of the cars, one of them a police car, the other belonging to the security guards; but the third, a souped-up Charger rust-bucket, was one he had never seen before. A uniformed cop got out and was followed by a youth and a young girl, both of them in jeans and leather jackets. The girl looked as if frightened for her life, but the youth had a brazen jauntiness about him that suggested that being hauled in by the police was a nightly occurrence.

'Who's this?' Malone said.

'We found 'em trying to get in over the far paddock,' said the senior constable, coming forward. 'We hailed 'em, but they jumped back into their car and took off like a rocket. I let go with a warning shot over the top of 'em and they pulled up.'

Malone looked at the youth. 'Let's see your driving licence, son.'

'It's in me other pants back home.' He could not have been more than nineteen or twenty, sallow-faced and blond-haired in the yellow glow of the big carriage-lamp mounted on the white post beside the path that led to the front door of the house. He had more confidence than was good for him; or anyway the appearance of it. 'Look, I don't have to take none of this shit —'

Malone turned to the girl. 'What's your name, miss?'

'Lily Azoulet.' She would have been pretty, Malone thought, if she took off half a kilo of mascara and make-up; in the lamp's glow she looked old enough to be the boy's mother. Fear didn't improve her appearance. 'Look, we was doing nothing — we just come out here for a bit of, well, you know —'

'They were up to more than that, Inspector.' The senior constable was named Curtis; he was in his mid-thirties, lanky and awkward, with country boy written all over him like a fashion label. His voice was a slow drawl, but he was shrewd and tough. 'This kid did everything but blow his horn to let us know he was there. Then the way he took off . . .'

'Bullshit,' said the youth.

'Bring 'em around the back,' said Malone.

He led the way round the side of the house and into the yard. He stepped over the dead gunman, reached inside the back door and switched on the light over the steps. The body lay on its back, the top of the head an ugly dark mess, the blank white face staring up with sightless eyes like that of a mime who had said all he had to say. He was in his late thirties and now, with the light falling pitilessly on him, Malone recognized him.

'This man just tried to kill my sergeant. He'd also come here to kill Mr O'Brien, who owns the stud. Do you know him?' he said to the girl.

She whimpered, shook her head and turned away, dry retching. Malone nodded to one of the security guards, who took her by the arm and led her back to the front of the house. Then Malone looked at the youth.

'You know him, don't you, son?'

The boy hadn't taken his eyes off the body; suddenly all the brazen confidence had drained out of him. The leather jacket with its metal studs was no longer his armour; he seemed to shrink inside it; it crumpled like black paper. He made a sound that was an echo of the girl's whimper and turned his back on the dead man. Malone waited patiently; the boy was going to start talking. Then he did, the words bubbling out: 'Look, I didn't know nothing about this, I mean, what he was gunna do. Holy shit, I been in trouble before, but nothing like this! I met him a coupla times, he used to run a stolen car racket –' He stopped. 'No, I'm not gunna tell you any more. Not till I seen a lawyer.'

'I think we can guess it, son. He came to you and offered you some money to come out here and create a disturbance, right? What did he pay you?'

'A coupla hundred – No, I'm not gunna say no more. Not till I seen a lawyer.'.

Malone looked at Curtis. 'Righto, take him into Camden and hold him. Better take the girl, too. Get the Crime Scene fellers out here. And Ballistics and Internal Affairs.'

'You want to be in charge?'

'No, this is Parramatta's region, let them handle it.' In the old days he would have resented having to hand over a case; now he was glad of regionalization, you could pass the buck and the paper-work. He reached down and, with his pen through the trigger-guard, picked up the dead man's gun and its silencer. 'A

263

silenced Ruger .22, a real pro's weapon. His name's Barry Fozel, he's got a record as long as my arm.'

He handed the gun to Curtis, who said, 'I'll have Parramatta and the Crime Scene guys here as soon's I can. Do you want to see them when they get here?'

'If I'm asleep, ask them to leave it till the morning. I haven't had the easiest of days.'

All at once he was glad that Lisa was miles away in Queensland. He would not have to climb into bed with her and tell her about today.

3

Malone fell asleep at one o'clock, after he had told Clements and O'Brien his surmise of what had happened. The long day, the after-shock, the drink of whisky, all hit him at once and he fell asleep as if he had been drugged. He woke at seven o'clock, still fully dressed, lying on the bed in one of the guest-rooms, and for a few moments he did not know where he was or how he had got there. Then he was aware of Russ Clements standing in the doorway.

'Breakfast's ready. And Kerry Swanson, from Parramatta, is out in the kitchen waiting to talk to you.'

'Give me ten minutes while I have a shower and wake up.'

When he walked into the big kitchen O'Brien, Clements and Detective-Sergeant Swanson were at the table and Mrs McIver, the foreman's wife, was busy at the stove. A small, busy-looking woman with a mop of red curls that made her look slightly clownish, she smiled at Malone. 'They're all having pork sausages and eggs. How about you, Mr Malone?'

'Why not?' It was the sort of breakfast Lisa would have forced on him after a day like yesterday.

Mrs McIver put a heaped plate of cereal, topped with fresh fruit, down in front of him. 'Get stuck into that first.'

'She thinks she's feeding the horses,' said O'Brien and Mrs McIver waved the back of her hand at him.

The men ate a hearty breakfast while they discussed the dead Barry Fozel and the boy and the girl who were still being held in the Camden lock-up. Mrs McIver listened with both ears pinned back, but kept busy at her stove and sink. Breakfast time in any normal Aussie home, Malone thought.

'We'll have to let the girl go, I don't think she had a clue what she was letting herself in for.' Swanson was a bony man of middle height, sandy-haired, with a thin bony face and the widest mouth Malone had ever seen. He had smiled occasionally during breakfast and it seemed each time that his ears were about to slide into the corners of his mouth. He was almost boringly phlegmatic, as unexcitable as a drugged sloth. Except that he was not slothful: he had been busy all night. 'The young cove, his name's Richie Cuppa, like in a cuppa tea, he's started to talk. We'll have to charge him, but we'll never be able to prove he knew what was going on. He's sticking to his story that he was paid to stage a diversion, while Fozel was supposed to come in from the other side and nobble one of the horses.'

'With a gun?' said Malone. 'If we're expected to believe that, we'll believe anything.'

'Cuppa says he didn't know anything about the gun. Anyway, juries believe anything,' said Swanson with the disillusion of a cop who had lost out too many times to the jury system.

Clements said, 'What about Fozel – anything on him that linked him to anyone?'

'Nothing.'

'Righto, Kerry, you handle it,' said Malone and took the cup of coffee Mrs McIver handed him. 'Anything new on Blizzard, Russ?'

Clements shook his head. 'I rang Andy Graham – he kipped down at Homicide last night. They've got a photo of Blizzard, or Malloy, whatever we want to call him, from Channel 15 and they've put it out for a run in the TV news and the papers. He's had a police artist do a sketch of Malloy without the beard and he's put that out, too.'

'The boy's going to have yours and my job before we know it.'

'Ain't it the way?' said Swanson, another middle-aged cop

who could feel the ambitious breath of youth on the back of his neck.

'There's no sign of his vehicle yet, the Nissan Patrol,' said Clements, 'but he's put out a description of that, too. My guess is that Blizzard has shaved off his beard, swapped the Patrol for something else and headed for Queensland till the heat dies down.'

Just don't let him get as far as Noosa, Malone prayed. He looked at O'Brien. 'What do you reckon, Brian?'

O'Brien took his time, slowly stirring a half-teaspoonful of sugar into his coffee. He had eaten less than any of the others, seemed almost unaware of the small bits of food that had gone into his mouth. 'I'm thinking about what you said Saturday morning. He's not suddenly going to get patient. He's on a run and he'll stay that way till he gets you and me.'

Mrs McIver dropped a plate into the sink; there was a smash of crockery as it broke two other plates. 'Oh, I'm sorry! I –'

'No, we're sorry, Mrs Mac.' O'Brien stood up, pressed her thin arm. 'We've upset you enough. We'll go into the living-room.'

'I haven't cleaned it up yet – gimme a coupla minutes and I'll run the Hoover through it –' She was struggling to sound normal.

'It's okay, Mrs Mac.'

The four men shook their heads and left the kitchen. In the living-room Swanson said, 'I'll be getting back. I've got enough on my plate without this cove Malloy. I've got Vietnamese killing each other, Syrians bashing each other up . . . Remember the good old days? Good luck, Scobie. Keep your head down.'

Clements showed him out of the house. Malone and O'Brien sat down on the checked tweed-covered chairs. Round the walls a carousel of stallions and mares posed behind glass; above the fireplace was a seventeenth-century painting of the Byerley Turk, the grandaddy of all thoroughbreds. It was a living-room designed for a man, not a hint of feminine taste in it. Neither man, however, was interested in what surrounded them.

'What do you think?' said O'Brien. 'You think he's going to have another go at us?'

Malone nodded. 'He's still somewhere around Sydney waiting to get at us. But I'm tired of sitting around waiting for him. I'm going to the funerals this morning, Jim Knoble's and Mardi Jack's.'

'You think he'll try his luck there?'

'No, not unless he's bent on suicide. Maybe he is, he knows his life is over, at least with his wife. But I'm going anyway.'

'So am I,' said O'Brien after a moment.

'No –' But then Malone gave up before taking the argument any further. 'Righto. But when we get there, if anyone bails me up for letting you come, you step in and get me off the hook. You're not my responsibility.' Then he added, more gently, 'I don't meant that the way it sounds.'

'I know.' There was a moment when all at once they were the closest of friends; but it was only a moment and both knew it could never last. Then O'Brien went on, 'I can't let Mardi be buried without me showing up. I guess I owe Jim Knoble something, too. I wasn't the one who split to the Superintendent about Blizzard cheating, but I was the one who started the hazing. I remember I went and got the fire hose –'

He shook his head at the folly of youth that could get you killed in middle age. Malone wondered if O'Brien appreciated the irony that the youth who had fire hosed another for cheating was now a middle-aged man under investigation by the NCSC for cheating. But now was not the time to mention it.

4

It was raining steadily by the time the two unmarked police cars reached Botany cemetery. As they drew in at the main entrance to the cemetery Malone saw the two SWOS vans and the four marked police cars lined up just outside the gates. Beyond them were four motor-cycle police and several TV vans and press cars.

A uniformed inspector, slicker glistening in the rain, came forward as Malone, Clements and O'Brien got out of their car. Malone and O'Brien were wearing raincoats and hats, but Clements had only an umbrella borrowed from Mrs McIver.

'We were told you were coming, Scobie.' The inspector was Neil Gittings, a twenty-four-year veteran like Malone and Clements, a graduate of the same year from the police academy but one who had escaped Blizzard's hatred and urge for revenge. He was tall and had a beefily handsome face and a ginger moustache that was now sequinned with raindrops. 'You're not too popular.'

'You think I'm playing hero, Neil?'

Gittings shrugged and a small waterfall tumbled off his slicker. 'No, I'm not saying that. But what if . . . ' He waved a hand at the bleak surroundings. 'What if Blizzard is somewhere out there in the sandhills, ready to have a go?'

'That's what I'm hoping for, Neil. How does that grab you?' Then Malone grinned. 'I'm sorry, mate. But Mr O'Brien and I feel we've waited long enough . . . Has Jim Knoble's funeral arrived yet?'

'No, it's due in about twenty minutes. They've just arrived with that other body, that girl Mardi Jack. They're over there on that hill.' He nodded towards a low hill in the middle of the cemetery. 'A lot of pop stars and show business people. Celebrities, is that what they call 'em? I wouldn't know. We had to bar the TV people and the press photographers – they'd have done a steeplechase over the graves to get up there.'

'I think I'd like to go up there,' said O'Brien and, without waiting for approval, moved off.

Malone glanced at Clements. 'I think we'd better go with him, Russ.'

'You're going to be right out in the open up there,' said Gittings. 'Like a shag on a rock.'

Malone looked after the quick-walking O'Brien. 'We'll be at least twenty yards apart. If he gets one of us, the other will have time to get behind a gravestone before Blizzard can take another bead on him.'

'You're out of your bloody head,' said Gittings. 'Don't get too close to him, Russ.'

'I'm only a sergeant,' said Clements. 'We're always several paces behind you inspectors.'

The humour was black, which was appropriate in the location. The cemetery had been laid out over rolling sandhills; where there were no graves there were scrubby shrubs, barricades of prickly lantana and several platoons of banksia trees, arthritic and bent by the wind. The long rows of graves looked like flat marble or stone beds; but the sleepers lay beneath them. Three pale green water-towers stood on the highest hill; through the rain Malone could make out the hazy shape of a SWOS marksman crouched on the top of one of them. To the south, in a hollow between the cemetery and the bay, were market gardens, green and neat as some military cemeteries Malone had seen, the crops laid out with the same precision as the rows of graves. A Chinese gardener stood motionless amongst the bright green, like an oilskin-clad scarecrow. Beyond the boundaries of the cemetery were the wharves of Port Botany: huge gantry cranes like the yellow skeletons of ancient giant birds, containers piled upon containers like massive red cedar coffins, corpses mass-delivered. The rain fell steadily on the whole scene, doing its best to wash the colour out of everything but not quite succeeding.

They were walking up a hill path past a row of mausoleums, like miniature Palladian villas. Malone remarked the names, all Italian; then suddenly he missed his step, putting his foot into a puddle without noticing it. There amidst all the Italian names, the Salvatores, the Buccionis, the Giuffres, was an Irish name: *Malone*. He stood, still with his foot in the puddle, the water leaking into his shoe, and Clements, coming up behind him, head bent under the umbrella, bumped into him.

'What's the matter?' Clements looked up wildly. 'You see him?'

'No.' Malone nodded at the name set in a marble plate on the iron door of the mausoleum. 'You think that's an omen?'

Clements frowned; then angrily pushed Malone on up the path. 'For Crissake, stop thinking like that! Jesus, you bloody Irish – always ready for a wake . . .'

Malone walked on, one shoe squelching, till he reached the

269

top of the hill and stopped. Ahead of him, down the slope the other side of the hill, Mardi Jack was being lowered into her grave. A sombre crowd of mourners, twenty or thirty of them, stood in a semicircle; their heads were bent and Malone recognized none of them. O'Brien had moved to one side, to a narrower path, and Malone turned his head and watched him from under the dripping brim of his hat. O'Brien had taken off his own hat: it was difficult to tell whether he had done it as a last gesture of respect for Mardi Jack or whether he was asking Frank Blizzard, somewhere out there in the rain, to recognize him and try to shoot him. Malone turned slowly, in a circle, looked around and felt the tightening in his gut and then the sweat breaking on him. If Blizzard was going to attempt to kill him or O'Brien or both, now was the moment. They were completely exposed on the top of the hill, so close to death that it seemed that Mardi Jack must be waiting for them to join her.

But the bullets did not come out of the grey curtain of rain and after a moment Malone called softly, 'Brian! Time we went back.'

As he spoke a girl looked up from amongst the mourners and stared at him, then at O'Brien. Then Gina Cazelli detached herself from the crowd around the grave, came up past O'Brien and stood in front of Malone. She was wearing a floppy-brimmed black hat made even floppier because it was soaked, a shiny black plastic raincoat that came almost to her ankles, and black patent leather boots. Her face was wet with tears and rain.

Don't shoot now, Blizzard, and maybe kill another innocent.

'Hallo, Gina. It's a sad day.'

'I heard you call that guy over there Brian. Is he the B. who was in Mardi's journal?'

'No,' he said without hesitation, protecting her and O'Brien from any further stirring of her feelings. 'He just owns the recording company, he thought he'd like to come up here and pay his respects. But he's really here with me to attend the other funeral, the policeman's. We were all old friends once.'

She looked at him doubtfully. Under the drooping brim of her

270

hat, her eyes puffed, her face devoid of make-up, she was even plainer than he had remembered her. He wondered if she had come alone to the funeral and if she would leave alone. The show business people were starting to leave the graveside and none of them was looking back for her.

'Did Mardi's father come down for the funeral?'

'No. There are some bastards in the world, fathers included.'

'Yes,' he said, who knew even better than she about the bastards of the world. *Our Father, Who art in Heaven, never let my kids say that about me* . . .

'Do you think you'll ever find the guy who killed her?'

He looked around the rain-drenched cemetery, then back at her. 'I hope so, Gina. For everybody's sake.'

Then she told him to take care of himself and moved off, stumbling up the slippery path as she tried to catch up with the departing mourners. That would be her life, he thought, always trying to catch up with those she hoped would be her friends.

He, Clements and O'Brien walked back down the hill without any word between them. The Knoble funeral had arrived; this time senior officers had come to the cemetery. Malone saw the Commissioner and several Assistant Commissioners, including A/C Falkender, who looked across and shook his head as if in disapproval of Malone's attendance. As soon as the coffin was lowered into the grave, Malone nodded to Clements and O'Brien.

'Let's get out of here. Otherwise I'm going to get my arse kicked for being here.'

They walked quickly out of the cemetery to where they had parked their car. As they got into it, Harry Danforth, puffing with the unaccustomed exertion, came hurrying out of the gates after them.

'You're in the shit, Scobie. The Commissioner's livid that you're here, especially after what happened last night. I'm supposed to tell you.'

'Righto, Harry, you just have. We're going back to Cossack Lodge now.'

271

'I'll follow you, we've gotta do some talking about what happens from here on. How's the new car going, Russ?'

'Fine, Chief,' said Clements. 'How's your old one?'

Danforth grunted and left them. Clements put the car into *Drive* and they went up past the TV vans and the press cars; some cameras swung round to follow them, but Malone did not care. He wondered if Malloy-Blizzard would have been here, camera at the ready, if they had not discovered who he was.

5

When the three men, Malone, O'Brien and the big detective Clements, had come out of the main house of the stud, Frank Blizzard had seen them from the cover of a thick stand of trees a mile and a half away. Sitting there on the hill, the powerful telescope trained on the main house, he had seen them come out and get into the unmarked police car. The car had gone down the driveway to the road, followed by another unmarked car with three armed men in it whom he took to be police. The cars turned in the direction of Sydney and a couple of minutes later passed below him within a couple of hundred yards.

He had remarked that no luggage had been brought out to the cars and that the other armed men, police or security guards, had remained at the stud. That meant Malone and O'Brien would be returning some time during the day. He was prepared to wait.

He had arrived here at six o'clock this morning, having spent last night at a motel at Bowral, seventy kilometres south of here. Yesterday afternoon he had driven the Nissan Patrol up Parramatta Road, passing several dealers till he saw a small used-car lot that had the look he was searching for, slightly rundown, its string of pennants as tattered as the flags of a defeated ship. The salesman who came out to greet him had much the same look, a matelot trying to stay afloat.

'How much for this?' said Blizzard. '1986, 35,000 k's genuine mileage.'

The salesman, thin and long-jawed, ran a crocodile eye over the vehicle. 'I dunno we're in the market for a Patrol, y'know, the downturn in the economy and all that. Leisure stuff, that's pretty hard to move these days, the yuppies are staying at home. The most I could offer would be, I dunno, I'd have to have a think about it –' He had to think, one of the quickest thoughts Blizzard had ever witnessed pass through a human head. 'I couldn't offer you any more than, say, twelve thousand tops.'

Blizzard knew it was worth at least fifteen. 'I'll take it.'

The crocodile eyes blinked: *Why wasn't the world full of mugs like this every day?*

'Just one thing. I want it in cash. I won't argue about the price, you don't argue about paying cash.'

'Ah gee, sport, waddia take me for? You could of pinched this from anyone – I don't handle hot vehicles –' He would handle a burning one if it meant a quick profit. 'You got your papers?'

'Everything. Registration, licence, my credit cards –'

'They could of been in the vehicle, sport –'

Blizzard produced his Channel 15 security card with his photo on it. It didn't matter showing his identity now; it would be at least four hours before his picture would go out on the news with the information that the police wanted him for questioning. By then he would be a long way from this salesman who was doing his best to hide his eagerness to make a cheap buy.

'Okay, you got a deal. You're lucky I got just that amount of cash in the safe – I just sold a Toyota, dirt cheap, beautiful bargain, to a guy who said he didn't trust banks –'

Sunday afternoon on Parramatta Road: Blizzard wondered how much cash was floating up and down the car lots, passing from hand to hand of men who didn't trust banks.

Ten minutes later he walked off the lot with $12,000 in his overnight bag, which was slung by its strap over his back. The telescope case hung by its strap from round his neck, in one hand he carried his camera box, in the other the gun-case. 'Geez, you're loaded, sport. You sure you don't wanna buy a smaller car? I got a beautiful bargain out there, a 1987 Honda Civic, one owner-driver, my aunt, as a matter of fact . . .'

Blizzard walked a hundred yards up the street and bought a motor-cycle, a Honda GL1000, for $4000. He also bought a helmet and gloves, strapped all his gear on the pillion rack and rode out of the lot and headed south.

He stopped at a McDonald's, bought two hamburgers and an apple slice, ate them and then rode on south again. Just before he got to Bowral he turned off the Hume Highway on to a side-road and pulled up beside a small creek. He scrambled down the bank, taking a mirror and shaving gear and scissors with him. There, over the next twenty minutes, he set about eliminating Colin Malloy from whatever remained of the rest of his life. When he had finished he looked at himself in the mirror and had no instant recognition of the man he saw there. The clean-shaven, balding man was a stranger; and for a moment he was terribly frightened. This was the madman who had killed five people and who had just wiped out Colin Malloy who, unlike Frank Blizzard, had experienced happiness. He had run his hand over his tender face like a blind man seeking to identify a stranger.

Now, standing in the timber, watching the two police cars go down the road towards Sydney, hearing the rain beginning to fall on the upper foliage of the trees, he was sane enough to know that he was suffering from some sort of madness. He had once read a poem, he couldn't remember who it was by, and a line had stood out: *There is a pleasure sure in being mad that none but madmen know.* Ah, but you would have to be really round the twist to get pleasure out of it. And he was far from that: he was sane enough to know that, too. All he hoped was that no one would call him a psychopath. He could not take an insult like that to the grave with him.

He stayed in the timber for another two hours, huddled in his anorak and helmet against the rain dripping steadily down through the filter of the branches high above him. The motor-cycle was hidden under bushes at the edge of the timber, though he was not expecting anyone to come searching for him, least of all a police helicopter on a day like this.

At last he went back to the motor-cycle, stripped the camou-flage away from it and rode it down the slippery hillside to a narrow dirt track that ran through the paddocks and parallel to the road. The rain had stopped, but the clouds were still full and low, moving slowly over the crest of distant hills like great flocks of sheep. He came to a gate, opened it and went through on to a gravel road that ran at right angles to the tarred Sydney road. A hundred yards along he came to another clump of trees; beyond it a narrow wooden bridge spanned a culvert through which the tarred road dipped and climbed. As he got off the motor-cycle, a pick-up truck came across the bridge, the timbers rattling like gunfire under it, the driver saluted and the truck went on up the gravel road.

Blizzard parked the motor-cycle under the trees, got out the gun-case and assembled the Tikka and the telescopic sight. Then he went back to the bridge, climbed over its low wooden railing and found a natural seat on a ledge of rock above the cutting. He sat down to wait, for as long as was necessary. The last of the six green bottles would come down the road . . . He began to hum the old song, sitting there in the steadily falling rain, which had started again, like a busker waiting for someone to come by and reward him. Then abruptly he began to weep and a terrible pain spread across the back of his head, where the rottenness had lain all those years. But it was an old pain and he could bear it. Maybe today would ease it for ever.

It was just after midday, with the rain still falling, when he saw the three cars coming along the road from the direction of Sydney. They were still half a mile away, approaching at a steady rate. He put the Tasco telescope to his eye, focused on the leading car and saw Malone in the front seat beside the driver, who looked like the big man Clements. He could not see who was in the rear seat, but if O'Brien was not there he was sure he was in one of the following cars.

He put down the Tasco, picked up the rifle, adjusted the 'scope sight and aimed at Malone as the leading car reached the top of the dip that led down under the bridge.

6

Clements didn't see the pot-hole till the last moment. He had had to swerve to miss several of them in the last mile or two; he had hit one of them and there had been a horrible thumping noise under the car. Now he swung the car to the left and that swerve saved Malone's life. The bullet went through the middle of the windscreen, right between Malone and Clements, and hit the rear door beside O'Brien as he lolled in the back seat. The windscreen was starred round the bullet-hole, but Clements' vision was not obscured. The car skidded back to the right of the narrow road, slipped on the greasy shoulder and hit the steep bank, scraping along its rock-ribs as it careered down the cutting. Had it not been for the steep wall of the bank, the car would have rolled over; as it was, it tilted over far enough for the side windows to be smashed as the car hit protruding rocks in the bank. The Commodore, still upright on all four wheels, was fifty yards down into the cutting before Clements managed to bring it to a halt.

Malone opened his door and fell out on to the roadway, drawing his gun and yelling at O'Brien to stay where he was in the back seat. He heard a second shot hit the car fender a foot from his head and he crawled round the back of the Commodore as the other two cars skidded to a stop behind him. On his feet now but crouched over, he chanced a look up between the wrecked car and the steep bank and saw the beardless man in the anorak aiming at him again. The bullet hit a projecting rock, sending a chip flying into Malone's cheek, stinging him so that he gasped, and went ricocheting away. Malone fired back, but his shot was hasty and went astray. Then he was up and running down the cutting, slipping once on the greasy road, and in under the bridge.

He heard the gunfire from behind him; the police had scrambled out of their car and were firing at Blizzard. Danforth's car was nose-to-tail against the police car, but Malone couldn't see the Chief Superintendent. Malone pulled up for a moment to get his breath; he put his hand to his cheek and felt the blood there. Then he went on under the bridge and up the other side of the cutting, keeping close to the overhang of the bank, slipping and stumbling in the mud of the shoulder but somehow managing to keep his feet. The rain had seemed to increase; or maybe it was only his imagination; he had no clear grasp of anything. The showdown with Blizzard had come at last and somehow he was not as prepared for it as he had expected to be. Maybe the waiting had gone on too long.

Another bullet ricocheted off a rock behind him, but the angle was too acute for Blizzard to get a clean shot at him. He kept running till he came up out of the culvert, swung off the shoulder and flopped into a shallow ditch beside a fallen tree, sending up a splash of muddy water as he did so. The rain now was pelting down, it was not his imagination; his hat was back in the car and the water swished across his face like a wet veil. He wiped his eyes, lay flat in the liquid mud of the ditch and looked back at the bridge.

Blizzard, seemingly careless of his own death, stood in the middle of the bridge, the rifle aimed straight at Malone. The latter fired an instant before Blizzard could squeeze the trigger of the Tikka. The rifle did go off, but it was pointed at the sodden sky as Blizzard fell backwards with Malone's bullet taking off the top of his skull. Malone would never fire a luckier shot; at the distance and in the rain, the bullet could have missed Blizzard by feet. Justice, often blind in one eye, occasionally has 20/20 vision in the other.

Malone lifted himself out of the ditch, wiped his face with a muddy hand. The whole front of him was black with mud; he looked primeval. But better primeval than dead. He walked back down the road, under the bridge and up to the wrecked Commodore. Clements, nursing an injured arm, and O'Brien were standing in the rain; Harry Danforth was standing with them, his gun in his hand. The three police officers had scrambled up the bank and were now on the bridge.

Danforth put his gun back in his holster. 'You okay, Scobie? Your cheek's bleeding.'

'Just a nick. I'm okay.'

Danforth then shouted to the officers up on the bridge. 'How is he?'

277

'Dead, Chief.'

'Good. Thank Christ it's all over.'

'How are you, Russ?' Malone looked with concern at Clements, who was tenderly holding his left arm.

'I think I've broken it. It's hurting like buggery. But we're alive, so why complain? It was Blizzard, wasn't it?'

Malone nodded. 'Pretty sure. I'll go up and have a look. You okay, Brian?'

'I dunno,' said O'Brien and leaned against the car. 'I thought I was. Now all of a sudden I've got no legs. I can't believe it's all over.'

Danforth looked at him carefully, then he said, 'I'll take you up to the stud, you can get a good stiff drink or a cuppa tea or something into you . . . You take charge here, Scobie – it's been your case all along. Better get an ambulance out here for Russ.'

Malone walked the few yards back along the road to Danforth's car with him and O'Brien. 'I'll be about half an hour, Brian. Have a whisky ready for me.'

'Sure. Well, we survived . . .' He wiped the rain from his face, the gesture of a weary man who had at last been able to stop running; or at least to drop to a slow trot. The downpour had eased and there was just a thin mist of moisture.

We've survived, Malone thought, up till now. But there was still tomorrow and he knew that O'Brien would be more aware of that than he was. O'Brien got into Danforth's car and Malone slammed the door shut after him. 'Have that whisky ready.'

'I'll join you,' said Danforth, who never said no to a drink, whether he was invited or not. He was already in behind the wheel. He reached to turn on the ignition, then sat back, lifting his big belly. He took his Smith & Wesson out of his waistband holster, leaned across and put it in the glove-box. 'I'm getting too fat to carry a gun. Well, see you in a while, Scobie. I'll come back as soon's I've delivered Mr O'Brien.'

He took the car down under the bridge and up towards the road that led to the stud. Malone looked at Clements. 'Get on the radio, Russ, call in all the necessary. Then sit there and don't move your arm.'

'What are you going to do?'

'I'm going up to have a look at Frank Blizzard. I still can't remember what he looked like twenty-three years ago.'

He went up and along the top of the bank and on to the bridge. The three officers, looking like oiled birds in their wet slickers, stood aside as he approached them. 'It's him, all right, Inspector. The rifle's a Tikka. There's ammo in his pockets, .243s. You can bet the bullets in your car will match the others ones you told us about.'

Malone looked down at the stranger. All that was familiar was the anorak; Malone had seen Malloy wearing it on at least two occasions. One of the policemen had pulled up the blood-stained hood to hide the horrible wound. All that was exposed was the beardless face, almost white below the cheeks, eyes shut tight against the rain or the pain, it was impossible to tell. The face was a mask, but with nobody that Malone knew behind it.

Then one of the officers said, 'Hallo, what's up? The Chief's coming back.'

Malone turned and looked up the road. Danforth's car was coming back, moving slowly, as if in bottom gear. It went down under the bridge, then up to the other two cars. Malone told one of the officers to stay with Blizzard's body, then he and the other two officers went running along the top of the bank and slid down to the roadway. Danforth still sat in his car, motionless and impassive. Beside him O'Brien lay against the car door, a red gaping hole in the side of his head, Danforth's Smith & Wesson held loosely in his hand.

Danforth blinked as Malone wrenched open the car door and O'Brien fell into his arms. 'For Crissake, what happened?'

'I dunno – it happened so quick . . . He took my gun outa the glove-box and blew his brains out before I could stop him . . .' His beefy hands were resting on the steering wheel, but they looked relaxed, not tight with tension. 'Why would he wanna do that?'

Malone looked down at the dead man in his arms. He tried not to look at the face; there was too much agony there. He gently eased O'Brien back into the seat, took off his own jacket and laid it over the head and face of the dead man. Then he looked at Danforth, making no attempt to disguise the accusation in his voice.

'Yeah,' he said. 'Why would he want to do that?'

7

Malone and Clements came out of Camden hospital, Clements with his arm in plaster and a sling, Malone with a dressing on his cheek. One of the police cars had gone on to the stud and then come back with Malone's bags; he had had a shower at the hospital and changed into clean clothes while the doctor had worked on Clements' broken arm. An understanding nurse had given each of them a heavy slug of medicinal brandy – 'courtesy of Medicare' – and the after-shock of the day's event was seeping out of them.

A local police car was waiting to drive them back to Sydney, but the two detectives didn't walk across to it immediately. They paused and looked at each other, reading the question in each other's mind. They had not mentioned Danforth in the past hour; the Chief Superintendent, pleading shock, had already gone back to the city. Now the question could not be avoided.

'Do you think he did it?' said Clements.

'Harry? Of course he bloody did it!' Malone said angrily; then controlled himself as a young nurse walked by and looked at him reproachfully. He waited till she had gone, then went on, 'Brian was never going to kill himself. He'd get depressed, I saw that a couple of times, but he wasn't suicidal, not as far as putting a gun to his own head. Harry did it, all right.'

'Someone paid him.'

'Of course. I can guess who. But we'll never be able to prove it. We'll never be able to prove anything. There'll be an enquiry and it'll be Harry's word against that of a dead man. With everything piling it on Brian, who's going to believe he didn't suicide? Harry will be ticked off for being careless with his gun, but that's all he'll get, a ticking off. He'll probably retire now,

280

go out with his full pension and whatever he was paid for killing Brian Boru O'Brien.'

'Jesus wept . . .' Clements looked west to where the rain had cleared and streaks of sunlit cloud lay like a silver reef in the pale blue-green sky. 'If I didn't have a cast-iron gut, I think I could spew.'

Malone's anger and disgust could not be relieved by vomiting. It was not just in his stomach but in every organ, bone, vein and muscle of his body. He was an honest man and honest men, too, are vulnerable to corruption. It doesn't reward them, just does its best to destroy them.

TWELVE

1

'What are you going to do?' said Joanna.

'What can I do? I'll stay with Philip.'

'Oh, for God's sake!' Joanna threw herself backwards, as if trying to hurl herself through the back of the couch; Anita had never seen her sister so physically angry. Joanna's usual temper emerged only through her tongue, which could be as sharp-edged and deadly as a scimitar; but now it seemed that her whole body was bursting with anger. 'Why do you have to subject yourself to *that*? Walk out – come back to Sydney – you'd have no trouble getting a job in radio or TV –'

'Darling, it would not be as easy as you think. You've never been in public life – you get out there and, whether you like it or not, you're trapped –' She played with the loose gold bracelet on her wrist; it seemed to her that in the two weeks since Brian's death, her wrist had got thinner. She *felt* thinner; or perhaps bonier was the word. As if all her flesh had become numb and all she could feel were her bones, which hurt terribly. 'How would I explain it? That I'd just become tired of living with the most popular man in Australia –'

'Oh, come off it! He's not that!'

'You read the wrong women's magazines. Anyway, Philip thinks he is and his minders have convinced most of the voters that he is. We're the Number One couple, Jo – I don't like it, but it's a fact. Since Philip has been PM and we've been travelling overseas, you'd be surprised at what I've found out about some presidents and prime ministers and their wives. They're farther apart than Philip and me, but they've had to stay together. Like

I told you, I'm stuck with him till at least the next election. All I can hope for is that he loses the election.'

'God, you're making the voters sound like a jury in the Family Court – if they have juries there.' She would never resort to the law courts to resolve her marital problems; she had given her previous husbands everything they had asked for without any public appearance on her part. Public opinion never troubled her, but she parted from her men in private. She reached forward to take her sister's hand. 'Well, then, all you can do is try to forget your lover. Bury him and forget him.'

'Could you do that?'

'I've done it,' said Joanna, but didn't say whom she had put out of her life and memory.

Anita shook her head. 'I'll never be able to do that. I remember reading a poem once on radio, I can't remember who by. It had a line in it that went something like –' She paused and her breath seemed to catch for a moment. *'The heart can never bury its dead.'*

2

Two weeks before, on that Monday evening, Harry Danforth had made a call from a public box. 'Jack, it's me. Harry.'

'No names, mate. You know what the police are like.' Jack Aldwych was sitting out on his verandah, feeling the cold but reluctant to go indoors; as if he knew he had a rapidly diminishing number of evenings and was trying to hold on to them. Jack Junior had brought him the telephone and he had taken it with irritation at being disturbed. 'They're likely to tap my phone, with or without a court order. What's on your mind?'

'Everything's been taken care of. You owe me for this one.'

'You mean we have nothing to worry about? Well, he won't be missed. Yeah, I do owe you. You can start thinking about retirement now, mate.'

'I been doing that, all afternoon. It's time I was getting out. A nice place up on the Gold Coast.'

'Leave it with me, mate. No more phone calls, no more visits. You understand? Look after yourself.'

Harry Danforth hung up and stepped out of the phone box. He suddenly felt cold, as if he had walked by a newly opened grave.

3

'Uncle Russ, what are you *doing*?'

Clements took the bottle away from his lips and grinned self-consciously. 'I was giving it mouth-to-mouth resuscitation. The wine wasn't breathing.'

Claire rolled her eyes and looked at her mother, who said, 'Who writes your jokes, Russ?'

Three months had passed and November was warming up into December. It was a Sunday and the Malones were having a barbecue beside their pool. Clements had brought six kilos of steak and three kilos of sausages, enough to feed a football team, and now, decked out in shorts, thongs and a brightly patterned shirt, an ocker Beau Brummel, he was supervising Maureen as she and Tom turned the steak and sausages on the barbecue. He had brought a girl with him; the nineteenth, Lisa, who kept count, had whispered to Malone. Her name was Sheila, a long-legged blonde who, Malone thought traitorously, looked too classy and intelligent for Russ but who obviously was more than just amused by him. Lisa was working overtime as matchmaker.

'You'll have to cure him of those dreadful jokes, Sheila. One can't live with a man like that.'

'Steady on,' said Clements through the smoke and sizzle of the barbecue. 'Sheila and I are just holding intellectual discussions, not living together.'

'What do you do, Sheila?' said Con Malone, one of the four other guests for lunch. He was wearing a bright green shirt and white slacks and, to Malone's delight, looked as if he were on his way to a St Patrick's Day celebration; the outfit had been a birthday gift from his daughter-in-law and he didn't like to tell her that he wore it only when he came to her place. Brigid, though she liked the green shirt, would have preferred him to wear his usual brown trousers. The white trousers, she thought, made him look like the oldest stroller on Oxford Street, a beat she had once ridden through on a bus with her eyes averted. 'Are you in the police?'

'I'm a pathologist in the Forensic Science bureau.'

Con, Brigid and the two elder Pretoriuses all looked impressed; the world today was a different one from the one they had grown up in. Russ, they all silently agreed, was a lucky man.

Lisa came and sat down on the bottom half of the sun lounge where Malone, in swim trunks, was stretched out. She turned her back on the others, as if closing a door on them. 'You're quiet.'

'That was Brian O'Brien's father on the phone.' He had gone inside to take a call ten minutes before.

'What did he want?'

'He said George Bousakis had been at him again. He asked me what I thought he should do.'

'What did you tell him?'

Malone put on his dark glasses, then took Lisa's hand and held it. 'I told him to tell Bousakis to get stuffed.'

A month ago Malone had been in his office at Police Centre when a call had come from the reception desk. 'There's a man here says he'd like to see you urgently, Inspector. A Mr O'Brien. He says it's about his son.'

When Horrie O'Brien Senior walked into his office Malone at once saw the resemblance: the son had been almost a carbon copy of his father. The same long lean face, the wide smile, the thick hair, almost white on the father: all that was missing was the quiet swagger of the son.

'I'm Horrie O'Brien, Inspector. I saw you at my son's funeral, but I didn't introduce m'self, I didn't want anyone taking pictures of me. Can I come straight to the point?'

'Go ahead, Mr O'Brien.'

'Well, I gather you know Brian and I didn't get along. He wrote me a long letter a coupla days before he was – he was killed. Or killed himself?' There was no mistaking that the last was a question.

Malone didn't commit himself; Harry Danforth had already resigned and left the Department. 'I think we'd better stick to the coroner's verdict, Mr O'Brien.'

Horrie O'Brien hesitated, then nodded. 'Yeah. Well . . . I got this letter, it was written on his stud's notepaper, it was almost like he had a premonition. He said he was sorry for what we'd missed between us and he hoped that, if everything went all right for him, we'd shake hands and let bygones be bygones. I might of, at that –' He looked down at his big hands; they were like his son's, wrapping and unwrapping each other. 'Being bitter doesn't get you very far, does it?' Malone didn't answer; and O'Brien went on, 'He said if anything happened to him I was to get in touch with his lawyers, he give me their name. I didn't do that, not till this week. I've been to see 'em this morning and they told me what's in his will. He left me everything, lock stock and barrel. I'm a bus driver, with overtime and shift work, I take home roughly five hundred bucks a week. And now he's made me a bloody millionaire!'

Malone felt a sudden warm glow of satisfaction. 'I think Brian would've been pleased.'

'I dunno. Because there's a problem or two, the lawyers tell me. The National something-or-other –'

'The NCSC?'

'Yeah, that's it. They want to grab what they can. I don't mind that, if Brian owed it to 'em. That was one of the things him and me disagreed about. I try to be honest . . .' He stopped and looked at Malone with embarrassment. 'Does that sound old-fashioned?'

'Not really. Not to me. But why did you come to me, Mr O'Brien?'

The older man's embarrassment didn't entirely fade. 'Because Brian spoke a lot about you in his letter. He said he'd made a friend, but too late – there was that premonition thing again, I guess. He mentioned a man named Bousakis, George Bousakis, a Greek he sounds like, and he said if I had any trouble with him I oughta come to you.'

286

'Are you having trouble with Mr Bousakis?'

'Not yet. I haven't met him so far. But the lawyers said he wants to buy out all Brian's holdings here in Australia. The lawyers say no one else will make me an offer and even if I wait I won't get anything better than Bousakis will offer me.'

'What do you think you'd like to do?'

'Mr Malone,' the older man said slowly and gravely, 'I'm due to retire – truth is, I'm past retiring age for a driver, but they don't know my real age. When the wife died I just wanted to keep working, keep my mind off her going like she did. I haven't got over losing her and now I'm trying to get used to the idea that I've just lost my son, my only kid. I'm not thinking too straight. The money don't mean that much to me. All I think I want to do is do what Brian asked. I disagreed with him enough when he was alive. Now he's dead, I'd like to make it up to him.'

Malone said nothing, looking at the man across the desk from him, seeing him fade into the younger O'Brien, Brian Boru, Horrie Junior. Then at last he said quietly, and he had to choke off the sweet venom in his voice, 'Mr O'Brien, I'd tell George Bousakis to get stuffed.'

And now, sitting beside the pool, he said, 'I told him what I told him a month ago. To tell George Bousakis to get stuffed.'

Lisa pressed his hand. 'So no one comes out a winner?'

'No one, at least as far as making money out of Brian's murder. It's just a pity he never got to name names to the NCSC, but you can't have everything.'

Lisa looked across the pool at the children, then back at him. 'I have everything.'

She leaned forward and kissed him on the forehead. Then she got up, went to the bucket of ice beside the back door and came back with a bottle of white wine and two glasses. She poured the wine, then saw the direction of his gaze.

'What are you looking at?'

'It's a green bottle. Have you got any more? Let's keep them as souvenirs.' As soon as he said it he knew it was a stupid, insensitive remark.

'No,' she said and bent down and kissed him again, this time on the lips. 'It's the last green bottle. And I'm going to break it when it's empty.'